# RECLAIMED BY HIS BILLION-DOLLAR RING

## JULIA JAMES

# ENGAGED TO LONDON'S WILDEST BILLIONAIRE

## KALI ANTHONY

MILLS & BOON

First published in Great Britain 2023
by Mills & Boon, an imprint of HarperCollins*Publishers* Ltd,
1 London Bridge Street, London, SE1 9GF

www.harpercollins.co.uk

HarperCollins*Publishers* Macken House, 39/40 Mayor Street Upper,
Dublin 1, D01 C9W8, Ireland

# RECLAIMED BY HIS BILLION-DOLLAR RING

JULIA JAMES

MILLS & BOON

Happy memories of our first family Greek holiday

# PROLOGUE

CALANTHE STOOD BESIDE her father, greeting their guests for the evening as they arrived in the banqueting suite of this top Athens hotel. All of Athens high society was here, and she was glad of it. Her father's sixtieth birthday was something to celebrate after all.

Her glance went sideways to him, a small frown forming. For all his bonhomie there was a look of strain about him, and his shoulders sagged as if he were making a visible effort. He did not look well.

Anxiety plucked at her. Her father had always been an ebullient character, strong-minded and forceful—characteristics that had made him a very wealthy man, whose property empire was worth a fortune. Though her own specialism was classical art, and she split her time between museums in London and Athens, Calanthe knew that as her father's only child she would one day inherit all his wealth. But she did not want that day to come too soon. She wanted her father to live longer than her mother had.

Grief shadowed her face... It was barely two years since her English mother had succumbed to the cancer she had fought so valiantly.

She shook the sadness from her. She was here as her father's hostess and she wanted to do him proud. She had already received approving smiles, and his praise of her had been heartfelt.

'*My darling child, how beautiful you look!*'

If she did, it was for him, she knew. For her position as the daughter of Georgios Petranakos.

She was gowned in a couture number, its pale blue silk a match for the grey-blue eyes inherited from her mother. Her dark hair and Mediterranean complexion came from her Greek genes. The artful bias cut of the gown showed her slender figure to perfection. With her perfect oval face, delicate nose and tender mouth, her hair in an elegant up-swept style and her father's gift of a simple yet extremely expensive diamond necklace around her swan-like neck, Calanthe knew that her beauty was assured.

It drew eyes and attention—and always had. But her smile was never more than gracious, her air always a lit-tle elusive. It exasperated her father, she knew. He wanted her to marry—and soon. But to marry required falling in love—and she had done that once before, when she had been young and naïve and trusting.

And she had her heart not just broken, but smashed to pieces—her illusions shattered in the cruellest way.

More guests were arriving, and she made herself pay at-tention to them, exchanging social chit-chat, being her fa-ther's gracious daughter as always. Soon they were moving away, and her eyes moved once more to the entrance to the banqueting suite, where new arrivals were being ushered in by the hotel staff.

One of the waiters glided up, proffering fresh glasses of champagne, and absently, with a smile of thanks, she took one, handing one to her father as well, while he conversed affably with yet another guest. Calanthe's gaze flicked back to the entrance. Surely everyone who had been invited was here by now? Dinner—a lavish buffet in the adjoining room—would soon be served.

She was just about to take a sip of her champagne when another guest made an appearance. Tall, wearing a tuxedo like all the other male guests, his face was averted from her as he spoke to a member of staff on the door. But there was something about him…

Suddenly, out of nowhere, every muscle in Calanthe's body tensed. Her breath froze in her throat, fingers convulsing on the stem of the champagne flute.

The new guest turned…looked into the crowded room.

Faintness drummed through Calanthe and she felt the blood drain from her face, a deathly coldness seize her.

# CHAPTER ONE

*Eight years earlier*

GINGERLY, CALANTHE EASED up the ceramic shard embedded in the hard, dry earth, delicately teasing it free with the tip of her trowel, calling across to Georgia, working beside her, to take a look with a more expert eye than her own.

It was Georgia who was studying archaeology, and was therefore well experienced on digs, whereas Calanthe was reading History of Art, which was a lot less hands-on with its subject matter. But she'd happily volunteered to join the student team which Georgia's professor had pulled together on a very tight timescale, to excavate a site newly revealed by the construction of a holiday resort on one of the myriad islands in the Aegean.

The students were a cheerful crowd, glad of a free, albeit working holiday in Greece—a sunny change from their *alma mater*, a rainy north country university in England.

Calanthe was pitching in willingly. She might have a wealthy Greek father, whom she'd visited twice yearly all her childhood, enjoying staying with him at his luxurious mansion on the outskirts of Athens, but she'd been raised in a quite ordinary way by her mother. Few knew she had a Greek surname as well as the English surname of her mother, which she was known by, and not even her close friends knew just how rich her father was.

'What do you think?' she asked Georgia now, holding the curved terracotta shard in the palm of her hand.

Georgia peered at it. 'Possibly Corinth ware? Let's see if there's more before we tell Prof,' she said enthusiastically, and set to with her trowel and brush.

A shadow fell over their kneeling forms.

'Find any gold or jewellery yet, ladies?' a deep voice enquired laconically in accented English.

Startled, Calanthe and Georgia lifted their bowed heads. Simultaneously, Calanthe was dimly aware, both their jaws dropped. The stranger looking down at them in their shallow trench was totally worth the reaction. Calanthe felt her breath catch. He stood there, towering over them—and not just because they were kneeling in a trench—booted feet apart, long legs encased in multi-pocketed khaki work trousers, heavily belted. He was narrow-hipped and broad-shouldered, his obviously muscled chest moulded by a dusty khaki tee, and he sported dark glasses that only emphasised the strong line of his jaw, already starting to darken this late in the afternoon, the sculpted mouth and the blade of a nose, and the dark, slightly over-long hair that feathered over his brow and at the nape of his strong neck.

The whole package was rough, tough and totally devastating...

Calanthe heard Georgia gulp and knew why.

'Just pottery so far,' Georgia managed to get out, scrambling to her feet.

Calanthe found she was doing likewise, suddenly burningly conscious that her comfy but baggy shorts were covered in soil, her own tee shirt damp with sweat, and her plaited hair screwed up unflatteringly on the top of her head.

Who *was* this guy? she found herself thinking, then answered her inchoate question herself. Pretty obviously, he was one of the workmen from the hotel construction site nearby. A second later she confirmed it—he was holding a yellow hard hat in one hand. However, what he was doing over here at the dig she had no idea. The excavation was out of bounds to all but the archaeology team.

'You're not supposed to be here,' she heard herself saying. It came out in a clipped voice, but that was from disconcertion, not in reproof.

Had he taken it as the latter? Something about his face seemed to harden a fraction, and even though he was wearing sunglasses Calanthe felt his gaze pierce her. She gulped, like Georgia, though hopefully more quietly.

'I was curious,' he informed her, in the same laconic fashion with which he'd asked his original question. 'This is, after all my country's history you're digging up,' he went on, and now his voice was less laconic, 'Not your own.'

Calanthe felt the pointedness of his remark and her chin lifted.

'Perhaps your country,' she said, echoing his tone deliberately, 'might show that it values its history more by banning the building of hotels all over it!'

This time the veiled gaze was definitely directed at her.

'The excavation site is being protected,' he shot back. 'And modern Greeks have to earn a living. Tourism is a major revenue source, so hotels are not a luxury but an essential necessity.'

His glance went to Georgia, and Calanthe felt as if she'd been dismissed from his attention. She wanted to bristle—but what he'd said was true.

He was speaking again, his voice back to being laconic

now. 'I was wondering if you could do with another volunteer, maybe, when I get off my shifts?' He glanced back at Calanthe, who felt herself flush again, and hated herself for it. 'Given the tight time scale you're working under.'

'You'll need to ask Prof,' Georgia said. 'He's over there.' She pointed.

The stranger nodded. 'Thanks. I will.'

He strode off, and Calanthe sank down on her knees again, deliberately not watching him stride away.

Georgia did, though—quite shamelessly.

'Oh, *wow*!' She heard Georgia sigh. 'Whatever he's got, he's got it two hundred per cent!'

'He's just a brickie,' Calanthe snapped.

Georgia's eyebrows rose. 'That sounds pretty snobbish,' she observed.

Calanthe shrugged. 'Well, what would some guy off a building site know about what we're doing?'

'He's interested,' Georgia said. 'Give him a chance.'

*To do what?* Calanthe heard the question in her head and didn't like that she'd asked it. Or wondered what the answer was.

'He could be wanting to filch stuff,' she argued. 'After all, he asked if we'd found gold or jewellery!'

'Everyone always asks that at digs,' Georgia replied mildly. 'Anyway, we're not going to find gold and jewellery—just pots. Speaking of which…let's see if we can find the rest of that pot. Come on—get stuck in!'

Calanthe did so with a will. It helped to put out of her head the workman who'd just volunteered to help out. But not, to her annoyance, very effectively.

Georgia, damn it, had been right. Whatever the man had, he had two hundred per cent of it…

\* \* \*

His name, so Georgia informed her that evening, when they set off with the other students to the cheap taverna near the harbour, was Nik.

'He's going to be working with Dave and Ken—when he can spare the time from being a *brickie*,' she said, pointedly using Calanthe's snobby description to mock it.

'Rather them than us,' answered Calanthe.

'Oh, come on—you're transparent!' Georgia quipped. 'You're only saying that because you fancy him rotten and don't want to admit it!'

Calanthe's face set, but Georgia wasn't done yet.

'Well, I fancy him rotten too—the voice alone, with that to-die-for accent…let alone the rest of him! But I'm honest enough to admit it. And…' she gave an exaggerated sigh '…also honest enough to know that I don't stand a chance. He's way out of my league.'

Calanthe snorted. 'Don't do yourself down!'

'I'm not,' said Georgia. 'I'm just being honest. Besides, I came out here hoping me and Dave might get it together— I've been after him for ever! On the other hand,' she mused as they gained the harbour area, glancing at Calanthe, who was looking a lot less dusty and work-worn now, in a loose-fitting cotton shift dress that skimmed her slender figure very nicely, her hair caught back in a ponytail that gleamed like mahogany, '*you*, my girl, definitely *are* in Nik the Greek's league! Nik the *Gorgeous* Greek…' She sighed extravagantly.

Calanthe snorted again. 'I have absolutely *no* interest, thank you—'

'Well, he'd be interested in you, I'll bet, with *your* looks! Greeks always fall for cool English girls! Of course, you're half-Greek yourself—I keep forgetting.'

'Georgia, please don't mention my Greek side to your precious Nik the Greek—'

Calanthe threw her friend a seriously warning look. She didn't want any questions about just who her father was. The surname was well known—and the wealth that went with it.

'Yeah, yeah… OK, I promise,' Georgia assured her airily. 'Now, come on—let's find the others and get some food. I'm starving.'

They quickened their pace, catching up with the others as they reached the quayside taverna which they frequented every night.

Joining the group of students—their professor and his deputy dined elsewhere, knowing their presence would only be restraining—Calanthe settled into the cheerful crowd, ordering a beer with the rest of them. Soon carafes of local wine and the usual local fare of *gyros* and *souvlakis* were all demolished. Conversation was lively, irreverent and familiar—discussing the day's dig and other archaeological matters, then segueing into universal topics of interest to their generation, from bands to politics to averting catastrophic climate change.

Their long table was outdoors, in the evening's cooler air, and everyone was relaxed and convivial. Calanthe sat back, glass in hand, wondering if she had room for one more of the sweet, sticky pastries that were the traditional dessert at tavernas such as this. She made a slight moue. Her father would be astounded to think of her dining in such humble surroundings. When she was with him in Athens fine dining was the order of the day, without exception, whether that was at home, courtesy of his in-house chef, or at the city's most expensive restaurants.

A wry smile tugged at her mouth as she took another mouthful of the wine, letting its rough but rich warmth fill her, enjoying the light breeze picking up and the sound of the sea lapping at the small boats in the harbour. She dipped her neck, rolling her shoulders slightly to release the muscles that had been hunched most of the day as she'd worked beside her fellow excavators.

'Need a massage?'

The low, deep voice spoke behind her. Laconic and accented. And familiar.

She jerked her head round, her expression altering immediately.

He might not be in his work clothes any more—he'd changed them for jeans and a fresh tee—but there was no mistaking who stood there. Tall, dark and devastating...

She felt a gulp form in her throat and suppressed it. *No*, she would *not* respond to the ridiculous impact this wretched man seemed to have on her—and every other female too. She was aware that Georgia had suddenly looked up from what had seemed to be a more-than-friendly tête-à-tête with Dave across the table, not to mention several other women further along, who were suddenly craning their necks to look at the tall figure now standing at the far end of the table.

'Nik—hi. Take a seat!' Ken called out from a few chairs along, waving in welcome.

To Calanthe's annoyance—and just why she was annoyed she didn't particularly want to think about—Nik casually swung a spare chair from a nearby table, and sat himself down, happy to let Ken reach for an unused glass and pour him a glassful of wine from the carafe.

'*Yammas*...' Nik said in the same casual fashion as he helped himself to the glass.

He glanced around the table, and then his gaze settled on her—again to Calanthe's annoyance, and this time she was more aware of the reason for it.

He tilted his glass at her. 'To finding treasure,' he said.

There was a glint in his dark eyes—eyes she would have preferred to still be shaded by sunglasses. Because unshaded they were…

She gave a silent gulp.

Dark and devastating, just like the rest of him…

Then he was saying something else. Not in English this time, but a murmur in Greek. She stilled.

'But I think I've just found it. Golden treasure…'

With an effort of intense will she kept her expression blank, as though she had not understood what he'd just said.

Or what he'd meant.

If she'd had any doubt, the glint in those dark and devastating eyes deepened, the sudden brush of his long lashes veiling it, but not before she'd read the meaning in it as clearly as she'd heard the words he'd just said.

For a second—or was it far longer than that?—she could not move. Not a muscle. Only sit there while those incredible eyes washed over her.

Marking her out…

For himself…

Out of nowhere, she could suddenly hear her own pulse, her own thudding heartbeat. Hear it and know why it was so suddenly, overpoweringly audible.

Then, breaking the moment, and breaking the look he was giving her, Georgia spoke.

'No treasure, Nik,' she said with a laugh. 'Just pots. And some bronze, if we're lucky.'

The dark, devastating gaze left Calanthe and she felt she could breathe again. Shakily, she reached for her wine, feeling the need for it.

What the hell had just happened?

She didn't want to think about it. Wanted to make herself

listen to what was being exchanged now…just stuff about the excavation.

Nik had clearly picked up on what Georgia had said. 'Bronze? No iron, then?'

'Maybe some,' Dave put in. 'But Prof says this site is likely to be on the cusp, timewise, between bronze and iron. Probably eleventh…maybe tenth century BC.'

Nik nodded. 'OK, so post-Mycenaean, then? More Dark Ages, pre-Archaic?'

Calanthe glanced at him, open surprise in her face at the knowledge he'd just displayed. For her pains she found herself on the receiving end of another glinting look from him. He was clearly aware of her surprise, and why it was there.

But now Dave and some of the others were launching into a discussion of just when the site might prove to date from, and what the implications of its location might be.

Nik, it seemed to Calanthe, was holding his own, although he was clearly no specialist. He made some remarks about building styles and methods in use in the period, and then Calanthe heard herself speak.

'You seem to have picked up a bit of historical knowledge by working on a modern construction site!' She spoke lightly, as if humorously, but his response was to throw another glinting look at her.

'No,' he replied pointedly, 'what knowledge I have of historical building styles and methods I've gained on my degree course in architecture—I did a module back in my third year on Classical Greek architecture.'

Calanthe felt her face stiffen. It had been a put-down, clear and obvious.

*And I deserved it. I put him down first, implying I was surprised that he should know anything intellectual since he's only a brickie on a building site…*

She picked up her glass, knocked back a mouthful of wine as a diversion, wondering why she'd felt the need to speak as she had. Seeking to keep him 'in his place'?

*To keep him at a distance—that's why I did it. Because...*

Her glance stole to him again. She heard him laugh at something one of the others had said, his dark head thrown back, his smile open and ready, displaying strong white teeth and carving lines around his mouth, crinkling his eyes.

Calanthe felt her breath catch. He really was the most in-credible-looking guy... With a sigh of defeat, she admitted it.

Georgia had turned away, diverted by Dave, and Calanthe leant forward, leaning her elbows on the table, wine glass in her hand, sipping from it, giving in to what she wanted to do. Just sit there and gaze at him...

After all, why *not* let herself gaze at him? Admit how gorgeous he was?

It was harmless enough, wasn't it?

Quite harmless...

*Athens: the present*

*Harmless...*

The word tolled in Calanthe's brain now, as she stood beside her father.

No, it had not been 'harmless' to indulge as she had wanted to do—as she had actually done—that long-ago summer, a wine glass lazily in her hands, letting her dreamy, wine-in-fused gaze self-indulgently rest on the man seated further along the taverna table, drinking him in as if he, too, were wine...

It had not been 'harmless' to have anything to do with him at all. Let alone—

She silenced her own inner, anguished voice. What use to tell herself what she should have done all those years ago? She hadn't—and her stupid, trusting heart had paid the price for it. She had been broken, and bitterly disillusioned by the man he'd turned out to be....

She heard, in her head, the echo of her father's voice, telling her just what Nik had done...what he had stooped to. How shamelessly, readily he had done so.

She tore her mind away—it was in the past and she would keep it that way.

Except that the past was now walking towards her. Purposefully heading towards her father and herself.

She had moments only to brace herself, to dredge up strength from somewhere deep inside her, and then he was there. Standing in front of her, a bare metre away. As tall and as head-turningly good-looking as he had ever been.

His evening dress was bespoke, hand-tailored to his broad, strong frame, superbly moulding his superb body. His hair was cut short and by an expert, feathering at the nape. His jaw was pristine, his skin smooth. He was svelte, groomed, immaculate, fitting in seamlessly with all the other svelte, groomed, immaculately clad rich men around him.

He stood in front of her. The eyes resting on her, not her father, were as dark, as long-lashed and as unreadable in their depths as they had ever been. With nothing in them except the bland civility befitting the occasion.

All her strength was going into standing there, every muscle taut, her fingertips tight around the stem of the champagne flute so that the skin around her lightly varnished nails was white. She had no strength left to analyse the something that flared to life in those unreadable depths—something that was not bland at all.

But then it was gone, and now he was speaking, that same bland civility in his voice.

'Hello, Calanthe, it's been a while.'

# CHAPTER TWO

NIKOS SAW HER FREEZE. Saw shock flash fleetingly across her face. Well, he hadn't been expecting to see her either. It had been impulse only, his instinct for taking opportunities as they presented themselves, that had made him walk in here.

His eyes went past Calanthe to the man beside her, who had registered his presence and now paused in his conversation with the man he'd been talking to, who nodded and moved away. There was a questioning look in Georgios Petranakos's eye, and Nikos spoke to allay it.

Even as he did he was conscious of a sense of biting irony. Georgios Petranakos had no idea who he was. The fixers he'd despatched eight years ago to protect his daughter would have recognised him, despite the different name he'd used back then...

Well, he was using his own name now.

'Nikos Kavadis,' he said, introducing himself.

He saw Georgios Petranakos mentally review the name, then nod in recognition. 'Ah, yes,' he said.

'I hope you will not mind my intruding like this, Kyrios Petranakos.' Nikos gave a smile that was a judiciously exact blend of confident and respectful. 'But I'm staying at this hotel at the moment, and I noticed your name listed on the function board in the lobby.'

The older man smiled genially. 'I am very glad you can join us.'

Nikos's social antennae, long honed, caught the note of genuine welcome in his host's voice. And, after all, why should he *not* be welcome?

His eyes darkened momentarily. Once, he would never have been welcome. Once, steps would have been taken—*had* been taken—ruthless and swift. His mouth twisted. Highly effective steps to dispose of him promptly.

But now... Oh, now he was completely eligible to move in such elite circles as Georgios Petranakos did. OK, so his own business affairs were not centred in Greece but ranged globally, wherever his specialist, innovative services were required—services so specialist, so innovative, that they had made him, in eight short years, a very wealthy man.

A man who could walk in, uninvited, to a rich man's private party with impunity. A man who could, with equal impunity, let his gaze go to the woman standing at Georgios Petranakos's side. A woman he'd had no idea he would set eyes on again. A woman he had once known, eight long years ago, as a very different person.

*But she was always the woman I see here now! Even back then.*

His thoughts darkened.

*But back then I did not know who she was. Not until—*

He pushed these thoughts away. When he'd found out who she was, everything had changed...

But as his gaze rested on her now he knew, with a surge of his blood, that one thing had not changed. A kick went through him, visceral and compelling. As visceral and as compelling as it had been the very first time he'd ever set eyes on her. Though here, in her couture gown, with her immaculate upswept hair, her perfectly made-up face, diamonds glinting at her throat, she could not have looked more different from the way he remembered her.

And yet…

*Her beauty is the same—as perfect now as it was then…*

He felt emotions well up in him—and memories… oh, definitely memories. Sensual, evocative and, sweeping over him in a way that was so very, very pleasurable…

For a moment he indulged them, gave them space to possess him. But then other memories came too. Memories less pleasurable. Unwelcome and jarring.

*Georgios Petranakos's fixers…making me that offer… spelling it out to me.*

Again, he pulled his thoughts away. His host was speaking, and Nikos gave his attention back to him, glad to pull away from thoughts he did not want to have…unpalatable memories.

'My daughter Calanthe,' Georgios Petranakos announced.

Had her father heard his murmured greeting a moment ago? Nikos gambled that he had not. Gambled, too, that Calanthe would make no reference to their prior acquaintance.

*Acquaintance?* The word mocked him silently inside his head. What he had had with Calanthe that summer long ago had been so much more than an 'acquaintance'…

'Kyrios Kavadis.' Her voice was cool, her expression cooler.

Yet she wasn't cool at all.

Nikos knew it. Could see it in the stiffness of her slender body, the way she held her head so high, the blankness in her face, her eyes. He felt again the emotions—untidy, irrelevant, unwelcome—that had made their presence felt as he'd walked towards her. As he'd registered her presence here, and that their paths were crossing like this after so long.

His gaze washed over her, expertly assessing. Eight years ago, not even out of her teens, she had had the natural loveliness of youth, but now…

*Now she has come into her full beauty.*

Exquisite—that was the only word for her now. The word echoed in his head. She was as exquisite in her beauty as her couture gown was exquisite, as the delicate diamonds at her throat and earlobes were exquisite, the diamond clip in her upswept hair. Chic and soignée, poised and elegant.

Memory thrust into his vision. Her coltish body in shorts, exposing her long, tanned legs, and a clinging tee shirt that moulded her breasts. Her hair in a plait hanging down her back, ready for a day working on the dig.

Then later, heading off to the taverna in a colourful, calf-length gathered cotton skirt and embroidered blouson, showing off her sun-kissed shoulders, her hair loosened into a tumbling cloud.

And later still, when he had taken her back to his room in the cheap *pensione*. Her lovely face lifted to his, her mouth tender as a newly ripened peach, her naked body arched and ardent beneath his, long limbs twining intimately with his, her hands winding around his bare back as he moved to take sweet possession of her…

Memory quickened in him.

And more than memory.

Desire.

It rose within him like a rich, potent liqueur, bringing the past into the present, fusing it, melding it, dispelling any doubts that had pulled at him moments ago as to whether it was wise to see her again like this. See her again after so many years. Here in her own refined, bejewelled milieu, a million miles from how she'd been when he'd first known her.

Yet again emotion plucked at him, unwelcome and jarring, but yet again he set it aside, dismissing what he did not wish to feel. Right now all he wanted was to let his gaze feast on her as she stood there, the poised and perfect daughter of one of Greece's richest men, taking in her exquisite beauty, savouring it, melding it with his memories.

But his host was addressing him once more. Requiring his attention.

'So what brings you to Athens? You are headquartered, I believe, in Switzerland?'

'Yes,' Nikos acknowledged, wresting his gaze and his mental focus away from where it wanted to be. 'Zurich. But I am here in Greece at the government's invitation, to consult on the current parliamentary enquiry—which of course you will know about—into reducing the cost of affordable housing whilst ensuring it is both environmentally low-impact in its construction and maintenance as well as earthquake-proof. It's based on work my company has undertaken recently in the Middle East, where similar constraints operate.'

He saw Georgios Petranakos nod knowledgably. 'Ah, yes, of course. I, myself, am likely to be involved marginally—though my remit is commercial rather than environmental.' He nodded. 'Perhaps we may find some discussion useful to us both while you are here?'

Nikos smiled politely with satisfaction. 'I would be more than happy to do so. When might suit you?'

'Come for lunch,' his host said expansively. He turned his head towards his daughter, who was standing rigidly, holding her glass of champagne. 'Calanthe, my darling one, you know my social diary better than my PA! Can we fit young Kavadis in for lunch this week? I was thinking, perhaps, of the day after tomorrow?'

His daughter's expression did not change. But Nikos knew with every fibre of his being that her father's invitation was not welcome to her.

That was understandable.

Again, memory pulled at him—but still he would allow it no ingress.

She did not blink. 'You are seeing your cardiologist that morning, Papa,' she said. Her voice was tight.

Georgios waved his hand impatiently. 'Plenty of time to get home for lunch!' he said airily. Then he turned his attention back to Nikos. 'We shall see you then?' He smiled genially, but dismissively.

Nikos nodded, the gesture encompassing Calanthe as well, and murmured his thanks. Then, knowing he had used up his host's attention span, he strolled away.

He was done here for tonight.

Thoughts flickered behind the unreadable mask of his face. So that was Georgios Petranakos in person. And *that*— once more that mix of honeyed memory and jarring awareness twisted in him—was his daughter Calanthe, in person.

Her name echoed in his head. He had had no thought of her when he'd followed his impulse to make himself known to her father. Yet now that he had seen her...

*More beautiful than ever.*

Eight years ago he had made the decision and done what he had done. But now the years had passed, changing so much, and what he had once let go of had just come into his life once more.

All his life he'd seized opportunities as they'd come by. It had taken him from a frugal rural life on a small Aegean island to diligent studying at school and entry to a lengthy architectural degree, on to venturing into business for himself, seeing those opportunities and capitalising on them, in the process making himself a wealthy man.

The journey had been intense and demanding, absorbing all his energies.

He had seized at those pleasurable carefree weeks with Calanthe just as he had seized at all the opportunities that came his way. And then the currents of his life had taken him onward...

*And now they have brought Calanthe back into my life. Into my reach.*

And this time...

His dark eyes glinted. Resolve filled him. A decision took shape in his mind.

The past had gone. But the present—oh, the present might yet be claimed for himself...

And this time—*this* time—there was no impediment to indulging that claim.

Calanthe lay in bed, her sleepless eyes staring upwards. Out of nowhere, with no warning, the past had opened up and walked into the present.

*Nik. The man I gave myself to—gave my stupid, stupid heart to. The heart he not only tossed aside but...*

A wash of humiliation swept over her. She had not felt it for years and yet it was here now, again, hot and humid and hideous. She could not bear to feel it...to remember it. To remember how her father, seeing her shed unstoppable tears over the man who had walked out on her, had taken her hands in his and told her just *why* Nik had walked out on her...

She heard her father's voice, kindly, but adamant.

*'A man who could do that, my dearest girl, is worth no tears—no tears at all!'*

She felt her face contort. No, Nik was worth no tears—yet she had shed them all the same.

She felt her hands clench at her sides in anger and in impotence. Then, deliberately, she stretched her fingers out, though they did not want to do so. Deliberately, she took a scything breath and set her mouth, a hardness forming in her unseeing eyes.

So Nik had walked back into her life again. The cold, disbelieving shock she'd felt as he'd headed towards her hammered into her once more. But she would not—*would not*—let him in again. She would keep him out with all the strength she possessed.

Her face twisted.

*He will never hurt me again—never. I won't allow it. I won't permit it. I won't ever be vulnerable to him again! Because I know him now as I did not then. I know him for what he is.*

That knowledge must keep her safe. It *must*.

Yet for all the bitterness that filled her, so did much, much more...

With a low, anguished groan she went on staring blindly at the ceiling, misery and memory filling her.

'Papa, what did the doctor say?'

Calanthe was waiting in the plush waiting room of the exclusive clinic where her reluctant father had been persuaded to see his eminent cardiologist.

'I'm perfectly fine! Just as I told you I was!' came the testy reply as her father marched out of the clinic into the waiting car.

'Really?' Calanthe said, not hiding the scepticism in her voice as the two of them settled back into the capacious seat and the chauffeur eased away. 'Then what did he say about the breathlessness? The pain that I *know*, Papa, sometimes strikes you in the chest?'

Her father waved an impatient hand. 'He's as much of a fusspot as you are! Tells me to cut down on work, lose some weight, take more exercise! As though I have time for any of that nonsense!'

'Papa, he's a doctor—he knows what he's talking about,' Calanthe began.

She could feel anxiety beating up in her. For her father even to admit the doctor had told him to do anything at all about his lifestyle was not a good sign.

'He wants to do more tests! I gave him short shrift. I've agreed to take some pills, but nothing more! And you, my daughter, are not to fuss over me. I can't abide it!'

Abruptly, her father changed the subject.

'Is everything ready for lunch today with young Kavadis?'

Calanthe stiffened immediately. For two days she'd been trying not to think of the coming lunch. Trying not to think about what had happened at her father's birthday party at all.

So Nik had crawled out of the woodwork—after eight long years. Crawled out, so it seemed, as a wealthy man—a man important enough to be consulted by the Greek government on building earthquake-proof, environmentally sustainable, low-cost housing.

Well, what was that to her? Nothing! Nik was in her past. And he would never, *never* be allowed to invade her life again.

Except…

'You will be joining us for lunch, will you not, Calanthe?'

She started at her father's question. 'Me? No. Of course not.'

'Why not?' His tone was bland.

'It's a business lunch, Papa,' she answered tightly.

Her father ignored her objection. 'He's a very good-looking young man, is he not?' he observed, his voice blander still. 'And financially very sound. Well-respected too.' He paused. 'Not married either,' her father said, 'so I am informed.'

Calanthe's fingers clenched. 'Papa...' she said warningly. But he would not be warned.

'Calanthe, my darling daughter, you know above all things I want your happiness! But the years are passing, and not just for me.' His voice changed, and something in it made her heart catch. 'Life does not last for ever, my dearest child. Your own mother was taken far too soon. As for me... Well, that quack just now has reminded me I am not immortal either—'

He broke off and Calanthe reached for his hands. Large and reassuring. The hands that had always protected her.

*Even when I did not know I needed it...*

Her thoughts swirled away. She knew just how much her father longed for her to marry, to choose one of the innumerable eligible potential husbands he had urged upon her. Knew how he wanted her settled, married with children. Happy... In love with the man she married.

*But I've done love. And it tore me to shreds.*

Her father's hands pressed hers, then released them with a pat.

'So,' he said, and his voice was bland again, 'will you join us for lunch today, hmm? Your ancient papa and the very handsome and eligible young Kyrios Kavadis?' He smiled. 'Look him over,' he said. 'That's all I ask.'

Nikos stepped out of the hotel limo that had brought him to the Villa Petranakos in the upmarket suburb of Kifissia and glanced up with an expression of appreciation as his architect's eye ran over it. These old mansions were worth preserving, and this one had been sympathetically restored, he could see.

The grand front doors were thrown open and Nikos strolled in, admiring the marbled interior as much as the exterior. But he was not here to admire an historic building. He was here for quite different reasons. A business association with Georgios Petranakos was potentially valuable. As the past had proved…

He slewed his mind away. Such barbed thoughts were not appropriate. His dark eyes veiled suddenly. Even though they came full circle to the present. To the other reason he was here today.

*Will she be here too?*

He couldn't call it. As the daughter of one of Greece's wealthiest men Calanthe would lead a hectic social life. She could be out and about right now…perhaps lunching with a lover—

The thought was a nail grating on a blackboard.

What did he know about her and the life she led now? Deliberately he had kept himself ignorant. Besides, he had had other things on his mind. Other priorities.

*I made my choice at the time. Took the only choice that was right for me.*

Took it? He had grabbed it with both hands.

He followed a manservant and was shown into a room opening off the spacious hall. Immediately, with a distinct kick to his pulse, he felt his eyes go straight to the woman standing by the window. Her stance was as stiff as it had been at her father's party, her face as expressionless. And every bit as exquisitely beautiful…

Her hair was confined into a knot at the nape of her neck.

There were stud pearls at her ears and a simple pearl rope around her neck, their colour matching the pale silk jersey top she was wearing. Her slender waist was belted, and she wore a thin, calf-length A-line skirt in soft dove-grey that went with her low-heeled shoes.

She did not move. And even though she was looking at him, she might as well have been made of marble.

Then his attention was called by her father, who was greeting him genially.

They took their places at the table. Nikos contented himself with merely nodding at Calanthe in a brief, civil gesture, murmuring a polite greeting, nothing more, and then looked across at his host as staff set the first course down, pouring wine and water for them all.

'I hope you will tell me something of the history of this most impressive mansion,' he said, with genuine appreciation in his voice. 'It has been superbly restored.'

His host smiled warmly, launching into the requisite account. Calanthe, Nikos saw from the outset, remained completely silent, merely eating and sipping water, her wine untouched. Tension radiated from her.

It did not deter him. He knew the reason for it. His gaze rested on her, veiled but measuring. He could hardly have expected a warm welcome from her, but that would not stop him.

*Not now that I have seen her again.*

He felt that kick in his pulse again…knew that he would not resist it. Would instead indulge it…

*And why not? Now I move in her circles…now I am no longer that penniless architecture student earning money during my vacations by doing back-breaking labour on a construction site… I have every right to make a move.*

Memory played in his head, enticing and alluring. From

the very first moment she'd looked up at him, startled, from that dusty excavation trench, and he'd seen the tell-tale dilation of her pupils which her prickly, snobbish rebuff of him had not been able to give the lie to, he'd felt that kick—and from then on he'd known he'd wanted her. Oh, she'd tried to hold him off—those snide put-downs had been meant to deter him—but he'd brushed them aside, knowing why she was sniping at him.

For the same reason she was now attempting to freeze him out.

*If she were not reacting to me as I am to her she would not bother freezing me out.*

His lidded eyes perused her as he gave half an ear to what her father was saying about the restoration of the villa.

*And if I were not reacting to her as I am then I would not be bothering to waste any time on her.*

Thoughts played in his head. Eight years ago it had ended. But now…?

*Now we could be good together—again…*

He realised his host had moved on to another subject and switched his full attention back to him.

'You have soared high very swiftly,' Georgios was now saying to Nikos with approval. 'You are still a young man, but you have achieved a great deal for environmental sustainability with your innovative designs and construction methods.' A shrewd glance came Nikos's way. 'It was perceptive of you to patent your materials and your method for low-energy concrete production.'

Nikos nodded, taking a mouthful of the excellent wine that had been served with the meal. Calanthe, he noticed, was still not drinking hers.

Memory slid like a knife between his synapses.

*That first night at the taverna—her knocking back the*

*cheap local wine we were all drinking. The glow it brought to her eyes...the way she kept looking at me...could not take her eyes from me. How hard I had to work not to look only at her, as I wanted to...*

He snapped the memory shut. Not now—not yet. There would be time for indulging in those memories. Maybe making new ones...

'Yes,' he answered his host. 'I saw no reason for others to benefit—perhaps those less responsibly-minded than I am determined to be. By patenting globally I can ensure they are used only in areas where it is environmentally appropriate. The continued use of concrete remains, of course, controversial, and is likely only to become increasingly so.'

His host addressed a technical question to him and Nikos followed his lead.

His eyes briefly encompassed Calanthe.

*There is no animation in her face. She is beautiful—exquisitely so—but like a statue. Not flesh and blood.*

Again, memory stabbed. More potent this time—much more potent.

*Her head thrown back, her hair cascading over the pillows, ecstasy in her face...*

With even more essential self-discipline, he snapped the memory shut. Returned to a discussion about reducing the energy requirements for making concrete and the commercial implications thereof.

His host's eyes rested speculatively on Nikos. 'Tell me, how long do you envisage being in Athens?'

'That will depend on how speedily the government officials decide to move during this consultation period,' Nikos replied drily.

'Hah, that means weeks!'

His host did not sound disapproving. Quite the reverse.

He sat back, with an air of genial relaxation about him and a decided look of satisfaction in his face.

Then the maid and manservant were returning, clearing away the finished plates, serving a summer tart for dessert. As they disappeared Georgios Petranakos visibly changed gear, launching into expressing his views on the government ministers Nikos was likely to encounter during the consultation process.

Nikos paid attention—this was useful information to him—but the scrape of a chair made him turn his head. Calanthe was getting to her feet, depositing her linen napkin on the table.

'Papa, if you will excuse me? I'm not sure I have either the stamina, or indeed the interest, to cope with the ins and outs of politicians. I must be off.' She glanced down at Nikos. Gave a tight, unrevealing smile. 'Kyrios Kavadis.'

She nodded.

And took her leave.

Her low heels clicked on the marble floor. She was not even waiting for her father and his guest to get to their feet and was gone in seconds.

Calanthe headed up to the curving staircase as fast as she could without actually running, clutching at the banister. It had taken all her strength to endure lunch—to sit there while Nikos Kavadis talked to her father barely more than a metre from her across the table.

Her expression contorted. And, worse, her father was obviously pleased that he'd be hanging around Athens for weeks! And she knew why he was pleased...

She pulled her thoughts away from the temptation simply to tell her father just why Nikos Kavadis was the very last man he should be encouraging in his endless matchmaking schemes. She felt her blood congeal at the thought of her father knowing...

She arrived at her bedroom and threw herself down on the bed, heart thudding. She wanted to pack...get out of Athens, get back to London. Get back to work. But her post at the museum was a job-sharing one, designed to give her time out here with her father and to put in some hours at one of the many Athenian museums on an exchange basis.

And now there was another reason to keep her in Greece. Calanthe felt an all too familiar anxiety biting at her. Her father might be playing down whatever it was his cardiologist had told him, but she could not dismiss it so easily. Her father was not well. So she could not run away just to get herself away from Nik.

She felt her hands claw into the bed-covering.

*I have to tough this out. I have to! He'll be here a while and then he'll go. Disappear again like he did before. But this time he'll disappear with my blessing—with my abject relief!*

If she could just hold out till then...

Then it would be over.

Like it had been before.

It was the only hope she could cling to.

# CHAPTER THREE

NIKOS CLIMBED INTO the hotel limo that was collecting him from the Petranakos mansion, his mood excellent for several reasons. Firstly, because he'd gained useful information about the politicians he was going to be dealing with here. And secondly, his host had more than once mentioned his latest birthday—a milestone that might make a man think seriously about stepping back from business, slowing the pace. Consider passing the burden on to young shoulders...

The words had been accompanied by a narrowed look directed at his guest. An assessing look... A speculative one...

Nikos might have made nothing of it, or little enough, except for the reaction of the other person present at the lunch. From his place at the foot of the table Nikos had heard Calanthe's knife and fork clatter to the plate. And then what surely had been an intake of breath that had been stifled as soon as it had been drawn.

Which could only mean...

The expression in his dark eyes was speculative...

Yes, precisely *what* could that mean?

Well, that was speculation and inward reflection for another time. For now it was time to focus on the third and most satisfying reason for his good mood.

Encountering Calanthe once more was proving as fortuitous as it had eight years ago. Seeing her again had brought that time vividly to his mind again. Eight years ago she had crossed his path and shared with him delights that had been memorable in his youth. Memorable, indeed…

His expression flickered.

It had been a golden summer in the weeks he'd spent with her at the excavation. A 'golden treasure' he had called her—and so she had proved.

Something changed in his eyes…hardened. Then he frowned. That was not why he'd called her his golden treasure. That had been because she herself had been such a find!

*I discovered her when I had no thought of doing so—no thought of anything that summer but hard work and putting aside money for my tuition fees.*

Then Calanthe—lovely, ardent and so, so giving—had appeared in his life and he had not been able to resist her…

Nor she him.

Once he had won her over she had given herself unstintingly and he had reciprocated—treasuring the gift she had given him, celebrating, with her, the transition from maiden to woman as she had trusted him to be her first lover.

His expression shadowed suddenly.

*She trusted me with her body but with nothing else. Not with who she really was…*

He pushed the thought aside. Not wanting to think about why she had proved such a golden treasure.

That didn't matter—not any more. All that mattered was how they had been together, he and Calanthe, that summer long ago, in each other's arms, passionate and carefree.

His expression changed again, became a frown again, but with a different cause. He was questioning himself.

Just what had been so good about those weeks with her before they had come to the end? Once she had stopped holding him at bay, accepted what was happening between them, she'd relaxed with him completely—and he with her. He'd singled her out, sitting beside her at the taverna in the evenings, interesting himself in her part of the dig. Interesting himself in her completely.

*Her ready laugh, her warmth… I could not keep my eyes from her, and nor could she keep hers from me.*

The other students had accepted what was happening—had treated them as a couple.

*And that is what we became.*

He'd revelled in the ardour of her lovemaking, the glow in her eyes. He had dedicated his time to her, had eyes for no other woman but her…

Reminiscence filled him and a frown plucked at his brows. Eight years had passed since he'd last seen her, but had there ever been anyone like her in his life? Women had always come easily to him, even when he was a penniless student. Now… His expression grew cynical. Now, of course, he thought caustically, he could have just about any woman he cast his eyes at. Except—

The frown deepened. Still he was questioning himself. There had been other attractive girls on that dig, but none had existed for him except for Calanthe. He tried to call up the images of any of the women he'd consorted with from time to time in his non-stop climb to fortune but none came to mind. Not any more—not since he'd seen Calanthe again.

In only a few days, out of nowhere, having never expected to see her again, he found she had totally imprinted herself on his consciousness.

*She is dominating my thoughts….my desires…*

The frown cleared from his face. That was hardly a problem—only a challenge.

A challenge he would meet gladly.

Determinedly.

Oh, she could freeze him out all she liked, but he knew better than to think he could not *un*freeze her. Reclaim the ardent, eager lover he had known, who had given herself so rapturously to him and would once more.

He was certain of it.

He settled back more comfortably into the deep leather car seat.

The only question was how and when to make his next move.

Calanthe set her coffee cup back on the tray, nestling back against her pillows. She was indulging in breakfast in bed, having been out late the night before. And the night before that. She was keeping busy—very busy—socialising to the hilt. Far more than she usually did when she was in Athens with her father.

Last night she'd been out to dinner with Yannis, one of her regular 'swains', as she wryly called the well-heeled young men who moved in her father's elite circles and would happily be a lot more to her than a mere dinner date if she ever showed the slightest inclination.

Her father, as she knew all too well, kept on hoping that one day she would choose one of them to marry. He made no secret of it. And as time had gone by she had come to accept that one day, eventually—though not yet!—she probably would accept a proposal from Yannis, or someone like him. Someone who was easy-going, pleasant company...who would make a loyal husband and an affectionate father to whatever children they might have.

Such a marriage—a marriage in which burning passion and heady desire played no role—was what she had come to reconcile herself to. It had come to seem...acceptable.

Except—

She pulled her thoughts away as emotion filled her—
emotion that she did not want, that she deplored, rejected.
No, she must *not* go down that dangerous path. Only one
man had ever set her passion on fire… Made her ache with
desire for him…

A man she must guard herself against with all her
strength.

And he had walked back into her life again.

Bleakly, she stared unseeingly into her bedroom, feeling
a restlessness seize her that had no right to be there.

For her father's sake she was stuck here in Athens, not
wanting to abandon him while she still had cause to worry
over his ill health, deny it as he insisted on doing. And
Nikos was here too. She knew that because her father kept
her informed of it. She'd dreaded this last week, lest her
father take it into his head to matchmake again and invite
Nikos for dinner. But she'd been blessedly spared that or-
deal. Even more blessedly, Nikos had not attempted to get
in touch with her.

*Maybe I have nothing to fear after all! Maybe he really is
only interested in a business acquaintance with my father!
It would be useful enough to him, after all.*

Her mouth twisted. Yes, her father's use to Nikos was
attested…

Again, she pulled her thoughts away. She would not think
of Nikos Kavadis—would not pay attention to the restlessness inside her. She would think, instead, of what she would
do today.

She might head into central Athens…put in some time
at the museum where she did some exchange work for her
London museum during her long stays in Greece visiting
her father.

Or perhaps one of her friends might suggest lunch some-where—maybe down on the Athenian Riviera at Glyfada… or they could take a boat from Piraeus out to one of the off-shore islands and make a day of it.

Even as she mulled over these possibilities the house phone on her bedside table rang. She picked it up, expecting it to be one of her friends—or Yannis, perhaps, thanking her for the evening before and suggesting another outing today.

But it was none of them. It was Nikos.

He had caught her off guard. He knew it the moment he spoke, by the sudden intake of breath at the other end of the line. Well, he wanted her off-guard—that was why he'd left it nearly a week before making contact with her.

OK, so he'd been full-on anyway, immersed in initial meetings with government officials as well as a whole slew of business meetings on his own account—including with Georgios Petranakos—which he was using his time in Athens to make the most of. But now he'd cleared his desk and another priority had taken over. The one he was focussing on today.

'Come to lunch,' he said, making no bones about it.

'I'm otherwise engaged,' came the immediate stiff reply.

'Your housekeeper says not,' Nikos riposted. 'I was think-ing,' he went on, 'of a leisurely jaunt out of the city. How about we go to Sounion? Take a picnic?' He paused deliberately. 'Your father thinks you've been burning the candle at both ends. He's suggested you need to slow the pace. With me.'

He could hear only silence on the line. He didn't let it last more than a microsecond, before speaking again.

'Good, that's settled. I'll pick you up at half-twelve.'

Then he rang off, a smile of satisfaction playing about his lips.

\* \* \*

She could have kept to her room. Cited a headache—a hang-over, even! Could have phoned her father at his office and rung a peal over his head for setting her up, as he so obviously had! Could have ripped into Elena the housekeeper for blabbing.

There were half a dozen things Calanthe knew she could have done—but she hadn't.

And she knew perfectly well why.

There were things that needed to be made clear.

Crystal-clear.

She emerged at the time Nikos had said to find him waiting in a low-slung, silver-grey, open-topped car sporting an Italian crest on its long bonnet. His own, or hired? She didn't know, and didn't care.

He leant across to open the passenger door for her, nodding a greeting as he did so, which she did not return. She had nothing civil to say to him. She slipped into the passenger seat, smoothing her pale green palazzo pants which she wore with their matching top. Like her, Nikos was wearing sunglasses, and she was glad of it. Perhaps they need never actually look at each other for the duration.

She sat back, pulling the seat belt across herself, burningly conscious of his presence beside her. Though she did not look at him she'd taken in that he was casually dressed in an open-necked shirt, cuffs turned back, his dark hair—so much shorter now than it had been that long-ago summer—slightly ruffled by the breeze. She felt her stomach clench as she caught the faint scent of aftershave.

Doggedly, she stared ahead, not letting herself look at him as he drove the car down the drive and turned out onto the highway, keeping deliberately silent. This was not a social outing—she did not even owe him courtesy.

Her face was set, more stony than ever.

He didn't speak either—only took the direction to Cape Sounion on the south-east of the Attica Peninsula, guiding the powerful car through the busy traffic until he could open the throttle clear of the city.

She was glad they were going to Sounion. It would be sufficiently out of the way for what she intended. Deliberately, she breathed slowly and evenly, refusing to let her tension show.

But she was as taut as a high-tension cable and she knew it. Did Nikos know it as well? If he did, he'd know why.

*And I want him to know—I damn well want him to know!*

Emotion rose in her. Emotion that had been suppressed for so long now that she might have thought it extinct. But it was no more extinct than the volcano on Thera had been extinct. It seethed like boiling magma, just below the rigidly composed air with which she sat so motionless beside Nikos.

He was so close…

Ripples like earth tremors vibrated within her. All she had to do was lift her hand to touch him…

Instead, she sat quite still, hands folded in her lap, gazing out through the windscreen, her expression impassive. Saying nothing. But feeling so much…

'What about here? It catches the breeze and the view is spectacular!'

Nikos's tone was inviting—deliberately so. He'd studiously ignored Calanthe's silence on the way here. It was, after all, to be expected. And he knew why.

*She's spoiling for a fight.*

That, he knew, was why she'd accepted his invitation. Why she was having anything to do with him. Why, indeed, he'd suggested driving out to Cape Sounion—way out of the city—taking with them the lavish picnic his hotel's kitchens had supplied him with, and which he now proceeded to unload from the small boot of the car.

It was a hire car, but he'd chosen and driven it with pleasure—even though the presence of Calanthe at his side, stony-faced and silent, had been a distraction from putting the car through its paces.

Closing the boot with a snap, he led the way to a picnic spot with panoramic views over the Cape and the Aegean Sea beyond. He spread out the blanket then hunkered down to open up the cool box, extracting a chilled bottle of white wine and one of sparkling water.

'Wine, water, or a spritzer?' he enquired genially.

'Water,' came the terse reply from Calanthe.

She was sitting herself down, carefully angling her legs away from him and keeping a good metre distant, towards the edge of the blanket. She did not remove her dark glasses, and neither did he take off his own. After all, the sun sparkling over the blue water beyond the cliff-edge was very bright. That was excuse enough.

The real reason, though, as Nikos well knew, was to give herself a sense of protection.

He carefully poured the chilled sparkling water into one of the glasses provided and handed it to her. She took it, scrupulously avoiding the slightest chance of their fingers brushing, and drank from its contents gracefully. Nikos mixed himself a spritzer and raised his glass.

'What shall we drink to?' he asked. His tone was deliberately bland.

He saw her lovely mouth tighten, her fingers around the glass do likewise.

'To never seeing each other again. *Again.*'

She knocked back another big mouthful of her water, difficult when it was effervescing so frenziedly in the heat, but the gesture served its purpose. As did her words.

The opening salvo.

Had she not been wearing her shades, Nikos knew she'd be glaring at him with a killing basilisk gaze. But his only response was to take up a deliberately relaxed pose, stretching out his legs, crossing them at the ankles and leaning back on his elbow.

Yet behind the relaxed pose he was bracing himself.

*The only accusation she can throw at me is that I left her. Nothing else.*

He had made sure of that—made it a condition to her father's fixers.

*And all that's in the past—long gone.*

So there was no point dwelling on it, was there? It was the present he was concerned with now. Only the present.

*I am not concerned that our affair ended—or why. I am only concerned with what I want there to be between us now.*

His eyes rested on her. Even with that net of tension over her, radiating her resistance and hostility towards him, she was still so beautiful it could take his breath away. He wanted to feast his gaze on her, drink her in... And then reach for her...feel her resistance to him melting away, feel her mouth opening to his, her arms coming around him, her body yielding to his...warm and ardent and eager...

Memories, delectable and enticing, were like tendrils in his mind, but he pushed them away. He was not there yet...

'Why?' he said, tilting his head to look directly at her, answering her with a tone of voice that was neither challenging nor countering, only enquiring. He was keeping his cool. Surely the best way to handle this.

He could see her expression change.

*'Why?'* she repeated.

It was like a bullet. Shot from her. Right at him.

She reared back. 'You have the almighty *nerve* to sit there and ask *why*!'

More bullets, spitting at him like machine gun fire.

'You think—you *really* think—that you can just, oh, so casually invite me out! Behave as though *nothing* had happened between us! As if—'

He cut across her. 'It did happen, Calanthe. Our time together that summer. And even if it hadn't...'

He changed his voice, his gaze never leaving hers. He wanted her to understand that she could protest all she liked but it would make no difference.

'Even if the very first time I'd ever set eyes on you had been at your father's birthday party I would still have asked you out. Still have wanted you here. Because...' his voice became a caress '...you are simply the most beautiful woman I have ever set eyes on.'

He saw her face work. 'Don't. Just...*don't.*'

Her words were not bullets now, but tight, like wire pulled to breaking strain.

He gave a shrug. 'Why not? Why not tell you the truth? You were irresistible eight years ago and you are even more so now.'

She shot forward, fury in the set of her shoulders.

'Oh, so damn irresistible that you walked out on me without a word! Walked out and—'

She broke off, twisting her head away, knocking back another gulp of water and then setting the glass down. He saw her take a breath, a deliberate one, to steady herself. Then she whipped her head back round. Returned to the attack.

But he did not let her speak. There was only one way he

could answer her, only one response he could make. Anything else was out of the question.

*She must never know why I left her.*

Not that what he was going to say to her was not the truth. He felt a flicker of emotion rise within him. It was just not *all* the truth...

'Calanthe, what we had together was good—memorably so! But,' he said, holding her unseen gaze, 'it was a summer romance. Wonderful while it lasted—but...' He paused, knowing he had to say this. 'Then it ended—just as the summer ended.'

He was speaking carefully. He knew that he was doing so, and knew why he was doing so. He was keeping to what he could say...explain.

To continue his defence, at least where he could, he went on, 'And, to set the record straight, I did not leave *"without a word"*. I told Georgia that I'd been unexpectedly called away and I left you a note. I'm sorry not to have told you in person, but I had to leave the island right away.'

He'd had no choice—her father's fixers had made that crystal-clear to him. No more contact.

*Not that I could have looked her in the face again...*

His mind pulled away. Those memories were too jarring. Emotion rose in him again. And besides, he'd had another pressing reason for leaving the island immediately...

'Why?' Her blunt question was still hostile. 'Just what was so pressing...so urgent?'

She was staring at him, her face immobile. He found himself wishing she was not wearing dark glasses, so he could see the expression in her eyes. See what she was thinking. He'd always been able to see what she was feeling...she'd never hidden her emotions from him...

His mouth tightened. No, she'd never done that, all right! But they'd been feelings that had only...complicated things.

And now—now he wanted things to be simple between them.

He wanted to put aside those elements of the past that jarred, whose memory was unwelcome—not let them get in the way now.

*Because what I want now is the present—only the present.*

His eyes washed over her again from behind the protection of his shades. And that was so very, very enticing...

Again he felt desire rise through him. The impact she'd had on him all those years ago was stronger now, so much stronger...

His own words that he'd spoken just now hung in his head—irrefutable and compelling.

'*You are the most beautiful woman I have ever set eyes on.*'

But he could not yet indulge himself. He still had to dispose of her anger to him. Get it out of the way. Explain— justify—his behaviour in the only way he could.

Her hidden gaze was still levelled at him. Her fingers still tight around her glass. Her body was still quite immobile. Tense.

'Family matters,' he replied. 'My grandmother...'

He left it at that. The only way he could leave it.

He saw her mouth thin, as if he'd uttered a typical self-exonerating excuse. He didn't want to hear her put that into words, so he took control of the moment instead.

'Calanthe, I know that the way we ended eight years ago upset you, but... Well, like I said, what we had was a summer romance. It was always going to end... You went back to your life.'

His voice hardened unconsciously. After all, her life—her

*real* life—had not been what she'd let him think. She had not been just another one of the bunch of British university students on a working holiday in Greece.

He continued, 'And I went back to mine. We went our separate ways.'

She was still keeping that hidden gaze levelled at him, immobile and tense.

He levered himself forward, looked directly at her. Said now what he wanted to say. What he wanted her to hear. What he had brought her here to say.

'But now I'm back.'

# CHAPTER FOUR

CALANTHE STARED AT HIM.

*'But now I'm back.'*

His words, so coolly uttered, stung like wasp stings on her bare arms. She felt emotion rise in her like boiling magma. But somehow she kept a lid on it. She was no longer that nineteen-year-old in the throes of agonising first love. She was a mature woman. Calm, composed, under control.

*My own control.*

'Back for what, Nik?' she asked.

Her voice was dry. As dry as sand.

She was aware far too late that she'd called him by the name she'd used eight years ago.

He smiled. It was a smile that reached back through the years. A smile she had not seen directed at her for those eight long years that divided them. A smile that divided her stupid, foolish ingenue self from the mature, capable, self-controlled woman she was now.

'For you, of course, Calanthe,' he said.

For a second—an endless, motionless second—the words hung in the air between them. Both of them looked at each other, their gazes veiled from the other.

Then he broke the moment. Set down his spritzer and leaned forward to examine the rest of the contents of the picnic box.

'I'm hungry,' he announced. 'Let's eat.'

She watched him busy himself extracting carefully wrapped parcels from the box, setting them out on the blanket, before peeling off the wrappings. Her mind was in turmoil. She wanted to yell at him, shout at him, throw everything she had buried so deep within her those long eight years ago when he had walked out on her…everything that had festered and burned and *hurt* so much…

And more than hurt.

Worse than hurt.

Once again, as she had the night after her father's birthday party, when she had lain sleepless in her bed, with Nik having just walked into her life again as he had, she felt the hot, humid drenching of humiliation rise up in her unbearably. She forced it from her. Refusing to give it entry.

Her expression hardened as she went on watching him unpack the picnic. Her mouth twisted. So Nik—rich and successful now—thought he could just move in on her again! Thought he could stroll into her life, driving his fancy car, staying in Athens' best hotel, flashing his cash around as casually as if it were candy. Thought he could just stroll right up to her and take up with her again!

He really thought that?

After what he'd done to her?

*Well, he can think again! Because it will never, never happen.*

She was safe from him. Had made herself so—painstakingly, painfully, assiduously and determinedly—with every year that separated her from that long-ago summer when she had been so vulnerable to him, so trusting…

*He can't get to me again. Not now.*

Because now, as the bitter taste in her mouth accentuated, she knew what kind of man he was. What he was prepared to stoop to…

A 'summer romance'. That was what he was calling what they'd had. Even though, for her, it had been so much more than that.

She felt her heart clench.

*I really thought myself in love—I truly, truly did…*

The pain inside her twisted, wrenching at her emotions.

*He looked me in the face and told me it was just a summer romance. That that was the only reason he ended it.*

But she knew better. Bitterly, bitterly so.

Again, the memory of her father's words to her as she'd sobbed her youthful heartbreak sounded in her head, telling her just what the man who'd romanced her all summer had done…what kind of man it had proved him to be.

*And he thinks I don't know. It's obvious he thinks that.*

Well, she would not enlighten him. Let him trot out whatever he liked about 'summer romance'!

*Because I can't bear to tell him that I know—I can't bear to feel again, in front of him, the humiliation of it…*

She screwed her eyes shut behind her dark glasses, grateful for them, schooling her emotions back under her control. She would not let them out again. Instead, she would deal with the situation as it presented itself. Behave as though he meant nothing to her. Because that would be the least painful to her, and protecting herself was her priority.

She took a silent breath, opened her eyes again, and watched him finish the unpacking, her expression impassive, making her features relax. She was safe from him— whatever he might so shamelessly, arrogantly think. That was what she had to hang on to.

He sat back, glancing up at her, and smiled. 'OK, what do you want to start with? It all looks good! There's seafood salad, chicken breast with some kind of dressing, Parma ham and smoked salmon—and any number of side salads!'

He indicated the spread with a sweep of his hand. His tone was genial, amicable, easy-going, his smile warm.

Out of nowhere, memory hit. She'd picnicked with Nik before, during their lunch breaks at the excavation, though nothing like this grand gourmet feast. They'd bought *gyros* at the harbour-side, clambered up the narrow goats' path to look down over the azure sea, settling themselves down.

Nik had smiled at her… Just as he was smiling now.

The pain was visceral, like a blow to her lungs. She forced it away. Forced the memory away. Forced away all memories of Nik from that time so many years ago. She would not give them oxygen to flare and burn her. Instead she dragged her eyes down to the repast spread on the dry ground. Against her volition she suddenly felt hungry. Breakfast had been a long time ago. Would it really kill her to eat some of this picnic?

She reached for one of the plates, hovering her fork over several of the dishes, then taking a little of each. She was hungry—she would eat. And the fact that she was doing so in the presence of the man she had never wanted to see again in her life she would completely ignore, with strength of will and absolute self-control.

*I won't let him get to me. I can't and I won't.*

Yet even as her eyes rested on him, still blessedly veiled by her dark glasses, and she sat back, making her position more comfortable and forking into the delicious food, she felt sensation sweep over her.

Nik at twenty-five had been a hunk of the first order— she hadn't needed Georgia's breathless admiration to tell her that. She'd had eyes in her head. Eyes that had wanted to do as she had done that first fateful night at the taverna: simply gaze and gaze and gaze...

As they still did.

She felt something squeeze inside her—something catch. Her gaze rested on him now as helplessly as it had eight long years ago.

*He's matured. That raw, rough toughness has matured into a lean strength. Smoothed itself. Honed itself. Then, he looked exactly what he was—a man in his mid-twenties, muscles pumped from hard physical labour, hair over-long, jawline roughened, hands callused. But now...*

Now the years sat on him well, as did his wealth. He might be lounging back on the cliffs of Cape Sounion, but there was a sophistication to him now, a cosmopolitan air that went with the expensive casual clothes, the impeccably groomed hair, the pristine jawline.

She felt again that tightening, that catching of something inside her. Eight years had passed, but one truth still forced itself upon her—however unwilling she was to hear it, however much she might bitterly resist it and resent it.

In her head, his words echoed.

*'You were irresistible eight years ago, and you are even more so now.'*

And, with a heaviness that seemed to crush her like a weight she could no longer bear, she knew that those words were true of her feelings too.

And the knowledge was unendurable.

Somehow she got through the rest of the picnic. For reasons she did not want to think about—because it was somehow easier on her not to do so...because letting Nikos know how hideously he'd hurt her was just too painful—she let Nikos behave as though this were just a normal occasion. As if he really was just a new business acquaintance of her father, inviting his daughter for this al fresco outing.

That, she knew, with a shiver of coldness, would, in fact, be what her father would assume.

*That I'm going out on a date with a new man. A man who, so far, has passed my father's eligibility test.*

The cold pool in the pit of her stomach chilled even more. If her father only knew—

She cut off her thoughts. No point giving room to them. No point doing anything but what she was doing now: having the semblance of a civil, social picnic with a man who was all but a stranger, who had obviously invited her out because she was Georgios Petranakos's very attractive daughter.

And his heiress.

The word tolled in her brain. With all its implications.

She shook them from her. They were irrelevant. Nikos Kavadis would not even get to first base with her, let alone meet whatever aspirations he might be contemplating giving house room to.

But what, exactly, was he after?

She felt the question in her head…felt herself shy away from it. Eight years ago he'd romanced her, not knowing whose daughter she was.

Now he did.

Again, her thoughts pulled away.

No, above all, she mustn't go there.

He was peeling a peach, then cutting it for her, offering her a slice. Carefully, she took the succulent fruit and slipped it into her mouth. There had been something unnervingly intimate in the way Nikos had offered it to her.

She swallowed it down, then reached for her water, nearly

finishing it off. She poured the rest over fingers that were sticky from the peach. Then she got to her feet.

'I haven't been to Sounion for a while—I might as well see the temple up close now I'm here,' she announced.

She kept her tone cool...impersonal.

Nikos stood up too.

'Do you want to stay for the sunset?' he asked. 'If so, I'm sure we can get a coffee at one of the hotels by the beach to while away the time.'

Calanthe shook her head. It was hours till sunset—the famous 'show' that tourists came to see, watching as it set behind the ancient ruins of the temple starkly outlined on the promontory.

'I'm going out this evening,' she said. 'I don't want to be back too late.'

'Who's the lucky man?' Nikos's enquiry was casual as he stooped to pack away the picnic things.

'A girlfriend,' Calanthe answered without thinking. Then she was cross that she hadn't said her evening out was to be with a man. 'A concert,' she added for good measure. 'Schubert.'

She watched as Nikos swung up the picnic box. Another memory darted into Calanthe's head—how he'd so effortlessly hefted a sack of dry cement into a waiting wheelbarrow on the construction site next to the dig. Georgia's eyes had gone to the ripped torso on display as he had done so and she'd given a sigh.

*'Oh, for your looks, Cal!'* she'd said. *'He only has eyes for you, you know.'*

Her expression changed. Hardened. In her head she heard again his declaration—that he had come back.

For her.

She felt a shiver go through her. A shiver that should not

be there. Yet there it was, all the same. A shiver of aware-ness…of vulnerability.

*Nik—back in my life. Wanting me again.*

She felt the power of his declaration—the declaration he'd so shamelessly, arrogantly made to her—and yet for all his shamelessness and arrogance she could feel its power.…

He held out a hand as if to guide her as they headed back to the car. She ignored it. That was the only sane thing to do. Ignore it. Ignore everything about him. Shut him out.

*I've said what I came here to say. Made it crystal-clear that I want absolutely nothing to do with him, ever again!*

And now she needn't.

That was all she must hang on to. Anything else was far too dangerous.


'Earth-shaker.' Nikos stood contemplating the ruins of the ancient temple to the powerful sea god Poseidon, brother of Zeus, patron of all seafarers.

Calanthe spoke at his side. '*Enosichthon*—that's what Homer calls him. Though there are variants on that.'

She was speaking civilly to him—that was something at least, Nikos allowed, bringing his gaze back to her. He was taking it carefully. She'd had her showdown with him—the one he'd braced himself for, knowing he needed to get it out of the way. Defuse the past so he could move on to the future.

His eyes rested on her. Every glance at her only con-firmed what he wanted. No matter how they'd parted eight years ago—or *why* they'd parted—right now he wanted only the immediate future with her.

He heard his own words to her echo in his head.

'*You were irresistible eight years ago and you are even more so now.*'

Nothing had ever been truer. She had swept him away—then and now.

He realised she was speaking again, and made himself pay attention to what she was saying.

'It's strange,' she mused, 'that a sea god should also be a god of earthquakes.'

'Well, we think of earthquakes as being of the land, but they're caused by the movement of the crust's tectonic plates, and many tectonic fault lines lie underwater or along coastlines,' Nikos explained. 'Greece is very vulnerable, sitting in the midst of some very complex plate boundaries. The whole area is moving and jolting as the plates grind together—hence the frequent earthquakes, some minor and some devastating, like the one that caught my parents—' He stopped.

Calanthe looked at him. He looked away. He should not have mentioned his parents, but it was too late now.

'They were killed in an earthquake when I was five,' he said.

He heard the intake of her breath.

'Nik… I didn't know. You never… You never mentioned that when we first—'

She broke off.

He looked at her, his expression veiled.

'There was quite a lot that didn't get mentioned,' he replied.

He shifted restlessly. There were things that perhaps they should have known about each other then. And things that should never be known…even now.

Especially now…

He walked a little way away, feeling the afternoon heat beating down. The blue of the sea was azure, brilliant in the sun, and the ceaseless chorus of cicadas was all around.

He had touched on a dangerous subject and wanted to move away from it.

'They put the temple here because it was the first glimpse of Attica for ships sailing home, didn't they?' he heard himself say, gazing around, wanting something totally neutral to say. 'Presumably by the time they could see the temple they were all but home and dry.'

'Seafaring was a dangerous business in those days,' she answered.

'Yet it was undertaken so much, all the same. All that trade constantly going on…taking goods back and forth across the Aegean and further. I remember from the dig that—'

He stopped again.

There was a pause. But then Calanthe picked up the thread, her tone of voice unexceptional.

'Yes, that was what pleased Prof so much—that the pots we dug up proved that trade with Corinth, even in that difficult era, had not disappeared.'

'What happened to all the finds?'

Nikos made sure his voice was simply civilly enquiring, glad that he could do so and that she could reply in kind. He wanted to be able to have a simple, normal conversation with her, not something charged with stressful emotions.

*Like fault lines between us, creating tension I do not want.*

She was answering his question, her voice as civil as his.

'After cataloguing and so on they ended up in the local museum. A couple of the more important pieces went to Corinth, I think.'

She wandered off, her attention apparently taken by the impressive row of columns marching along the flanks of the temple ruins. Nikos strolled after her, placing the palm of his hand on one of the fluted columns experimentally.

'The marble is quite coarse-grained,' he informed her, wanting to keep this normal conversation going. 'As you'll know, the current temple is built on the ruins of an older, Archaic period temple, which was made of limestone. The two have been very skilfully integrated.'

He pointed out areas where it was possible to discern, with a trained eye, what he meant, and saw that she was listening. It called to his mind how she'd listened at that first taverna meal all those years ago, as he'd discoursed on building methods in the ancient world.

*Was that what made me want to make her think differently about me? Make her want to want me?*

He looked covertly at her now. Her whole appearance was so different from what it had been eight years ago, when she was a teenager. Her outfit alone—from some pricey boutique in Kolonaki, no doubt—and her chic, poised elegance were a world away from the way she'd looked back then.

*Like she was just one of those run-of-the-mill students... Not even letting on she was half-Greek. Let alone whose daughter she was.*

That was definitely one of the things that had never got mentioned...

He felt emotion twist in him. Pushed it aside. He didn't want the past making things complicated now, in the present. He'd called their affair a summer romance—and that was what it had had to be.

But now...?

*Now I'm part of her world.*

It had taken long studies, non-stop hard work and taking risks, unsure if they'd pay off. But they had—more than handsomely. And now he was reaping the rewards.

He gave a silent nod to himself. He was doing some good in the world as well.

As if she'd caught his thoughts, Calanthe spoke. Her voice was different, somehow, from her impersonal conversational tone as they'd explored the temple ruins.

'What you told me just now... I didn't know about the earthquake in your childhood. That's why you specialise in earthquake-proof housing, isn't it, Nik?'

Her question was softly spoken, and for the first time since their paths had crossed again there was sympathy in it.

'Because of your parents.' She paused, a slight frown forming. 'What happened to you after...after your parents were killed?'

'I went to live with my maternal grandmother,' he answered. 'She...she was very important to me.'

He stopped. This was dangerous territory again.

Abruptly, he glanced at his watch. Changed the subject just as abruptly.

'If you're going out tonight I'd better run you back. I haven't forgotten how vicious the Athens traffic is.'

He headed back down towards the car park and Calanthe followed him. As he walked he put the past behind him. His parents were long gone, his grandmother had died three years ago—he felt emotion stab at him for a moment—and his youthful romance with Calanthe had come to the end it had. For the reasons it had had to...

*But those reasons no longer stand in the way. That is what I welcome. So the way ahead with her is clear.*

All he had to do was convince her of that. And he would, too.

His gaze went sideways to Calanthe. Even at the end of a hot day outdoors she still looked cool and elegant. And so breathtakingly beautiful!

One thing was certain, however many years had passed. And his own words to her over lunch echoed in his head.

*'You were the most beautiful woman I'd ever set eyes on.'*

And she still was. As irresistible now as she had been then…

# CHAPTER FIVE

CALANTHE LEANT ON the ferry's railings, gazing back at the port of Piraeus as it receded into the distance, the churning wake of the ferry showing its path. She was glad to be out of Athens, even if only for the weekend. She was heading for an island villa belonging to a friend who was throwing a lavish party.

Most of the guests were being flown out there, or would arrive in private yachts. Calanthe, however, was taking the public ferry quite deliberately. She lived in two worlds and always had. Her mother's middle-class world of taking public transport and her father's wealthy VIP world of limos, yachts and helicopters.

She'd always moved easily between the two, depending on whether she was in the UK or in Athens. The only exception had been that fateful dig during her student days, when she had brought her UK self to Greece for the summer.

*No wonder Nikos didn't have any idea about whose daughter I was.*

And she'd wanted to keep it that way. Hadn't wanted her father's wealth impacting on what she'd had with Nik that glorious summer. Complicating things…

Painful emotion plucked at her she watched Piraeus recede across the widening gap of sea, her mind going yet again to their picnic at Cape Sounion. Her expression hardened. Nikos had claimed that what had been between them had been nothing more than a summer romance. Never intended to last. And that that was why it had ended the way it had.

She felt herself waver. Almost...*almost*...she could believe him.

Her mouth twisted.

Except that she knew otherwise. Bitterly, savagely knew otherwise...

Restlessly, she moved away from the rail, heading for a seating area. Had she been wise to go to Sounion with Nik? Yes, she'd been able to let rip at him, make it clear she wanted nothing more to do with him. But just seeing him, spending time in his company, however tense, had made her ultra-aware of him all over again—of his sheer masculinity, of how strong the magnetism was that he somehow exerted over her.

And she'd been made aware of more than that. Made aware of that pang of sympathy that had smote her as he'd told her about the sad fate of his parents. She'd seen him as a little boy, bereft and orphaned, being taken in by his grandmother to grow up with her.

She pulled her thoughts away. She didn't want to think of Nikos like that. Deserving her sympathy. It was as if she was letting her guard down about him, and she could not risk that. Could not risk it at all.

Since that day at Sounion she'd come to terms with Nik's return to Greece. Had decided she would put the past behind her, but would not let Nik back into her life. That would be an act of insanity...

Had he accepted that whatever it was he wanted of her now—all that he had said to her at Sounion—was impossible? Perhaps he had. It was over ten days since then, and he'd made no attempt to see her again or ask her out.

She was relieved—of course she was. What else should she be? No other emotion was permissible. Her father, too, had said nothing, and she was relieved at that, too. She did not want him thinking of Nik as any possible kind of suitor.

*I don't want to have to tell him who Nik is—who he once was. He's clearly made no connection, and I don't want him to.*

No, the past had to stay in the past. That was the only way she could cope with the present.

*And the only way I can cope with having seen Nik again is by not seeing him!*

That was the safest way. To wait it out until he left Athens and she was safe from the danger of running into him again. It was her major reason for looking forward to the coming weekend villa party—it would get her out of the city...help get Nik out of her head.

Determinedly, she sat herself down on one of the benches on the cooler, more shady side of the deck, extracting from her bag one of the specialist art history journals she subscribed to, intending to while away the ferry crossing.

She had barely opened it when a shadow fell over her. She glanced up.

Froze.

It was Nik.

Shock was stark in her face. Nik saw it instantly. More than shock. Dismay. And something more than that. The flash in her eyes told him that all her anger, all her rejection of him, all her scathing repudiation, all her blanking of him... all of that was a lie.

He felt a tight, justified stab of satisfaction.

He sat down opposite her.

'What the *hell*,' she spat at him, 'are you doing here?'

He crossed one leg over the other in a leisurely, relaxed fashion.

'The same as you are. Heading for the Volous party.'

'You don't know Marina Volous!'

'No, I know her husband. A business association... He's in finance, as I'm sure you know, and a useful contact. He invited me. Tell me something...' his tone changed '...why are you travelling on the public ferry and not taking one of the private transfers laid on for guests?'

There was an edge in his voice—he could hear it. Knew why it was there.

'Do you enjoy play-acting that you're just an ordinary member of the public? The way you pretended when you were a student on that dig?'

He saw her face tighten.

'There was no pretence, Nikos. And, although it's absolutely none of your business, my English mother—as you may recall me telling you that summer—raised me on her own, and always insisted I should be able to live without relying on my father. She earned her own living—she was a hairdresser and beautician—and apart from visits to Greece during school holidays I lived a perfectly ordinary life. Not poor, but not rich either. My father paid for my university course, but that was all.'

His expression was sceptical. 'She wasn't a wealthy divorcee?' he challenged.

'She wasn't a divorcee at all!' came the riposte. 'She never married my father—she didn't want to. Her choice, not his. She didn't want to be tied down in marriage. But my father insisted on acknowledging me as his daughter on my birth certificate, so I have dual nationality and two passports.

I'm Calanthe Reynolds, as you knew me, and Calanthe Petranakos as well.'

He saw her expression change. Harden with suspicion.

'How did you know I was taking the ferry?' she asked.

He smiled, eyes glinting. 'Your housekeeper told me when I phoned this morning to offer to escort you to the party,' he said.

Calanthe's eyes flashed angrily. 'I neither need nor want your escort!' Her face worked. 'Leave me *alone*, Nik. I don't want *anything* to do with you ever again! I made that clear enough at Sounion. Our "summer romance", as you call it, was over eight years ago. You saw to that.' The bitterness in her voice was audible, and something hardened in her eyes. 'You're not getting another one.'

He met her flashing eyes full-on. This time neither of them was wearing shades, and he could see the angry depths of her grey-blue eyes…eyes that had once gazed at him meltingly, filled with warmth and desire and passion and something more than that…

'Maybe,' he said slowly, his eyes never leaving hers, 'a summer romance is no longer what I want. Maybe I've moved on, Calanthe. Maybe I want something more.'

It was strange to say it. Strange to put it into words. But as he did so, he knew he meant it. Although just what 'more' was it that he wanted?

That he did not know. Not yet…

But his words had drawn a reaction from her—an instant withdrawal. He heard her sharp intake of breath. Then he saw her shoulders hunch as she flicked open the journal she was clutching.

She didn't look up as she threw her reply at him. 'Too bad, Nik. Because you will never do to me again what you did before. *Never.*'

There was anger in her voice. And more than anger. A bleakness that was like a knife twisting in his guts. He frowned inwardly, suddenly on edge. He masked his expression, relieved she wasn't looking at him. Felt the twist in his guts come again. Urgently he tried to untwist it. To reassure himself.

*She can't know—I made it clear that she must never know. Never.*

She must never know what he had done that summer long ago...

Calanthe heard the bleakness in her own voice and knew why it was there. The words on the page of her journal blurred, then resolved into focus again. A focus she must keep now, doggedly, despite the turmoil in her brain.

Her nerves were totally overset. She had accepted Marina's invitation as an opportunity to get her away from Athens, away from Nikos—and now here he was, sitting right opposite her, heading to the very destination she was. She could not bear it.

Determinedly, she buried herself in her journal, totally ignoring the man sitting opposite her. Yet she was aware that he had got his phone out, was perusing the screen, occupying himself as she was.

After a while, he got to his feet. 'I think I'll stretch my legs,' he remarked.

Calanthe made no reply, conscious that she could now minutely relax. To her relief he didn't come back—not even when the ferry finally docked.

She hung back deliberately, hoping he'd take a taxi up to the Volous villa, but when she did disembark—for the ferry was about to set off to the next island on its itinerary—to her dismay there he was, down on the dock, leaning casually against the door of a svelte saloon car that had drawn up on the cobbles.

He waved as she walked off the ferry, carrying her overnight bag with her. 'Our hosts have sent a car to collect us,' he said, opening the rear passenger door and relieving her of her bag, though she had not asked him to.

Stiffly, she got in, murmuring something to the driver, and was grateful that Nikos got into the front passenger seat. The car set off, nosing down the narrow streets to gain the open road and then head along the coast road towards the Volous villa.

Calanthe had been there once before, the previous year, when her friend Marina had first married, and she knew it to be large and luxurious, set above its own private beach, with a multitude of guest rooms. She would ensure hers was far away from Nikos.

Her face set stonily. Nikos was chatting to the driver in an easy-going fashion and memory assailed her. Nik had always chatted easily to anyone—he'd fitted in with the student crowd that summer, been accepted by them as one of their own, and now he was chatting easily to a man who earned his living working as a driver for a very wealthy couple.

*But then, that is Nik's own background, isn't it? Nothing grand or privileged...*

Unease flickered through her. On the ferry she'd thrown at him the way she'd been raised by her mother. Yet he had thought her to be faking it—faking the person she'd presented herself as during that summer.

*Should I have told him who I was?*

Her expression hardened. It would have made no difference, though, would it? Not in the end...

The car drove through electronically controlled gates,

crunched along a driveway and pulled up. The driver came round to open Calanthe's door. She got out, murmuring her thanks, feeling the heat hit her after the air-conditioning of the car. The driver was getting her bag, hefting out another one too—Nikos's, she assumed—and then taking the car away to wherever the garages were. The front door of the grand villa was opening, and a member of staff was welcoming them in.

Saying not a word to Nikos, Calanthe hurried forward, eager to gain the sanctuary of her own room. Eager, above all, to be nowhere near the man she wanted absolutely nothing to do with.

'Calanthe! Darling! *Wonderful* to see you here!'

Marina, who had always been the exuberant type, sailed forward, her red and gold kaftan billowing in the breeze that lifted up from the beach to reach the wide marbled pool terrace already thronged with arriving guests gathering for afternoon cocktails.

Calanthe, having finally reluctantly emerged from her room, knowing she could not hide there for ever, was gushingly embraced, and then Marina stood back, her dark eyes gleaming with blatant curiosity.

'So, darling, tell me *all* about that absolutely *gorgeous* hunk of a man you've brought with you! Theo tells me he invited him—but it's you he arrived with! So, tell *all*!'

Calanthe stepped back from Marina's embrace, feigning indifference. 'We just came in the same car, that's all. He's a business acquaintance of my father—that's how I know him.'

Marina's gleam intensified. 'Playing it cool, are you? Well, no change there, then! Except...' her voice became conspiratorial '...the absolutely *gorgeous* Nikos Kavadis is in a league of his own compared with all your usual boy-friends!'

'He is *not* my boyfriend!' The words snapped from Calanthe. 'I told you—I hardly know him.'

'Hardly know him *yet*,' Marina amended. 'And tonight will be the *perfect* time to remedy that. Mind you,' she added, 'you'll have to move fast. He's already being sized up by every predatory female here!'

'They are totally welcome to him,' Calanthe informed her. 'Marina, please… Don't try and…well, you know.'

Her friend threw her hands up. 'You'll fall one day, darling! Even you! Little Miss Cool will melt eventually… I warn you!'

Calanthe remained expressionless, but emotion knifed inside her. Marina's warning was far too late. Eight years too late.

Involuntarily, her eyes went to the far side of the swimming pool. Nikos was there, talking to Marina's husband and several other people. Talking as easily as he'd talked to the driver on the way up here. Quite at home in these wealthy surroundings. Just as he'd been quite at home in Athens' most expensive hotel, where her father had held his birthday celebration.

And he was looking as devastating as he always did.

Always had.

Whether he was in his rough work clothes on the construction site or, as now, in the kind of eye-wateringly expensive designer label casual clothes suitable for a high society villa party in the Aegean. And Marina was right—many female eyes were going his way. Eyeing him up. Wondering if he was available…

A sour expression crossed Calanthe's face.

*Help yourself, ladies! You'll be doing me a favour.*

Marina was asking her what she'd like to drink, and beckoning a circling member of her staff.

Calanthe shook her head. 'Actually, what I'd really like to do is catch a swim,' she said.

'Darling, of course! There's the pool!' Marina gestured expansively.

'Oh, no—I was thinking of the beach. The sea looks so inviting. I'll just run down...'

She slipped away. Under the sundress she'd changed into in her room she'd put on a one-piece swimsuit. Towels would be supplied at the beach, she knew. She could hide there until it was time to come in and dress for the evening.

The path down to the beach zigzagged through the garden, opening up eventually onto clear pebbled sand. Sun loungers had been set out under parasols, each with a bale of towels. There was a little changing room as well, to one side, as well as a small and pretty blue-shuttered beach house, set back from the beach.

But all Calanthe had to do was pull off her sundress, and head for the water. It was cool and refreshing and she gave a sigh of relief as it embraced her. Slowly, she swam out to sea, wanting to calm her ragged nerves. She was stuck here till tomorrow morning at the earliest. If she cut and ran now Marina would want to know why, and that would cause yet more of the speculation that was the last thing Calanthe wanted to encourage.

*Please, please, let Nik pair off with someone else! Let him accept I won't have anything to do with him again and find consolation elsewhere.*

There would certainly be women ready to offer that consolation. And Nik could pull any of them.

*He always could. Even when he was just a penniless student. No woman could resist him... Least of all me...*

She turned on her back, letting her hair float out around her, and lifted her face to the westering sun, feeling its rays warming her cheeks even though the water was keeping the rest of her cool. As she drifted, arms splayed out for buoyancy, eyes closed against the bright sun, cradled by the warm Aegean sea, a memory seeped into her synapses.

A memory she could not hold at bay.

A memory she could not resist…

Even as she had not been able to resist Nik.

Their first night of passion…incandescent…unforgettable…

*He'd been wooing her for a week. Seducing her slowly but surely. She knew it—welcomed it. Gloried in it. And now, this Friday night, she pulled out all the stops for him.*

*She and Georgia had been shopping, each determined to dress up for the evening, giggling as they made their choices.*

*Georgia wore a mini-dress, showing off her long legs, but Calanthe had opted for a vermilion floaty, calf-length peasant-style gathered skirt and an embroidered blouson, worn off her shoulders, and espadrilles to make her taller. She was letting her glorious hair cascade freely down her back. And when she saw the look in Nik's eyes as she approached she knew with every female instinct that tonight… oh, tonight…the kisses she had come to yearn for would become so much more…*

*When the lively meal finally ended, and only the hardcore students remained, she and Nikos stood up from the table. Georgia and Dave were leaning close, heads together, murmuring sweet nothings to each other, and she was glad for them.*

*Gladder still for herself.*

*Was she in love? She didn't know. She only knew the wonder that netted her and the way her heart lifted every time she saw Nik. The way her pulse quickened, her breathing became shallow, and the way she longed for him to sweep her up to him, wind his strong arms around her, bend his mouth to hers...*

*And she knew that he, and he alone, was all that she wanted and craved...*

*They wandered through the warm Aegean night, his arm around her waist, she leaning into him, down the cobbled streets to where his little pensione was. He was taking her to his place, for she knew that Georgia would want the room they shared in their own little apartment for herself and Dave.*

*And she was ready for this—totally, completely ready.*

*He kissed her in the doorway, slow and sensuous, arousing, then asked, 'Is this what you want? You must be sure, Calanthe.'*

*His dark eyes poured into hers.*

*She wound her arms around his neck.*

*'Yes,' she breathed. 'Oh...yes!'*

*He smiled and led her indoors, up the narrow wooden stairs. Inside his room it was warm, but a thread of cooling breeze came through the open window overlooking the harbour. The narrow bed awaited them—with just room for two.*

*He turned her to him, smiled down at her. 'This week,' he said huskily, 'has been an eternity.'*

*Then slowly, very slowly, he eased down the loosely gathered neckline of her blouson, slipping it over her shoulders...exposing her breasts...lowering his mouth to graze their ripening mounds.*

*She gave a moan of pleasure, leaning back, and felt her*

*nipples cresting. Each gliding soft caress of his mouth, of the tingling tip of his tongue as it laved her, sent ripples of exquisite bliss through her.*

*Her moan came again, and then, as he lifted his mouth away from her, it became a cry of loss.*

*He smiled. 'Oh, sweet Calanthe, the feast has only just begun...'*

*And he showed her.*

*He slid the blouson from her...slid down, too, the gathered skirt, so that it fell in a dark pool to the floor. She stood there with only her wispy panties remaining. He reached out a finger to her, never taking his eyes from hers, and ran it along the waistline of the material. She thought she must die of bliss.*

*But the bliss, like the feast, had only just begun.*

*He eased the material down and she stepped out of it. Her heart was beating like a drum, her pulse throbbing in her veins. She heard his breath catch.*

*'So beautiful...' There was a husk in his voice...a rasp.*

*She smiled. 'Your turn,' she said.*

*She reached for him, slid open each button of his shirt one by one, achingly and arousingly slowly, easing the shirt away to let her fingertips explore beneath. He stood stock-still, and with an instinct as old as Eve, she knew he was exerting every inch of his self-control to stand there while she slid the shirt from him.*

*Then she turned her hands to the belt around his waist. As she undid the buckle, feeling her way in the dim light, she gave a sudden gasp of shock. Her hands had felt, unmistakably, just how much self-control he was exerting.*

*A low laugh broke from him, but there was urgency in his voice when he spoke. 'This is a torment such as I do not think I can endure,' he said.*

*He lifted her hands away with his own strong hands, callused and rough from his work on the building site. Swiftly, he finished what she had started, and as he shucked himself free of his trousers and his shorts she gave another gasp. Instinctively turned away.*

*He caught her in his arms, scooped her up effortlessly against his muscled frame, then crossed over to the bed, pulled back the covering sheet and laid her down as gently as if she were made of porcelain.*

*Then he lowered himself beside her. 'Shall we begin?' he asked.*

*His voice was low and accented, filled with what she knew with all her being to be desire.*

*His hand glided along her flank, shaping her breast, leisurely exploring it, then moved over the soft, slender mound of her belly to slip his questing fingers over her thighs, between them...*

*They slackened at his touch and she gave another low, instinctive moan. What he was doing to her was exquisite—unbearable...*

*Sensation such as she had not known existed, had not known possible, teased through her, and she felt her hands clench into the bedding. She felt arousal sweeten inside her and knew that he was readying her body for his possession.*

*He moved his strong, hard thighs over hers, widened her legs...*

*'Nik—I... I've never...'*

*The words broke from her and he stilled. Gazed down at her. For a few seconds he did not speak, and for a dreadful moment, she thought he would draw back.*

*Then he lowered his mouth to hers. 'You give me a gift,' he said, 'that any man would treasure.' He grazed her mouth again, the smile at his lips rueful. 'I will be as gentle as I can,' he told her.*

*He was true to his promise. There was pain, as she knew there must be, but it lasted such a little time compared with the eternity of bliss he gave her...*

*Again and again, and yet again, she felt her spine arch in ecstasy as he held her trembling body in his arms. Her own arms wound around him tightly, as if she would never, never let him go. It was bliss, it was wonder, and it was beyond all she had imagined such a time would be.*

*And then finally, as her own bliss ebbed and she felt the low throb of her own body enclosing his, drawing him in deeper, and deeper yet, he lifted his body from her and drove, with strong, powerful thrusts, to bring his own release.*

*As he did so, her body convulsed around his yet again... more intensely, more searingly. She cried out—she could not help it—her hands clutching at him, feeling the strain of his muscles, seeing his throat tensing as his body experienced what she was experiencing yet again. A groan broke from him, low and harsh, and his forehead lowered to hers as if in salutation.*

*She took him into her embrace, feeling a wonder and a joy and a happiness so great she could not measure it. He folded into her and she cradled him, feeling the sweet weight of his body on hers, smoothing his dampened hair, his muscled shoulders, soothing him, caressing him, cherishing him...*

*Loving him...*

Was it tears in her eyes now, or simply the sea water wetting her cheeks? Well, what did it matter? The Nik she had known then—or thought she had known—was gone with the years.

She would not let him back in.

Dared not.

Whatever the temptation.

The word was in her head before she could stop it. Shocking her. Dismaying her.

With a gasp, she jack-knifed in the water, her wet hair clinging to her shoulders, and trod water rapidly. No, no—of *course* she wasn't being tempted by him! How could she even think it?

For a moment she threshed in the water, pushing her soggy hair out of her eyes, and then, with an effort, duck dived into the clear sea. She had drifted quite far out. There were rocks below, on the seabed, small fishes darting, and she could feel the swell of open water.

Arcing around, she surfaced, looking back to shore. Only to see, with deeper dismay, as she blinked the water from her lashes, the tall figure of Nikos standing by the shoreline.

He was looking directly at her.

Nikos put his hands around his mouth to amplify his voice. 'You're very far out! Need a tow back in?'

He lowered his hands as he saw her strike out towards the shore in a strong freestyle. He'd wondered whether to go in and fetch her, but she was doing OK. He watched until she was back within her depth. She was clearly reluctant to get out of the water with him watching. Should he do the gentlemanly thing and turn his back? Let her reach her lounger and wrap a towel around her?

No. He would not. But what he did do was fetch the towel for her, shake it open.

'Think of me as a beach valet,' he informed her drily.

Expressionlessly, she waded out. Not looking at him.

It was something he found he could not reciprocate. Instead, he fastened his gaze on her, in her clinging one-piece.

Her coltish figure had matured into a softer, richer form, yet her legs were still as toned, her body still as slender. The simple swimsuit moulded her body to perfection, and the cold of the water had done delectable things to her nipples…

He felt a kick in his pulse that he could not stop…felt arousal stir and knew he must turn away, just as she was doing, having snatched the towel from him.

Rigorously she wrapped it around herself, busying herself with squeezing out her dripping hair. 'I don't appreciate you following me down here!' she snapped.

He was back in control of himself.

'I did not follow you,' he informed her. 'As a late invite, I've been put in the beach house.' He gestured to the small stone-built building set back from the beach, its whitewashed walls and blue shutters and door lit by the rich late-afternoon sunshine. 'Simple accommodation, no staff service, but ideal for midnight swims,' he said good-humouredly. His eyes glinted. 'Perhaps you'll join me for one tonight?'

She glowered fiercely at him, but he was not put off.

'Lighten up, Calanthe—this is a weekend to enjoy.' He made his voice still humorous, but there was a message in it all the same.

She was yanking at her hair, starting to rapidly and roughly plait it.

'So enjoy it!' she told him. 'Just not with me! There are any number of women all too willing to help you do so, I'm sure!'

His eyes rested on her face. 'The thing is, Calanthe, the only one I want is you…'

He had softened his voice. Made it a caress.

An invitation.

A promise.

He felt emotions move within him. Desire, yes—for who could not feel desire as she stood there? Even with the beach towel obliterating her figure and her fingers working on her dripping hair, her face shining with sea water and bereft of any make-up. His breath caught. Whatever it was about her, he could not take his eyes from her. Could not stop these strange emotions welling up within him.

*This time... This time we'll make it come right between us.*

That was the promise in his head.

To himself.

To her.

She'd stilled, her fingers still entwined in her half-plaited her. He changed his expression. Became reminiscent, softened his tone more.

'You used to plait your hair like that in the morning when we were getting up together. You were heading back to the dig and I was putting in my shift at the construction site. You'd pin it up, and I'd have to wait all day until finally I could take those damn pins out, unplait it, and let it tumble around your shoulders. We'd fall into bed, then shower, then get dressed and go and join the others at the taverna. You would look...oh, so lovely. Your eyes glowing from our lovemaking...your skin honey from the sun... And we'd sit together at the table, and you'd sneak some of my deep-fried aubergines, which you never ordered for yourself because you said they were too fattening. But somehow nicking mine wasn't fattening at all...'

He gave a low laugh, memory vivid in his head.

'Don't—' Her voice was low. Strained. 'There's no point remembering, Nik. It was eight years ago. It's not coming back.'

He shook his head. 'No, it's not coming back. But...' He

changed his voice again and felt his arm lifting of its own volition, as if to reach for her. 'But we can—'

'Can what?' She cut across him, and her voice was like a blade. 'Pick up where we left off? Is that your idea? You bump into me, eight years on, and think, *Hey, she's still fanciable...why don't I take another tour?*'

She was standing so close he'd only have to take a step towards her to reach for her, but her stance was rigid...chin lifted, eyes stony.

'It's not like that,' he said tightly. 'Look...' he frowned '...eight years ago I had nothing—nothing except responsibilities. Responsibilities to complete my training, make something of myself any way I could...'

He saw something changing in her face, but he ignored it. This was important—he had to make her understand. Understand that now was not then.

'And now I have! I'm a wealthy man. And, whilst I still have a great deal I want to do with my life, things that I want to achieve—as you do, I'm sure, in your own field—I've got time now. Real time to want more than I wanted eight years ago. And what I want...*who* I want...' his voice softened again as his eyes rested on her unflinchingly, openly '...is you.' He took a breath. 'I told you that at Sounion. Told you that even if I'd never known you before I would want you now. And, no—not just for a summer romance! Calanthe, this...between us...could be something else. Something that might prove really important...in my life.' He paused. 'You're important to me, Calanthe—I want you to know that.'

She didn't answer. Her hands had fallen to her sides as he'd spoken to her, saying the things he knew he had to say. He could not read her face, though he searched her eyes. Then she took a breath.

'I'm going up to shower and change,' she said.

She walked to where her sundress was lying on the lounger, picked it up. Turned back to him as she slipped her feet into flat sandals. Took another breath and looked straight at him. Face expressionless.

'Stay away from me tonight,' she told him.

Then she turned and headed for the path, making her way up through the gardens.

Nikos watched her till she was lost to sight.

*'Stay away from me tonight.'*

Her words echoed in his head, and his own answer echoed too.

*I can't.*

# CHAPTER SIX

CALANTHE GAVE HER appearance once last check, relieved that she had brought this particular dress to wear this evening. It was Grecian-style, a pale column of finely pleated ivory silk, the bodice draping over her torso, and it made her look cool and elegant.

Statuesque.

Not in the least enticing.

That was the last thing she wanted.

But once…

Memory flickered like a flame she wanted to quench, yet still flickered for all that.

That vivid vermilion peasant skirt…the off-the-shoulder embroidered blouson…her hair loose and tumbling…

All to lure Nik.

There was a sour taste in her mouth. Oh, Nik had got lucky that summer, all right! She'd fallen for him totally, given herself to him totally, wanting nothing more in all the world than him! And he… Well, he'd helped himself to her—to more than what she'd offered him so very gladly…

She pulled her mind away, out of the past. She could not bear to think about it now.

Back in the present, his words on the beach hung in the space between herself and her reflection.

*'You're important to me, Calanthe.'*

Her expression steeled. Yet in the pit of her stomach she could feel what she'd never wanted to feel ever again. The wash of hot, humid humiliation that she could not bear to acknowledge, to face, or to admit. She turned away, not wanting to see the woman in the mirror...the woman who could be 'important' to Nikos Kavadis.

She would not be that woman.

Reluctantly, she crossed to the bedroom door. She had taken refuge in her room, performing lengthy ablutions, taking for ever over her hair, even though it was simply coiled in a soft chignon at her nape, and a long time over her make-up, even though it was the bare minimum for such an evening.

She had taken as long as she could, even asking one of the maids to bring her some Earl Grey tea as she dressed for the evening, but she could delay no longer—or Marina would send out a search party. Already she could hear music coming in through the glass doors to her balcony.

Nerving herself, she went to join the party.

Nikos stood at the far end of the terrace, looking out over the darkened sea beyond. His mood was strange. He had accepted the invitation to this party for one reason only—because he knew, from Georgios Petranakos, that Calanthe had been invited too.

Georgios was being assiduous in letting him know his daughter's social diary. Nikos's eyes narrowed. He knew there was a reason for Georgios's co-operation in his pursuit of Calanthe. Georgios hadn't spelt it out—he hadn't needed to—but Nikos had got the message. It was common knowledge that without a son—and given that Calanthe had no interest in her father's business herself—Georgios Petranakos would be on the lookout for a son-in-law of suffi-cient calibre to take over the running of his property empire when his time was up.

*And I may just make the grade.*

There was an irony to that which was not lost on him. Eight years had changed his prospects radically. If Georgios Petranakos really was assessing him in the way he might be, it should reassure him—show him that this time his interest in Georgios's daughter would not be opposed. Not if he carried it through to the conclusion that Georgios might just have in mind.

*But do I have it in mind? Is it something I would consider?*

He felt his thoughts move over the question. He had told Calanthe down on the beach now veiled in the darkness of the evening that she was important to him. But what had he meant by that? He did not know—not yet.

*I need to make her mine again—need to claim her back. I need to hold her in my arms...to know...discover again... what she is to me.*

He shifted restlessly, feeling his thoughts just as restless. Sightlessly, he gazed out over the darkened sea stretching to the horizon. There were no lights to steer by, only the stars above, and someone would have to know the constellations to navigate by them.

For him, it was his own future he was trying to reach— would it be Calanthe's too?

His unease sharpened. What if the past had already blighted the future?

His hands tightened over the stone balustrade and he lifted his head. Determination fired in his eyes. He must steer his course by his own judgement. He had always done so and would not change now.

Taking a breath, he lifted his hands away and headed

back along the terrace to where the bright lights of the party were beckoning him.

And where Calanthe awaited him.

Calanthe was surrounding herself with people all dressed up for the evening, the men in white dinner jackets, the women in silky evening gowns. Most of those she was with she already knew, so after greetings had been exchanged it meant she could get away with contributing little to the general conversation. She was sipping at champagne, but making a glass last a long time, then swapping it for sparkling mineral water.

Always she knew where Nikos was.

Right now he was on the far side of the pool, in another circle of people. To her relief he had made no attempt to talk to her, or even approach her. Nor did he move in on the people she was with. To her even greater relief he was clearly being targeted by a very determined woman, bejewelled to the nines, with bleached blonde hair, too much make-up, and a very clinging short dress.

Nikos was welcome to her.

*Please let him content himself with whoever that is throwing herself at him! Please let me just get through enough of the evening to be able to retire without Marina coming to drag me out again! And please don't let her think there is anything at all between me and Nikos Kavadis!*

To aid herself in this plea Calanthe knew that she, too, must display some diversionary tactics. Provide a decoy. Yannis, as it happened, was not here—he was away in New York on business—but an even better decoy was on hand. Bastian.

Bastian was ideal. He was a long-time admirer but, since he was also one of Athens' most assiduous playboys, his pursuit of her would be for one purpose only—another notch on his very well-notched bedpost. But he was also good-humoured and easy-going, and she knew all she had to do was let him know she was trying to avoid a particular man here and he would co-operate happily.

An hour later he was doing just that.

A lavish buffet was being served, and everyone was taking their places at the tables set out under colourful lights strung overhead.

A covert glance from Calanthe showed her that Nikos and the bleached blonde were at a table as far away from where she was as it was possible to be. Sitting herself down beside Bastian, finding their own table lively in the extreme, she finally started to relax. Helped, she knew, by the second glass of champagne Bastian had presented her with.

'Drink up, my sweet,' he murmured shamelessly in her ear. 'Then I might finally stand a chance with you this evening...'

She pushed him away good-humouredly and took another sip of her champagne, feeling the net of unbearable tension easing from her. She would get through supper, dance a couple of times with Bastian, and then escape. Plead a headache...whatever... It didn't matter. And tomorrow she would head back to Athens.

All she had to do was get through the rest of the evening.

As for Nikos—

She cut off her thoughts. Banned them from her head. She laughed, instead, at something one of her friends at the table had just said, taking more sips of champagne in between mouthfuls of the delicious gourmet buffet Marina's chef had provided.

*I can do this. I can do it because I must. Just as, when I'm back in Athens, I can keep doing it. If Nikos tries to*

*contact me again I will simply stonewall him. I will have*
*nothing more to do with him. Nothing. Not tonight...not in*
*Athens. Not ever.*

Yet even as she made the vow to herself she felt her eyes
slipping sideways as she reached again for her champagne
glass...slipping across the array of candlelit tables to the
one where Nikos was seated.

She didn't want to look, yet some kind of compulsion
made her do it all the same, and he was sitting so that she
could see his profile...see him lean a little towards the
woman at his side...see him smile at her.

A needle slid into her heart. Once it had been her he'd
smiled at and her alone. A private smile, warm and intimate,
full of promise and fulfilment.

She felt an ache arise inside her, a longing...

Her fingers convulsed over the slender stem of her champagne flute. Dear God, she must not allow such memories!
So painful, so aching... So dangerous.

She felt a hand touch her bare forearm and started.

'If I were the jealous type...' Bastian trailed off, an eyebrow lifting, his eyes slanting to where she had been looking.

She gave a sharp shake of her head. Dismissing the in-
sinuation. She took another mouthful of champagne and set
down the glass, resuming her meal. Doggedly, for the rest
of supper, she refused to let her eyes go anywhere near the
one man in all the world she must not look at.

Must not have anything to do with ever again.

Must not crave...

Nikos smiled at the woman beside him. He wished her no
ill, but she was wasting her time. She'd already told him she
was newly divorced, her unfaithful ex-husband set aside,

and that all she wanted right now was to feel good about herself again in the aftermath by reminding herself that she could still draw male attention.

Well, he had a solution to her predicament—but it was not going to be himself.

His eyes narrowed. Watching—or rather *not* watching Calanthe devote herself to a man who all of Athens knew to be a notorious playboy was not an enjoyable process. His only comfort was that he knew why she was doing it. And he knew what he was going to do about it.

But he must pick his time carefully. Get it just right. And then—

He cut his thoughts off. He must not rush ahead of himself—must not make assumptions or take it for granted that he would achieve what he was set upon.

A wry expression formed in his eyes. Eight years ago he had known that Calanthe's initial prickly attitude to him had been a disguise for her response to him. Known that once he got past that—as he had so very easily in the end—she would yield to her response to him…yield to his desire for her. The desire with which he'd kindled hers, set it aflame…

But she was fighting him now every centimetre of the way—he could take nothing for granted.

*I only know that she is fighting not just me, but herself as well…*

Well, he would not give up on her.

Not this time.

This time he would make it all come right between them.

Calanthe was dancing with Bastian. She'd lingered at the supper table, not wanting to exert herself in the upbeat dance numbers that the live band had struck up with, waiting for something slower. Now she was wishing she hadn't. She'd made it clear to Bastian that she only wanted him as a decoy, nothing else, but he'd been knocking back the champagne, and now he was making every effort to get up close and personal with her, however often she drew herself away from him.

The moment the number ended she'd make her excuses and leave.

She didn't get the chance.

'Time to trade partners,' said a cool, deep voice behind her.

She froze, but it was too late. Nikos had simply disengaged Bastian's hands from around her waist and blatantly put them around the waist of his own partner—the bleached blonde, Calanthe saw instantly. She also saw that both the blonde and Bastian were taken aback, but then, as they eyed each other up, were swiftly reconciled to the exchange. She heard Bastian pay his new partner an extravagant compliment, saw her toss her head and smile encouragingly, and then they were away.

As for herself…

'Finally,' said Nikos, in the same cool, deep voice.

And took her into his arms.

She was as rigid as the marble statue she resembled. Yet the hands that had come to rest automatically on his shoulders were trembling—he could feel it through the linen of his white tuxedo jacket. Just as he could feel the warmth of her body through the delicate plissé material of her dress as his hands rested at her waist.

Sensation washed through him.

To hold her again…have her in his arms…

With an effort that cost him more than he wanted to exert, he kept his touch as light as he could, resisting the overpowering temptation to draw her to him, feel the soft length of her body moulded against his.

She was far, far too tense for that.

And she was pulling away from him. Oh, not obviously, but her spine was arching back, her feet moving back the maximum distance they could, given he was holding her and dancing.

For a second she looked at him, her eyes wide with shock. Then she yanked her gaze past him.

'Let me go,' she said.

Her voice was as tight as the drawstring of a bow.

'Dance with me,' he said.

His voice was low in pitch, for her ears alone.

He felt her straining back and thought she would pull free of him—which she could easily do, for his hands were barely touching her waist. Yet she did not.

'I won't make a scene,' she said, her voice still bowstring-tight, still looking straight past him. 'That's the only reason.'

'That's good enough for me,' Nikos murmured, his voice relaxing, his stance relaxing.

Carefully, he started to move, picking up on the slow, familiar melody from the band as the singer started to croon the lyrics of an old sentimental song.

They danced, but hardly moved. To his side, almost out of his sightline, Nikos could see the divorced blonde draping herself over a very willing Bastian, whose hands were now freely running up and down her back. He wished them well. Wished everyone in the entire world well.

For one reason only.

Calanthe was in his arms.

The only place he wanted her to be.

How she got through the dance she didn't know. It seemed to go on for an eternity. Or perhaps eternity was being in Nikos's arms...

Yet he was barely touching her, his hands hardly skimming the fabric of her gown, and her own hands were barely skimming the fabric of his jacket. Nor was she looking at him. She could not. Dared not.

Yet her consciousness of what she was doing—what he was doing—was like an enveloping flame…a flame that licked at her senses, flickered along her nerves, grazed her bare skin.

A line from the Ancient Greek, old and familiar, came to her:

*…subtle fire runs like a thief through my body…*

The poetess Sappho, whose lost verses remained only in shattered fragments.

*As my love for Nikos was shattered.*

But she could not think of that—could not feel that now. Could only feel what it was to be here, in his arms, in an embrace that was barely there. Yet she could catch the scent of his aftershave, the scent of his body, and knew that all she had to do was step closer to him, fold her hands over his strong shoulders, let his hands fasten around her pliant waist, bend her to him, turn her head so that his mouth could catch at hers…

Fire and faintness…faintness and fire…yearning and wanting…wanting and yearning.

There was nothing else…nothing in all the world, all the universe. Only this slow eternal dance.

And then it ended. The music stopped. Though the pulse in her veins did not. Nor did the fire still running through her body like the thief it was…

She felt his hands drop from her…let her own hands fall…let her eyes finally meet his.

And in them she saw what she must not accept, must not acknowledge. Must not permit.

Instinctively she moved away. She saw the dark outline of the path that led off the terrace, away from the light, away from the party…away from Nikos. It offered refuge from him, from the pulse of her own veins, the fire stealing her senses and her sense.

The sound of the cicadas in the lush, irrigated vegetation was loud in her ears as the noise of the party dimmed. All around, the heady scent of jasmine infused her senses. A little way along, the path widened into a miniature terrace, only a few metres square, with a stone bench at one side. She sank down on it, looking out towards the night-black sea, still feeling that heady pulse in her veins, the flicker of fire that she could not put out.

Footsteps on the path leading to the little terrace stayed her. A figure emerged. Tall and dark. Only the white of his jacket visible in the starlight. Her breath caught.

'Calanthe…' said Nikos.

His voice was as velvet as the night.


She did not move, and yet he heard the low intake of her breath, saw her eyes going to his in the dim light spilling through the leaves from the party above.

He walked towards her, his pace unhurried.

She got to her feet, stood there as if poised for flight. But she made no move.

Her eyes had flared wide…her lips had parted. She stood stock-still, as still as a marble column, in her ivory silk gown, her arms slender, her throat exposed, hair in tendrils around her face.

He lifted a hand to her, his fingers drifting with infinite slowness down the smooth length of her bare arm, and took her nerveless hand in his. He felt her tremble at his touch.

His gaze burned into her widened eyes. Her lips were still parted. Motionless. And she was so exquisitely beautiful that his muscles clenched, holding his body taut.

Slowly, infinitely slowly, he drew drifting fingers down her other arm, took her other hand in his, hearing another intake of her breath. Her hands were warm and trembling in his clasp.

'Nikos...'

It was a breath of air, no more than that. A whisper. A plea.

'Don't—please...*please* don't...'

He gazed down at her.

'Don't what, Calanthe?'

His voice was husky now, his whole body held under such control that it racked him.

'Don't tell you how beautiful you are? How I desire you?' That half-smile, mocking himself, twisted at his mouth again. 'I wanted you then, all those years ago—and I want you now.'

He felt his want rise within him, flushing his veins like a slow, ineluctable tide, infusing his senses. The scent of jasmine was drowning the perfumed air. From above, the low throb of music pulsed.

He saw her eyes dip closed, then open again, with a new pleading in them.

'Nikos—I can't. I won't—' She broke off and half turned away, drawing one hand away from his.

With his freed hand he cupped her averted cheek, felt her skin like satin.

'Don't turn away.' The huskiness was stronger now, the self-control more urgent. 'Don't turn away from this. From what this is. From what has always been between us. From the very first...'

Slowly, carefully, he turned her to look at him again. Her eyes were flared so wide he could see into their depths. See, with a stab of triumph, the distension of her pupils.

Her words might deny him.

Her body could not…

He said her name again, husky and lingering. Bent his mouth to hers. Felt the tender softness of her lips. She made no resistance and triumph came again. But it dissolved even as it came, liquefying into desire, drumming at his senses, flooding his blood, his brain, with its power and potency.

All evening he'd seen her, so near and yet so far. He'd known he would close in on her. Known that was the reason he was here at all. Known it was his purpose. His intent.

And now…*now* it was happening. He was claiming her back…

Had he been a fool, eight years ago, to part with her as he had? Whatever the reason he had done so? He didn't know—could not answer…could not care. His senses were reeling, the exertion of holding his body in check bringing agony to his muscles.

He heard through the drumming of his pulse her breathing his name again. But nothing else. No protest. No denial.

*Only yielding… To my desire. To her own desire.*

His kiss deepened on her tremulous lips, opening her mouth, oh, so softly to his.

He felt his body surge. His hand tightened on hers as he drew his mouth away. He lifted his fingers to her still-parted lips, tracing their outline. Slowly, lingeringly. She gazed up at him, making no move away from him.

He smiled. A smile for her and her alone in this moment which had come at last.

'Come,' he said.

\* \* \*

He led her on down the sloping path to the beach below. Dimly she was aware of the soft sound of wavelets breaking gently on the pebbled shore, of the starlight high above them, the cradling darkness of the night. She could not speak, could not think…could do nothing but let him lead her.

Why she was doing this she did not know. It made no sense. It was everything she had said she must not yield to. And yet she was yielding.

Fragments of thought fleeted through her mind as he led her onwards.

*This time he cannot hurt me—because this time I know him for what he is…know the hurt he did me. So if I yield to him—yield to all that I can deny no longer, all that I crave for myself—then surely it will be for me alone, with no illusions. Only desire.*

Desire she could no longer deny, or resist, or in any way do anything but yield to now, in this moment, in this night…

Her hand in his, they reached the little stone beach house and he pushed open the door. Drew her inside. Into his arms.

They lit no lamps. Needed no light. Only the dim reflection from the phosphorescence off the sea through the single window beside the wide bed. Her ivory gown was skimmed from her trembling body, his own impeding clothes ruthlessly, impatiently discarded, and he drew her down, laying her softly on the white sheet, lowering his lean, hard body beside her.

Covering her body with his.

As he had done before, so long ago.

And now he did it again.

She was silk and satin, her body slender still, but softer in the fullness of her womanhood. She was everything he remembered and so much more.

With slow sensuality he explored every part of her, drowning in his own pleasure as he did so, drawing from her a pleasure that showed in her eyes fluttering shut, in the low, helpless moans from her throat.

He moved over her, cupping her breasts, feeling them engorge at his touch, her nipples cresting between his gently scissoring fingers. Her eyes flew open, then fluttered shut again, and he saw pleasure flush her face, arch her neck. He lowered his mouth to her breast, suckling at her with slow swirls of his tongue, lingering and leisurely, then administered the same to her other breast.

He reared back to gaze at her. A smile curved his lips as he looked down at her lying there, splayed on his bed, head back, breasts ripened by his touch, hands outstretched, fingers curved into the sheet. A low, husky laugh of triumph and desire, arousal and possession came from him, and then he was lowering himself to her again, easing his body so that his hands could cup her hips, letting his lips glide over the soft curve of her waistline and further still.

He slipped one hand from her hip, parting her thighs, cupping the secret V between with the heel of his hand. He heard her moan again, felt her hands folding over his shoulders, her nails indenting into his muscled flesh. He moulded her with the heel of his hand, feeling her body's response.

Then he lifted his hand away.

Lowered his mouth instead.

His conscious mind was in white-out. There was nothing in the universe except this and now. Heat was burning up his own body as his tongue and lips feasted where, when he had readied her, he would possess her fully. Her moans were coming faster now, more helpless. He heard her head thrashing on the pillow, felt her thighs widen and slacken, her hips lifting in automatic, instinctive and overpowering pleading. He heard her say his name. Low and incoherent. Arousal was coursing through him, so powerful it was impossible to restrain himself any longer, not for a moment, not an instant…

He lifted his head away and reared over her, his hands sliding over her hips, lifting her to him, his thighs thrust between hers, widening them further still. His heart was pounding, deafening him, drumming every sense into meltdown. Her hands snaked around his waist, pulling him down towards her as she arched her spine up to him, saying his name, her voice husky and helpless.

'Nikos—now… Oh, God! Now…just *now*—'

He gave her what she was pleading for. With a surge of triumph he thrust into her, deep and deeper yet. She cried out, high-pitched, and just for a second past and present seemed to blur and merge.

She had cried out like that the very first time…when he had known he must be as gentle as it was possible for a man to be, taking a woman from virgin to lover.

Then it was gone, and the roaring fire of sexual passion was consuming him in its furnace, and he was thrusting and thrusting again, and then, with another surge of triumph, he felt her convulse and liquefy around him. He heard her cry out again…a gasp, a sob…as his heat flooded her, fusing her to him. Her body was enclosing him, drawing him further in with wave after wave of breaking pleasure. It was drowning through him, obliterating everything in existence except this moment of absolute release, absolute consummation, absolute satiation.

How long it lasted he did not know—could not know, for time had ceased.

Then oblivion receded and his body became heavy and inert, drained. Chest heaving, he let his body slacken, felt her arms, warm against the sudden chill in his muscles, draw him softly against her, cradling him as his exhausted limbs became torpid.

He was dimly aware that he could still feel after-tremors in her body, slowly ebbing away. Dimly aware that of all the places in all the world where he might be, here was the only place. Dimly aware of a heaviness pressing him down, as if gravity had suddenly quadrupled and there was no strength left in him.

He said her name. It was all he could do.

And then sleep took him.


Calanthe lay with Nikos's sleeping body in her arms. Her own body was still and cold. So very cold.

And yet the night was warm.

She gazed with blank eyes at the white-painted ceiling. A single thought was circling in her head. Pulsing in her stricken limbs now slack and exhausted.

*What have I done? Dear God, what have I done?*

But she knew the answer. No matter how many times the question circled endlessly in her sleepless brain.

The fire she had let run so fatefully—so fatally—had burned away all sense. But now that fire was cold, cold ash.

Memory swept over her. Not of the night that had just passed, but of nights so long ago.

How many times had she held him like this in the aftermath of passion, his body deep in heavy slumber, still embracing hers? Countless times in that long-ago lost summer. Until the very last time…

But now… Now there was a new last time. There must be.

Slowly, she pressed her mouth to his sinewed shoulder as he lay half across her, making her farewell. What she had once thought she had with Nik had never truly been

at all—nor was this true now. Carefully…very carefully…
she eased her body from his, drew herself away. Got to her
feet, swaying slightly, pushing back her loosened tresses,
and reached for her discarded clothes.

And when Homer's rosy-fingered dawn crept out over
his wine-dark sea beyond the pebbled beach she had already gone.

Leaving Nikos to wake alone.

# CHAPTER SEVEN

'I WAS THINKING, PAPA, of perhaps heading back to London a little earlier than planned,' Calanthe ventured tentatively.

She eyed her father across the dinner table. She'd arrived back in Athens before lunch, having taken the first ferry of the morning, terrified that Nikos would wake and come after her. But she'd made it back home, had heard nothing from him since, and all she could feel was abjectly grateful.

Her father paused in the act of raising his wine glass.

'Oh, my darling girl, why?'

There was dismay in his voice and Calanthe felt doubly bad. She didn't want to leave her father early. Especially right now. She frowned, her eyes resting on him.

Her gaze skimmed his face. He'd told her he'd be cutting back on the rich food, reducing his intake of wine and alcohol in general, but she'd seen no sign of it yet. Tonight's dinner was rich roast lamb, the wine heavy and plentiful. His colour was high, and her announcement just now had made his cheeks flush more. She wanted to ask him—yet again—whether he'd made an appointment for the further tests that he'd admitted his cardiologist had recommended. But he always waved the question away, getting tetchy and irritated, changing the subject determinedly.

Well, tonight the subject was changed, all right. And clearly it wasn't one he welcomed.

'I've a lot to get on with,' she said, hoping he wouldn't ask for details.

His shrewd gaze rested on her and Calanthe wished it wouldn't. She braced herself for his questioning, yet it did not come. Instead, his expression changed, became bland.

'Well, stay at least until next weekend,' he said. 'I had in mind a dinner party for this coming Friday.'

He mentioned some familiar names of his own generation. None, Calanthe thought thankfully, with sons who might make potential husbands for her.

*I can last out till the weekend. And if Nikos tries to make contact, then...*

She would give instructions that no call from him should be put through, and she would bury herself at the museum till Friday and stay totally out of circulation.

Above all, she must not think about the insanity she'd committed. Must not feel...must not remember. Because what else was it except insanity?

It could be nothing else. A moment of self-indulgence... succumbing to the soft music and the velvet night, to the bliss of feeling his arms around her once more after so long, to his lips on hers... To the fire he set running in her veins, to all that she had once had and had never thought could be hers again.

It had been a final chance to take and taste and claim all that she had once thought might be hers for ever.

From a man who had never been the man she'd thought he was.

That was all she had to remember. Not that night of madness in his arms that she should never, never have allowed...

* * *

Nikos glanced up at the imposing building that housed the headquarters of Georgios Petranakos' property empire, in the business suburb of Marousi, close to Kifissia.

He'd been summoned there to a meeting.

OK, 'summoned' had not been the word used by Georgios's efficient-sounding PA. 'Graciously invited' fitted the bill better. But it was a summons for all that.

And Nikos was very, very interested in knowing why.

There could, he well knew, be any number of reasons. But there was only one he wanted it to be.

He felt his solar plexus clench as he swung through the glass revolving doors into the air-conditioned lobby, giving his name at the reception desk.

He could see the receptionist glance at him appreciatively from under her eyelashes. Normally he would have bestowed a winning smile upon her—after all, why not? But today he refrained for two reasons. One because of the tension building up inside him as to why Georgios had asked him to come and see him, and another reason far more compelling.

Because the very attractive receptionist could, for all he noticed, be as boot-faced as a harpy.

Women no longer existed for him.

*Apart from one.*

Emotion roiled in him like bilgewater in the hull of a boat, weighing him down. Destabilising him. Words stabbed at him. Cutting into his flesh. Drawing blood.

*She walked out on me.*

Stark, brutal words. Stabbing again.

She'd walked out after everything that night at the beach house had brought—after the passion and desire, after he'd won her to him, after her body had yielded to his more than ever he remembered, after the sensual bliss that had possessed them both, after he had folded her trembling body against his, his heart hammering, holding her close, so close...

To wake in a cold, empty bed.

The pre-dawn beach house had been chill. Deserted. Silent. At first, with a grabbing of hope, he'd thought she might be in the attached shower room, but that had been deserted too. So had the pebbled beach when he'd yanked open the door.

Then, staring back inside the bleak and silent beach house, he'd realised, with a blow to his guts, that her gown was no longer carelessly thrown over a chair...was no longer visible at all. Only his own crumpled and tossed aside evening clothes cascaded on to the floor, his dress shoes kicked off at the foot of the bed.

She'd gone.

Now only one question burned in his head. Consuming him like a fire within, giving him no peace, no rest.

*How do I get her back?*

Because getting her back was vital. That night with her— that unforgettable night when he'd rediscovered everything he had ever wanted and so much more—had focussed his entire world on a single name.

Calanthe.

*I want her. I want her back. I want her again. I want her in every way. I want her in my life. For my life.*

It should have come as a shock for him to realise that, yet it did not. Because it seemed, quite simply, like the truth. Simple, straightforward, obvious. That unforgettable night with her had made that truth undeniable.

All he had to do now was find out how to achieve it.

He stepped into the executive lift that would whisk him straight up to Georgios's office.

And by the time he left his dark eyes were glittering and the set of his mouth was aslant with satisfaction.

'Calanthe, my dear, how well you look. Glowing as ever!'

The compliment coming her way was undeserved. Calanthe knew that despite her carefully applied make-up her cheeks were wan, her colour pale. But she smiled appropriately, greeting the wife of one of her father's oldest friends, then turning to greet the next arrivals for the dinner party.

It would be slightly unbalanced in numbers, for her father had told her that the sister of one of his married guests was visiting Athens and had been included in the invitation. But they would be just under a dozen at the table, and since all the guests knew each other as well as they knew her father, Calanthe envisaged that her role would be minimal. She would probably slip away once coffee had been served in the salon after dinner, and leave her father's generation to their own amusements.

With everyone present, and pre-dinner drinks consumed, dinner itself was announced, and she led the way through to the dining room. She gave a little frown. An extra place had been set. She was about to murmur to the staff that it should be removed when she heard the front door opening again. Heard a voice she would have paid a year's salary—paid any amount—not to hear again.

Her eyes flew to her father. Dismay flooded her, as realisation did likewise. This was his doing—*his*! But he was busy settling the guest on his right-hand side, paying her no attention. Paying no attention to the arrival of this latest extra guest until he walked in.

And then: 'Ah, my boy, I'm so glad you could make it! Such short notice... Come, come—here is your place.' He smiled genially, encompassing both Nikos Kavadis and his daughter. 'You two young people!' he said, beaming, and gestured that Nikos should take the seat next to Calanthe.

There was nothing she could do. Nothing short of throwing a fit, or fainting, or simply charging out of the room, grabbing her handbag and her passport and heading for the airport to take the last flight that night to London—or anywhere else in the entire world that was not her father's house in Athens, with Nikos Kavadis sitting next to her for dinner.

Frozen with numbness, she lowered herself jerkily into her chair. Nikos paused while she seated herself, then sat down beside her.

He turned to her with a smile.

Bland. Unreadable.

And it cut her like a knife.

She hadn't known he'd be here. That was obvious. She looked as if she were about to pass out on the spot. As he smiled at her, two spots of hectic colour burned in her whitened cheeks.

'So we meet again,' he said pleasantly, shaking out his linen napkin.

She didn't answer—only swallowed. Everyone around the table continued to chatter, their conversation easy and convivial. Obviously, all the guests knew each other well.

A sudden memory shafted through him. That first evening in the taverna, when he'd inserted himself into the throng of students spending their summer vacation excavating the site beside the resort where he had been working as a builder. The crowd there had been chattering and convivial, easy-going and sociable, welcoming him in.

All except Calanthe.

She'd tried to freeze him out.

Just as she would now, if she could.

But that wasn't going to be possible, was it? Not at her father's dinner table, in the middle of all his guests.

The woman at his left was addressing him, and he turned his attention to her, smiling politely, and answering what she'd asked about who he was, and how he knew Georgios.

And his daughter.

'So nice of Georgios to have invited you for her!' The woman smiled. A glint of open curiosity showed in her eyes. 'Dear Calanthe…always so many admirers! But no one *special* as yet,' she trilled.

The question hung in the air. Athens was a hotbed of gossip. And gossip could be a powerful engine sometimes.

Nikos smiled. 'As yet,' he echoed.

The woman's glint came again. 'Ah! So we must hope…' she trailed openly. 'I know just how much Georgios longs for the dear girl to settle down and finally make her choice. My own son married last year, and my daughter is engaged. It's such a comfort to any parent, but for Georgios, without a son to take over…well, of course, Calanthe's eventual choice will be *so* important—don't you agree?'

'Indeed,' agreed Nikos dutifully, on cue.

He changed the subject, politely asking what line her son was in—he was a commercial property lawyer, it seemed, and her daughter worked for a management consultancy.

'Their father and I are so very proud of their achievements!' the woman enthused. 'They've had to work very hard to get where they are today!'

Nikos veiled his eyes. Memory overwhelmed him again. How, unlike the children of wealthy parents such as these, he'd had to put in long working days during every university vacation, evenings too during term time, earning money to fund his studies.

Working his way through university had not been suffi-cient, though, to see him right to the end of his long archi-tectural qualifications.

He'd needed extra help.

And he'd got it...

He cleared his thoughts, made some remark about all professions being crowded, and asked what law firm her son worked at. He was conscious that, at his side, Calanthe was conversing with the male guest on her right. Her voice sounded strained, though, her answers stilted.

But it was not her voice he was most conscious of. It was her closeness to him. Her dress was long-sleeved, in a dark blue, with a modest neckline, and she was adorned with a pearl necklace and stud earrings, her hair in its customary upswept style. Just right for a sedate dinner party with her father's friends. But, sedate though her appearance might be, it still had the power to overwhelm his senses, inflame them...to fill him with longing for her.

As they ate, he could feel from time to time the edge of her wide sleeve brush against the sleeve of his jacket. Could catch her perfume, light and floral. Her closeness was a torment—and a temptation. It was tantalising, testing to the limit his iron self-control, being so close to her and yet behaving as if their incandescent night together had never happened. As if he were nothing more than a polite dinner guest in her father's house.

Well, he was going to be more—far more!—than that. Now, thanks to Georgios, he had the green light to go ahead. To take Calanthe into his life.

All he had to do was convince her of it...

And in that he would succeed.

He must, for his happiness depended on it.

Someone across the table asked him something about his

business, and then Georgios asked how his dealings with the government officials were going. Conversation became general, focussing on business and politics—things that Nikos had learnt how to handle with ease and confidence. He was, after all, despite his origins, one of them now. Worth a fortune, just as they were.

His glance went to Georgios, veiled again as he remembered what had been discussed in his office. And why…

At his side, Calanthe was silent, focussing on her meal. It was a very rich duck casserole, and he was aware she was only picking at it. She wasn't touching her wine either. Georgios, however, was enjoying himself heartily, beckoning for a refill of his wine glass.

Nikos frowned. Georgios's colour was high, his breathing heavy as he conversed convivially with his friends. As if in slow motion, Nikos saw it happen. Saw Georgios stall, his hand suddenly going to his chest, his wine glass falling to the table. A gasp broke from him and Nikos saw his hand clench over his chest. His heart. Saw him start to keel over sideways.

Nikos was on his feet in seconds, yelling for someone to phone an ambulance as he took Georgios's heavy, slumping weight, lowering him unconscious to the floor to try and take the pressure off his labouring heart which was trying to pump blood to his brain. Cries of consternation were all around, but Nikos only ripped open the front of Georgios's shirt, desperately feeling for a heartbeat.

Then Calanthe was there, crouched down on the other side of her father, whose eyes had now rolled back. Her face was contorted in terror and she clutched at her father's hand.

'There's a pulse,' Nikos said, his voice strained. 'But it's faint.'

'The ambulance is on its way,' someone said, and handed

him a phone so he could talk to the emergency call handler about what best to do till it arrived.

It seemed to take an eternity, but then the paramedics were there, taking over. Getting Georgios on a stretcher, then whisking him away in a wail of sirens.

Nikos turned to Calanthe, who'd staggered to her feet and was now swaying, white-faced.

'I'll come with you to the hospital,' he said.

He took her hand. It was as cold as ice.

Nikos was in San Francisco, giving a presentation at a seismology and civil planning conference, but his mind was seven thousand miles away in Athens—where Georgios Petranakos was recuperating from the triple bypass that had been performed after his emergency admission to hospital. His coronary arteries were shot to pieces. Recovery was proving slow.

He had not heard that from Calanthe—had not heard *anything* from her—but from Georgios's finance director. The fact that he was telling Nikos was significant. As were the implications to be drawn from it.

The conference over, and some useful business meetings attended in the Bay area, he returned to Zurich, put in hand an array of measures that would enable him to be absent from his desk for a good while, then flew down to Athens.

He would wait no longer.

'Papa, won't you consider that convalescent home the cardiologist recommended? Being there would help get you back on your feet, with careful exercise and therapy.'

Calanthe tried to make her tone persuasive, but it did not seem to be working. Even though he'd been discharged from hospital, there was a new weariness in her father, and she did not think it was just because he was still recovering—slowly—from major heart surgery. His eyes were sunken, his cheeks hollow.

She felt anxiety nip at her. It reminded her, painfully, of how she'd tried to rally her mother in her final days, intent on keeping her going, not letting her succumb to the dreaded disease gradually taking her over from the inside.

It had been a losing battle...

But this battle for her father must not be lost!

There was no reason for it to be lost. Many men survived bypass surgery well—he would too, surely?

Her father shook his head. He seemed fretful, as if he was waiting for something, but she knew not what.

He looked at her, eyes searching. 'Are you going back to London sometime?' he asked.

She shook her head. 'I've taken indefinite compassionate leave,' she said. 'I want to see you well first.'

'What are you doing this evening?' her father asked, as if her assurance that she would not be leaving Athens any time soon was what he'd wanted to hear. 'Anything nice?'

'Yes,' she said, trying to rally him. 'I'm having dinner with you, Papa.'

He made an impatient sound in his throat.

'You should go out!' he said. 'Night after night you are in...'

'Of course I am,' she said. 'I wouldn't dream of abandoning you!'

'I have staff to look out for me—and that nurse you insisted on!' he said. 'But you—you should be out and about. Choosing a man to marry.'

Calanthe's heart sank, but her father was speaking still.

'I've had my warning!' he told her. 'The next attack could finish me off.'

'Oh, Papa don't speak like that!' she said immediately.

He ignored her. 'So I want it settled! Is that too much to ask?'

Calanthe looked at him in consternation. He was not putting this on. He had never been manipulative of her in such a way—had never used emotional blackmail on her.

'Papa—' she began, dismay in her voice. And then broke off. What could she say to him? What could she possibly say when what he wanted was impossible?

The house phone on her bedside table was ringing and Calanthe picked it up. Her earlier conversation with her father was still in her head, fretting at her. The voice at the other end of the line wiped it from her thoughts.

'Before you hang up on me, listen—please.'

Nikos's voice was brisk and businesslike. That, and that alone, kept her on the line.

'Well?' she replied, her voice tight.

'I want you to have dinner with me.'

Her hand clenched over the handset. 'Are you mad?'

'Far from it.' The brisk, businesslike tones were clear down the line. 'There's a matter I need to discuss with you.' There was an infinitesimal pause. 'It concerns your father.'

She stiffened even more. 'In what way?'

'I shall discuss that with you over dinner.'

He gave the name of the restaurant, set the time, and rang off.

Calanthe stared at the phone in her hand, then slowly lowered it.

Conscious that she could hear the thud of her heart.

Hating it that she could.

The restaurant Nikos had chosen was quiet, and discreet. Warily, Calanthe took a seat at the table as he stood up at her approach. He was in a superbly tailored charcoal lounge suit, with a dark grey tie. Every inch the businessman. Not the lover. It might have reassured her, but it didn't. She herself had dressed sombrely, in an olive-green dress with a high neckline and no jewellery.

She had not seen Nikos since that fateful dinner party where her father had nearly died. Why had he asked her here?

That was the question she put to him once the waiters had left them alone, after fussing endlessly, it seemed to Calanthe, with menus and iced water and bread rolls and wine lists.

His answer, when he disclosed his reason, froze her in disbelief.

# CHAPTER EIGHT

'YOU WOULD BE doing it for your father,' Nikos heard his own voice saying.

'Would I?' Calanthe's tone was scathing.

'There would be other reasons, too.'

His eyes rested on her. Her face had closed, her mouth was pinched, and her eyes were steely.

'Really? You mean apart from handing my father's company to you on a plate.' She gave an acid smile that didn't alter the expression on her face. 'And myself as well.'

He lifted his glass to his mouth. Felt himself relax.

'It is what your father wants,' he said smoothly. 'You surely know that.'

Her face stayed rigid. Then she cut to the chase.

'Why you?'

He eased his knife through the tender fillet of chicken, cut himself a slice.

'He believes me capable of running his company...finding synergies with my own, to our mutual advantage.' He paused. 'He spelt it out quite clearly to me when he all but interviewed me for the role the week of that dinner party.'

Her eyes were gimlets. 'Which role would that be? CEO or son-in-law?' Again, her words were acid.

'Both.' He forked up the chicken. 'That's the whole point, Calanthe.'

He let his eyes rest on her again. Rejection radiated from her like a force field. It might have been a sign to be taken negatively, but he knew it for the opposite. Knew why she was radiating rejection on all frequencies.

A small smile formed briefly at his mouth as he watched her bristle like a porcupine at his words. Her sole was barely touched, her utensils gripped in nerveless hands.

'You saw at that dinner party with his friends and peers how acceptable the notion was to him,' he went on. 'How expected. It was always going to be so—one day his daughter would marry suitably, and his son-in-law would carry his business forward.'

He tilted an eyebrow.

'You have no interest in doing so—he made that clear to me—and he also made clear he would have welcomed it had you done so. But he respects your choice of career. However...'

He paused again, his gaze levelling with hers.

'He will not willingly see his life's work discontinued. Without a competent and suitable son-in-law, after his days have passed, the assets would be disposed of and the company either liquidated or sold on. No matter how much money that would leave you with, what he has spent his life building up would be dissipated. He does not want that. Hence this solution. It suits everyone all round.'

Her eyes narrowed. 'Except me,' she said.

Nikos's expression changed, his eyelids half veiling his gaze. 'You say that to me after our night together?' he said.

There was a caress in his voice, he knew. A promise.

Her knife and fork clattered to the tablecloth. Her head shot back. 'That night should never have happened. Never!'

He held her gaze without concession. There had been something more in it than repudiation—something revealing.

*She cannot deny what our night together brought her! What it meant for her...for both of us...*

He had to make her see it and accept it. Accept everything that went with it. Everything he had brought her here to accept.

'But it did, Calanthe—it did happen. And it proved just how good we are together—deny it all you will! I told you there, on the beach, how important you were becoming to me, and now—'

A choke broke from her.

He did not let it stop him.

'Now I have the chance to tell you again...to tell you how...how special you have become to me. Eight years ago you were too young, and I had my way to make in the world. The time was not right for us. But now, Calanthe, *now* the time *is* right. So very right.'

His voice was a caress again. He wanted, *needed* her to accept what he was telling her.

'Had your father not collapsed as he did, I would have taken the time to woo you properly...win you over to me. But your father needs the reassurance we can give him now. Would you begrudge him that?'

She stared across at him, her face still closed. 'It's not him I begrudge,' she said. Her voice was tight, her mouth pinched.

He reached his hand across the table. Touched her fingers with his. Leant towards her. Her face was still leaden, and he didn't want it that way. He didn't want words like bullets, the freezing off and the rejection. He didn't want that at all.

He wanted the woman he'd led down that scented pathway to the private darkness of the beach house...the woman he'd taken into his arms, her body aflame for him, trembling with a desire that answered his own, surging in his body, urging his possession of her.

He felt desire quicken in him again now, as his hand closed over hers, felt hers beneath it.

His voice was low once more when he spoke again. 'What is between us—what has *always* been between us—cannot be denied! Be honest with yourself. Be honest with me as I am honest with you.'

Something came into her eyes. A flash. Dark like black lightning. Had he really seen it? Or had it been a trick of the light?

He felt her hand drawing back from his, withdrew his own.

Frustration filled him and made him speak more bluntly than he wanted. 'Calanthe, this would protect your father! He just isn't well enough to go back into harness. His heart is weakened—you cannot want to risk another attack! Not when it is so easy for you to remove that risk.'

He saw his warning hit home...pressed further.

'When he outlined his hopes to me he told me about your mother, Calanthe. That she had died far too young. Deprived of old age. Don't let that happen to your father too. Not when it would be so easy to prevent it.'

For one long last moment he let his gaze rest on her, met her veiled, oblique regard of him. Then she spoke, with no expression in her voice.

'I'd like to go home now, Nikos,' she said. 'No, don't get up. I'll get a taxi. Finish your dinner. I'm sorry I only picked at mine.'

She got to her feet, walked stiffly away, as though tension racked her body. He watched her leave the restaurant, then sat back, unconsciously reaching for his wine glass.

He caught the lingering fragrance of her perfume. All that was left of her presence there.

*What will she decide?*

He did not know.

Knew only that there was only one answer he could bear to hear from her.

'Your father is asking for you,' the housekeeper informed Calanthe as she stepped through the doorway.

Calanthe bit her lip. The last thing she could face right now was seeing her father. Her brain was in meltdown, churning with thoughts, emotions and feelings that she could not process, that had turned her upside down and inside out.

*I didn't see it coming.*

But it had—like a bomb exploding inside her.

She hurried up the stairs, knowing she must face her father—but not, dear God, with the true extent of her feelings.

*Not that I even know what they are. I'm all in pieces—completely in pieces!*

Her father was in bed, and the massive bed frame was dwarfing him, she realised with a pang, as it had never done previously. He looked frail and ill. The pang in her heart struck more deeply, but she put a cheerful smile on her face, moving across to kiss his sunken cheek.

'How are you feeling?' she asked brightly.

'That depends on you,' came the laboured reply. 'You have been to dinner with young Kavadis? Of course I knew! He asked my permission first! So...' he levelled his sunken eyes on her '...what answer have you given him?'

Dismay flushed through her. She could see in his eyes what she did not want to see. Expectation...and hope.

She felt her stomach clench.

'Papa, I—' Her mouth was dry suddenly. 'It…it was… out of the blue.'

She sounded like a Victorian maiden, she thought wildly, trotting out the traditional *Oh, this is so sudden!* prevarication.

The expression in her father's eyes changed. It was knowing now—amused, even. As though his daughter was an open book to him. And Nikos too.

'Really?' he riposted sceptically. 'The man hasn't been able to take his eyes off you! Right from when he walked into my party! Do you think I can't tell when a man has been struck by lightning? Oh, you may play the ice queen,' he said, the amusement deepening, 'but that can be alluring to a man like him. He's a man who knows what he wants. He's made himself something from nothing—achieved everything he wanted. And now…' his eyes rested on Calanthe and she could not escape their message '…he wants you.'

She felt her face tighten. 'What he *wants*, Papa, is your company!' she bit out.

He waved his hand again. 'Of course he does! I would not respect him if he didn't!' His voice changed, and there was shrewdness in his face once more. 'And I would not contemplate him coming within a hundred metres of it if I didn't think he had three essential qualities. One—ambition. The way *I* had it, Calanthe, when I started out in business. The kind of ambition to make something of myself—as he has already proved he has. The second is competence. I will not let what I have spent my life building up be in the hands of someone who isn't capable. And the third…'

Calanthe saw his expression change, soften.

'The third is obvious.'

He held his hand out to her. Automatically she took it, feeling its warmth, its cherishing. A lump rose in her throat.

'He will make a good husband for you, *pethi mou*. Truly he will. To him, you are a prize in yourself—not just because you are my daughter! He values you as a man *should* value the woman he marries.'

He shut his eyes for a moment, then opened them again. Naked longing was clear in them for her to see.

'It's all I want for you, my darling, dearest daughter. To see you settled and happy. With a man who is worthy of you.'

She heard his words. Felt ice pool in her stomach.

Worthy.

Nikos Kavadis was 'worthy' of her...

The ice in her stomach chilled even more.

She felt her father squeeze her hand, then release it. He looked tired suddenly, and weary, and ill. The lump in her throat thickened, and fear clutched at her. What if he never recovered from his bypass? What if his ailing heart failed again? This time for ever...

Ice pooled in her again—but not because of Nikos.

'I just long to see you settled,' her father said again, and in his voice there was longing and hope—and fear. Fear that she might not, not even now, when he was lying there, stricken and frail, his brush with death narrowly escaped.

Heaviness filled her, and a sense of the room closing in on her. It left nothing but herself, sitting on her father's bed, looking at his face filled with all that he wanted for her.

Slowly, she got to her feet. 'I know, Papa, I know,' she said softly.

Love was in her eyes, and pity too—and anguish.

She bent to kiss his cheek, to murmur goodnight to him. But as she turned and left the room there was something else in her eyes.

Resolve.

And the heaviness inside her was like a concrete weight. Dragging her to the bottom of the sea. The deep and drowning sea…

Nikos sat at the desk in his hotel room, attempting to focus his thoughts on own business affairs. But he hadn't touched the keyboard on his laptop for ten minutes.

Since she'd left him at dinner last night there had been nothing from Calanthe. Nor from Georgios Petranakos either. He would give it another twenty-four hours, then head back to Zurich.

But every atom of his being resisted such action.

He stared at the blank wall in front of him, feeling emotions shift and shape within him.

Surely Calanthe would accept him? And not just for her father's sake, but for her own too? Surely now she would finally let the past go? Would accept what had brought them back together after so long? How much he wanted her and she him?

Longing filled him. Memories of that night at the beach house tormented him.

Waking to an empty bed had been unbearable.

*All I want is her—Calanthe.*

Her name rang in his head.

A ping sounded from his laptop—an email arriving. Another one. He'd ignored most of them, his mind too distracted to pay them any attention. But he cast a cursory glance down to see who this one was from and suddenly his entire attention was on it.

It was from Calanthe.

He clicked it open. Conscious that his heart rate had increased. Conscious that he resented the fact that it had.

Conscious that he did not know how to predict just what her answer would be. Or even if she was prepared to give it.

It seemed she was.

The email was brief.

I accept.

*Yes!* He wanted to punch the air in triumph.

Then, just below, in parentheses, he saw she'd written something else.

(Ts and Cs apply. To be discussed and confirmed.)

He didn't care. He snatched up his phone, to call the Petranakos mansion immediately, but before he could the hotel phone rang.

He wanted to ignore it, but didn't.

'Yes?' His tone was impatient.

It was Calanthe.

'Nikos?' She sounded brisk. Businesslike, even. 'You have my email now. Meet me for lunch in forty-five minutes.'

She named a restaurant, and the street it was on.

He frowned. That was the same street as Petranakos HQ. But he made no demur—only agreed. He made no mention of her email, or what it contained, making his voice smooth and co-operative.

'Of course. I'll see you there.'

She rang off and he sat back. That sense of triumph was still coursing through him.

Triumph—and more than triumph.

A sense of achievement so intense it filled him completely.

* * *

It was like déjà vu, Calanthe thought as she sat down at the table in the restaurant she'd stipulated. But this time she wasn't going to be sideswiped. For a start, she was at the restaurant first. Secondly, she was well briefed this time around.

As Nikos would discover.

She ordered an elderflower spritzer from the hovering waiter, who was being very attentive, knowing she was the daughter of one of their most regular patrons, and then settled back to watch for Nikos's arrival.

He turned up dead on time, making straight for her table, wearing the same darkly formidable charcoal business suit and grey tie as he had the previous night. It had the same impact on her—the one she didn't want it to have but could not prevent. She felt her hands clench in her lap. Well, she must, that was all. Too much depended on it.

An image hung in her mind of the way her father had reached for her hand last night, his frailty tugging at her, her love for him squeezing her heart.

Nikos sat himself down, smiled pleasantly at her, greeted her civilly. But his expression was unreadable. The waiter was there again, and Calanthe noted that Nikos had ordered a martini. Dry—but potent. It gave her the slight sense of an edge over him. An edge she would need, she knew.

For the next few minutes there was the business of menus, and ordering, and iced water, and bread rolls, but finally they were left to themselves. It was a relatively early lunch, so the restaurant was quiet.

Nikos glanced at her. 'Why this particular restaurant?' he asked. 'I'd have happily come out to Kifissia…met you somewhere there.'

It was a leading question, and Calanthe acknowledged it.

'It was the most convenient,' she said. 'I've just spent the morning with my father's financial director.'

If Nikos was surprised, he hid it.

'He seems a sound man,' he commented.

She knew he'd already met the man, and that her father had introduced him to several of the other senior directors. Nikos would have wanted to meet the executive team—there was no way he could step into Georgios's shoes on any other terms. He would have to show himself to be approving of the calibre of the senior executives, and, indeed, agree to co-operate with them.

Calanthe nodded. She knew her father's FD personally, as a frequent dinner guest with his wife, along with several other board members. But her meeting with him that morning had been of a specific nature. So had her conversation with her father earlier that day.

'I've also talked to my father,' she said now. She looked straight across at Nikos. 'I wanted to be sure I understand exactly the terms on which you will be taking the burden of running his company from him—and,' she added pointedly, 'what his senior team think of it. Also, crucially...' she held Nikos's unrevealing gaze '...what they think of you.'

Nikos's martini arrived, and he took a ruminative sip as the waiter glided away.

'And...?' he posed to Calanthe.

She took a breath. 'It seems both my father's notion, and you yourself, are deemed sound,' she said.

'I'm glad to see you reassured,' Nikos said.

His voice was smooth. Too smooth for her liking.

She took a mouthful of her spritzer, for her mouth was suddenly dry. She was doing her level best to be Little Miss Cool, but her senses kept trying to distract her. Kept trying to get her gaze to fix on just what it was about him that seemed to quicken the blood in her veins, make her heart beat faster. But she had to stay cool.

'However, I did tell my father, and his senior team, that if we go ahead with my father's plan I will join the board.'

Nikos stilled. She saw it. Felt it giving her an edge again. He hadn't seen that coming.

'I may not be a born businesswoman, but I won't totally abstain from any degree of responsibility or commitment. I want a seat on the board, so that I am involved in some capacity. My father and his team have no objection,' she said pointedly.

She watched Nikos pick up his martini again, revolve the glass slowly in his fingers.

'You want to keep an eye on me?' he said.

She nodded. *Because you've got previous, Nik...*

He cocked an eyebrow at her. 'Any other Ts and Cs on your list?'

For a second, Calanthe could not stop her expression hardening. Yes, she had some more—but she would not disclose them now. Not yet. Not till the time was right.

She felt Nikos's gaze narrow assessingly. She made her expression relax. 'Some more may occur to me, but for now that's it. After all...' she looked at him straight '...right now we're only talking about an engagement. Nothing is fixed until we marry and you sign whatever paperwork my father has had drawn up for you.'

He sat back, lifting his martini glass, eyes resting on her. 'Thinking of jilting me at the altar?' he said casually.

Was there humour in his voice? Baiting? Teasing, even?

She wouldn't rise to it. She was feeling a sense of relief—a reaction to the tension that had gripped her since he'd walked up to the table—and now the effect of his physical presence was there again, impacting her, overwhelming her, making her blood kick, her breath quicken…mixing memory and desire…

*No!*

Slamming down on that oh-so-dangerous word, she said instead, 'No altar, Nikos. A civil wedding only.'

He frowned. 'Won't your father want the full works?'

'Let's keep this simple, Nikos,' she said.

Her voice was low. She felt the tremble in it. A tremble she didn't want. Her eyes dropped to the tablecloth.

Suddenly, she felt her arm being touched. The briefest gesture on her bare forearm.

'Calanthe…' she heard him say. His voice was soft. Almost tender.

She looked up, blinking. He was gazing at her—openly so. She couldn't bear it…but she could not look away.

'You will not regret this,' he said. 'I have rushed you, I know, because of your father's illness. But even if I cannot woo you properly before our wedding, I will woo you after.'

His smile was a caress, a promise…

She felt colour beat up in her—and heat. His eyes, so dark, so drowning, were telling her how beautiful he found her, how desirable, how he could not resist her…

Nor could she resist him.

She heard herself speak. A mere breath of air. Saying his name. 'Nikos…' A sigh, an exhalation.

Heat flushed her body, filling it with longing, with desire. He took her hand, cradled it in his. His eyes didn't leave her. He turned her hand over in his and then, the tender skin of her inner wrist exposed, drew it to his mouth. Grazed its silken surface with his lips. Weakness drowned through her…

*'Mademoiselle…'*

It was the waiter, arriving with their first courses.

She yanked her hand away, cheeks burning. Nikos gave a low laugh, leaning back as the waiter deposited his *assiette*, having bestowed Calanthe's upon her.

'Is there anything else?' the waiter asked politely.

Nikos glanced up at him. 'A glass of champagne for each of us,' he announced.

As the waiter murmured his assent, Nikos's glance turned to Calanthe. 'To celebrate,' he said.

The waiter glided away, and Nikos reached inside his jacket, drawing out a small, distinctive box, flicking it open.

'And not just with champagne,' he murmured. His gaze rested on her, sending a message to her, along with the contents of the box. A message it was impossible for her to deny—though it made her own gaze veil, her throat tighten suddenly.

Calanthe's eyes dropped to the ring he was placing in front of her. The diamond solitaire—worth a fortune, she knew—glittered at her, its message clear. Nikos, staking his claim to her.

*Re*-claiming her, after eight long years...

And never, *never*, had it rung so bitter.

So achingly hollow...

The wedding was to be as quiet as Calanthe could make it.

She wanted minimum stress on her father.

And on herself.

Her mind slid sideways, as it had been doing ever since she had sent that fateful email of acceptance to Nikos.

A feeling of complete unreality had settled over her as she'd gone through the motions required for organising the civil wedding she'd insisted on.

Despite her father's objections she'd held adamant on that

point. She'd also been adamant that no announcement at all would be made of the forthcoming wedding. She would, she'd informed her father, tell their friends afterwards, justifying her decision by revealing her father's ill health.

There was one other thing she had remained adamant about. Nikos had moved out of his hotel and into a rented flat, near enough to both Marousi and Kiffisia, but he would live in it on his own until the wedding. Calanthe had been crystal-clear about that.

'My father will expect it,' she told Nikos. 'And nor do I want to leave him at this time, while he is still so weak.'

Nikos hadn't liked it—but had gone along with it. Besides, he'd been busy too, she knew. He was running his own company remotely—albeit with one quick trip back to Zurich—and immersing himself in the running of her father's company too.

She, too, had alterations to make in her life. She knew she would have to give up her job in London...see if she could take up full-time work of a comparable nature here in Athens.

Keeping busy had helped. Helped her stop thinking about what she was doing. Helped her stop thinking about Nikos.

She was holding him at bay, she knew. And she knew why too. She was keeping their time together at a minimum, citing her own desire to spend as much time with her father as she could before moving out of his home. Again, Nikos hadn't liked it—but had gone along with it.

His words from the lunch where she had given in to what he wanted echoed in her head.

'...if I cannot woo you properly before our wedding, I will woo you after...'

She pulled her mind away. She could not think about 'after' until it came.

\* \* \*

Nikos said the words he needed to say. Heard Calanthe say hers. Heard the officiant speak his part.

Apart from the necessary witnesses and officials, the only other person present at Kifissia's town hall was Georgios Petranakos. Drawn and ill as he still was, there was a look on the older man's face that was one of satisfaction. Relief.

It was something Nikos could echo—and far more intensely.

Finally, Calanthe was his!

Eight years ago he'd left her—

His thoughts pulled away from the memory like a plane hitting turbulence.

But now…

*Now I will never walk away again.*

Emotion welled within him, inchoate but powerful. He did not know what it was—only that it made him turn and look at her now, feeling it rise within him again, catching at his lungs.

How much she moved him!

Just to look at her was a delight.

She wore a simple cream dress, narrow-cut, knee-length, and with cap sleeves. Expensive, obviously, but not showy— discreetly elegant. Also low-heeled court shoes and pearls at her ears and throat, with her hair in a coiled chignon set with pearl combs. Her make-up was subtle, but enhanced her natural beauty. In her hands was a small bouquet of cream-coloured flowers, delicately scented, hand-tied with cream satin ribbons.

Nikos's breath caught again as he felt that strange emotion well up in him once more. She looked, he thought, like perfection itself.

The slightest frown formed between his brows.

But her expression was grave...tense, even.

He gave a forbearing mental shake. Well, that was to be expected. She had nearly lost her father—his health was still a major concern to her—and she had been rushed into marriage because of it.

His words to her—the promise that he had made when she had finally accepted the necessity of their rapid marriage—came back to him.

He had, indeed, had no time to woo her.

His wooing, as he had promised, would come after their wedding.

He felt anticipation flush through him.

Starting tonight...

The celebrant was speaking again. Solemn, binding words. Uniting them in matrimony. Binding them together—he to her, she to him.

And it was done.

He turned towards her, smiled down at her. She was as pale as her dress, her expression unreadable. But he did not mind. Nerves were understandable on a bride's wedding day.

He murmured her name—a caress in itself. Lowered his head to brush her lips with his.

They were as cold as marble.

Anticipation flared within him. Soon... Ah, soon he would warm those lips. And all that he had rediscovered on that glorious night at the beach house would be theirs again.

He could not wait.

Calanthe kissed her father goodnight. They had dined at home, after the wedding. Her father and Nikos would have far preferred dining out, but she had put her foot down, claiming it would be too tiring for her father after the exertion of attending the wedding.

It had been a strained affair—both the wedding itself and dinner *à trois*—but she had coped. Most of the conversation over dinner had been between her father and Nikos, and she had been relieved. She had only been able to pick at her food and had hardly touched her wine.

Nerves had racked her, and now, as she bade goodnight to her father, they racked her even more.

She was trying not to think—not to let any thoughts into her head at all. Keeping her mind as blank as she could. Trying, above all, not to let the one question that clamoured to be released pound in her head.

*What have I done? Dear God, what have I done?*

Because there was no point letting it out.

She knew what she had done.

She had married Nikos Kavadis.

The man who had broken her heart eight years ago was now her husband.

Nikos could feel the tension in him mounting. The car was pulling up outside the modern apartment block…the driver was getting out to open the door for them. He got out first, nodding at the driver, holding out his hand to help Calanthe. She got out without taking it, murmuring her thanks to the driver, then walked to the apartment block entrance.

Nikos dismissed the car, extracting from his jacket pocket the key card that would open the doors for them. They slid aside and he stepped in with Calanthe, the air-con in the lobby chill after the external temperature.

He was glad they were repairing straight to his apartment. There was no need to fuss with wedding nights in flash hotels, and because of Georgios's poor health a honeymoon away right now was out of the question.

Besides, now that he was officially Georgios Petranakos's son-in-law there was a great deal of work to be done in stepping fully into the CEO's shoes. A honeymoon could come later—the Maldives, the Seychelles, maybe even the South Seas...

Until then...

His eyes glinted, his gaze going to Calanthe now as she stood beside him in the elevator. It was carrying another passenger—a neighbour, Nikos presumed—so conversation between himself and Calanthe was absent. They got out at his floor, and Nikos readied the key card.

Calanthe was already familiar with the apartment—he'd brought her here before the wedding, to show it to her. He opened the door for her now, and she stepped inside. She seemed, he thought, on edge. Well, so was he. But his weeks of tortuous self-denial were about to end...

'Coffee?' he said to her now.

It was not what he wanted—there was only one thing he wanted—but he could be patient if she wanted to collapse for a while...put her feet up, knock back a coffee, maybe even linger over a liqueur.

She shook her head. 'Thank you, no,' she said.

There was something different in her voice. Nikos frowned. She was walking through into the large reception room, with its stylish modern furniture. He followed her in, and as he did so she turned.

'I have something to say to you,' she said.

He paused, looking at her. There was something different in her face, too. Something in the set of her shoulders, the lift of her chin.

Out of nowhere, Niko felt his expression change—grow tense.

And then she was speaking. Her voice no longer merely crisp, but cutting like a knife. Slicing to the bone.

Her face was like a stone. 'Whatever you expected of this marriage, Nikos, understand this. It will be a marriage in name only,' she said, and her eyes were like gimlets, sharp and piercing. 'You will not be laying a finger on me.' She drew a breath—a harsh, hard sound, as hard as her expression. 'Not now. Not ever,' she said. '*Never* again.'

Calanthe felt weakness flood through her, debilitating and depleting—the aftermath of the tension that had racked her body from the moment she had sat alone in the car with Nikos.

She had said it—dear God, she had actually said it! Said what she had been waiting to say ever since she had given in to her terror for her father, yielded to what he longed for, what she dared not refuse when his brush with death had come so close and might yet come closer still.

What it had been absolutely essential for her to say had now been said. For Nikos to hear.

*What I never wanted to tell him.*

He was looking at her as if she were from another planet. She wanted to laugh, but laughter might break her apart, and she had used up all her strength today—the very last of it. She could take no more.

He made a start towards her, but she stepped back, a jerking, instinctive movement, forcing her legs to do so.

Then: 'Why the *hell*,' he said, 'are you saying that?'

The incomprehension in his voice was absolute. She saw his face work.

'Calanthe—what is going on? I know you're tired—exhausted, probably…any wedding day is a strain.' He took a breath—a ragged one. 'Look, you can call it a day, OK? I'll make some coffee and you can take it to bed with you. Have a shower, take your make-up off, get into bed.' He took another breath. 'I'll sleep in the spare room. Give you peace and quiet. Give you space. Give you time.'

She looked at him. Keeping her face like stone. Her eyes like granite. Expressionless. Unyielding.

'You could give me eternity, Nikos, and it wouldn't be enough. You see…' She heard the words coming from her. Words that had been eight years in the making. 'You are the very last man on this earth that I would *ever* soil myself on or let near me again.'

She saw his expression change, his brows snap together.

'Why?' he said bluntly.

His face had closed, like a guillotine slicing down over it.

'Because of what you did eight years ago,' she answered.

Her legs would hardly hold her upright, but she forced them to do so.

His eyes flashed. She could see, as clear as day, that he was veiling what was in them.

*He knows—he knows why I've said what I have. I can see it and he cannot hide it from me.*

Bitterness filled her. And all the more when he said what he said next.

'Because I ended things with you?'

He was making his voice sound open—but she knew that was the very last thing it was…

'Calanthe, I told you—I said to you that very first day at Cape Sounion why I did it. I thought it was a summer romance only…feared that maybe…'

He drew another breath, keeping his eyes fixed on her. She could see that he wanted her to believe what he was saying.

'Maybe you were reading more into it—it was your first romance, and I knew that. Yes, I regret that I left you so abruptly, but I've explained why. I had to get back to my grandmother. That was the reason I left the island.'

She shut her eyes as if to shut him out of existence. Shut out what he had just trotted out to her.

Then: *'Don't lie to me!'* The words were spat from her. Her hands clenched at her sides. A blinding pain came in her head, making her sway. 'You didn't leave the island because of your grandmother! You didn't leave me because you thought it was just a summer romance!'

Her eyes narrowed to slits. The fury in her now possessed her utterly, in an overpowering tide that had been banked for eight long, endless years. She spoke again, every word deadly. Each one finding its mark.

'You left me, Nikos,' she said, 'for one reason and one reason only.'

Her eyes were like knives. Stabbing right into him.

'Because my father *paid* you to leave me.'

# CHAPTER NINE

IT WAS SAID. Said in words that could never be unsaid. Words she had stored within herself all these years. That had eaten into her, eaten into the heart she had broken over him. Over a man who had taken her father's money to walk out on her.

Pain twisted inside her like torsion in her guts. He was standing there, stock-still, the blood drained from his face.

She went on speaking, saying what had been buried in the deepest part of her for so long. 'When did you find out who I was?'

Even now she dreaded the answer. Dreaded to hear that he had known all along. That he had seduced her knowingly...

*Because if that were so then...*

Then she would not even have those precious memories of their time together to cling to.

There was no expression in his face as he answered her. 'When your father's fixers arrived. Just before—just before I left you.'

His voice had no emotion in it—none. And then something dark and deadly flashed in his eyes.

'Calanthe, for God's sake—if you have known all along, why wait till now to throw it at me?'

The words broke from him, raw and uncomprehending.

Her face contorted. 'Confront you with the ultimate humiliation a woman can endure?' Her voice twisted and she had to force the words from her, each one burning like acid in her throat.

*It hurts—oh, God, how it hurts! To know what he did... To know that money—my father's money—was more important to him than I was! After all we had together! After he held me in his arms, kissed me, made love to me—laughed with me and held my hands. We were together, a couple, him and me...*

But it had meant nothing at all to him.

Nothing.

All that had been important to him was the money her father had offered to get rid of him...

And he'd taken the money.

Condemning himself for ever.

She saw his expression tighten.

Words gritted from him. 'I told your father's fixers that you must never know—'

He broke off.

She could not bear to look at him. Could not bear it.

'No, it's not something you'd want known about yourself! Just what you stooped to!' she shot at him. 'Well, my father told me,' she said flatly. 'He said...he said I needed to know.' There was a stone in her lungs, so that she couldn't breathe. 'That I needed to know I would always be a target for unscrupulous men who would romance me, seduce me, tell me anything I wanted to hear—but whatever they did, whatever they said, all they would want would be his money.'

Her voice was as hollow as his now, her eyes dead. She shifted restlessly, as if moving might untwist the torsion in her guts, but it only tightened it, making it agonising to endure.

'And now his money is what you have again, Nik,' she said, unconsciously using the name she'd called him by all those years ago, when the world had been a wonderful place and Nik the most wonderful man in that wonderful world. 'And much, much more of it this time! By bringing you in to run his company he's made you richer than even you've made yourself. Oh, you'll work for it, I'm sure—hard and well—and you'll earn your share of the profits that will accrue now.'

She forced a ragged, razored breath into her stone-filled lungs, forced herself to look at him. He was standing there, so close—and yet so infinitely far away—with shock still immobilising him. Because what else could he feel but shock at what she'd thrown at him, that she'd known about him all along, shock that was making his face grey like ash?

'You've told me twice now, Nik, that I am "important" to you—and I know I am. I always was, from the minute you knew I was my father's daughter.'

He started forward. 'Calanthe—that's not why! You're important to me because—'

Her hand slashed upwards, silencing him. 'Don't try and make it right, Nik! It cannot be made right! Because *nothing* can justify what you did! Oh, you might well have left me anyway—I know that. That's the line you've trotted out to me—that it was a summer romance, that I was so young, that you had your way to make in the world. But you found a good way to make it easier for yourself, didn't you? *Didn't you?* With my father's money. The pay-off you took to walk out on me.'

Bitterness and pain and burning humiliation consumed her.

'You wanted my father's money. Not me.' She took another razored breath. 'Well, that's what you've got now, too.'

She made herself look at him again. He hadn't moved—not a muscle. Somehow she made herself walk past him, head to the front door of the apartment. There she paused and turned back to him.

'I won't be living with you here, Nikos. I've rented the apartment next door. So far as my father is concerned I'm with you. And the world can think that too. I'll socialise with you, keep up appearances—for my father's sake, you understand. I'll stick this out until he's well enough to hear that we've split up, that I married in haste and repented all too quickly.' Her voice twisted. 'He knows, you see, that I make mistakes when it comes to falling for men. As for his company—well, as I say, I'm sure you'll run it well, and make money both for him and yourself, and everyone will be happy because of it.'

She frowned.

'Not much has changed, has it, Nik? Eight years ago my father paid you to leave me. Now, because he wants you to run his company and be the son-in-law he's been waiting years for, he's paying you to stay with me. He bought you off—now he's buying you in.'

She took a breath…it was a like a razor in her throat.

'Well, enjoy it, Nik—enjoy all the Petranakos money coming your way now. This time around it's all you'll get.'

She pulled open the door, stepped through…

And was gone.

Calanthe watched the lights around Gatwick get closer as the plane descended. She had been desperate to get away, right out of Greece, so she'd walked out of the apartment block and headed for Eleftheriou Airport, taken the first flight to London. She'd land after midnight but she didn't care. She'd head for her flat and take refuge there.

Like a wounded animal…

She closed her eyes, saw that monstrous scene in Nik's

apartment playing and replaying in her head. Saw herself throwing at him the accusation that had burned within her for so long, shameful and shaming. The thing that she had *never* wanted to admit to. The ultimate humiliation.

She had turned it into anger—anger that was utterly justified—and condemned him for what he'd done. But it had taken all her strength to face the man who had taken money to leave her, to look him in the eyes and tell him she knew she had been *nothing* to him...

She gave a sob of misery.

*I loved him! I loved him with all my stupid, stupid heart!*

Her hands twisted in her lap, nails digging into her palms. And now she was facing the worst pain of all. The pain she could not bear to face. But she had to.

If she had never set eyes on Nikos again she might have survived his betrayal eight years ago. But he had walked back into her life with devastating consequences—that night in the beach house, in his arms, finding again the bliss she had once known with him when she had first loved him.

And she knew, with another anguished sob, that she loved him again...

Nikos stood on the balcony of his apartment in Zurich, overlooking the lake. The air off the mountains was cool. Autumn would fall sooner here than in Greece, and then the winter's snows would come. But he already dwelled in the land of winter...the land of perpetual ice and snow. It was a land he had not expected ever to be exiled to. And he might never escape. Not even if—

He cut off his thoughts.

Too dangerous. Far, far too dangerous.

Better to accept the perpetual ice and snow.

It was all he deserved.

His thoughts were bitter, like acid in his throat.

*I never wanted her to know. Never wanted her to know what I had done.*

But she had known all along. Known even in that moment he'd set eyes on her again, walking up to her at her father's birthday party.

*Every time she looked at me she knew.*

He stared blindly out over the dark waters of the lake. No wonder she had left him that morning, after their night together in the beach house...the night he had believed had brought them back together again. When all along...

He wrenched his hands from the wooden balustrade, turned sharply away, strode back indoors. He needed a drink. Any drink. Anything at all that might dull the rawness inside him, which felt as if the skin had been torn from his flesh.

He yanked open his cocktail cabinet, splashed out a slug of malt whisky, knocked it back as if it were water. It burned as it went down his throat and he poured another.

But he did not drink it. He put the glass down roughly instead. Felt his jaw set like steel as a thought came to him.

He had one chance—one only.

One hope—one only.

And everything...*everything*...depended on it.

Calanthe was in Berlin, attending a conference on Late Antiquity which her former boss at the London museum had agreed she could still go to if she reported back on it. She'd gone straight from London, and it would mop up a few days.

She'd emailed her father when she'd arrived in London, saying she had some loose ends to tie up in clearing her desk, sorting out her flat and bringing over what she would need for a permanent stay in Athens.

As for Nikos, she'd simply tersely texted him to say she was in London. He would know why, and that it had nothing to do with what she'd told her father.

It was simply to avoid him.

He would be busy, anyway, she knew. He had a lot to take over at her father's company, and he had his own to run as well. He was in Zurich right now, and she was glad of it. It would give her some time in Athens without him.

But she could not avoid him for ever. She knew that. She had meant what she'd said when she'd told him that she would appear as his wife in public, for the sake of her father. Yet she dreaded it with all her being.

To stand beside him…to be Kyria Kavadis, accepting congratulations, having her girlfriends eager to know all about how she'd finally succumbed to love and marriage…

She felt her throat close, painful and tight. How could she have come to do what she had done? Let herself fall in love with him again? When this time around she *knew* what kind of man he was! How could she have let her stupid, stupid heart betray her as it had?

And yet it had.

And it was agony to know it.

Nikos stood in Arrivals at Eleftheriou, tension in every muscle of his body. Calanthe's flight from Berlin had landed. She would be deplaning now. He knew she was returning to Athens because her father's housekeeper had mentioned it when he'd put in his daily call to Georgios, reporting back on his company's affairs.

Calanthe herself had not informed him. She had kept ruthlessly silent since leaving for London.

Her absence had given him the essential time he'd needed…

His muscles tensed again. So much depended on this. *Everything—my whole life...*

But he would not—must not—let that show. He must stay...detached.

He craned his neck as another bevy of arriving passengers issued through from Customs. And there she was— walking swiftly forward, wearing a smart business suit in dark blue, low-heeled shoes, pulling a wheeled carry-on suitcase.

He stepped forward and he saw her face whiten with shock. He took her arm with one hand, relieved her of her carry-on with the other. She had stiffened at his touch, but he ignored it.

'How was your flight?' he asked her.

He kept his tone even, neutral, and she answered in kind. 'Fine,' she said.

She made to pull away, but he kept his hand on her forearm. It was as tense as steel.

'Good,' he said. 'Well, there's another one ahead of you.'

He started to guide her forward, but she balked.

'What do you mean?'

He paused, looking down at her. 'I mean,' he said, still keeping his voice neutral, 'we are going on our honeymoon.'

He saw her face whiten even more.

He cut across the protest rising on her lips. 'I have things to say to you, and they cannot be said in Athens.'

Rebuff flashed in her eyes. 'I don't want to hear them!'

'Tough,' he said.

He was in no mood to give any quarter. He'd steeled himself for this and he would see it through. He *must*.

He took a swift, incisive breath. 'You're going to hear them even if I have to shout them out loud to you in the middle of this airport, for all the world to hear! But the best place to hear them requires a flight—a short one—by helicopter.'

She was resistant still. That was obvious. And it was obvious why. He didn't care.

'Well?' he demanded. 'Are you going to agree? Or do we stand here arguing in the middle of Arrivals?'

Her face was set, but she made no more verbal resistance.

'Good,' he said again. 'The heliport is this way.'

He guided her forward, still in possession of her carry-on. His touch was light, but insistent.

Essential.

Just like the destination they were heading to.

Calanthe strained away from Nikos in the close confines of the helicopter now speeding its way across the Aegean. Where they were heading, she neither knew nor cared. A profound weariness was washing over her and it was not just to do with the flight from Berlin that morning. It was a weariness of the spirit that went so deep inside her it was part of her very being.

It had been a part of her for a long, long time.

For eight long years.

Dully, she gazed out of the window. An island group was nearing, and the helicopter started to dip down towards one of the islands. It touched down on a characteristic large H, with nothing much around it except a marina. It looked gleaming and new, with the Greek flag flying jauntily from the harbourmaster's office and expensive motor yachts bobbing at their moorings, as well as some sailing craft.

A sudden fear struck her—please don't let Nikos be thinking of taking her on a yacht! In such tiny confines, with a crew all around them...or, worse, no crew at all, just her and Nikos...

As she jumped down from the helicopter after him, ignoring his outstretched hand, he led the way to a waiting taxi. She got in as Nikos stashed her carry-on and his own grip bag in the boot. As the taxi drove off she shut her eyes, glad that Nikos made no attempt to talk to her. But she had to open them perforce, a short while later, when the taxi drew to a halt outside what was clearly a resort hotel.

Though attractively designed—only two storeys high and set in landscaped grounds, with the sea just visible beyond—it did not look particularly upmarket, but more for general tourist visitors. Not something Nikos would choose at all.

She went inside, where the entrance gave way to a large, airy atrium—again, attractively styled, but in no way at the level of a luxury hotel.

She turned back to Nikos, who was coming in after her with the luggage. 'Where is this?' she asked.

He paused. Looked at her. His gaze was veiled. 'Don't you recognise it?'

She looked at him blankly and shook her head.

'Ah, well,' he said, 'no reason you should. The last time you saw it, it was a building site.'

For a moment what he'd said made no sense. Then realisation flooded in. She gave a gasp. Of what, she wasn't quite sure.

He gave another nod as it dawned on her. 'Yes,' he said dryly, 'one and the same.' He glanced around him. 'Strange to think some of this is here due to my efforts. The foundations, mostly, and maybe part of the first storey.'

She was feeling faint. Faint with shock. It was washing over her in great waves.

What was she *doing* here? Why had she just numbly let Nik bring her here? And why did he want to be here?

Cold iced through her.

*Please, please don't let him think he can recreate our time here eight years ago—pretend that what he did to me never happened...*

He was speaking again, still in that same everyday tone of voice, as if her presence here was completely normal.

'I'll check us in. I've reserved a villa near the pool. Two bedrooms.'

She felt a fraction of the cold that had iced through her dissipate.

She glanced out of the tinted plate glass windows that looked out over gardens in which was set a massive pool—thronged, she could see, with children. On the far side, to the right, beyond more gardens, she could see tennis courts. She knew that underneath was the excavated archaeological site.

Time telescoped...past and present. She could almost see them all...students in two long rows, hunched over on their kneelers, flat pointed trowels teasing away the dry earth and stones, carefully, assiduously, patiently trying to reveal the past of three thousand years ago...

Eight years was nothing in that timeframe. The blink of an eyelid. But so, so long ago to her...

'Calanthe?'

Nikos's voice brought her back to the present. The present she did not want and could not avoid. Could not escape. He had a folder with their keys in it and was holding open the wide doors leading out to the gardens and the pool area. She walked forward, feeling the heat slam into her as they lost the air-con of the atrium.

She followed Nikos along a wide paved path, lined with bougainvillea, hibiscus and oleander, all attractively planted, with stone benches and ironwork chairs and tables set along it, and parasols against the sun. They skirted the pool widely, heading, she realised, for a semicircle of little stone villas curving away from the pool area, overlooking the sea.

Each semi-detached villa was attractively built, with a balcony fronting the upper storey and a private terrace created in front at ground level, and hedging between the villas for privacy. As they passed one she heard gleeful laughter coming out, and children's cries in English.

'Come on, Dad! Let's get to the pool! I can't wait!'

She smiled in spite of herself. Children on holiday, families on holiday...far from soggy England which was having a wet summer.

'This is ours,' Nikos said, as they approached the end villa.

He set their baggage down at the wooden front door, painted Greek blue, just like the shutters and window frames, and opened the door, hefting up the luggage again.

There was something in the way his body moved that lanced memory through her. How easily, eight years ago, his muscled body had tackled all that heavy lifting at the building site, as if what he was carrying was papier-mâché. She shook the thought from her...told herself instead that it was a wonder that a man as rich as Nikos was should lower himself to carry his own luggage.

He gestured for her to go in and she did so. Immediately cool air enveloped her, and she was glad. They were in a sitting/dining room that occupied the whole ground floor, with an open-plan kitchenette at the rear and a staircase against the left-hand wall. It was attractively furnished in blue and white—but, again, it was just an ordinary family resort.

It was homely. Comfortable. Appealing.

Against her volition she liked it.

'Do you want to choose your bedroom?' Nikos said, poised at the foot of the wooden staircase.

She nodded briefly, following him upstairs. The room at the front was larger—a double with a balcony—but she chose the smaller one at the back, a twin. Nik was welcome to the double bed. Welcome to its solitary vastness.

She relieved him of her suitcase, closed the door on him. Went and sat down on one of the beds.

She was feeling entirely blank.


Nikos stepped out onto the balcony that opened off his bedroom. There was a partial sea view, and if he craned his head he could see part of the huge central swimming pool, but not the main resort building to the rear. It was strange to be back here—though 'strange' was an understatement...

Eight years ago he'd been a labourer here, turning a dirt field into a hotel.

Now he was staying here.

With his bride.

The word rang like a hollow, mocking joke, and he shifted restlessly. Had he been mad to bring Calanthe here? Yet somehow this place had seemed...appropriate.

*It's where I first set eyes on her.*

He felt the tension that racked him tighten unbearably. This place might also prove to be the last place he would ever set eyes on her.

Unless...

*Tomorrow—tomorrow I will find out what my fate is to be.*

He pulled his thoughts away. There was this evening to get through first.

# CHAPTER TEN

'THERE ARE TWO restaurants here. The main one in the hotel, and then a more informal bistro-type near the pool.'

Nikos looked at her impassively and Calanthe tried to react similarly. But it was hard. Far harder than she wanted it to be.

To be here, in his company was hard, when the last time she had seen him it had been to hurl at him all those bitter, savage accusations that had eaten at her for all those years.

But not only was it hard for that reason. But for the very opposite.

Her gaze, still as impassive as she could make it, rested on him as they stood in the sitting room of the little villa. His presence was making itself felt on her consciousness... her senses. He was casually dressed, in chinos and an open-necked shirt, deck shoes and turned-back cuffs. Casual— devastating.

*Irresistible.*

The word he'd used about her now hovered in her head about him. Memory added to it. The clothes he was wearing now were way more expensive than those he'd worn when they'd gone out in the evenings eight years ago, but he wore them to the same effect. Her helpless gaze had clung to him then. It clung to him now.

'Or,' he was saying, as she tried to veil her treacherous—

irrelevant—reaction to him, 'we could stay in. The restaurant has a delivery service that we could use if you wish.' He paused. 'Your call,' he said.

In her head, Calanthe heard the words *None of the above!* But for reasons she did not want to admit to. Because she didn't want to have dinner with Nikos at all. It would be just too...

*Dangerous. That's what it would be.*

Dangerous to spend any time with him at all. Dangerous to be with him. To gaze at him. Dangerous to be exposed to him...as if he carried an infection she knew she would be unresistant to.

*What if he—?*

She broke off her thought. What Nikos might try and do now that he had her to himself again was not to be given space inside her head.

'The poolside bistro,' she heard herself say.

That seemed the least bad option. Eating here, with him, was out of the question. And dining in the main restaurant, conscious of eyes all over the place, was not what she wanted either. So maybe the smaller bistro was preferable? Less showy?

*More intimate?*

No! Don't think of that. This was a family hotel, not a place for romantic couples. Surely that must reassure her?

He nodded. 'Bistro it is, then,' he said.

He crossed to the door, holding it open for her. She walked past him, burningly conscious suddenly of what she was wearing. Her suitcase contained only clothes appropriate for a conference, not a holiday resort. So she'd been glad to discover from the hotel guide left in the villa that there was a beach shop off the central atrium.

She'd waited until she'd heard Nikos leave the villa—he'd

called out, in a deceptively casual tone, that he was going to catch a swim—and then warily made her way up to the hotel. She'd had to walk past the huge oval pool that dominated the gardens. There had still been some people in it, although not many at that late hour of the afternoon, but the only one she'd had eyes for was the swimmer who had been steadily ploughing the long length of it with a rhythmic, powerful freestyle.

Her breath had caught. His scything arms had sent up showers of water that caught the light of the lowering sun, creating a halo around his head, turning alternately left and right to draw breath as he swam. His powerful legs had threshed the water. She hadn't been able to see his body beneath the water. Only his shoulders, the upper part of his back. Bare and sculpted.

And so, so familiar.

She'd wrenched her gaze away, hurried her footsteps. As she'd walked up the shallow steps that led up to the terrace in front of the hotel she'd glanced sideways, catching a glimpse of the fencing around the tennis courts in the distance. Beneath their black surface lay the excavated remains of the dig, its contours mapped, its layout recorded, contents salvaged, and its presence now protected by the layer of hard standing carefully covering it.

But it was still there, deep beneath.

The past was always present, however deeply buried by the years…

Emotion had plucked at her, seeking entrance, but she'd held it back. Not giving it entrance. Nikos had brought her here, to a place she would never have set foot in again, and she had come, unknowing until it had been too late. But that did not mean she would not do her desperate best to protect herself. However hopeless the prospect.

The beach shop off the atrium had been full of buckets and spades, snorkelling kits and swimsuits. But there had also been some beachwear, and she had made her selection. She was wearing it now—a light cotton sundress in blue, with an elasticated waist and shoulder line.

The trouble was, she realised with a shimmer of dismay, the sundress was far too much like the outfit she'd worn to wow Nikos all those years ago.

Had he spotted the resemblance? She did not know and would not let herself care. He knew now, after what she had hurled at him on that hideous farce of a wedding night, that what he had done to her had exploded, for ever, whatever arrogant ambitions he'd had to win her back.

As for herself... Oh, dear God—now she was to suffer all over again. Eight years ago she had loved Nik, not knowing the depths to which he would stoop. And now—now she didn't even have that comfort...

The knowledge tortured her. But she must endure it.

Emotions swirled within her, powerful and chaotic and unnameable, each and every one of them unbearable.

'It's along here,' she heard Nikos say as he guided them forward, back up towards the pool, glowing iridescently now with underwater lights. There were a few last swimmers splashing around in it before it closed for the night.

Nikos led the way in the other direction from where the distant tennis courts lay, down a pathway that meandered and then opened into a clearing in which a kiosk-style building declared itself to be the bistro. An appetising smell wafted from it.

'It seems to specialise in pizzas,' Nikos said wryly. 'Do you mind?'

Calanthe shook her head and he pulled out a chair for her at one of the outdoor tables set on a spacious circular paved area edged by oleander and bougainvillea. It was prettily lit by the lights strung around and suspended from wooden poles where more fairy lights were wound. Most of the tables were occupied by families, and she could catch various languages—from Greek and Italian to English and German.

She glanced across at the other diners. Happy people, happy families, on happy holidays...

Did her expression change as she looked at them...wondering, with a stab she wished she did not feel, whether she would ever have that herself?

*Will it ever be mine? A husband to love me as I love him, and children for us both to love and make happy childhoods for?*

Her expression hardened, and there was anguish in her suddenly averted eyes. Well, it would never be with Nik.

That stab of anguish was like a dagger in her heart—her stupid heart, broken all over again.

'Looks like this is a popular place—it's nice to see holidaymakers enjoying themselves,' she heard Nikos remark as a smiling young waitress plopped laminated menus down in front of them, ready to take their drinks order.

'We do our best.' The waitress smiled. 'The season's ending now, but we've been full on all summer.'

Nikos smiled at her. 'That's good,' he said.

Calanthe could see the waitress revelling in the impact of Nikos's smile.

*He made me feel beautiful—warmed me with his smile... beguiled me with his kisses... Until—*

She cut off her thoughts. There was no point remembering now. She knew what he was. And he knew that she knew.

He was relaxing back in his chair, still smiling at the young woman. 'I'll take a slice of the credit, I think. I

worked here years ago, when it was nothing but a building site!'

The waitress's eyes widened. 'You?' she said.

Like Calanthe, she'd seen at once that he was wearing expensive clothes, an expensive wristwatch, handmade deck
shoes—not the kind of things belonging a man who'd ever
hauled bricks on a construction site.

He gave a laugh. 'It was hard work—and hot! But...' He
nodded. 'Looks like we did a good job. And I'm glad the
resort is doing well.'

He glanced across at Calanthe and she had a sudden fear
that he might tell the waitress that she, too, had once worked
here—on an excavation. But he simply asked her what she
might like to drink. She opted for sparkling water, and Nikos
ordered a beer. The waitress smiled, and Calanthe could see
her eyes lingering on Nikos as she headed off. Eyes would
always linger on him.

*Just as they did eight years ago. Like Georgia gazed after
him, and all the other girls too.*

And herself, most fatally of all.

'So, what kind of pizza?' Nikos asked.

He sounded enthusiastic, and Calanthe wondered at it.
Pizza was a universe away from the gourmet meals he could
now enjoy.

She glanced at the colourful menu, designed, obviously,
to appeal to parents and children.

*'Pizza al funghi,'* she said, and set down the menu.

'OK. I'm going for pepperoni, chorizo, peppers and double cheese,' Nikos replied.

'Very authentic,' Calanthe heard herself say, her tone
ironic.

He gave a half-laugh. 'Well, pizzas have evolved since
Naples.'

The waitress was returning, depositing Calanthe's water bottle and Nikos's half-litre glass of lager, glistening golden and beading gently.

He thanked the waitress, gave her their pizza orders. Then added: 'And a carafe of red—whatever's local.' He smiled.

She headed off again, throwing yet another lingering glance at Nikos.

He lifted his beer glass. *'Yammas,'* he said, and took a draught.

Calanthe poured a glass of fizzing water for herself, which tasted thin and prickling in her mouth. She did not return his casual toast.

She looked away, deliberately, towards a family a little way off. The father had a beer, like Nikos, and the mother a glass of white wine, fizzy drinks for the two children. They looked primary school age, she thought, and were busy working on the colouring sheets provided for their entertainment while waiting for their pizzas to arrive. The children were bickering, but amicably, clearly content and enjoying their holiday, and their parents were chatting to each other. Relaxed, carefree—on holiday and happy. She saw the dad lean forward for a moment, gently brush the mum's cheek. There was a soft look in his eyes, returned in full by his wife.

Unaccountably, she felt tears prick at the backs of her eyes. Blinked them away.

She envied them.

The arrival of their pizzas was timely, and their aroma mouth-watering. She busied herself with the cutting wheel, slicing up the massive thick-crusted pizza, and Nikos did likewise. The waitress came back with a carafe of red wine and two glasses, taking her time filling each—as if,

Calanthe thought, she wanted to maximise her time spent close to such a devastatingly attractive man as Nikos.

He thanked her with another melting smile, and Calanthe saw the girl's expression take on a smitten look.

*The way I used to gaze at him.*

Her expression hardened. Well, much good it had done her.

Defiantly, she picked up her knife and fork and attacked a slice of pizza with venomous vigour, dropping her gaze down to it, looking away from Nikos. And the girl gazing so helplessly at him.

'Is there anything else?' the waitress asked Nikos, clearly hoping there was.

But he simply smiled again, shaking his head. 'It's all perfect,' he said. 'Thank you.'

And she coloured on cue, finally taking her leave.

Calanthe got stuck in to eating, realising, as she did so, that she'd swapped from drinking water to reaching for a wine glass. She hadn't intended to drink any alcohol, but it was good, robust wine, and it went excellently with the pizza.

Nikos, too, had finished his beer and started on the wine.

He tilted his head slightly. 'The wine hasn't changed in eight years,' he said. 'Rough, but good for all that.'

She didn't answer, only took another mouthful of the wine. Feeling its impact on her. Giving her courage. She set down her glass, looked straight across at him.

'You dragged me here, Nikos, to this place, because you said you had "things to say" to me. So, what are they?' she challenged.

Yet even as she challenged him she felt a weariness of spirit assail her. What was the point of any of this? She felt a familiar pain squeeze her heart. Eight long years ago Nik had broken it. Now it would be broken all over again. This time because of her own stupidity.

*This time around I knew what he was—but I still let it happen...*

Her throat tightened with a familiar choking. And what good did that do her? None. Just as the ocean of tears she'd wept for him so long ago had never done her any good.

Nikos was answering her. His voice tight. 'This is not the time. Tomorrow.'

She looked across at him. Felt that weariness encompass her, that heaviness dull her senses.

'Whatever,' she said, and gave an indifferent shrug.

Then went back to eating her pizza. Went back to listening to the happy chatter of families on holiday...happy couples, with happy children.

She reached for her wine glass again, drained it, picked up the carafe, refilled her glass, poured the rest of the carafe's contents into Nikos's glass, then set the empty carafe back on the wooden table.

'You used to do that,' Nikos said slowly, watching her. 'Tell me to finish it off...that you'd had enough. Then you'd gaze across at me and I'd see in your eyes what any man would give a fortune to see.'

'But you didn't give a fortune, did you, Nik?' she heard herself answer. 'That besotted gaze of mine *gained* you a fortune. Or, if not a fortune, then at least a hefty pay-out.' She paused. 'My father told me exactly how much you cost him. Told me you doubled what you'd first been offered to leave me.'

She emptied her voice of emotion, because the emotion that would have been in it otherwise would have been unendurable to feel again.

'He told me that though you drove a hard bargain, and

took him for more than he'd intended to pay, it had been worth every cent. He paid you willingly whatever it took to keep me safe from you.'

His face had closed. As if a steel shutter had come down over it. She saw him reach for his refilled wine glass, drain it to the dregs. As if he needed it. His cheekbones were stark, his mouth like a whipped line, his eyes completely masked. As if he could not bear to let her see what was in them.

And for a second—just the barest, briefest second— she wanted to see. Because there had been a flash—just a flash—of *something*. An emotion revealed, then instantly gone.

It might have been guilt.

Or even shame.

If he'd been capable of either.

But it had been neither.

For that brief second she had seen what surely should not be there—surely *could* not be there. What made no sense being there.

Pain.

# CHAPTER ELEVEN

NIKOS'S HANDS WERE grimly steering the hire car along the winding coast road—not towards the new marina, with its heliport for the yacht owners, but to the island's main town, where the ferry port was.

The little harbour town along the coast from the resort and the former excavation site was not large enough for anything other than fishing craft and the vessels that had once plied their mercantile trade three thousand years ago across the eastern Mediterranean, leaving behind, millennia later, only the bare outline of their dwellings and warehouses, their bronze and ceramic household goods, their great amphorae that had once carried olive oil and wine, the cargo of the times.

His thoughts went to the resort hotel he'd taken Calanthe to—the one that he'd helped build with his bare hands. One day, in millennia to come, would the archaeologists of the future be excavating the site? Unearthing remnants of the people who had once been there? Not traders any longer, but holidaymakers. Every life a tale to tell...

A tale long lost.

How hard it was to tell a tale that was lost.

How easy it was for tales to be lost.

To sink away into the past. Even the recent past. A mere eight years—an eye-blink—separated him and the woman now sitting silent, withdrawn and hostile beside him and the man and woman they had once been.

But tales that could not be told—that had not yet been told—could fester and corrupt.

*Eight years of festering and corruption...*

'Are you going to tell me where you're taking me?'

Calanthe's cold voice pierced his circling, brooding thoughts.

'As we get there,' was all he would say.

She fell silent again, simply gazing out of the window. The road was vaguely familiar to him. Was it to Calanthe? She'd have left the island this way, heading to the ferry port as they were doing now.

He joined the queue and they drove slowly through the town into the bowels of the waiting ferry. It was only a short crossing to the next island in the chain, hardly worth getting out of the car. He said as much to Calanthe, but she undid her seat belt.

'Too claustrophobic,' she said, and got out, heading for the deck.

He did not follow her. Instead, he sat back, head against the headrest, gazing at nothing.

She came back just as the ferry docked at its destination, getting into the hire car and doing up her seat belt.

'Why have we come to this island?' she asked, as the hold doors slid slowly open and the cars started to emerge on to the quayside.

'To show you something,' was all Nikos said.

They drove out through the ferry port—very similar to the one they'd left, but larger, for this whole island was larger, if not by much. This island was familiar to him— long familiar.

Once again, he opted for the coast road, heading east. He

did not look at Calanthe, but within a few kilometres of the town he saw her turn her head as they passed a road sign.

'*Aerodromio?*' she said. There was a clear question in her voice. 'Nikos, don't tell me we're *flying* somewhere now!'

'No,' he said.

He knew his voice was terse. But he was banking a lot down. And it was taking all his strength, his nerve, to keep it banked down. He felt his emotions stress and strain, like fractured plates in the earth's crust, rubbing and grinding against each other. The pressure building up, unable to be released.

As they approached the airport he didn't take the road that branched off to the entrance, nor did he keep to the main road that followed the coastline, a half-kilometre or so to their right. Instead, he slowed and took an unmarked dirt road leading off the left.

He knew exactly where it went.

It circled the northern perimeter fence, the high mesh that separated the airport area from the countryside around it.

He drove between the fence to his right and the olive groves that stretched to the left, hectare after hectare, spreading widely inland. A few houses were dotted around, and some stone sheds, but not many. The trees were heavy with olives—in a few weeks the harvest would begin. The whole area was extensive, marked off by old stone walls, many crumbling now, into holdings owned by any number of islanders.

When it was time for harvest, it was usually a communal affair. He remembered it well from his youth, with neighbours pitching in to help each other, all hands on, including his own hands, even when he was a small child.

The children always enjoyed themselves—it was almost like a party. Someone would bring a football, and there would be a kick-around when the adults were busy or had no tasks for them. Then someone would call them, and the children who were old enough, but not too heavy, would shin up the olive trees to help knock down any recalcitrant fruit on to the waiting nets spread out below to catch them.

'Where are we going?'

Calanthe's question recalled him to the present.

'We're nearly there,' he said.

He drove a little further, careful of the wheels on the rutted track. Then, at a spot he knew well, he stopped, cut the engine.

'I want to show you something,' he said.

He got out of the car, feeling those tectonic plates inside him again, fractured and cracked, grinding against each other. Still seeking release.

Soon, but not quite yet.

She got out as well, and in the silence the immediate chorus of cicadas was all about them as the mid-morning sun beat down. There was a tumbling stone wall less than a metre high to their left, and he stepped through a gap, turning so that both the car and the airport's perimeter fence were in front of him.

Without him asking, Calanthe came and stood beside him. But she was not looking at the airport—rather at the olive trees all around.

'Looks like there'll be a good harvest,' she said, as if searching for something to say.

'Yes. I've given a hand here many a time…helping my grandmother.' He paused. 'She owned a good few hectares of olive trees.'

Calanthe glanced around her. 'Which were hers?' she asked.

He nodded towards the airport. 'Over there,' he said.

* * *

Calanthe frowned. 'Oh, that's a shame!' she exclaimed. 'But I guess maybe the island wanted an airport?'

'It did,' Nikos confirmed. 'It was controversial at the time—a dozen years ago or so—and I remember a lot of debate, with a lot of pros and cons thrashed out in the local newspapers and in the bars and tavernas. In the end, as you can see, it went ahead.' His voice changed a little. 'It's helped to encourage more tourism, and helped develop the island economically—reduce its dependence on farming and fishing.'

'Isn't that a good thing?'

Though there was a question in her voice, she knew it was not just about the subject under discussion. Why was it under discussion at all. What was going on?

'Overall, yes. Except that when there are projects like this, issues like this, there are always winners…' He paused. 'And losers.'

He walked away, along the line of the old tumbling wall, and Calanthe followed him, placing her footsteps carefully in the rough grass. Some way ahead of her, Nikos stopped again. She caught up with him and he nodded towards the section of airport behind a white two-storey building.

Beyond it was a single runway. As well as the cicadas all around, Calanthe started to hear the noise of a plane's engines, approaching from over the sea, its port and starboard lights blinking at the edges of its wings as it came into view, its descent quickening. It wasn't a large plane, just a standard tourist charter, easily capable of using the scale of runway here. It banked, and then landed with a deafening roar, engines in noisy retro thrust to slow its speed.

Calanthe put her hands over her ears until the engines cut

out. 'Well, anyone living too close to that would definitely be one of the losers!' she exclaimed.

'Not that much,' Nikos said. 'Except in high season there aren't many flights. There were other losers, though.'

She looked at him. His voice had changed. Taken on an edge.

'And winners,' he went on, with the same edge in his voice. He nodded to the building in front of them. 'Old Stavros was one of the winners. He was a shrewd old boy, and he owned as many hectares of olive trees as my grandmother. All of them are now under the other half of the airport, abutting my grandmother's land. Stavros liked to keep his ear to the ground...keep an eye on what people were doing. Including my grandmother,' he said, and now there was a heavy note in his voice. He paused. 'He played his cards very close to his chest, though. Few people got the better of him.'

Calanthe looked at him. There must be some point to this, but she had no idea what. Was Nikos about to tell her why he'd brought her here?

It seemed not.

He turned on his heel, his back towards her.

'Let's get back to the car,' he said.

There seemed to be tension in his voice now, and his face was set.

She frowned, but followed him, stepping through the gap in the wall and getting back into the car.

He turned it around, heading back the way they'd come. Once on the main road he drove back towards the ferry port and then, a few kilometres along, turned inland onto a metalled but narrow road, towards the island's hilly centre.

They drove through a small village with a little church, a single bar, a mini-supermarket and a pharmacy, and out the other side, all the time gaining height. Then, about a kilometre beyond the village, a stone wall extended to their right, with a wooden gate in it. Inset into the wall was a ceramic plaque declaring, in both Greek and Roman lettering, *Villa Irene*.

'Irene,' Nikos remarked, 'was the name of my grandmother.'

He drove slowly through the gate, between oleander bushes, and pulled up outside a solid-looking house with white-painted shutters and a white door. It looked neat and attractive, with large glazed ceramic pots either side of the front door, vivid with red geraniums.

'This is her house,' Nikos announced, cutting the car's engine.

He got out, and Calanthe did likewise. She was aware that her heartrate had quickened a little.

'It's very pretty,' she said, politely and truthfully.

'I grew up here,' Nikos said. 'It was just my grandmother and me. After she died—three years ago—I kept it. It needed doing up a bit… She always refused to modernise, even when she knew I could easily afford it. Nowadays I let it out—it's marketed as a "rustic retreat", for those wanting to get away from it all and experience what's left of authentic rural life.'

'It suits that perfectly.' Calanthe nodded appreciatively.

'A neighbour looks after it—sees to the garden, cleans inside and so on. There's no one staying at the moment, though.'

He stooped to retrieve a large, old-fashioned key from under one of the flowerpots, and opened the door. It was cool inside, because of the thick walls, and simply decorated, in keeping with the building's style. Calanthe could not help but like it.

*How strange to think of Nikos as a young boy, growing up here.*

She frowned. How had he come from being here—a local lad, helping out with the olive harvest, part of a village community with traditional values—to behaving as he had. Being paid off by a rich man...paid to desert his infatuated daughter...

*Was the temptation too great for him to resist? He was putting himself through university...working on building sites during vacations. When my father offered him so much money could he just not bring himself to refuse it?*

And if that were so...her frown deepened...was that excuse enough?

She thought back to her own upbringing. OK, she had always known that she had a rich father in the background—had experienced the luxury he enjoyed when she visited him during school holidays—but her mother had raised her with sound principles that befitted their modest circumstances.

*What if our roles had been reversed? What if Nikos had been an infatuated young man and his rich father had thought me a scheming gold-digger...tried to pay me off?*

Would she have taken the money?

She knew the answer. Knew it clear and confirmed. No, she would not. There were things decent people did, and things they didn't. What Nikos had done was one of them.

Her expression hardened.

He was heading into what was clearly the main room, with a fireplace set in one wall, flanked by comfortable-looking traditional-style seating, and with a wooden dining table and solid-looking chairs at the far side, next to a door going through to what she could see was the kitchen.

The whole room had a welcoming ambience, and she liked it instinctively. There was a large, handsome armoire against another wall—made out of olive wood, she guessed, and beautifully painted with ornamental flowers and scrolls in ultra-traditional style. An original piece, she reckoned, and felt drawn to it automatically.

'This is beautiful!' she exclaimed.

'Part of my grandmother's dowry when she married. It had been her grandmother's before. There is some similar painted furniture upstairs—one of the old beds and another armoire, and some smaller pieces too.'

'How lovely that they're still here,' Calanthe could not help saying.

She looked around her. There were some paintings on the wall, in a rustic style. One showed an ancient ruin and a girl sitting in traditional Greek costume from several hundred years ago. Another showed a large, handsome goat—presumably a prized animal from long ago. Yet another was a still-life, of a ceramic jug full of flowers.

She heard Nikos opening the armoire and turned. He was extracting a box file, and after closing the door he crossed the room to deposit it on the table. Calanthe watched him, half curious, half frowning, conscious that her heartrate was still raised.

Wondering why, exactly.

Her eyes rested on Nikos. She tried to see him as he must once have been, growing up here, a strong lad, tall for his age—already showing, she was sure, the devastating good-looks he would have as a teenager.

Had he broken local hearts? she wondered.

*As well as mine?*

'I'd like to show you something.'

Nikos's words were a welcome interruption to thoughts that were pointless to have. As pointless as her thinking now, as she crossed to where he stood, how good he looked in that open-necked shirt, the same one he'd worn last night, the cuffs not turned back this time, how his dark hair feathered at the nape of his strong neck, how his long eyelashes dipped over his dark eyes, how his sculpted mouth brought back memories she must not indulge…

Yet they pressed for ingress all the same.

So many, many memories…

An ache opened inside her, raw and intense. Anguished was tearing at her. To see Nikos here, in the house he grew up in, to remember how he'd been that golden summer of her youth, how totally she'd fallen for him, how ardently she'd given herself to him, wanting nothing more than for that summer to go on and on…never to end.

Never—dear God—to end as it had.

*He took my father's money. Let himself be paid off. Shameful and despicable.*

Her eyes were shadowed as she walked towards the table. Nikos had reappeared in her life, out of the blue, and made clear that she had once again aroused in him the same fire of desire that had flared before.

As had he, so fatally, in her, that night at the beach hut.

*But I was strong then. At least afterwards—in the morning. Strong enough to leave him.*

And to regret, bitterly, her weakness.

But not strong enough to stop herself doing what she should never have allowed herself to do again…

She felt her heart squeeze with pain.

'Calanthe—'

His voice penetrated the fog of her hopeless thoughts. A wave of that familiar heavy weariness swept over her again. All this traipsing around from island to island. A helicopter, a taxi, a hire car, a ferry… An olive grove, an airport and now his grandmother's old house.

What was it for?

What purpose could it serve?

*He is who he is. Venal and corrupt. There is nothing more. I have to accept it.*

But she was here now, and she would see it through.

He was lifting two documents out of the box file. They had a formal, legal look to them, and were both very similar.

She drew closer and he placed one of them in front of her. It was a contract of sale. She glanced at it, frowning, not knowing what she was supposed to be seeing.

'I mentioned Stavros to you when we were down by the airport. I told you he was shrewd old guy…that few ever got the better of him. This contract shows it.'

He paused, pointing to where the legalese was interrupted by the typed identification of a specific piece of land.

'This is his olive grove. The one that is now under half of the airport.' He paused. Pointed at another typed-in line. 'This is the sum he received for it.'

Calanthe's eyebrows rose. It was an extremely large sum for just an olive grove. Except, of course, she realised, it was no longer an olive grove but part of a commercial airport.

Nikos was moving the document aside, replacing it with the other one. 'Take a look at this one,' he said.

It was identical to the first, except for two things—the identity of the plot of land and the sum paid for it. She frowned. Massively less than the first.

'The two plots were the same size,' Nikos was saying.

There was something strange about his voice. She looked at him, still frowning.

He lifted away the top page of each document, revealing the pages behind. Another couple of paragraphs of legalese, and then two sets of signatures. One was common to both—somebody from an outfit called Venture Land. The other was different on each.

One was Stavros's signature.

The other was Irene's—Nikos's grandmother.

'Look at the dates,' Nikos was saying now.

She did. His grandmother's contract was dated three months before Stavros's.

She looked up at Nikos, still not understanding. 'So?' she said.

His voice was hollow as he answered her. 'Agreement to build the new airport was made public a fortnight after my grandmother sold her olive grove to Venture Land. Had she waited a mere two weeks it would have been worth what Old Stavros got for his—way more than she received!'

Calanthe swallowed. 'That *is* wretched,' she allowed. 'But if no one knew whether the airport would get planning permission when she sold, then wasn't the buyer taking a risk buying her land at all? He might have ended up with just another olive grove.'

'Unlikely.' Nikos's voice was hard as iron.

He drew out another document—this time, Calanthe could see, it was the printout of an email.

'You see, the date stamp on this email shows that the sender had received private information—a copy of a signed document from a key member of the planning committee saying that the airport was definitely getting the go-ahead. The vote had already been taken and, crucially, the exact site it would occupy confirmed. It was just a question of timing the announcement. The sender, therefore, had inside knowledge. As, therefore, did the recipient.' He thrust the email printout at her. 'Take a look at who that is.'

She saw the name—it meant nothing to her. But then she saw who the email had been copied to.

Her eyes flew to Nikos. Stricken. 'My *father*?'

Her voice was as stricken as her face.

'The very same.' There was a dark savagery in Nikos's voice.

She dropped the printout as if it were toxic. 'But…but… Venture Land…' She floundered, trying to make sense of it. 'I've never heard of it. What's it got to do with Petranakos?'

'It's a subsidiary. A small one—one of several. A major company such as Petranakos, Calanthe, can find it…useful sometimes not to declare an interest in a particular piece of land. After all,' he went on, with the same savagery in his voice, 'if someone turned up at your door to buy a perfectly ordinary olive grove and they were from Petranakos Property… Well, even the simplest person might wonder what their interest was. But if it was just a small company called Venture Land, operating in just these few islands, who said they had an interest in working with olive oil producers— nothing large-scale, just adding to their holdings here and there as plots became available… My grandmother had already made clear in the village that hers was for sale—why would she think anything of it? She was offered a fair price for an olive grove of that size, number of trees and general yield. Why would she refuse?'

His voice changed. 'You see,' he said, 'she wanted to make it easier for me to pursue my studies. Architecture is a long course, and she knew it would take me a long time to qualify.'

'She sold the grove to help you,' Calanthe said.

She could feel her stomach churning, things rearranging themselves in her head. Things she did not want to be rearranged.

'Yes. I didn't want her to, but she was adamant. She was so proud that I'd got on the course—a village boy, on a top architectural course! I was already at university when she went ahead with the sale.'

Calanthe saw his fists clench.

'She did it without telling me. Without warning me. If I'd known—' He broke off.

Something in his eyes made Calanthe blench.

'She was a simple, decent woman. An honourable woman. Selling part of her inheritance for my sake... Selling it, so she thought, for a fair price, to a fair buyer... And all along—' He thrust the contract of sale for Stavros's holding at her. '*This* was the fair price of her land! *This* was what Stavros held out for! He saw how much my grandmother got and sat tight. Refused to part with his land.' He inhaled sharply. 'He didn't sell until the announcement was made confirming the airport would be built and the site. Then the price of his land rocketed. And Stavros got the true market value.'

He sat down abruptly, yanking the box file closed, replacing everything he'd taken out of it. Then he looked at Calanthe.

'I find it ironic,' he said, 'that it is only because I now have access to all the Petranakos business records that I can present you with the evidence I needed to show you. Oh, I've got my grandmother's paperwork for this and all her other affairs, such as they were, in a safety deposit box in the local bank here. But without proof that Venture Land is part of Petranakos—without their copy of the contract of sale for Stavros's holding and without the email trail showing that Venture Land and Petranakos had insider knowledge about the airport—you would just have dismissed all this.'

He paused, laying his hands flat on the closed box file.

'Perhaps there is one other thing that it may be...helpful... for you to know.'

He rested his eyes on her as she stood there, stomach still churning, thoughts in chaos, dismay roiling within her. His gaze was dark and cold, and it cut her like a knife.

'My grandmother sold her olive grove for the sum you saw on her contract. Stavros sold his for the sum on his. Take one from the other. What number comes up? You do the maths.'

He paused—a deadly pause.

'Does that precise amount sound familiar to you?'

She shut her eyes. There was a drumming in her ears.

'It's what my father paid you,' she said.

Her voice seemed to come from a very long way away.

Nikos smiled. 'Got it in one,' he said.

# CHAPTER TWELVE

SO HE HAD told her. Told her just why, eight years ago, when Georgios Petranakos had sent his fixers in to put it to him that he might like to consider the offer they were willing to make him, he had not sent them packing.

Now, eight years later, he pushed aside the box file, looked up at Calanthe. 'You'd better sit down,' he said. 'I don't want you passing out on me, and you've gone white as a sheet.'

He watched her numbly collapse down on one of his grandmother's dining chairs. She put her hands on the table, holding them tightly together, so the knuckles showed as white as her face.

'You were just evening the score,' she said, and he could see what each word was costing her.

'Yes,' said. 'I was just evening the score. Your father's fixers weren't happy—they wanted me to accept the sum they'd offered me. But I held out. It was peanuts for your father—I knew that and they knew that—but they were careful with his money all the same. For me, the sum I got out of them was simply...justice.'

He sat back, ran a hand through his hair. Tiredness filled him, and a sense not of vindication but simply of resignation.

'Does it make any difference to you?' he asked.

His voice was tired. He was tired of all this. Tired because he suspected none of it was of any use. Not even what he now asked her.

'Does it make any difference to you, Calanthe, if I say the rest of it? That your father's fixers needn't have bothered to offer me anything at all.' His eyes rested on her. 'Because they could have achieved their ends without costing your father a cent.'

He frowned, fingering the edge of the box file, looking down at the surface of the table where he had eaten all his meals as a child, so familiar that if he listened hard enough he could almost hear his grandmother moving around in the kitchen, putting pots and pans away, not letting him help, telling him he must get on with his homework instead.

*'Studying is important, Nikki—with education, the world is yours!'*

He had believed her—and it was true. The world was his. He had achieved so much—for himself, certainly, and even something for the world as well. Safer housing and offices and factories for those threatened by earthquakes.

His eyes lifted to the woman sitting opposite him. So beautiful, even with her face so pale, her eyes so stricken. She had caught his eye from the very first, but she had not liked his attention…had resisted him at first.

But he'd won her round. Won her, full stop. Made her his. And to him she'd entrusted her virginity—a gift he'd cherished. Honoured.

*What did I feel for her then, all those years ago?*

Even now he was not sure.

But of one thing he *was* sure, and he would tell her so.

He drew a breath, spoke again. 'Your father didn't need to pay me off.' He met her eyes. 'You see, the moment I realised who you were I knew I had to end it.'

He saw her eyes widen. Saw her not understanding.

He took another breath. 'Calanthe, there's a name for poor men who make up to the daughters of rich men. It's not a name I ever wanted. And had your father been *any* rich man other than the man he was his fixers would have got short shrift from me! But all the same I'd have done what they wanted. Finished with you and left you. But instead...' his eyes would not let hers drop '...because of who he was, and because of what he'd done to my grandmother, I took his money—everything that I held out for. And then I left you. Left you to go back to my grandmother. To give her the cheque they'd given me, made out to her, not me.'

His voice changed, tightened. There was bitterness in it now.

'So your father has never known that I am the man he paid off all those years ago. My grandmother took the cheque because I told her that I'd confronted the head honcho of the company that had bought her olive grove and demanded from them its true value—and got it.'

She spoke finally, her voice low and stricken. 'I've always thought my father an honourable man who made his money fairly—' She broke off.

'Maybe he did—mostly,' Nikos said. 'For all I know, in this particular instance, his Venture Land front man simply tried it on and got away with it. Maybe that email I showed you with your father's name on it was never read by him. Maybe it was just filed by his PA along with hundreds of others. My grandmother's olive grove was small fry...even the airport was small fry—just one of scores of other land deals your father has struck in his time through the people he employs and the subsidiaries he's set up.'

She looked at him, anguish in her eyes. 'Or maybe you might just be...be trying to make it easier for me.'

'Maybe I am,' he said, his voice weary. 'But does it? If

it counts at all, the reason I told your father's men that you must never know was that I didn't want you hurt. But your father...' He sighed. 'Your father thought it best you were hurt. To protect you from the man he thought I was.'

*And am I that man, after all?*

Tiredness washed over him again. He had staked everything on this moment, on trying to justify what he'd done. And now—

Abruptly, she pushed back her chair. It scraped on the stone floor. 'I need... I need...'

She didn't finish. Only walked rapidly from the room. He heard the front door open, and then silence.

He picked up the box file, replaced it in the painted armoire that had been there all his life, as solid and sound as the house he'd grown up in, as the grandmother who'd raised him.

He followed Calanthe out into the garden. She was standing with her back to him, arms folded defensively, her shoulders hunched. He came up behind her, but not too close.

Keeping his distance.

That was essential.

'I don't know whether I did right or wrong in taking your father's money as I did,' he said slowly. 'But this I do know. I never regretted it. I regret a lot—but not that.'

She turned, her arms still tightly folded as if to protect herself, keep him at bay. 'Do you regret things, Nikos? What do you regret?'

Her voice was low. Sunlight was playing on her hair. Gilding the honey of her skin. How beautiful she was— how breathtakingly, wondrously beautiful...

As she had always been.

From the very first to the very last.

As this, surely, was the last.

'I regret having to leave you that golden summertime,' he said. 'I've told myself I would have left you anyway, even had I never known whose daughter you were, because you were just a summer romance. You were so young, and I had to make my way in the world. I had nothing to offer you then. Yet for all that I would still have left you with regret. Wishing I did not have to. Wishing...' He took a breath, ready to say now, all these years later, what he had told himself was not so. 'Wishing I could ask you to wait for me.'

It was said—what he had barely given head space for.

He had told himself that what they had was only a summer romance, that it could not last, could never be more than that.

*And when I discovered who she was I had to cling to that fiction.*

Her eyes were on him, her folded arms still keeping him at bay. Still protecting herself, as if stanching a wound. Then she spoke, her voice low and anguished.

'I would have waited, Nikos. Because I was in love with you.'

Her eyes were pained, and no longer because of what he'd told her at his grandmother's dining table. He could see there were other reasons now. Reasons beyond that.

'I was in love with you, and it broke my heart when you left me. And I would have gone on yearning for you...hoping and hopeless...wanting you back. So my father told me what you'd done.' Her voice hollowed. 'So that I could stop loving you—and hate you instead.'

She looked away for a moment, then back at him.

'But I have no cause to hate you, Nik. Not now.'

She looked around her and he saw her expression—so drawn and stark and stricken—soften a fraction.

'I shall think of you here, Nikos. That will be good, I

think. Because this is a good house, and your grandmother was a good woman, and she raised you, as I now know, to be a good man. I've wasted years hating you. Now at least I can let that go. What a waste it all was,' she said sadly.

He saw her dip her head, saw the sun burnishing her hair, setting a halo around it. Saw, too, slow tears oozing down her cheeks.

He felt himself step forward. Reach out his hand. Touch her lowered cheek with his outstretched finger.

'Don't weep,' he said. His voice was low. 'Don't weep for the waste of it. I was never worth it. But you...you, Calanthe, have always been worth it—always! In that golden summer *and* now. Above all now.'

He let his hand fall away, felt his fingertip wet with her slow tears.

'Eight years ago it did not matter what I felt for you. You were Georgios Petranakos's daughter and you were beyond me. And my duty...' he drew a heavy breath '...my duty was to my grandmother, to ensure she was no longer cheated of what was her due. Then, when I saw you again in Athens, at your father's side, even more beautiful than you had ever been, I knew that all I had wanted that summer long ago was what I wanted again. You in my arms again. In my bed. And when your father needed me...then it all seemed so perfect for me. Until—'

He broke off. Then he made himself say what he must.

'Before, it was you who loved me and I who turned my back on you. Now, all these years later, it is you who has turned your back on me.'

He paused, frowning. Looking away from her. Not able to bear to look at her.

'I thought,' he said, and he heard a bleakness in his own voice that tore him in pieces, 'that in marrying you I was getting everything I wanted. But...' his voice was ragged now '...in fact I was losing it all.'

He made himself look at her, meet her stricken eyes with his.

'Losing you, Calanthe, the woman that this time I knew with all my heart I had come to love.'

He heard a cry break from her. Break from her heart broken so long ago as his was newly broken. Tears were pouring down her face. Tears he could not bear to see. Tears he must wipe away. Kiss away.

She came into his arms. Clinging to him with broken sobs. His hands framed her face, his fingers clutching at her, and he was bending to kiss her eyes urgently, desperately.

'Do you mean it, Nikos?' Her voice was a whisper...a plea.

'With all my being,' he told her, and his voice was rich with emotion. 'At first I thought that all I felt was desire,' he said, and his voice was different now, stronger and full of wonder. 'A desire I could now fulfil, for I belonged to your world...had earned my place in it. But then...' He took a breath, ragged and raw. 'It took your denunciation of me on our wedding night, your rejection of me, to show me the truth of what I felt for you! Desire, yes—oh, yes, always and for ever! But also—oh, my most adored Calanthe—so, so much more.'

His name broke from her and he swept her to him. Emotion was rising in him like a tsunami, and he held her tightly, fiercely, against him.

She was gazing up at him, and what he saw in her eyes made him reel.

'I never stopped loving you,' she said. 'I tried... I tried and failed. Whatever my father told me...whatever I told myself. Even though I knew and believed that what you had done was torture to me—still I went on loving you. Though I buried it as deep as it was possible to do. Until—'

She broke off. Spoke again.

'When you came back into my life—oh, dear God—I felt it all start again. Hating you and loving you. And I could not bear it! But now…'

There was something new in her voice, like a bird breaking free of a cage after beating its wings in vain.

'Oh, Nik, my dearest, darling one, now I need only love you.'

The joy in her voice turned his heart over. He kissed her slowly, gently, his senses still reeling, and she kissed him back. Softly, lovingly…

'What happens now, Nikos?' she asked, her voice low, as she drew back from him a little.

'Will you stay with me?' he asked, his voice just as low. 'Will you stay with me, my bride, my wife…my love?'

She gazed up at him, her eyes shining like stars. 'Oh, yes,' she breathed. 'Oh, *yes*.'

It was the answer he craved. The only answer he could bear to hear. Now and for ever. It took him to heaven on wings of gold. And he was flying there with her.

'This,' Calanthe declared, 'is the best pizza ever—it's official!'

'It's the same one you ordered last night,' Nikos pointed out, lifting a slice of his own—also exactly the same as he'd ordered the night before.

'It's completely different!' she riposted. 'Because…' she reached a hand across the wooden table at the poolside bistro, her other hand precariously holding a slice of fully loaded *pizza al funghi*, threads of melted mozzarella trailing '… *I* am completely different!'

She shut her eyes. Could happiness such as this truly be real? It radiated from her like sunshine, brighter than anything she had ever known. Filled her from within. Every cell in her body...every fibre of her being.

She gazed across the table at him as he took a mouthful of his own pizza, cocking a quizzical eyebrow at her as he did so. He was smiling, his eyes alight with a warmth that took her breath away. Not letting her gaze drop for even a second, an instant, she bit into her own pizza slice.

At the table next to theirs was seated the same family as last night, the two children filling in their colouring sheets, their parents smiling at each other with fondness, secure in their love for each other.

Calanthe felt her heart squeeze.

Last night she had thought such happiness could never be hers—and now it was. Hers for ever.

It swept over her, wave after wave, as she steadily demolished the pizza, washing it down with the robust local red wine. Nikos did likewise. What they talked about she hardly knew...except that conversation came as easily now as it once had all those years ago.

'How long can we stay here? At the resort?' she asked him as, replete with pizza, she finally pushed the denuded wooden platter aside, reaching for her wine glass and leaning back comfortably in her chair.

'As long as we like,' Nikos answered. He refilled his glass, then realised that he'd drained the carafe. 'Shall we order more wine?' he asked.

She shook her head. 'You finish it,' she said. She frowned. 'But what about work?'

'What about it?' he returned easily. He leant forward. 'It can wait—both your father's company and my own. Because this, my adored Calanthe, is our honeymoon.' His voice was husky as he looked around him. 'Mind you, I had envisaged somewhere more glamorous, I must say. I was planning for the Seychelles, the Maldives...the South Seas, even.'

She waved away such possibilities. They were unnecessary and irrelevant.

'Here,' she said, 'is perfect.'

She looked around. It *was* perfect. Perfect because it was a happy place, for happy families having a happy holiday. Perfect because she was here with Nikos and he was all she needed and would ever need to be happy.

She felt her heart turn over. She gazed at him, her eyes filled with lovelight. All that she had once dreamed of... yearned for...longed for...was now hers.

She finished her wine, setting her glass back on the table. She saw the young waitress bringing the family next to them their pizzas, heard the happy exclamations of the children, their colouring sheets set swiftly aside.

She and Nikos had dined early—and she knew why. She watched as Nikos finished off his own wine, then looked across at her. He said not a word—only got to his feet. She did likewise. She waited while he reached into his pocket, drew out his wallet, put down a generous tip for the young waitress, slipping it under his wooden platter, then repocketed his wallet.

He held out his hand to Calanthe and she took it, folding her fingers into his warm, strong hand.

They walked away down the dim path, night-scented with honeysuckle, the cicadas serenading them as they headed back to their little villa. They stepped inside, still hand in hand, wordless and unhurried, for neither words nor haste were necessary now.

At the top of the stairs Nikos turned to her and said simply, 'My bed is larger.'

She gave a laugh, low and happy. 'Perfect,' she said.
And it was.
Quite, quite perfect.

She was velvet in his arms. Velvet and silk and satin. And
her mouth was honey and peach. Anything and everything
that was sweet and wonderful and wondrous.

With languorous kisses and leisurely caresses he roused
her to all that she desired, receiving back from her, with her
gliding hands and sweetest lips, all that he could ever desire for himself. Until, holding back no longer, he claimed
her in his burning desire and found something he had never
known before.

His newfound love for her consumed him, consumed them
both. And as their moment of union came...as their bodies fused into one glorious, transcendent whole, possessed
by ecstasy...he heard her cry out, sobbing even as it broke
through him like a tumultuous wave. He threw back his head
to echo her cry, deeper and louder, as her body convulsed
around him and her arms clung to him, her thighs wrapping
round his to hold him to her, never to let him go, rocking him
in the cradle of her hips as her body shuddered beneath his.

And as she quietened, tremor after tremor still quivering through her, he smoothed her tumbled hair with a shaky
hand, every muscle in his body slackening. His heart was
still thundering, and hers was beating against his, and he
drew her with him as he slipped from her, letting his head
rest on the pillow beside her, lifting a hand to trace, with
wondering gentleness, the contours of her parted lips.

He gazed into her eyes, knew there was wonder in his
as in hers.

'I never knew...' he said. 'I never knew the difference
love makes.'

She gave a choke, a smothered cry, burying her face in his chest and wrapping her arms around him more tightly yet.

He stroked her hair softly and tenderly, felt wonder and gratitude filling him. And love…such love…possessing him…

Slowly, driftingly, as they were held in each other's arms, sleep finally took them.

And love held them close for ever.

# EPILOGUE

'MY DEAREST, DEAREST DAUGHTER...' Georgios Petranakos's voice was warm, and rich with emotion. His glance went to Nikos. 'And you, whose love for her will always keep her safe!'

He was lifting a glass of vintage champagne, tilting it towards them both. He was looking well, his recovery from major surgery definitely underway. True, he wasn't supposed to be drinking alcohol for a good while yet, but Calanthe hadn't the heart to stop him on this particular day.

Her wedding day.

Her *second* wedding day.

Her *proper* wedding day, as both her father and her husband called it.

And she did too.

She lifted her own glass to Nikos now, and he did the same to her.

'My adored bride,' Nikos said softly, lovelight in his eyes.

'My darling husband,' she murmured in return, her eyes shining with love and happiness.

Their church wedding earlier that day had been a quiet affair—both she and Nikos had insisted on it. They did not want to risk any over-exertion by her father. Later, when he was stronger still, they would hold a lavish wedding party, invite all of Athens, but for now what both she and Nikos

truly valued was having made their vows to each other—
vows of love and matrimony that could never be broken.

Love filled her. So much love for her beloved Nikos. Hers
now for ever and ever!

It was a love that her father understood—endorsed. They
had told him everything—all that had estranged them. He
had found it hard to accept that Nikos was, indeed, the
same young man he had wanted to protect her from all
those years ago, but when they'd told him just why he had
accepted Georgios's money it had been her father's turn to
be abashed. To Calanthe's intense relief, the explanation
that Nikos had ventured—that perhaps Georgios himself
had not known of how Nikos's grandmother had been un-
derpaid so shamefully—had been confirmed by her father.

'My boy, believe me from my heart,' he'd said to Nikos,
taking his hand. 'Never, *never* would I have knowingly
cheated anyone of a fair price for their land! The man who
did so no longer works for me.'

It had been all that she and Nikos needed to hear. Now
only a golden future in endless love and happiness awaited
them.

And one more joy.

As her father toasted them both again, wreathed in beaming smiles, she took another sip from her champagne flute.
But only a small one.

'You are not the only one who must abstain from alcohol
for a while, Papa,' she said, lowering her glass. 'You see…'

She turned to Nikos, and a secret smile passed between
them.

'Shall we?' she murmured.

He took a mouthful of his champagne. 'Most certainly,'
he assured her, his eyes entwining with hers.

She took a breath…looked at her expectant father.

'You must get as well as you can, Papa, as fast as you can,' she told him. 'Because Nikos and I want you to be as active and vigorous a grandfather as your forthcoming grandchild will need… In fact, we insist!'

A shout of delight broke from Georgios and he enveloped Calanthe in a bear hug that made her catch her breath. Then he was seizing Nik's hand and pumping it excitedly.

He stood back. 'You have given me the greatest happiness,' he said, addressing them both. His eyes went from one to the other, reading each of them, 'And you will give each other the greatest happiness too.'

He gave a sigh of satisfaction, looked again at his daughter.

'How right I was, my darling girl, to want young Kavadis for you!'

Calanthe slipped her hand into Nik's, squeezing it as tightly as his was squeezing hers. She leant forward, brushed her father's cheek and smiled.

'Yes, Papa—so, very, very right,' she said.

'And I,' said Nikos, raising his glass again, 'completely agree.'

He lifted Calanthe's hand in his, brushing his lips across her knuckles. Then he clinked his glass against hers.

'To us both,' he said.

He glanced at Georgios, his father-in-law, then back at Calanthe. Love blazed in his face as he lowered their still-clasped hands to where, safe and secret within her, their baby was growing.

'To us *all*,' he said.

\* \* \* \* \*

# ENGAGED TO LONDON'S WILDEST BILLIONAIRE

KALI ANTHONY

MILLS & BOON

To those who were told to settle,
but instead waited for the person who could
make them laugh and their heart sing.
This story's for you.

# CHAPTER ONE

'EARTH TO EARTH, ashes to ashes, dust to dust...'

Sara stood at the edge of the royal mausoleum as the priest intoned the committal service. A small group of mourners and official witnesses, as required by Lauritania's constitution, huddled round on a day that outside was too bright and beautiful to contemplate the three grand coffins of King, Queen and Crown Prince, waiting to be interred.

She paid little attention to the people around her, her focus entirely on the coffin holding the earthly remains of Crown Prince Ferdinand Betencourt. Their country's flag was draped over the top, bedecked with lilies, their scent cloying in the still morning air. A mere ten days ago she'd been Lady Sara Conrad, his fiancée. A woman one day destined to ascend the throne by his side...

The hysterical sound bubbled from her before she could stifle it. She clutched a handkerchief to her mouth to try and cover up the barely suppressed laugh at how foolish she'd been. She'd never believed ignorance could be bliss, but had learned a powerful lesson.

*'You'll be by his side, you'll bear his heirs, but you'll never have his heart...'*

Poisonous words whispered in a ballroom just a few months earlier. Words spoken by some woman, tall and elegant and worldly and everything Sara wasn't, telling her exactly where her place was in the hierarchy of Ferdinand's needs.

She frantically dabbed her eyes with a handkerchief, pretending her laugh was a grief-stricken sob. Had anyone noticed the sound of near hysterical disbelief? Because, in truth, she'd grieved the loss of Ferdinand months before his untimely death. The destruction of her immature dream that once they were married he might find the time to love her. She kept the handkerchief to her face, chancing a furtive glance at the assembled group. As she did so, a prickle of awareness tripped along her spine. She turned to her right and caught a man she didn't know staring at her. A stranger in the tiny band of familiar faces. She hadn't noticed him before in the throng of black-bedecked mourners and cronies at the funeral.

There was no missing him now.

He stood out. From his imposing height to the perfect cut of his dark suit and his undeniably authoritative presence. All screaming bespoke tailoring and old money. The only thing out of place was the expression of bored indifference on his face, while those around them were in the clutches of sorrow. A face that was square-jawed, cleft-chinned, sculpted perfection. His intense focus made her feel too small for her skin. As if she wanted to split from it, shed the dour black clothing she wore and morph into something brighter, more beautiful. *Changed.*

How inappropriate, considering she was supposed to be mourning her fiancé today. Yet there was no controlling how her body reacted to this captivating stranger. Much like she couldn't control the seething anger that twisted down to the pit of her soul—anger at the charade everyone had maintained around her. Perpetuating the vicious lie that she could ever have had a 'devoted' relationship with the

Crown Prince. Theirs had been no growing love match, as she'd kidded herself to believe, but one of absolute indifference—on his part at least.

And then the stranger cocked his head and raised an eyebrow, the curve of his perfect mouth hitching in a way that said, *I see what you did.*

That look flashed over her, hot and potent. Petrol thrown onto the smouldering coals of her long-suppressed desires. She went up in flames, the heat roaring through her, incandescent and overwhelming. *He* knew she wasn't grieving like the rest of them. Her heart tangoed to an inexplicable thrilling beat in a way it had never done before.

Sara looked away before her lips quirked in return at his knowing look, which would have been highly improper and a complete disregard for her now worthless royal training.

Sometimes you knew things about yourself, and Sara knew she wouldn't have made a good Queen. It was no wonder Ferdinand couldn't love her. Not with all the 'unseemly' emotion that threatened to burst from her, which her parents, and the courtiers who'd been tasked with turning her into the perfect future monarch, had required her to ruthlessly contain.

*'You need to try harder, Sara...'* Their constant refrain at some misplaced smile or, heaven help her, laugh. All of them had seemed intent on squashing the joy right out of her.

They'd very nearly succeeded.

The same problem didn't appear to afflict her best friend, the only surviving immediate member of Lauritania's doomed royal family. Annalise stood across from her, expressionless, a slender, lonely figure. Did she suffer the same drowning sensation as she faced being Queen that Sara had experienced at the mere prospect of taking on the role? The frantic desire to escape the golden handcuffs of the palace?

Sara couldn't tell. The Lauritanian Queen was required to

marry. Now, Annalise was unlikely to find the love match she'd once dreamed of. And yet there she stood, stoic and impassive, as a queen should. Not noticing Sara's inner turmoil at all.

Sara stared at the floor once more as she twisted the now tortured handkerchief in her hands, not willing to risk her friend seeing the ugly truth. That she'd been overcome by emotion, just not the one expected of her. Sara should be mourning the loss of her future, yet everything seemed lighter because she was…free. Of the expectations that had bound her for as long as she could remember.

She'd been betrothed to the Crown Prince at birth. Sara had known from the moment of first conscious thought that she was destined for one man, fated to be his Queen. Now, for the first time in her twenty-three years, her life was her own. Not tied to a person she'd come to learn was many things, but none of them what he seemed. It had been on the night of that ill-fated ball when she'd finally realised he would never love her. Any naïve hope that he could, quelled by his words when she'd confronted him. How he saw their forthcoming marriage as a duty to his country and nothing more. No promise of fidelity, just an expectation of long, lonely years trapped in a marriage without any feeling. Back then, there'd been no escaping the juggernaut of a royal wedding bearing down on her.

Now? Relief she shouldn't feel wrapped round her like a blanket. It made her a wicked, wicked person. Thinking of herself when her country's monarchy had almost been obliterated. Yet when had she ever had that luxury? Being a queen sounded nice when you were a little girl craving tiaras and ball gowns, until the reality of it hit like an avalanche. The relentless press, the jealousy of others, the absence of true friends. Till all you could foresee was a lonely future buried under the cold weight of expectation...

Still, that blistering sense of *awareness* hadn't lessened. She lifted her gaze once more. The man's eyes remained fixed on her, his mouth still holding its amused curve. A honeyed heat drizzled over her and she basked in it, the sensation new and illicit. What would it be like to kiss that mouth?

If another future had been hers, she might have been brave, done something about it. But as much as she craved to give in to it, such feelings screamed *danger*. Because powerful men like Ferdinand and this alluring stranger didn't really see women as individuals. She was more than a mere accessory, despite how she'd been treated when her engagement was formally announced. The sacrificial virgin for the royal dragon. The monarchical behemoth had threatened to swallow her alive the longer she'd stayed in its clutches. And she'd concluded that was all people saw for her future. To be a pretty little bauble on the Crown Prince's arm. To smile on cue, to bear equally pretty children and quietly fade into the background when not required.

No more.

She shut down her random musings. Turned away from yet another handsome man who made her dream of things that would remain better in fantasy than reality. Instead, she focused on her friend. Annalise walked forward to her family's coffins, yet as she reached them she looked at Sara. Eyes strained and weary. Mouth pinched and trembling from suppressed sobs. Tears forbidden to fall. Sara wished the world wasn't watching and she could console her friend rather than being required to stand remote from her Queen. And for a moment the weight of it all threatened to crush her.

Because they were both young women who'd lost the

world they'd expected to wake up to each day. Their lives had changed for ever.

Sara bowed her head, saying a silent goodbye to the monarchy she'd thought she'd known but now realised she hadn't ever really understood. There was no fairy tale to be found here, no happy ending. Still, life was hers for the taking. All she could do was bide her time until her chance came. And now she had all the time in the world.

Lance loathed funerals. It wasn't the sadness that bothered him. Life was an unending parade of grief and lost chances. No. It was the hypocrisy. The exalted dead bearing little resemblance to the people they'd been in real life. The three individuals whose lives they'd been remembering today were that sort. Beloved of their people, but a mere fantasy. One he had no interest in remembering or promoting.

He'd been invited to be official witness to the interment, as the antiquated Lauritanian constitution required. Returning to the place of his blighted high school education during his father's long tenure as British Ambassador here. Lance supposed he should have felt privileged. His not so dearly departed dad had cultivated a close friendship with Lauritania's royal family, thinking it might assist his son's fortunes as the future Duke of Bedmore. But in truth Lance would never have returned to this conservative little country, even with a direct invitation from the Queen, had his best friend and business partner Rafe De Villiers not requested it.

He and Rafe had met at the prestigious Kings' Academy here, both fighting against the Lauritanian aristocracy in their own way. Those bleak years had forged an unassailable comradeship and a rule that if one asked for assistance the other would always answer the request without question. A promise made when they'd been abused at the school because they were 'other'. Rafe for being a commoner. Lance because he wasn't *from here*.

So here he stood, sipping champagne at the wake surrounded by a dour sea of people. Tasked with reporting back to Rafe on the political machinations of the aristocracy because, as a commoner, his friend would never have been allowed to grace this hallowed occasion. Lance had no desire to reacquaint himself with these people, many of whom had tried to bully him at school, before he and Rafe had joined forces—and the other boys had realised they were a force to be reckoned with. It was a stultifying task, especially since a few of them tried to rewrite history and talk to him as if their past disdain didn't matter. Anyhow, his lineage was finer than the rest of them put together. Because inheriting a dukedom had some advantages, no matter how determined he was to squander them.

Still, being here pricked at Lance's keen senses. Rafe was up to something, hinting at a curious interest in the new Queen—a monarch who needed to find a husband, and quickly, as the constitution dictated. Right now, all the royal family's hangers-on were surrounding her with knives carefully sheathed, waiting to stab each other's backs at the earliest opportunity in a fight to be named King. He catalogued their names, the ones watching her with avarice, jockeying for an auspicious marriage. Some things never changed. Lauritania was steeped in the past. The future terrified the people here, and it was staring down at them with both barrels today.

Lance downed the dregs of his champagne and grabbed another frosted flute from a passing waiter. The young Queen, pretty as she was, held no interest for him other than an academic one. As his deliberately lazy gaze drifted over the room what he sought was something far more alluring. The flash of golden female brilliance he'd glimpsed earlier at the mausoleum.

Even swathed in black like the rest of them, she'd been impossible to miss. He supposed laughing at a funeral tended to draw people's attention, but it seemed no one else had noticed the well-covered slip. Lance hadn't been able to help himself. She'd stood out because she seemed so *unaffected* by the misery surrounding them. A diamond amongst these lumps of coal, and he adored bright, sparkly things that grabbed his attention and held. Only because in his life they were so very rare.

When he'd caught her eye she'd almost smiled. On a day when there was not a glimmer of hope to be had, she seemed filled to the brim with it. He'd sensed something a little wild and unbridled about her that in ordinary circumstances he'd like to get to know for a few hours in a large bed of tangled sheets. Or maybe the not so ordinary circumstances were perfect...

Another glance across the room and he spied her, the bright beacon he'd been searching for, golden hair an unruly tangle under her black hat. He began to move, dodging the crush to get to her. Luckily, he was a head taller than most of them so it was hard for her to disappear even as she slipped in and out of the groups of people around her. He quickened his pace, his heart thumping hard at the pursuit. There was no way he'd let her escape him. The universe should allow him some small compensation for coming here.

She wasn't looking in his direction, staring somewhere into the crowd with a soft, almost questioning look on her face. Watching the throng of people circling about her as if she was somehow separate from the grief here. Yet for all the oppressive misery in the room, her back was ramrod-straight and she held her head high as if the room was hers to own and rule.

A perfectly fitted conservative black dress skimmed her gentle curves, the skirt ending at the backs of her knees, showing off the swell of her calves. Her hair was pulled up from the back of her slender neck, curls drifting loose. Lance wanted to brush them away and drop his lips to the elegant sweep of pale skin at the junction of her shoulder. Skim his mouth along the warm flesh. See if he could get a smile out of her then. Or, even better, a gasp of pleasure.

Lance realised now, as he made his way closer, how small and delicate she was. Even in those modest heels she'd tuck neatly under his chin if he held her. He couldn't help thinking she'd be the perfect fit. As he reached her, he pitched his voice low, dropped his head and murmured for her ears alone, 'You've been a very bad girl.'

She whipped round, a flush of pink washing over her cheeks, a glorious wide-eyed beauty, too innocent for the jaded man he'd become.

He'd left the womb a cynic, his mother claimed. That wasn't *quite* right. He'd become an incurable cynic the day his parents sold off his sister, Victoria, to the highest bidder to further his father's career. Now, Lance's preference was for someone as world-weary as him. Not this fresh burst of perfection that made her little part of the room shine.

It was as if he were hypnotised, unable to take his eyes from her. Of course beautiful women were everywhere. He was a glutton for them and not known for his self-control. But he'd never met someone who made the room simply stop and melt away.

She tilted her head and looked up at him with huge blue eyes, so pale and cool they were like the spring meltwater from the mountains. Her mouth perfection in petal pink. She might have been the one blushing, but he was left speechless.

'And why is that?' Her voice was soft and musical, with the lilt of an accent that told him she was native Lauritanian.

No *I beg your pardon*. Or, perhaps, *Who the hell are you?* Because he was sure this woman had secrets and he wanted to mine them all. He saw it in the wide shock of her eyes—that someone might have seen what she was trying to hide. Her rosebud lips parted and she took in a shaky breath. God, how he wanted to kiss her. Right here and now. Might have been passable at a wedding reception. Grossly inappropriate at a wake. Though he'd spent most of his adult life being inappropriate. Disappointing his father had once been his greatest mission. Now the man was dead, but Lance still had a reputation to uphold.

And he hadn't answered her question. She raised her slender, pale eyebrows. As he closed in, he dropped his head again as if to impart something illicit. Then he caught the scent of her. Apples and blossom. So crisp and fresh he wanted to take a bite.

'You were trying not to laugh.'

The blush swept across her cheeks again. He'd been right. For her there was something about today that didn't match the grief of everyone else here. She placed an elegant, gloved hand to her chest.

'If true, that would have been incredibly improper of me.'

Lance loved that she didn't deny it. What a glorious mystery she was. Yet as she looked up at him tears shimmered in her eyes. Whilst he spent his life pretending not to be a gentleman, Lance still retained some manners. He whipped out a handkerchief and handed it to her.

He hated women's tears. Especially when there was not a damn thing he could do about them. She gave him a soft smile of thanks, took the sharply pressed linen and dabbed her eyes.

'Perhaps, but then I'm improper all the time, so I judge everyone by my own low standards. I always say if you can't laugh at something, life's no fun.' He was renowned in the press for taking very little seriously, which showed how un- derestimated he was. It was a carefully cultivated illusion on his part. Some things were deadly serious, like his sister's cur- rent circumstances. Everything else was simply unimportant.

The woman in front of him brightened a little then, a tiny quirk of her lips. He supposed he should introduce himself, but there was something about the mystery between them that carried an illicit kind of thrill.

Then she pursed her lips a fraction, blinking with long lashes fanning her cheeks. 'You were at the interment. Should I know you?'

He put his hand to his chest and staggered back as if she'd mortally wounded him. 'Of course you should know who I am. Everybody does.'

No hint of a smile this time, but her eyes gleamed, their corners crinkling with amusement. Good. Better than the glittering tears threatening to mar her face. 'Lance Astill. My father was British Ambassador to Lauritania for many years. And you are?'

He held out his hand. She placed hers in his. It was so slender he felt he might crush it. Yet the delicate bones had a surprisingly firm grip. He turned her hand and bowed over it, although not allowing his lips to touch the smooth silk of her black gloves, no matter how much he wanted to. Today was all about games, and he loved to play. He stood back and released her, her eyes wide and mouth open in a tiny 'Oh' that could have been shock or surprise. At least there were no more tears.

'Sara Conrad.' The name sounded familiar. A Conrad boy at school had been one of his more persistent tormen- tors... 'I was the Crown Prince's fiancée.'

Lance froze. He'd known Ferdinand had become engaged to some aristocrat, but couldn't fathom it being this woman. She was too full of life to be squashed down by the strictures of the palace. And the Crown Prince was never known for his fidelity. Lance didn't imagine he'd have taken his marriage vows seriously.

'I'm so sorry,' he said. He wasn't. She'd had a fortuitous escape.

Sara looked up at him, a slight frown creasing her brow. 'Don't be. I'm not.' The words tumbled out of her. She raised a gloved hand to her mouth as if trying to shove the errant syllables back in, her eyes wide. 'I shouldn't have said that. Ignore me. I… It's the grief talking.'

He took her by the elbow and manoeuvred her towards a potted palm, out of earshot of most others. On the way he grabbed a glass of wine from a passing waiter. She needed fortifying. This woman was too open and honest. She'd be eaten alive by the crowd here, who gloried in each other's humiliation and loss, the bunch of them competitive to a fault. Right now, most of them were grappling to court the new Queen. This bright and beautiful woman in front of him would be a casualty along the way.

'You didn't appear particularly grief-stricken. Your laughter was somewhat of a giveaway…'

'It was hysteria more than anything.'

'You don't strike me as prone to hysterics. Should I have a vial of smelling salts handy in case you're overcome and swoon into me?'

The corners of her mouth trembled upwards and she sank her teeth into her lower lip as if trying to stop a smile breaking free. He wanted her to lose her inhibitions. To claim her errant smiles all for himself.

She glanced about the room as if searching for something

or someone. 'Have you ever been in a situation where you realised everything you thought you knew was a lie?'

He looked into her smooth, now impassive face, fighting so hard not to show any trace of happiness. Yes. He knew exactly what she was talking about. He nodded.

She kept going. 'I was born to be a consort and look at me.' She waved her hands up and down her body. The wine in her glass sloshed about but didn't spill. She took a gulp and winced. 'Talking to some stranger, showing...*feelings*. There's nothing regal about me. I'm sure I would have been a disappointment. A terrible Queen. No wonder he...'

She bit her lip again, but not to halt a smile this time. Lance didn't need to be told who 'he' was. He'd bet his considerable fortune that the Crown Prince, and the rest of the aristocracy Lance loathed, had tried to crush the wings of this glorious being in front of him.

'Angel.' It suited her. She looked as if she should be adorning some classical artwork. Paint her perfect pale skin against the backdrop of a morning sky, with a pair of wings, and she could be a heavenly being to match any he'd ever seen on a fresco. 'I was born to be a duke and I've been disappointing them for years.' Her eyes widened and the tilt of her lips gave her an ethereal beauty that would have stopped everyone in the room, had anyone else been able to see them. Luckily, dark corners behind well placed potted plants were useful for concealment. 'The trick is, you need to own the role, not fight against it. You're untouchable if you don't care.'

'And you don't?'

Once, he'd cared too much. Not any more, not for years. Caring didn't matter when there were things he couldn't fix. Victoria bore the brunt of his greatest failing. Phone calls hurriedly ended when her husband arrived home. Strange bruises she claimed to have suffered because she was 'clumsy', when that had never been a problem which afflicted her in the past. The terrible suspicions he harboured, which had grown and grown in the years she'd been married. He shouldn't be trusted with any woman's happiness.

'All I care about is thrilling them in the tabloids.'

How they loved plastering him on the front page, each story more overblown than the last, when there was a mundane truth no one wanted to hear. Most of it was little more than fiction.

The smile on Sara's face was glorious and wide. *Unrestrained.* A warmth kindled in his chest. Better a smile than tears for a man he knew didn't deserve her. Now, if he could remove her hat, unleash her golden curls from the thick chignon at the base of her head. Brush the strands through his fingers. Stroke away her hurt and her fears until she flushed rosy with pleasure…

'You're a…a scoundrel.'

A reminder of who he truly was. He needed to stop his heated imaginings. Innocents had no place in his life. He tended to crush them with thoughtlessness. Victoria was his first victim. He didn't want there to be any others.

He bowed. 'At your service. The Astills are notorious for their vices.'

'Really?' The question was breathy and curious. Against all better judgement, he was glad that he'd piqued her interest.

'My forebears have spent centuries squandering our fortune. We come from a long line of drinkers, gamblers, adulterers and fornicators. I've a family history to live up to and I take my role as its current head seriously.'

'And in that illustrious list, what vices do you choose?'

'The marital bed is sacrosanct and safe from me. Otherwise, take your pick.'

Her sharp intake of breath made his heart rate spike. Her

cool blue eyes twinkled with fascination. Lance dipped his head to her ear.

'Although of late gambling and drinking have lost their appeal.' His voice was a murmur, breath whispering along her neck. 'If I want to maintain the scandalous reputation of the Astill family, there's really only one choice left…'

Lance revelled in the wash of pink that once again tinted her face like sunrise over snow. A tremor shuddered through her. He moved closer. Couldn't help himself. Not that Lance would touch a woman so…untainted by life. But still, one could dream for a moment that things were different.

'Perhaps that's what I need,' her voice whispered, thick and breathy.

His heart pumped a bit harder. 'What?'

'My life…it's been so…' She fluttered her hand about again, as if trying to shake free the words.

'Controlled?' Which, in other circumstances, he would have enjoyed pursuing, especially when that careful control snapped in a torrent of passion…

'Yes. Perhaps a scandal would make things more interesting.'

She looked up at him as if he were the answer to every prayer. Very few people interested him. Fewer held his attention. At the moment, this diminutive creature in front of him had him thrumming like a tuning fork, all to her song. As if he were the hero she searched for. It sounded as if the beautiful Sara Conrad needed the fantasy of an escape, even if he could never give her that.

'Oh, angel.'

Her pupils dilated. Wide, dark reflections of her desires. All he saw in them was himself.

Lance's voice pitched even lower. Rough and unrecognisable. 'Scandal I can do.'

Her lips parted. She licked them. 'Please.'

That one whispered word exploded to life. Left him hard and aching. More like an untried boy than a man who'd been unashamedly sampling beautiful women since his late teens. The power of her request coursed through him like a drug. Intoxicating. Addicting.

*Temptation, thy name is Sara.*

He should move away, yet here, cloistered from the crowd, with unspoken desire thick and heady around them, there was nowhere he'd rather be. Lance was lost in a world centring on her.

'Sara!' Her back stiffened. Her head dropped. Lance looked over at a pinched-looking older couple. They turned their sour attention to him. 'Who are you?'

'I'm Astill, the Duke of Bedmore, but you will call me Your Grace.' Lance stood to his full height, towering over the couple as he glared down on them. 'And who the hell are you?'

Their eyes widened and that look he was so familiar with, the avarice of aristocracy, swept across their faces at the mention of his title. Mamas had been trying to marry their daughters off to him for years, to make a duchess out of them. This pair's interest would pass. They'd work out who he was soon enough. What he loathed, more than the people before him, was that Sara stood there, still and silent. It was as if all the life had been bled out of her.

'My parents, Count and Countess Conrad,' she said.

Her father spoke first. 'Why do you have our daughter sequestered behind this shrubbery?'

Lance did nothing bar raise an eyebrow. 'I would have thought it obvious, considering today was the funeral of her *fiancé.*' He hated having to pretend she was grieving that wastrel, but he'd protect Sara's reputation. It wasn't his to destroy. 'Lady Sara was overwrought. As a *gentleman*, it was my duty to assist her.'

Her mother simply stared at him. Then she narrowed her eyes. Ah, there it was. She knew.

'*You.*'

He smiled. The moment of recognition always amused him. As if standing too close to any woman would ruin her for ever.

'Lance Astill. You—you're the...the Debauched Duke.' The woman spat out the words. Lance was quite proud of the title coined by the tabloids, although he didn't think it was their most creative moniker. He didn't discourage the nicknames since they kept most people at a sensible distance.

'Frankly, I prefer the Dilettante Duke myself. But I own whatever name they give me.' He leaned forwards conspiratorially and gave a leering wink. 'Since it's mostly true.'

The pair blanched. Her father turned. 'Sara, come with us!'

The beautiful Sara had her head down, shoulders hunched and shaking. His handkerchief was firmly pressed to her mouth. She could be crying. But he didn't think so. If he wasn't much mistaken, she gave a delightful little snort of amusement.

'Now look what you've done,' he said. 'She's upset again. After all my valiant efforts.'

'You've done quite enough,' her mother said.

He raised an imperious eyebrow.

She hesitated. 'Your Grace.'

He took her capitulation as a win. Baiting bluebloods was his favourite game, after all.

'As have you. Upsetting your daughter on this most terrible of days. You should take her home immediately, tuck her into bed with a warm cocoa.'

Sara coughed from behind her hand.

He lowered his voice conspiratorially. 'That's what *I'd* do.'

At the mention of a bed and Sara in the same breath, her father turned a ripe shade of puce. 'Come, Sara. We'll take our leave.'

Good. Get her away from the vultures who circled here. Though he doubted her parents were any better.

Lance turned to the glorious woman before him. 'Lady Sara?' The way he'd positioned himself meant her back was now to her parents. She removed the handkerchief. Tears of mirth smeared her cheeks, her eyes aglow. A perfect smile lit up her whole face.

Time simply stopped.

Lance took her hand in his. 'It's been a pleasure, although I'm sorry it's in such unfortunate circumstances. I hope we meet again…soon.' There was no chance of that. He rarely came to Lauritania and had little expectation of being invited to the new Queen's wedding. Still, he relished the small fantasy curling between them that a second meeting was inevitable. *Fated.*

She didn't remove her hand from his. The warmth of her fingers seeped through her glove. They were lingering too long and they both knew it. She curtsied deep and low, holding his gaze. 'The pleasure has likewise been mine. Thank you for your attentions, Your Grace.'

And, for the first time since inheriting it, he gloried in the sound of his wretched title spilling from someone's lips.

# CHAPTER TWO

IT WAS SOME cruel kind of irony that had Sara sitting at her new Queen's wedding reception some two months after the death of the Crown Prince. On a wedding day that had been marked as her own. Though the room didn't much feel like a wedding reception. Yes, there were flowers, grand table decorations and a cake, but this place held all the joy of the wake.

'That should have been you,' her mother whispered. True enough. Still, it was a heartless comment if her parents accepted the fantasy that she could be upset by today. That it wasn't her sitting at the bridal table with Ferdinand as her husband. But Sara had come to realise over the past weeks that they really didn't consider her thoughts much at all.

'Well, Mother, it's not.'

'They could at least have made fresh choices. This was all meant to be yours,' her mother hissed.

No. This had never been for her, she knew it now. She'd fooled herself for years, despite the niggling doubts that perhaps this wasn't what she wanted for herself. The flowers in the centrepiece of the tables were exquisite hothouse orchids, which hadn't been her choice, but the most expensive and fitting for a royal wedding, or so the planner had dictated. The cake was a ten-tier monolith of baked engineering and fondant icing. She recognised it all because none of what had been ordered for her and Ferdinand's intended nuptials had been wasted, all recycled for Annalise's wedding.

Relief ran over her like a warm shower, though Sara wasn't sure it boded well for her best friend. The monarch who'd married a commoner, surprising everyone except Sara, because Annalise had mastered the art of quiet rebellion.

Unlike herself. She was a master of nothing, really. She didn't rebel at all. It was an alien concept. She was always behaving, doing what she'd been instructed to do. Even as a teen her only act approaching defiance was to grab a pair of scissors and hack her hair short in a fit of pique, a ridiculous thing to do because it had made her blonde curls tighten so she looked something akin to a dandelion. Not a great success, and in the end only made her feel foolish. In fact, she wondered what rebellion truly felt like. Was it a quiet thrill or something loud that got the blood coursing? Was it terrifying or exhilarating?

She glanced over at the top table. To the best man. The man whose white handkerchief embroidered with his initials was kept in the drawer beside her bed. A shiver ran through her. She'd never expected to see him again, whilst hoping against hope that she would. But he was sitting there in morning dress with a stern, aristocratic demeanour, the perfect tailoring of a silver waistcoat gripping his powerful chest, that torso accentuated by the best Italian superfine wool and Savile Row tailoring money could buy. He stared out at the crowd with a supercilious air, as if they should bow down before him. As if he was above them all. Her stomach swooped and her heart took off on a race of its own, throbbing as if it were fighting to escape from behind the ribs caging it in.

She might not be sure what rebellion felt like, but she knew what its name was.

Lance Astill.

Goosebumps raced over her skin at the memory of his murmured words, the caress of warm breath at her ear.

*You've been a very bad girl.*

Her toes curled whenever she thought about that moment, and it crept into her consciousness *often*. She'd fooled everyone else at the funeral. They all thought she'd been overcome by emotion at the loss of Ferdinand. A man who had never been hers to begin with.

Not Lance.

Because he understood. He'd owned her the moment he'd whispered those words in her ear. He was rebellion all wrapped in a tall, muscular package with broad shoulders and narrow hips.

Ferdinand might have been born to be King, and he'd been an attractive man in his own way—God rest his soul. But Lance? She twisted the napkin in her lap.

He ruled the room absolutely, with no effort.

She'd watched people attempting to talk with him. Men, the young heirs to their father's titles. His contemporaries. He'd cut them all with a glance till they shrank away and he stood alone. The only one he spoke to was the new King, Rafe De Villiers. She'd heard her parents hissing that they were best friends. That together they'd bring the country into disrepute. They'd been wanton boys and worse adults. They had to be stopped.

All of that only made him *more* interesting. It had been bad enough googling him. But after she'd left the wake with her parents, Sara couldn't help herself. One tiny peek was all she'd allow herself. One illicit glimpse at that powerful body with defined muscles carved by the hand of a generous creator, as Lance stood slick and wet from a swim on the deck of some yacht in the Riviera. Or the action shot of him on horseback, powerful thighs gripping a polo pony as he was snapped mid-swing. The tremble in her fingers as she scrolled down the screen at the more salacious pictures. The scandalous headlines. The exquisite women.

It shouldn't have thrilled her. It shouldn't.

But it did.

Lance could teach her all about rebellion. He could teach her to be a *very bad girl*, and part of her coveted that with a secret desire she'd locked away deep inside of her.

But what was she doing, staring at him like a lovesick puppy? He hadn't looked at her, not once. It was no wonder, really. Her own fiancé had shown no interest. Lance Astill? She wasn't at all like the beauties who usually adorned his arm: tall, all slender limbs and perfectly tamed gleaming hair. The type of elegant, worldly women who wandered up to hopelessly naïve girls in ballrooms and told them what the world was really like, sending their carefully stitched-together fantasies crashing down. She could fool herself any way she liked, but the reality would remain the same.

*You'll never have his heart.*

She tore her eyes away from him. They sat at a table with people her parents knew from some of the older titled families here, where she was the only person under fifty. A few of them watched her with interest. Of course they might simply think she'd been staring at the top table, perhaps grieving over what they thought she'd lost.

As far as she was concerned she was the winner on this day.

'Look at her, wearing black,' her mother said, glaring at the top table once more. There were a few murmurs of assent. 'What was she thinking?'

The lack of respect for their new Queen shocked Sara. She ignored it. Her parents were obviously still smarting because their daughter wasn't sitting there now. As for the rest of the aristocracy at this table, she wasn't sure why any of it mattered. The world had changed and they needed to change with it. In Sara's view, the dress was a masterpiece of royal wedding finery, even if it wasn't virginal white. Sara mused that Annalise had given a lot of thought to the colour. Her choice was a devastating one.

'Her Majesty's been forced to marry when she's still in mourning. I think the colour is beautiful and respectful. Anyhow, *you're* wearing black.'

And so was she. It seemed fitting. Proper, even.

'That's different. It's her wedding day. She should be celebrating.'

'When her family has only lately been placed in a grave?'

Her mother crossed herself, then sniffed. 'She's Queen. Appearances must be maintained. And I thought at least you'd be bridesmaid. A deliberate slight. You would have done better.'

Sara was glad she wasn't bridesmaid. Then she'd have to be next to Lance. Would have to dance with him when the time came. The thought of his arms around her, her body pressed up against all that height and hard muscle… She put her hand to her chest as her heart fluttered beneath it. Took a sip of water to cool the flame that had lit deep inside her at the mere thought.

That man was too much for her.

'I told you, it wasn't like that.' Annalise had believed too that Sara was upset. She'd told Sara she hadn't wanted her imagined grief paraded before the world. It wasn't a slight of any kind but an act of deep kindness and friendship.

Some music started, the lilting strains of a string ensemble. The Queen stood, and so did the rest of the room. Then Annalise and her husband walked to the dance floor and a waltz began. Sara loved the waltz, one of the many dances she'd learned during her royal training. The structure, the rise and fall of it.

'Don't worry,' her mother whispered, shrewd eyes on some unattractive man at another table as they all sat once more. 'Your time will come. Sooner than you may think.'

Sara didn't like the scheming tone. It set her heart beating fast in a way that wasn't at all pleasant. Instead, she indulged in watching the new King and Queen sweep across the dance floor, thanking the universe that it wasn't her at this moment, all the while wishing she was in another man's arms.

She turned away from the scene. There was nothing to be gained from hoping for things that would never be. She blinked back threatened tears as a shadow fell across her.

'Lady Sara.'

The low burr of that voice caressed like velvet over her skin. A woman who'd spent her life training to be Queen didn't fall off her chair. But Sara almost did, having to grip the seat of the elaborately swathed piece of furniture in tight fingers to steady herself.

*Rebellion had found her.*

The whole table turned towards Lance. He was glorious, his throbbing physical energy barely constrained by his formal dress. The height of aristocratic perfection. And when she looked at him she didn't see the barely tamed man he tried to present but someone swashbuckling, swinging from the rigging of ships, cutlass in hand, duelling at dawn or riding a joust. Her silly, childish fantasies getting her into trouble again, but right now she didn't care one little bit. He cast his gaze across the table, jaw hard, eyes narrowed in a look of disdain so singeing it was a wonder the people around him didn't simply self-immolate and shrivel to ashes.

Then he held out his hand, palm up.

'Would you care to dance?'

She stared at it for a moment as the whispers hissed around the table, her heart thumping in a frantic rhythm. All she could do was look up at him, at his stern face and quirked eyebrow, and grab this tiny moment for herself.

He tucked her arm in his own and led her to the dance floor, where the new Queen and King still seemed to be waging their own silent battle. Lance seemed to be fighting his own. Nothing about him was soft today. His jaw was hard, eyes scanning the crowd sharp as cut glass, a tension rippling through him that trembled through her too. He slipped his arm round her, she placed her hand on his shoulder, the heat of him burning into her palm through the layers of fine wool. It was enough to cause her first steps to falter, until the sheer force of him led her into the dance. And whilst all eyes should have been on the newly wed royals, they were on her. Like shards of glass spiking her skin. So she stiffened her spine, raised her head as she'd been trained to do and gave them something to talk about.

'You look beautiful,' Lance murmured. 'Although shouldn't you be out of mourning?'

His hold on her was relaxed. He moved as if he were born to dance, not a step out of place. The push and pull as he led her round the floor. She wanted to close her eyes, relax and allow him to sweep her away from this place.

'Isn't today supposed to be all about the bride?'

'You were meant to be the bride today,' he said through gritted teeth, but the look he gave her was full of concern as they spun across the floor. His sympathy almost undid her. The sense of loss, not for something she'd wanted but for the future she'd expected, almost overwhelming. Could he sense it?

Lance's arms firmed, holding her tighter, holding her together. She recognised that feeling. The pounding heart. The sick ache in her stomach. She'd always known where she was headed in life, never questioning it. Now, she had no idea what was in store for her, and she was afraid of what might come.

'How did you know?'

The papers could be cruel but most of them hadn't been gauche enough to mention it, too busy commemorating the new King and Queen to ask questions about her.

He nodded towards the new couple, a frown on his face. 'I have friends in high places.'

'You don't seem happy about the marriage,' she said.

He stiffened under her hands. 'I loathe any situation in which people are forced to do things out of duty rather than desire.'

'The press say it's a love match.'

Before her family's deaths, Annalise had confided in Sara that she had a secret admirer. She'd never told Sara his name, but Sara suspected it was the man to whom she was now married. The way he held her close as they danced, as if she were something precious, breakable, his eyes never leaving her face...

'How delightfully naïve. Tabloids lie. Or print what they're told to.'

She'd never expected he'd direct his air of disdain towards her, and found it stung. Still, she didn't need to meekly accept it. She'd accepted far too much without a fight. No longer.

'So the myriad stories about you are untrue?'

Lance raised a supercilious eyebrow. 'Checking up on me?'

The heat raced to her cheeks like an inferno as the corner of his perfect lips began to curl into a grin. She couldn't lie, she'd experienced enough of that in her short life. The unvarnished truth was far better.

'Perhaps…a little?'

'They tell exactly the right story about me. Disappointed?' Then his mouth broke into a wicked smile that caused a complicated dance in her belly.

'Thrilled.'

He laughed, a deep, throaty sound which rolled right through her in a glorious rumble.

Lance lifted his arm and twirled her in a perfectly executed spin that left her divinely light-headed. Or perhaps it was the man himself. Then he drew her close with an arm a touch lower than the polite height of her shoulder blade, his fingers splayed firm against the fabric of her dress.

'And what else have you learned about me through your avid investigations?'

That he had the body of a god, the face of an angel and the reputation of a tomcat. She couldn't help wanting to know *all* of him.

'Is there anything else to know, other than the apparent truth of what they tell?'

A look flashed across his face, a tightness around his eyes, and then it slid away as he twirled her in a giddy dance across the floor, the chandelier sparkling above her. In his arms she felt more of a queen than she'd ever done when she really had a chance of being one.

'You seem to have my measure, then,' he said. She couldn't miss the hollow, flat sound of the words.

She wasn't sure of it at all. The man was known as a rake, and if that were true he should have been whisking her off into a darkened alcove. Yet all he'd ever been was kind, which in her world was something novel.

Lance looked over her head, at the watching crowd. 'Want to give that lot something to talk about?' he asked, and she nodded. Then his hand slid down low on her waist, an impolite position for the polite company of a Lauritanian royal ballroom. His arm tightened and dragged her against him. The air pushed out of her with an 'oof'.

He held her tight against his rock-hard body. The murmur of the crowd grew louder as the strains of the music changed to something slower. A rumba beat, her dance teacher would have said. *A dance that represents desire and yearning between partners.* She couldn't comprehend why she should learn it at the time. If her parents had known, they would have thought it the height of scandal. But her dance teacher, preparing her for ballrooms across the world and many dances with a king, had told her that one day she'd understand. She lost the sultry rhythm and stumbled a step.

Lance dropped his mouth to her ear. A whisper of breath across her throat washed goosebumps over her. 'Let me lead you.'

Sara shouldn't, but she *wanted*. Craved the promise in his voice. Craved to melt into him.

Then he moved, and *how* he moved with her. As if they were created for one another. She let him take her, only a sliver of air between them, yet it was as if they were one person. The sublime push and pull as her body did everything his wanted, so perfectly in tune her mind blanked to all else bar him. The hiss of the crowd, the cloying scent of perfumes mixed with orchids. It all melted into the distant background as she concentrated on how they danced together, the heat of his body against hers. She felt dizzy in that joyous way she had when as a child she'd been allowed one ride on a carousel.

Lance looked down on her intently and the...*want* in his

gaze froze the breath in her lungs. She could bathe in that look because it made her feel as if she were the only woman left in the world. She knew then that she was glimpsing the man the tabloids loved to hate.

And she finally understood what her dance teacher had talked about. Yearning and desire. The beating pulse of it, the ache deep at her core for things that couldn't be. It almost undid her in front of a crowd of hundreds. Sara sensed a movement next to them, an intrusion, and that glorious spell cast over her by the sinuous sway of their bodies faltered.

'Lady Sara, may I have the pleasure?' A voice she didn't know, the man she'd seen at the other table. She didn't want to leave this dance, the breathless sensation of being in Lance's arms. And Lance didn't relinquish her. He looked down at the stranger, all authority and menace.

'No.' A tremor ran through her as he swept her away in a turn, leaving the man standing on the floor alone. 'Unless you want to, of course. But I thought I might save you a trying time. He looked dull.'

'Thank you.' Sadly, the space had increased between them to something eminently more respectable. 'My hero.'

'That's something I have never been accused of.'

The music changed again. More people joined the floor as he led her away, snatching two drinks from a passing waiter and handing one to her. She took a sip of the cold beverage with perfect bubbles.

'So what do you do when not being rakish or heroic?' she asked. She had to regain her equilibrium where Lance Astill was concerned or she'd dissolve here in front of him out of heat and *need*.

He raised an eyebrow. 'I'm a duke. That's usually enough for most people.'

She looked around the room. All eyes were on her, full

of avarice and intrigue. A place she'd never really fitted in, she realised now. How could she ever have thought she did? They'd probably be chattering about her for days. She'd never liked the attention before, but now she relished the sly glances.

'I'm a little over the aristocracy and their intrigues.'

'A woman after my own heart.'

She shrugged. 'I just think there's more to Lance Astill than...' she waved her hand up and down in front of him, signalling his clothes and general appearance of wicked perfection '...this.'

Lance's face was inscrutable as he regarded her, then his head cocked the tiniest fraction.

'I'm a second-hand dealer. Or at least that's what my dear old dad used to call me.'

The champagne caught in Sara's throat and she started coughing, her eyes watering. How mortifying, but she hadn't expected him to say *that*, even though she'd suspected there was more to the man than the image he portrayed.

'And yours was his *exact* reaction when I told my father my plans. He couldn't abide any sort of trade. Thought being a duke should have been enough. Though I did enjoy meeting his exceptionally low expectations of me.' Lance reached round and patted her firmly on the back to settle her coughing. 'Are you all right or are you going to expire on me here in the corner from shock? I'd hate to add that to my scandalous résumé.'

'I'm fine,' she said, her voice a little hoarse. She collected herself, wiped at her eyes, thankful for the waterproof mascara she'd worn today. 'Ignore what your father called you. What do you call yourself?'

He reached into the front inside pocket of his suit and handed her a fine white card, elegantly embossed in gold: *Astill's Auctions*. She cradled it in her palm.

'He loathed me using the family name. If he could have disinherited me, he would have.'

'That seems harsh.'

'He claimed I was a stain on the title of Bedmore, conveniently forgetting our wicked ancestors. But I'm the heir, no matter how disappointing. In the end, the dukedom won, as it always does. Anyhow, I told him I was merely refilling the family coffers, what with all the gamblers in our history happily emptying them.'

'What do you auction?'

'The possessions of the rich and recently deceased. They seem to trust one of their own coming into their homes and poking about their secrets, especially if death duties start biting at the family heels. Luckily, most of them have no idea what treasures their attics and dusty corners are hiding, which is where I come in. It's all rather grubby, but I'm the soul of discretion there at least.'

She couldn't see it as grubby. She saw him as before, a swashbuckling figure swooping into their homes. A pirate, definitely a pirate with his good looks and swagger, looking for treasure. What had this man seen in all the times he'd searched grand manors?

Sara loved beautiful old things. The lure of finding some dusty object that turned out to be an item of value. On the rare occasion she shoved a hat on her head and sneaked away, she would haunt the Morenburg antique markets to see what she could discover. Her excuse was that she'd been encouraged by her tutor to hone her skills. For her, it was the excitement of the chase.

'Have you ever found anything incredible?'

'Perhaps.' A fire lit in his eyes, and the cold containment of him was dispelled again. 'However, it's a secret.'

An expectant silence stretched between them.

'I won't tell. Don't make me wait.'

Lance's mouth curved into a sly smile. Then he lowered his head towards her and her breath caught.

'It's *all* about the thrill of waiting, angel,' he murmured. They stood close again, bodies a whisper away from each other, 'That's what makes anticipation such fun.'

Everything slowed. She looked up at him, deep into his hazel eyes flecked with gold, the pupils dark with intent. All his attention was focused on her, the moment sparking with a kind of magic. Then he took a small step back and a long swig of his champagne, and whatever was between them faded like morning mist in the sunshine.

'I'm sorry to disappoint,' Lance went on. 'What I've found requires authentication first. But when it is it'll set the art world alight and make my auction house notorious. One more thing for my father to roll over in his grave about.'

She wanted him close. She wanted secrets between them. She wanted to…hold onto this sensation that shivered through her, one she had trouble understanding.

'You know the palace has a Michelangelo,' Sara said. 'Or so it's claimed. I don't think it's real.'

'It's not. It was painted by one of his students. But they like to pretend. How did you know?'

'I know the difference between a Rembrandt and a Rubens.'

Lance raised his eyebrows. 'I should hope so, they're entirely different eras.'

She rolled her eyes. 'I was going for the alliteration.'

He smiled again. The wry curve of his lip was back. The wicked gleam in his eyes speared her and she felt the heated stab of it right down to the tip of her toes.

'Still hasn't answered my question,' he said. 'Or do you enjoy…punishing me by keeping me in suspense?'

She could keep him languishing for hours if it would keep them like this, together, for a little longer. In the end she took pity on him.

'I studied fine arts. I wanted to help curate the palace's collection when I was...' *Queen.* Her tutor had thought she had an aptitude for it, an innate ability to pick real from fake. Something she wouldn't need now. Now, she had nothing. It was as if she were a blank notebook, yet she didn't know what she wanted to write inside. She had no idea what to do with herself any more. Initially that sensation of being adrift was freeing. Now, her lack of purpose and whatever new plans her parents were hinting at for her sat like curdled milk in her belly... She shook the feeling off. She had here. She had now. And she'd live in this precious and perfect moment.

'Anyhow,' she said, 'I wanted to do something useful. Something I loved.'

Lance gazed down on her in a way she had never seen Ferdinand look at her. Her former fiancé had been all cool reserve and disinterest. Now, she was being observed as if she were some precious bejewelled thing this man wanted to pluck from a shelf, lock in a vault and keep to himself.

'Who'd have thought in this godforsaken country I'd find someone like you?'

There was some movement to the side and Lance turned his head. She didn't take her eyes from him. She couldn't. His profile, the perfect straight nose. Transfixed by the curve of his lips. His strong, angular jaw. She noticed then a thin white line just under his ear.

'You have a scar.'

His head whipped round, his eyes widening a fraction before his lips thinned. 'Don't we all?'

She shook her head. 'No. Here...'

Sara couldn't help it. She reached out to touch and he jerked away. Foolish girl. Those unseemly emotions had run away with her again. This, between them, meant nothing. It was a dalliance for him before he returned to the UK and forgot all about her.

*You'll never have his heart...*

That was fine. She could accept a man like Lance wouldn't really be interested in her. Anyhow, after her crushing engagement to the Crown Prince she didn't need some dashing duke in her life. She needed to find herself, find her way. Flirtation might be on the agenda. Attaching herself to another man like a limpet, only to have him prise her off? No way.

Sara took a deep breath. She should go, back to that stultifying table with her parents. She was about to step away when Lance moved first.

'I think we've done enough to ensure you're talked about for a while.'

She looked up at him and his expression now conveyed the same polite disinterest Ferdinand's had. She didn't know why the realisation hurt so much. She had no claim on Lance. She didn't really know him at all.

'That's a good thing?' she asked.

'You wanted scandal. This is as much as I can do for you. And now I should take my leave.' He turned his head again and she saw there was movement at the bridal table. 'The King and Queen appear done, and I won't keep royalty waiting.'

Lance clasped his hands behind his back and gave her a small bow. Then he turned and walked away, leaving her clutching his business card in her hand.

# CHAPTER THREE

LANCE WALKED THROUGH the cobbled back lanes of Morenburg old town. One more night here in Lauritania's capital and he'd be gone. He'd done his duty. He'd wished Rafe felicitations in his marriage but any hopes for his future happiness were a fiction.

Acid burned in his gut. Rafe was now one of them. Part of the Lauritanian aristocracy that had scorned them for years, though in the end Lance had sought their disapprobation. He supposed he couldn't fault his friend's choices. The chance to be a king didn't come round every day. Rafe had been on a quest for power even when they'd been teenagers. It had driven him to become almost the richest man in Europe. Still, that hadn't seemed to gain him the acceptance he craved. Not when the near feudal nature of this society was so ingrained.

Lance didn't care about acceptance. He'd tried once, but being the black sheep suited him better. His father might have fought to change the tide, but that man's respectability had only been surface-deep. Scratch it and he'd been as tarnished as the rest of them. He'd been mad for power too, would have done anything to ensure his family's fortune, his own career, even at the expense of his daughter. Vic had been shunted from boarding school to boarding school, whilst Lance had been dragged along to learn lessons from his father on politics, diplomacy and being 'a man'.

His father had once aspired to be prime minister. He'd never attained that lofty office, the family's chequered past not completely rehabilitated in his lifetime. In Lance, his father had hoped that dream would come true. As heir, Lance might have played along…until his parents had shown the contempt they truly had for their children's choices. He'd refused to engage with their machinations when pushed in the direction of a young woman his parents thought would kick-start a political career with an excellent wife from the right family. In truth, he'd been too interested in sampling the delights of many women rather than settling down with one for a career he wasn't sure he wanted. And, since he hadn't done his duty, Victoria had been forced into marriage.

He knew she'd done it to gain their approval. The girl who'd always been left behind whilst the family travelled for his father's postings. Searching for love and acceptance from people who didn't really see her value. He knew she'd attempted to buy those by agreeing to marry the man her parents had chosen for her. When Lance hadn't tried hard enough to stop her she'd promised things would be okay, that it was what she wanted.

But the deepest, darkest truth was that her marriage had got his parents off his back. The price she'd paid for his failings had been too high. The way she'd seemed to diminish over the years, from a vibrant young woman to something… *less*. Wilting under her husband's constant criticism, packaged as loving care. Lance's deepest fear was that the hurt wasn't only emotional.

That had set him on this path of destruction he so relished. Lance had gloried in his father's disappointment right up to the day the man had died. Even now he was mouldering in the family crypt, Lance hoped he didn't rest easy. Not after what he'd done to Victoria. The life she now lived. The bitter person who had replaced the hopeful young woman she'd once been. How he'd failed her was a wound that would never heal. As a child she'd adored him, followed him round whenever they'd been together. She would look at him as if he were some kind of hero when he'd tried to teach her how to fence or fly-fish.

He kicked at the ground with his foot as he walked, the anger always on a low simmer deep inside. This country brought back those thoughts—dark ones with no light in them. It made him far too introspective for his liking.

Except there was a flash of light here. A golden-haired angel who fitted in his arms as if she'd been made for him. He'd never really enjoyed dancing. He knew how to dance properly, because that had been expected of him, but he'd never seen the point of it when what he was really after was the main game of a woman horizontal. Until the reception last night, when what had started as thumbing his nose at the parents who'd turned her skin pale at the wake morphed into something else entirely. She was a woman to whom his body moulded seamlessly. He'd relished the light resting of her hand on his shoulder, the delicate grip of her other in his palm. Her slender waist and the way they moved together so perfectly. The time he'd spent with her had been more erotic fully clothed than anything he'd ever done naked.

Damn if he wasn't getting hard thinking about it. The lust washed away his bitterness and anger, replacing it with a thrum of anticipation he couldn't deny. If she were anyone else he might have stayed, sought her out and explored the blistering attraction, purely chemical and delectably rare. He knew she felt it too, from her dilated pupils and short breaths when he'd held her close, all soft and pliant as they moved together. They'd talked about the thrill of waiting. Of anticipation... All of that coursed, rich and heavy, through him. He could show her everything, hold her on a delicious edge for hours till she panted his name. But she was too innocent and *never* for him. She deserved a knight in shining armour. Not a wastrel. She'd already been engaged to one of those.

He exited the back streets into the bright autumn light of the main square with its emerald grass and flower gardens and fountains, making his way to the Hotel Grande Morenburg, its opulent sandstone façade dominating the street. As he did so, his phone vibrated in his pocket. He drew it out. The call was from his long-standing and, some might say, long-suffering butler.

'Is there a problem, George?'

Most of the time his estate and business interests ran smoothly, his trusted staff knowing exactly what he required and carrying out his wishes without question.

'Sir, the Snow family's rent is in arrears. Your agent is talking eviction. I thought you'd wish to know.'

Lance stalked into the hotel foyer through glass doors held open for him by gloved doormen who bowed as he passed.

'Mr Snow's unwell again?'

The family had been residents of the village for generations, proud people who didn't ask for help, even when they needed it.

'Yes, sir. In hospital.'

'The family require rent relief, not eviction. Ensure my wishes are made explicit. If the agent doesn't like it, make discreet enquiries about finding a new one.'

'Of course. Are you returning to London tomorrow?'

'Yes. There's nothing here to stop me.'

* * *

Lance hung up. The hotel hadn't changed since his first time here in his teens. Still gleaming gold with cream marble and massive urns of flowers adorning the foyer, the hush of opulence cocooning everyone privileged enough to be able to walk through. Time stood still here, like most of the country.

Well, he moved forward relentlessly. Hell, he wasn't going to stop for anything or anyone. He strode to the lifts. One more day, that was all he had here. Then he was gone. Leaving Rafe to his wealth and power and Sara Conrad safely untouched.

Near the lifts he caught a shadow, lurking behind one of the lush potted palms strategically placed all around the foyer, giving this place the illusion of an oasis away from the masses outside. A small figure all in black. Whilst he wasn't a stranger to illicit assignations, it was uncommon for him to find a woman loitering behind a plant in a foyer. But this alluring figure…a glimpse of golden curls escaping from under a black hat pulled low over her face… His heart kicked up a beat and his feet carried him to the palms in more of a hurry than his brain liked.

'Sara?'

She whipped round, her face pale and eyes wide as she seemed to falter and sway on her feet. He grabbed her elbow and steadied her. 'What are you doing here?'

She backed up against the wall, everything about her wound tight. That pulse of heat deep inside him started up again. The irrational flash of hope that her being here meant something. The curl of tightness in his gut making him crave to touch her skin, draw her close.

'I… I need to talk to you.'

Propositions were made to him all the time, business and erotic, by self-assured people as jaded and hungry as he was. They were always searching for something. That wasn't Sara, but part of him hoped, and feared in equal measure, that what she wanted was as dark and dirty as where his thoughts headed.

That she wanted *him*.

'Of course.' He motioned to gleaming French doors which led to the world-famous café where everyone who was anyone came to be seen. It was safer there—because the idea that they wanted one another had taken hold like a weed that couldn't be dug out. 'We can go—'

'No!' He didn't think she could get any paler, but somehow she had. Clutching an oversized bag close to her with whitened knuckles, her other hand curled tight into a fist. 'In private. Please.'

He held her gaze for a few heartbeats. It was impossible to tell what was going on behind those pale blue eyes of hers. But he knew fear when he saw it. The over-bright glitter of her gaze. A forced smile that wasn't for him, but for the world at large. There was nowhere private in this place to talk, and hiding behind a plant meant she didn't want to be seen. Really, there was only one option. Even if it started a pulse deep and low in his body, which he desperately fought to ignore.

'We can go to my room.'

Sara wilted a fraction, then straightened. Began walking to the lifts, all stiff and severe. He guided her to one, separate from the others. The gleaming gold doors whispered open and they walked inside. It was a small space— too small when she edged to the opposite corner and all he could smell were the flowers of some perfume he'd remember for ever as the scent of her. She slumped against the wall.

'The Presidential Suite?' she asked, her voice soft and lilting.

'It's always reserved for members of my family if we ever come here.' One of the benefits of being a friend of the deceased King. He loathed it, but still used it.

'Do you often?'

'No.' And he suspected after tomorrow he'd be here even less often than before.

The lift slid in a quiet rush to the top floor and the door opened with an elegant chime. Lance motioned for her to exit and slid his key card into the lock of a glossy white door, which released with a quiet click. He beckoned her in.

Sara walked ahead of him, through the parquetry entrance hall with its opulent vase of flowers, which didn't smell as delicious as her, towards an expanse of mullioned windows overlooking the old city. A view of tiled roofs swept down to Lake Morenburg, which sat in the middle of the scene like a livid blue inkblot staining the landscape, rimmed by the brooding Alps behind.

She stood at the panelled glass, staring out at the capital, the brilliant, bright day outside at odds with the gloomy dark clothing she wore. He hated that she appeared to still mourn a man who'd never deserved her.

'Would you like something? A drink? Coffee, perhaps?'

She shook her head then turned her back on the city and walked to the couch, falling onto it. Slid her bag from her shoulder and dropped it to the carpet with a thud. He wanted to go to her. Instead, he stood behind an armchair with his fingers gripping the back, pressing into the fine brocade fabric. Far safer here as she took the hat from her head and placed it on the table in front of her.

Sara ran her fingers distractedly through her hair to tame the curls that now spilled around her shoulders. He didn't want to be standing behind a damned armchair. He wanted to walk over to her, bury his hands into that unruly tangle and drag her to him like some caveman who had no place in her life. He'd crush this fragile creature who looked as if she could grow wings and flutter away from it all. So he didn't move.

'What do you want to talk about?'

He tried for cool, impassive. It seemed to jolt her out of some sort of inertia. She sat forwards, picking some lint from her black coat.

'Scandal.' There was nothing cool or impassive about her words. She blurted them out a little too loud and a lot too breathy. 'You said you could do that and I need one.'

Those words stabbed like a blade. Of course she didn't really want *him*. Anyone could give her a scandal. He didn't know why that hurt. He'd never cared before. That sort of question usually had him leaping in feet first with indecent enthusiasm.

Lance moved to sit in the armchair to her right, at the head of the coffee table. He was up for many things, but he loathed being used. When he walked into anything it was with eyes wide open, usually as the instigator. He couldn't abide secrets and lies from someone who wouldn't say what she *really* wanted. He demanded honesty at all times.

'What sort of scandal?'

Her eyes widened a fraction. 'Pardon?'

He crossed his leg, slung one ankle over his knee and sprawled there, not taking his eyes from her. 'Do you need a tiny garden-variety scandal that will excite a few gossips over their afternoon tea and cake? Or a monstrous scandal that threatens to tear the fabric of your known universe and leave everyone ducking for cover?'

'Something…in between, I suppose.'

The flame burning in his gut flared a bit brighter and

angrier. 'If you don't know what sort of scandal you want, I can't help you.'

She wasn't expecting that, he could tell. A small frown troubled her brow, her fingers restlessly smoothing over her dark trousers when she wouldn't look him in the eye.

Coward.

'Total ruin. Give me that.'

He gritted his teeth. He'd been thinking about the way she fitted in his arms, how she might feel the same, and she'd obviously been thinking about using him for her own mysterious ends. He wasn't sure why he found that so… disappointing.

'This isn't some bodice-ripper of a story you've pulled from under your bed, no matter what the tabloids say about me.'

She looked at him then, bold and bright, the Sara he'd dreamed she might be for real, rather than the woman she was showing him now—too much like the rest of them here in this abhorrent country. Wanting, expecting but not truly asking.

'I don't want my bodice ripped.'

At least she was prepared to tell him what she didn't want. Still. He leaned forwards, forearms on his knees, the curdle of disappointment rising in his throat. 'That tells me you have no idea what you're asking for. I'm no corruptor of innocents.'

'I'm not exactly innocent.'

He'd seen debauchery at its best and its worst. The aristocracy ran rife with it, and he'd partaken in plenty of the best. She didn't have a clue what she was talking about. He aimed to show her exactly how clueless she was, whilst she danced about him, playing games he detested.

'You either are or you aren't. There's no in-between. Some chaste kiss in a dark corner doesn't count.'

'It wasn't chaste. It was…' She looked at her hands, her fingernails. Anywhere bar at him. 'Moist.'

Which sounded like a hellish kiss, but a twist started in his gut nonetheless. She'd been engaged, but the thought of anyone kissing her… He didn't stop to question why the acid sensation felt a lot like jealousy. Anyhow, what did it matter? He'd made a rule long ago. Only deal with those as jaded and worldly as he was. He had no time or patience for anything else, no matter how tempting the package it was wrapped in.

'Chaste, moist…it's still only a kiss. Defiling virgins is not part of my repertoire.'

She looked at him then, eyes narrow and mouth pinched. She'd ignite tinder, the sparks flashing from her as she barely suppressed her anger.

'I don't know. It sounds like a fine addition to your business card. Purveyor of antiques, corruptor of innocents, defiler of virgins. Perfect for all you claim to be.' Slashes of red bled out over her cheeks. 'Except I'm not exactly a virgin, I suppose.'

Every person in this country would have expected Sara to enter her marriage to the Crown Prince a total innocent in all respects. Lance couldn't understand why the heat burned like lava in his gut, out of control and possessive. Still, he'd never show it. He leaned back in the chair as if he didn't care at all.

'No virgin sacrifice on the marriage bed, then. The Crown Prince would have been disappointed.'

The woman in question dropped her head again, as if she were embarrassed about the admission.

'He was.' She chewed her bottom lip almost hard enough to draw blood. 'He thought it would be a good idea to try before we married because… He said it would make the marriage night less…'

Lance clenched his fists. 'What a romantic. And did His Exalted Highness live up to all your expectations?'

He knew all about young women being forced into loveless marriages.

A shudder rippled through her. Her throat convulsed in a swallow.

'I had no expectations.' She held her head high and looked at him with bright, brimming eyes. 'Why are you being so cruel?'

Because he was furious. That she still hadn't asked him for what she truly desired, but seemed to think he was some kind of toy she could play with and discard. That a man who didn't deserve her had touched her, had made her first time awful, if her reaction was anything to go by, when it should have been world-ending.

The sooner he was out of this country with all its machinations, the better.

'Haven't you worked it out? I am who I am. Pick a descriptor. Despicable. Diabolical. I'm the Duke of them all.' Lance's jaw tightened. His hands clenched then relaxed. He stood and strode to a cabinet at the far side of the room—he needed a drink. It was past midday, so he wasn't being completely uncivilised. He grabbed a decanter and poured some whisky into a glass, tossing it down and relishing the burn. There was nothing more to be said. 'Go home, Sara.'

'No!' She launched herself from the couch and moved to the window again. Whipped round with her hair flailing about her shoulders, eyes wide. She looked exquisite. Untamed. Unattainable. Still innocent, no matter what she said about herself. He'd always adored a challenge, but she wasn't the challenge for him. 'I… I thought this would be easier. Being here. You're confusing me.'

A double shot of neat whisky so long after breakfast slid through his blood, but it wasn't the alcohol intoxicating him now. He stalked towards her.

'What about me confuses you?'

He didn't need her to answer. He knew exactly what she found confusing about him. It was written all over her. Her quickened breaths. Her eyes were wide, her lips parted, a pulse beating at the hollow of her neck. Something about it all made him reckless. Why *should* he care about her so much? She wanted a scandal. He could give it to her.

He reached out to all the spun-gold hair that fell around her shoulders. Took a thick curl and twisted it round his finger, before letting the gloriously silken strands slide free. He ached to plunge his hands into all that radiant hair. Tilt her head to his. Draw her close and kiss her like he'd wanted to from the moment she'd come into his arms on the dance floor. From the moment he'd seen her at the funeral, if he was being truthful. And he could show her many things. Obliterate any stuttering memory of awful sex with some bastard of a prince until the only word on her lips was the sigh of his name as she came again and again. Who was he to deny himself?

So he slid his hand along her jaw, relished the quickening breaths, her parted lips. He'd have her. The sex would be superlative and give her every bit of the scandal she craved, evidenced by the dilation of her pupils in those meltwater-blue eyes. Except another truth shone out from them which made him stop and pull back, even though his body screamed at him to continue. A pleading look that told him she was searching for someone to save her, when he was no saviour—for anyone. He'd failed his first test long ago, and had continued to fail ever since. A woman like Sara should not trust herself to his care, trust him for *anything.*

Lance pulled away and Sara swayed on her feet. Those dark shadows under her eyes, which he'd been too distracted to notice before, were telling. Had she been kept awake, reliving that dance and craving something more, as he had? After all the worldly delights he'd sampled over the years, it was hard to imagine that one ridiculously chaste turn around a dance floor could make a jaded man like him hot under the collar, but it had nonetheless.

'You don't know what you're asking for,' he said, his voice rough. He cleared his throat. It was tempting to walk over and drown himself in more drink, but that had never been his poison of choice, no matter what the tabloids liked to write about him. Now, drowning himself in her… He shut his errant thoughts down.

'Yes, I do. My parents…' she took a deep breath, as if she were fortifying herself for something '… I suspect they want me to marry.'

He stilled. A vision of Victoria's face swam into his head. Pale as her bridal whites, walking down the cathedral aisle on her wedding day. A tense smile, her eyes moist, shot at him as she'd neared the altar. He'd made a half-hearted offer to bundle her into a car and drive her away. To ignore what their parents wanted. But he'd joked about it and she hadn't realised how serious he'd been. Then again, he'd also neglected to investigate the exalted man they'd chosen for her. If he'd asked even a few questions he'd have discovered her future husband was not someone who should be allowed near women. He'd failed to extricate her from a terrible situation, one he feared became worse as each blighted year passed. But no. None of this was his business.

Attempt to help and he'd fail again. It was better that Sara stood up for herself.

'You've just escaped one marriage. They've tried that before. It ended in disaster. And you're still in mourning, if your black clothes are anything to go by.'

'That doesn't matter to them… Our dance. They said I was running wild, that what I did was disgraceful…'

Lance barked out a laugh. 'A dance—disgraceful? Your parents have no idea.' The hypocrisy of it, when they were happy to offer their daughter to all and sundry, was astonishing.

'They say I'm to work on the man's art collection but, from the way they keep hinting, I *know* it's more. And the man they want for me…he looks like a toad.' She glanced up at him in a shy kind of way from behind veiled lashes, reminding him of how truly innocent she was. 'You don't. You're not toad-like at all.'

That admission of hers, in that hesitant voice, sent a sinuous curl of desire through him once more. He ignored it, knowing no good would come of this. 'Maybe you'll turn him into a prince with a kiss.'

She crossed her arms and glared at him. 'That only works with frogs. *Not* toads. And I don't want a *prince*.'

The words were left hanging in the air, unspoken. *I want you.* He ignored every inclination to give in to temptation.

'I don't see how a supposed scandal is going to help.'

'You know how it is here. People like him, they want someone above reproach. If I'm not… But look.' She ran over to her bag and rummaged around. Pulled out a large blue velvet box and opened it. Inside sat the exquisite amethysts and diamonds of an antique parure, the fat gemstones glittering in the natural light. 'I can pay you if you help me.'

Little shocked him, but this rendered him close to speechless. 'What the hell are you asking?' He'd never been offered payment before. It made him feel as grubby as he pretended to be. Lance grabbed the box from her and closed the lid. Thrust it back towards her. 'They're not part of the Crown Jewels, are they?'

Sara shook her head, took back her jewels. 'My twenty-first birthday present. But I don't wear the parure, since I loathe purple.'

'You loathe purple?' He snorted a mocking laugh. When he'd glimpsed her in the foyer he'd had high hopes, but now they'd descended into farce. 'I have money of my own. How do you think I'm in the Presidential Suite?'

She at least had the good grace to blush. 'I thought you said you needed to replenish the family coffers, what with all the gambling.'

He gritted his teeth. Hissed the words through them. 'My father quite successfully rehabilitated the Astill name and fortune…' through canny politics and beneficially marrying off his only daughter '…and I'm sure all our ancestors, rakes and wastrels as they were, are rolling in their graves in horror. I've come along to rectify his errors, not continue them. And I certainly don't take money from women for my services. I will not sleep with you.'

She looked up at him, her eyes big and bright with unshed tears. 'You won't help me?'

'No means no, even in Lauritania. I suggest you try using the word on your parents.'

'I have, once before. When I found out Ferdinand didn't love me.' Sara gave a shaky laugh. 'I'm not sure he even liked me. I told them and it didn't matter. All that mattered to them was me being Queen one day. The power they'd gain. And they want it now.'

'You're looking for a hero, Sara.' She wasn't his responsibility. He'd failed at caring for anything, cultivated by years of selfishness. 'I'm not that man. I never was.'

'I need to leave the country and I don't really have money of my own.' She bent down and picked up her bag. Placing her hat on her head, she asked, 'How much do you think the parure is worth?'

'For the complete set, about fifty thousand euros, give or take.'

'Then I'll sell it. I'm sure there's someone who'll take it.'

'A shark might, for a quarter of that.'

'I understand. I'll go.' She hitched the bag high on her shoulder. He didn't want her to leave. She couldn't stay. 'Thank you for your time, Your Grace.'

The words hung bitter in the air, mocking him, as she no doubt knew they would.

'Sara.'

She walked to the door, turned and looked up at him with brimming blue eyes. 'It's fine. I'm sure it'll be fine.'

*It'll be fine, Lance.* Victoria had said those words too, moments prior to agreeing to her engagement, which had been beneficial to everyone bar the woman herself. He should have done more to stop her. To convince her to ignore their parents and refuse. But Vic had been the good child. Sweet and kind...once. Full of life, riding her beloved horses and caring for any orphaned or abandoned creatures she found. But not now. All the life and caring in her had bled away. She'd done what had been asked of her when Lance had refused a political marriage. And nothing about her life had been fine since.

Sara began to open the door. He had no doubt she'd say no to her parents. But what if that didn't change anything? If he read in the papers that she'd ended up with the toad she feared her parents wanted her to marry? Lance knew he'd never forgive himself.

He hadn't been able to save Victoria, but he could try to save another woman. Getting her out of the country would be easy, he had a private jet waiting for him at the airport. In the end, some small redemption might come from the golden-haired angel in front of him.

'Stay. Please.' He walked towards her and put his hand on the door above her head, gently closing it. Keeping her in. Hopefully keeping her safe. 'I'll help you get away.'

Sara slumped against the door. Lance stood perilously close, his hand above her head, crowding her. As he had when he'd stalked towards her with intent and cupped her cheek as if he was going to kiss her. She took a deep breath, overwhelmed by the warmth of his body. The scent of him. The hint of leather from his casual jacket, which still seemed to cling to his skin, and another scent, something earthy and intoxicating. She closed her eyes for a moment, wishing he'd drop his mouth to hers. Show her what a kiss could truly be like. But she didn't think she'd survive it. Not at the moment, when every cell in her body was exhausted. As if she could slide down the cool wood of the door and simply curl up on the floor.

Instead of doing that, she turned in the cage of his body and looked up at him. His eyes were searching her face. She sensed everything was fragile—this seeming truce, his agreement to help her. She wanted to ask why, after being so cruel to her, but she couldn't. If she said anything he might send her away again, and she couldn't go back.

'Thank you.' The words were soft and breathy, hardly sounding like hers at all because she almost couldn't get enough air with him so close.

He pushed away from her and walked over to the cabinet again. She felt as if all the light and warmth had been taken from her. She wanted it back.

'I'm having another drink.' He held up a glass, raised his eyebrows. He looked more casual today, in jeans that hung low on his narrow hips, a crisp white shirt moulding to the expanse of his muscular chest. The dark leather jacket made him look in some way almost…dangerous. 'Want one?'

Sara nodded, unable to say anything. She walked over to the couch and sank into it again. Leaning back into the down-stuffed cushions, her eyelids felt heavy. If she closed them, she could sleep for a hundred years.

Lance strolled over to her calmly, with his long, swaggering gait. He looked so relaxed it was as if this sort of thing happened to him every day—being begged for assistance by damsels in distress. He handed her a glass with a long pour of amber fluid. She took it and sipped. The peaty taste burned her throat, making her cough, but she didn't care. This might numb all those feelings, and she wanted to feel numb, for a little while. Feelings were overrated.

Lance sprawled in the armchair opposite her. 'Why do you think your parents are planning another marriage for you?'

Sara toyed with the sparkling crystal tumbler. The reasons were many. She'd guessed her parents' coffers were running low. Paintings had mysteriously gone missing from walls, rooms looking a little bare as furniture disappeared. The hint that her engagement ring didn't need to go back to the royal vault, that it could stay with them. She wasn't a fool—she knew what that meant. She'd just never thought they'd sell her off. More than once, anyhow.

'Well, none of my parents' friends trust the Queen, and the King—'

'Oh, I know what they think of him.'

'But it's more. If I'd been Queen it would have given them the ultimate power and prestige. Opened even more doors. Now that's all gone. They're afraid of losing what they'd come to expect. And they can't afford to lose any more. They might say it's only a job they want me to take, a chance to finally use my art degree, but I *know* it's more. They made hints at the wedding. It's also the way that man looks at me. Like I'm a…' Sara shuddered again.

She was no fool. The man looked at her as if she were a smorgasbord and he was starving. As if he were *entitled* to her, talking about a long and bountiful future she didn't want and had no interest in.

'Who's your new intended?' Lance's voice was cold as a winter ice storm.

'Lord Scharf.'

He took a long slug of his drink. Raked a hand through his hair. 'The man's over forty.'

'I know.'

'You're right, he looks exactly like a toad. We can't have you marrying that. You deserve someone dashing.' Sara trembled. The liquid in her glass quivered. She took another sip, yet the shaking wouldn't stop. A slight crease formed between Lance's brows. 'Do you want a blanket?'

Sara wanted to curl up in something soft, and sleep. Instead she inclined her glass to him. 'This'll warm me up. And I don't need to marry anyone.'

She wanted to live her life on her own terms for once. Not be beholden to a man, to any person. She'd had enough of being compliant, of not speaking up, for a lifetime. All she wanted was room to be herself for a while. Deciding what she really wanted could come later.

'A woman after my own heart. What *do* you need?'

Lance might have looked as if he were lounging in the chair, slouching in a masculine kind of way. Yet there was a tension about him, like a wildcat ready to spring.

What she needed was some fun and adventure. To experience more of the feeling she'd had when she'd danced with him. The thrill of doing things she shouldn't. Of not being perfect all the time. Taking a little for herself. Of having a *choice*, not being dictated to by others. Being held in the arms of a man who looked at her as if she were the centre of his universe. She needed *lots* of things. But she hadn't really prepared for any of them beyond finding Lance and convincing him to help her. All she'd really done was grab the parure as she'd fled the only home she'd ever known.

Here, she was weak, completely worn down and fragile from the years of having no real control over her life. She supposed she could go to the Queen to ask for help, but Annalise was newly married—and what could she say? *Your brother didn't love me and he was cheating on me. My parents didn't care. They want me to marry someone else.* Lise had only just buried her family. Sara wouldn't add to the complications in her friend's life, or to her grief.

She took a final sip of her drink. 'I need a place to…hide for a little while.'

Lance blew out a long breath and looked about the room, then to her oversized tote. 'Have you got another bag? Clothes?'

'No. I… I grabbed some…' her cheeks heated '…underwear.'

She'd not planned in the end, just snatched some things and fled.

He snorted a laugh. 'Thank God for clean underwear then. Well. Clothes we can—'

A knock sounded at the door. Sara leapt from her seat,

her drink sloshing onto her hand. She placed the glass on the table, her heart pounding so hard it felt as if it could burst from her chest. No one should have access to the Presidential Suite other than staff at the hotel, and Lance hadn't called them for anything. The room also looked like housekeeping had already been. No breakfast plates left on the dining table in front of the windows. Everything in its place.

'They're looking for me.' Her breathing came out in gasps, as if she couldn't get any air. They were here for her. She knew it.

'Why?'

He had no idea. Her days were diarised to the last second, and she was always trailed by someone. For a long time she hadn't left the house without an army of people knowing exactly where she was headed, ostensibly for protection, but after the Crown Prince had died she wasn't sure what the need was. She wasn't important any more.

'I always have security. Today I...left.' Without a word to anyone.

'Does anyone know you're here?'

'I asked for you at Reception.'

Lance rose from his chair, calm and slow. Took another long sip of his drink. Pinned her with a hard stare, pointing over her shoulder. 'Bedroom. That way. Take your things.'

His voice was low and authoritative. Too soft for someone outside the room to hear, but to her it screamed loud as a shout. That he seemed to believe what she said was telling.

She grabbed her coat, hat and bag and hurried out through a doorway, closing it behind her. Then she remembered she'd left her glass on the coffee table. She opened the door a crack. Perhaps she could get it. But the murmur of voices signalled it was too late.

She tried to slow her breathing, but it came in thready

gasps. She couldn't hear much, only snatches of words like *'value'* and *'jewels'*. *'No'* and *'search'*?

Sara backed away from the door without thinking. Her chest heaving, she scanned the room for somewhere to hide and spotted a closet. She wrenched open the door and backed inside, closing it after her. Dropping her bag to the floor. She shouldered through hangers and clothes. Slid down the back wall till she sat on the carpeted floor. Wrapped her arms round her legs and huddled as tight as she could make herself. Every sound was muffled in the darkness of the closet. She tried to tamp down the sick feeling burning in her throat, the fear that they'd find her and take her home. She swallowed. Lance was a duke. His father had been respected here. Whatever he said, they'd believe.

But what if he gave her up to avoid trouble? She hugged her knees even tighter. He wouldn't do that. Would he? The silence crushed her as she tried to curl into herself, make herself as small and insignificant as possible. To embrace in physical form how she'd felt for years, with nothing but the cocooning blackness around her and the slight sliver of light shining through the crack between the doors. Then she dropped her head onto her knees so she couldn't even see that. Waiting for what seemed so long. Too long...

Sara jerked her head up at the cool breeze of the door opening. Coat hangers scraped on the bar above her as two arms reached in and pushed them back.

'Oh, angel.' Lance leaned forwards and reached out his right hand. 'Come here.'

She placed her hand in his as he pulled her upwards and she threw herself into his muscular chest, one sob after another cracking the veneer she'd presented to the world. He wrapped his arms round her, drew her tight as she gripped the front of his shirt and held on, all that strength cradling her as she wept in his arms.

'It's okay,' he murmured, cradling the back of her head with his hand. 'They're gone now. I'll look after you.'

She felt safe for the first time in longer than she could remember. The sobs petered out to hiccups, and then to sniffs as Lance held her, whispering gentle words she couldn't make sense of, till she came back into herself. Relishing the comfort of being truly held, pressed against his hard, strong body, she became aware of her ragged breaths and how his hand stroked up and down her back, soothing her. She could stay here all day, but she lifted her head, looking into his concerned face. He loosened his arms then and she pulled back and wiped her face. His shirt was a crushed, damp mess.

'I'm sorry.' She reached out and began smoothing the creases in the previously pristine cotton. The taut curve of the muscles underneath distracted her, the tight nubs of his nipples as she brushed her hands over them. He put his hands over hers to still them and his nostrils flared.

'A shirt I can have laundered.' If only washing away what had hurt her was so easy. 'Are you all right now?' His voice sounded strangely rough.

She nodded, his body hot under her palms. She pulled her hands away and wrapped them round herself.

'They were looking for me?'

'Yes. But I gave them enough truth to make the lie believable.'

'Which was?'

'You came to ask for a valuation of a piece of jewellery you'd been given for your twenty-first birthday. I valued it, and you left. Told them you'd asked for suggestions for a few pawn shops in the city where you might be able to sell it. Hopefully they're on a wild goose chase.'

'Thank you.'

He frowned. 'They were persistent and came with a man who looked like personal security.'

She shivered. He walked towards her and took her by the arm, guiding her to the vast bed. 'Sit. Before you fall.'

She shook her head. 'I need to keep moving. What if they look at the security cameras? They won't stop looking until they find me. I've brought trouble to your door.'

'Is your phone turned off?'

She nodded. 'When I left home.'

'Then keep it off. And you needn't worry. They'll believe me and, even if they don't, I enjoy trouble and loathe bullies. But are you certain you want a scandal?'

'Even when I have no idea what kind of scandal I want?'

He smiled then, a wicked smirk that made her overheated and trembling. Once again, here was the man she'd read about in the media. The bad boy they loved to write about.

'Luckily I'm an expert. I can guide you. How about one where you're protected? You'll look naïve at the end, but you can walk away with your head held high. And you'll be untouchable.'

'That sounds perfect. What are you planning?'

'An engagement.'

She sat on the edge of the bed then, because the shock at his comment meant her legs couldn't be trusted to support her. 'What?'

'Of convenience. Your parents seem to be worried you've fallen under my spell. Let's make it real. If we're pulled up here or at the airport, we'll say it was love at first sight and we're engaged. The press will lap up the story of a romance out of the ashes of your heartbreak. No one will try to take you away from me after that. Once you've found your feet, you can break the engagement off and give a tearful interview to the press.'

'Saying you had an affair?'

He frowned. 'No matter what the tabloids claim, I'd never be unfaithful. You could simply confirm I'm the wastrel they say I am. You'll look a little naïve and I'll look like the cad.'

'But you're not.'

'The press say I'm the Dastardly Duke.'

It was her turn to frown. She didn't care what the press thought of him really. She wondered what Lance thought of *himself*, though. 'In my opinion Dashing Duke would be a better description.'

He shrugged. 'Whatever the adjective, it solves a problem. I can appear suitably heartbroken for a while before returning to my old ways. What do you say? My jet's scheduled to fly out tomorrow morning. We can be in London by lunchtime, with the scandal well underway.'

It sounded thrilling, it was everything she'd been hoping for, except... She dropped her head to her hands and groaned.

'I'd like to say, *Let's go!* But I don't have my passport.'

'You have clean underwear but no means of escape.' He chuckled, the sound deep and throaty as it rumbled right through her. 'Well, I *have* been in stickier situations. Leave it with me. Since I happen to know Lauritania's King.'

# CHAPTER FOUR

LANCE SAT BACK on one of the deep, comfortable seats of the jet, watching the sleeping form of Sara in front of him. She was lying still in her reclined chair, her chest rising and falling gently, her pale lashes fanning her cheeks. Rose-coloured lips were slightly parted. Her knees barely brushed his. At least the dark smudges under her eyes were halfway gone after she'd fallen exhausted into his bed the night before.

He'd been a gentleman for once and taken the couch. Lying back, he thought how delectable and fragile she'd looked wearing one of his shirts, since she'd brought nothing with her except clean underwear, which he steadfastly refused to think about any more, because visions of whether they were lace or plain, matching or contrasting, conservative or risqué had plagued his thoughts for most of the night. At least he'd had work to do, things to keep him occupied. Usually his escapades were unplanned adventures, where he relished the spontaneity. This type of scandal required planning, so he'd put his wakefulness to good use. He only hoped Sara would be pleased with his efforts.

Their escape in the morning, such as it was, had gone smoothly. No one had questioned her as Sara had crept from the hotel to a waiting car whilst he checked out. The cloak-and-dagger nature of it had set his heart racing. Even for him, helping a damsel in distress flee a country was something new. Her passport was freshly minted and delivered early morning via special courier. Lance smiled. Knowing a king proved to have some benefits, even though Rafe had been somewhat chastened and mysteriously wandering about the palace cellars when Lance had arrived. There was a story there that one day he might try to discover, but not now. He had better things to turn his attention to. Putting a smile back on Sara's beautiful face was one of them.

She needed some joy, that was clear. If he still had a heart, finding her huddled in the cupboard behind his clothes would have broken it. As it was, all he could do for the woman in front of him was hold her as she sobbed. And wasn't he the bastard to relish the emotion that brought her into his arms again? Clutching at him as if he were the only thing keeping her afloat. All soft and sweet-smelling, like a flower garden. Then when she'd started petting him like a cat he'd wanted to purr under her fingers. Have her touch bare skin rather than a cursed shirt.

Those insidious thoughts burrowed deep and low. Enticing imaginings that would have had him undoing the top button on his shirt, had he been dressed more formally. As it was, Lance adjusted himself in his seat. The whole episode had been entirely innocent from her perspective. Nothing to get excited about, but still he anticipated the next moment when Sara might look at him as if he were her eternal saviour...

The seatbelt light flicked on with a chime. The flight attendant walked through to remind them to return their seat backs to the upright position as they prepared for landing. Sara opened bleary eyes, blinked a few times and stretched like a kitten in the sunshine.

'Almost there,' he said. She arched her arms back above her head, the sombre shirt she wore stretching tight over her breasts in a way that was far too distracting. He took a final mouthful of the champagne they'd been given to carry them through the three-hour flight. 'Are you ready for what's to come?'

'What's that?'

Perhaps he should simply have helped her escape the country and then let her go. But she still carried a pale, haunted look that spoke of her family's, and perhaps the world's, betrayal. He'd couldn't leave her to whatever wolves might lurk out there, wanting to take a bite of this pretty little lamb.

'The press. A fiancée's going to cause a certain stir. I'm an avowed bachelor who doesn't want to do his ducal duty and breed.'

In a flash, he could see Sara's children. Little moppets with blonde curls and blue eyes, as angelic as her. He didn't know why that strange thought assailed him at that moment. Or why the vision of her cradling those beautiful children, the ones she deserved, left him feeling a little…wistful.

Sara wrapped her arms round her waist and stared out of the window as the pilot announced their descent. 'I'm used to the press.'

He wasn't sure she knew what she was letting herself in for, but he'd shield her from the worst of it for a little while. Before the storm truly took hold and they were ripped along in its maelstrom.

'There's no press like the tabloids in the UK. The Lauritanian media are collared and caged by comparison. At home they roam vicious and wild, free to write what they want, and they love writing about me.'

'I know. Your exploits are popular.' Something inside him stirred. He liked it that she'd researched him, but loathed what she might have found. Most of it was an exaggeration he did nothing to discourage, because it suited his purposes. Only the most cynical tried to get close to the Debauched

Duke. 'Why a bachelor? No children? They seem like normal things to want for most people.'

Here was that hoary little chestnut which got some women stuck, no matter his brutal honesty with them. Convinced they could change him. He clenched his fists. Flexed his fingers. These were the questions he'd been asked by more than a few women who'd looked at him, pretending to be wide-eyed and innocent, when he could see the hopeful gleam shining in their eyes, revealing their desire to become the Duchess of Bedmore. Though Sara seemed to have lost any gleam altogether, sitting opposite him looking tired and washed out. Not at all hopeful. He suspected that her enquiry was guileless, with no hidden agenda.

'The world does not require any more Astills,' he said.

His father had wanted to make the name *great* again, and Lance was witness to where coveting greatness could lead. To his shame, in his early twenties, thoughts of his destiny and inheritance had been heady ones. Whilst he eschewed it now, when he'd left Lauritania and returned to England he'd caught up with friends like himself, with power and privilege, wielding it whichever way they wished. He hadn't been true to himself or the promises he and Rafe had made at school. He'd succumbed to the allure of wealth and the benefits of privilege. It had almost entirely corrupted him.

Until Victoria.

She'd suffered, being only a tool used along the way to further his father's quest for reflected greatness—the true victim of his parents' schemes. Now, it didn't matter that his father was dead. His life's quest was to tear down what had been built and toss the tiny pieces to the four winds.

'Why? Yours is one of the oldest families in the country. You have a long history, some of it…eccentric. But doesn't that mean anything?'

He tugged at the cuffs of his shirt. He supposed it was hard for her to understand after a life devoted to duty and expectation. He was the perfect person to show her. Still, the prick of what he suspected was disapprobation stung. Lance wasn't sure why. It wasn't as if he usually cared what anyone thought.

'It means *nothing*. I've told you what a pack of wastrels we all are. Remind me to take you to the portrait gallery at Astill Hall and tell you some of the stories. It'll make your hair curl.'

'I don't need my hair any curlier, thank you.' Sara reached to her wrist and took a hair tie from round it, restraining all those glorious strands. The band left a slight mark on her pale skin. He reached out to smooth it away, then stopped himself.

'I thought you said your father had rehabilitated the family?' she asked.

Lance swallowed, to equalise the pressure in his ears. With him not wanting children and Victoria being unable to have them, no matter how hard she'd tried, the earth would be washed clean of their blood. There'd be nothing left *to* rehabilitate.

'Nothing can take away the stain of all those black sheep. The best thing to do is put us all out of our misery. But enough about me.' Their interactions weren't meant to be about deep and meaningful questions. For her, at least, it was about injecting some fun into her life—and he knew *all* about fun. Still, on that front, they had work to do. 'Our first job is to get you some clothes. Then we'll take the helicopter to Astill Hall.'

She'd like that. Shopping, then a sightseeing flight over London on their way to the country, keeping her away from the capital, where the worst of the tabloids lurked. At least in his ancestral home he could maintain some control and privacy. Hell knew when he'd become so considerate. It was an unfamiliar sensation.

Sara smoothed her hands over the exquisitely tailored but dreadful black trousers. He wanted to burn every black item of clothing she owned. Dress her in jewelled colours so she couldn't pretend to grieve any longer.

Sara shook her head. A rogue curl fell free over her face. She tucked it behind her ear.

'I don't have any money for shopping.'

'I do.' Lance shrugged. 'No fiancée of mine is ever going to pay for her own things. It's one of the perks of being with me, even in a sham engagement.'

None of the women he'd been with who *weren't* his fiancée had complained about his generosity. In fact, they'd seemed ecstatic. He enjoyed making people happy, *especially* women. But Sara fixed him with a glare that would have slapped down even royalty.

'I need to sell the parure and I need a job.'

'If you really want to offload the jewels, they'll be taken care of today. As for work, you don't have the right visa, so that poses a problem. But you don't need a job immediately.'

'So you expect your fiancée to sit at home and take care of the manor?'

Strangely, that idea suddenly had boundless appeal. Someone there other than staff and the lonely halls, half of which he'd shut down because he didn't use them. A beautiful, smiling face welcoming him home, with little blonde cherubs running behind her when she opened the door to greet him as he…

An odd warmth ignited in his chest at the thought. He slammed those thoughts into the vault of his imagination.

'Of course not.' The damned champagne was addling his brain. He should have stuck to water.

'Then I need to do something.'

With her lack of experience and a fine arts degree, he suspected there weren't many places who would take her, *except...* 'You can work with me.'

'I can't take your clothes or your money!'

'You can't continue to wear what you're wearing now, since it's all you have.' The vision of her in one of his shirts the night before drifted lazily through his consciousness. It had swamped her. She'd looked impossibly alluring, scrubbed clean of make-up, all mussed up as if they'd just had... Once again he tried to shut down his errant imagination. When had it become so fertile? 'And if not money, didn't Ferdinand give you gifts?'

He didn't know why the words hissed out so vehemently.

'No. The only thing he ever gave me was the engagement ring.'

With all the Crown's riches, her fiancé should have draped her in gems, spread glittering trinkets over her flawless, naked flesh...

He *really* needed to stick to business.

'You won't be taking my money. You'll be earning it, in a way. Whilst I can't officially employ you, we can come to some sort of arrangement. I'm always looking for treasure. You might be able to help me find some.'

She sat up a bit straighter and a beaming smile broke out over her face, as beautiful as the first rays of sunshine spilling over the horizon. A man could be quite dazzled by her, if he allowed himself.

'I used to do that in the Morenburg markets.'

Undiscovered antiques were the only thing of worth in Lauritania, as far as he was concerned.

'Did you find any treasures?'

Sara cocked her head to the side, her eyes narrowed, the corner of her mouth curling till she looked quite sly.

'It's a...secret.'

He saw what she was doing. The thrill of it was like a lick of fire igniting in his belly. 'Don't keep me waiting.'

Sara put her finger to her lips and tapped, as if she were thinking. 'I seem to recall someone telling me it was *all* about the excitement of waiting.'

She thought to turn those tables on him? He chuckled. 'One day, angel, I'll truly teach you about waiting for what you crave. That'll be one hell of a lesson.'

Her face softened, and her mouth opened as if it was too hard to take in air. Her pupils flared, big and dark, in the pale blue of her eyes. She shifted in her seat as his words were left hanging in the air. What was he playing at? This game was about saving Sara, not seducing her.

'How about we make a deal?' he asked, wrestling the conversation back on track.

'O...okay?'

He tried to ignore her little stutter. The way the word came out all soft and hopeful.

'You tell me, and I'll tell you.'

She laughed and it seemed as if the whole day brightened around him again.

'It's not much, really. A miniature teapot in pristine condition, which I think is antique Meissen porcelain. My art history tutor was having it appraised. He believes it's quite rare.'

Whilst she said it wasn't much, Sara sat up straighter, her face alight, gaze distant as if she was recalling the moment she'd found it. He understood that electric sensation, discovering something others had forgotten about or didn't value.

'Well done,' he said. 'Highly collectible.'

She shrugged. 'It's impossibly pretty, and I was lucky.'

Then she leaned forwards, hands clasped in front of her. 'Now it's your turn.'

'Remember, it's yet to be authenticated.' But it would be, he was certain of it. Lance leaned back in his chair, stretching the moment out, his heart beating a little faster even now, his recollection of that moment twelve months before when he'd unwrapped a filthy oilcloth and uncovered a masterpiece.

'A Caravaggio. Found it in someone's attic.'

Her eyes widened. *'No.'*

How he wanted to reach forwards, cup her face in his hands and brush his lips across hers. Take their mutual excitement and channel it into something messier and hotter. But Sara wasn't for him. She was looking at him as if he were some miracle when his life was littered with failings.

'Yes. And *when* it's authenticated it'll cause a huge stir.'

'But that's worth...'

'It's priceless.'

In so many ways. Most importantly, in creating an escape plan for his sister. She'd refused all offers of money to help her leave her husband, claiming it was somehow tainted. She wouldn't take anything from a fortune bestowed on him by the family that had hurt her so terribly. That meant any financial assistance he offered had to come from what he *earned* in his business. With the sale of the Caravaggio, he'd have proof that the funds had come from his work and not the family coffers. That painting was a way to help Vic, make her safe.

'I wish I could find something like that. It would feel amazing.' She was looking up at him in wonder now. As if he held the secrets of the universe. He wanted to keep that look on her face, even though he didn't deserve it.

'It did. Which brings me back to you and your need for

finances. Help me, and if you locate anything of value I'll gift you the equivalent of the buyer's premium at auction when our arrangement ends. Fifteen percent.'

'I— What? Wait.' Sara held up her hands. 'You say you're buying my clothes. Now this? I can't take charity.'

'It's not charity. I own an auction house. I find hidden treasure and sell it. You have the right qualifications and want to find treasure too. It's perfect.'

She shook her head. Another golden corkscrew of hair tumbled free. She blew it out of her eyes. 'Even if I can't be an employee, I want to be paid as if I were.'

'I don't have another employee like you.'

'*Exactly.* It isn't a commercial arrangement. I… I'll take two percent.'

'Accepting that would be robbery on my part. I have the funds, why won't you take them?'

'I need to learn to look after myself. What about when we're not together? What then?'

Lance frowned. In these moments she sounded so much like Vic… Yet he understood pride. He needed to play smart here. He shrugged.

'I suspect it will cost me nothing, since you're unlikely to find anything of value at all. But if you're concerned… twelve percent.'

Sara's eyes narrowed, and her lips pursed. Ah, he had her now.

'Of *course* I'll find something. Five.'

'Ten.'

'Seven and a half. And that's *final.*'

It wasn't enough, but he'd give it to her. He sensed she needed a win of her own.

'You strike a hard deal, Lady Sara.' Lance held out his hand and she slipped her cool palm into his as they shook in agreement. He should let her go but marvelled at how it was the perfect fit. Their eyes met, palms locked between them. Her eyes widened.

Then the plane jolted with a bump on the tarmac and began taxiing to the terminal. She pulled her hand from his. He missed the warmth of her soft skin on his own. Craved it like some beacon in the darkness, when in truth the darkness was where he belonged.

Moments after they left the plane, everything had become a blur of activity. Sara's head still spun. After some short time to freshen up, they'd been collected by car to travel to London. She'd exchanged details with his secretary so she could sync Sara and Lance's diaries. When she briefly turned on her phone to check the coming days' events, multiple message alerts angrily pinged at her. She turned it off, dropping it into her bag.

Lance looked up from his phone, on which he'd been assiduously working, cocking one eyebrow. 'Trouble?'

Most of the messages had come from her parents and brother. But there was one from Annalise. Her family, she wouldn't deal with. Lise, she *couldn't*. How could she admit what was going on to her friend?

She shrugged. 'It's to be expected. Where are we going now?'

She and Lance had come to a kind of agreement about her clothes. He'd arranged for someone to meet them at Astill Hall that very afternoon and had handed over his phone so she could speak to a lovely woman who'd asked what she was looking for in terms of style. 'Economical and fun' was what Sara wanted. Lance had taken the phone and insisted that not an item of clothing was to be black. Sara didn't really care. He was paying, after all. But when her parure was sold, she'd pay him back. Anything else didn't seem right, especially when she needed to take care of herself.

The car began to slow, and then came to a stop. The chauffeur opened his door.

'Could you give us a few moments?' Lance asked.

The driver nodded and left the vehicle, standing close by.

'The minute we step out of this car, the game begins.' Lance's voice was low and steady, in some ways reassuring. And still her heart skipped a few beats.

'What game?'

His responding slow grin was pure wickedness. If it could be bottled, it would corrupt millions and send the world into chaos. 'The tabloid media—one of my favourite amusements. Are you ready to play?'

'Yes.'

He clapped his hands together. 'Excellent! Now, what's your favourite food? Not something ordinary. Your guilty pleasure.'

She looked at him, sitting there in a magnificent pin-striped suit and pristine sky-blue shirt. His hair gleamed like burnished gold. This man, *he* could become her guilty pleasure. It would be so easy to lose her head around him. But he didn't want her. He'd made that clear. It wasn't what he was asking for…

'Sacher torte.'

'Excellent choice. Now…' He nodded to the driver, who opened Lance's door. Lance hopped out and bent down to look at her. 'Look at me like you look at a slice of Sacher torte. You know you want it but shouldn't have it. It's decadent. It's *sinful*. You're going to eat it anyhow.'

She didn't know what to say. Her mouth dropped open, because the idea of thinking of him like that was now filling her brain. He frowned.

'You look like you've come down with indigestion.'

She shut her eyes. 'Okay. Right.' She took a deep breath, because she knew how to act. She'd spent a lifetime doing so. When she opened her eyes again she allowed herself to admire the tempting hint of chest where he wore no tie. Wondered how his skin would feel there. If she'd be able to feel the beat of his heart under her palm…

'Perfect. Just like that,' he murmured, his gaze softening. 'Good girl.'

The words made her feel like a *bad girl*. If a human being could self-combust, she would have lit up like a torch. She wasn't sure her legs would work right now. Everything about her simply melted.

He seemed to realise she needed a bit of help, reaching his hand into the car, palm up. She placed hers into it and he squeezed, then assisted her out. He slipped his arm round her waist and led her down a narrow, cobbled lane to a small midnight-blue door. The only sign on the premises was a name, John T Smith, in gleaming gold.

'What is this place?' she asked.

'Somewhere we can find a man who can help with your amethysts.'

'Is John Smith really his name?'

The corner of Lance's mouth curved up into a sly smile. 'I've never been impolite enough to ask.'

As he pushed the door open a little bell tinkled. They walked into the dimly lit room, which glittered with sparkling glass display cabinets full of gold, silver and porcelain. The walls were adorned with magnificent artworks in ancient gilded frames.

'Oh.' It was all she could say. She knew the value of some of the pieces here. It was an incredible collection of rare and valuable objects.

'Thought you'd appreciate it,' Lance murmured.

A man walked out from behind a curtain. He was wiry and small like a jockey, with a beaming smile for Lance.

'Your Grace, how good to see you again.' His voice sounded overly deferential, but he winked at Sara, and she smiled back at him.

'Cut it, John.'

'I'm trying to be properly polite to my betters.'

Lance sighed. 'When have you ever thought me better than you?'

'Never.' He turned his attention to Sara then. 'But this vision before me. She's better than the both of us combined.'

'She is indeed.' Lance squeezed her hand and introduced them. 'You know why we're here.'

'The parure. May I see it?'

Sara dug into her bag and handed over the box. The man behind the counter opened it. He pulled out a jeweller's eyeglass and began looking the piece over.

'Well, then.'

'You know my thoughts,' Lance said.

'I think you're a bit light on in your valuation. Losing your touch.' John Smith looked at Sara and frowned. 'This is a valuable suite of jewels and amethysts are all the rage at the moment. Are you sure you want to sell?'

She'd never been more certain in her life. 'Yes. How much do you think it's worth?'

'Well. Your fiancé here thinks it's worth fifty. I believe a bit more, but after buyer's premium you could get fifty-five.' He turned his attention to Lance. 'You're not going to auction it?'

'That wouldn't be proper.'

John narrowed his eyes at her. 'No, I'm guessing not. Want me to arrange things?'

'Please. Now, what else do you have for us?'

John took a bundle of tinkling keys from his belt and unlocked a drawer. 'A couple of items you might be interested in. Did you hear old Fothergill's dead?'

He fiddled with the drawer and pulled out two small satin bags.

'No,' Lance said. 'How's young Lady Fothergill coping?'

'She was in here the other day. Think things are tight in that big, lonely estate of hers. She was selling off some trinkets. I asked if she wanted you to call and she does. I can text you her number.'

'As always, thank you.'

'Now, here is what I was talking about.'

He pulled out a velvet-covered tray, opened the little pouches and spilled two glittering rings onto the inky surface.

Sara's heart stuttered, before beating a little faster. 'What's this?' she said as if her voice wasn't her own.

'If we're engaged, you need a ring.'

John smiled like the Cheshire cat. 'He told me all about you. Asked me for the most interesting ones I have. And here they are.'

He waved them over with a flourish. Lance picked up the first, an enormous sapphire the colour of worn denim, with tiny diamonds surrounding it. It was old, outstanding. He twirled it under the lights then picked up the other ring, which was smaller but no less beautiful. An oval opal which shone like a rainbow. Again, surrounded by diamonds with a carved gold band. The sapphire was magnificent, but the opal...

It took her breath away.

'This,' Lance murmured. She held her breath as he twisted it under the lights and it changed colour with every turn. 'Beautiful and complex, like you.'

He looked at her, in that second entirely inscrutable, unknowable. 'Let's see what it looks like in natural light.'

Lance took her hand again, the warm grasp of it unusual, unnecessary, and it sent a shimmer of pleasure right through her. He led her out of the shop, the little bell tinkling its quaint tinny sound as they walked into the lane once more. A chill breeze blew as leaves skittered around them. Something about this felt…important. Far more significant than it all really was. And she didn't want to look at Lance, or the exquisite piece of jewellery he held. The morning had seemed fun, the fantasy of it all. But this was all too much, too real. She looked up at the grey sky, which always seemed to follow them here, and wrapped her coat a little more tightly round her.

'Autumn's coming earlier this year.'

Lance chuckled. 'I'm not out here to talk about the weather. Do you like it?'

He held out his hand, the ring pinched between his thumb and forefinger. She looked down at the exquisite opal, full of fire with pinks and greens and blues, the muted gleam of old cut diamonds framing the edge of the gemstone. It took her breath away, this ring. How could she not love everything about it? Still she shook her head.

'You prefer the sapphire?'

He'd compared the opal to her. *Beautiful and complex*. It had so much meaning. Too much, if she let her imagination run wild. 'Aren't opals supposed to be bad luck?'

'Only for the faithless, apparently. Which I suppose means I'm doomed.'

She looked up at him, staring down at her with earnest hazel eyes. 'You said you'd never be unfaithful.'

'That's true. Perhaps there's a meagre chance for me after all.' He chuckled. 'So, what do you think? Will it do?'

'It's too much. Surely you have something in some vault you could use?'

'The traditional engagement ring in my family would be the Astill Amethyst.' He smiled. 'You hate purple. If you don't like the opal, we can find something else.'

Something clenched deep inside her. Her parents hadn't remembered she hated purple when they'd presented her with the parure on her twenty-first birthday. Or perhaps they didn't care. She looked at the ring, still held between them by Lance's long, elegant fingers.

'It's perfect,' Sara whispered.

'Then it's yours.'

He slid the jewel into the pocket of his trousers and took her left hand. Lifted it to his lips and kissed. A flush of heat flooded her cheeks.

'There's really no need—'

'Hush.' He pulled her into him. Leaned down. This close, with all his vibrancy and vigour and strength, the man was too much. Sara closed her eyes, absorbing the heat of him. His earthy scent that twisted her insides into complicated knots. He murmured in her ear, 'I may be the Dastardly Duke, but I do believe in doing things properly. Even this.'

Lance released her and she wavered. She sucked in a deep breath, trying to remind herself this was all fake. Men like him didn't fall for women like her. Then he took both of her hands in his, his warm, solid grip holding her steady. He stared deep into her eyes and she lost herself in the fathomless green of his, the golden fleck in them that gleamed like the opal in his pocket. So serious, so sincere. She had trouble breathing, getting any air.

'Sara.' His voice hit her like a shot of schnapps, sliding through her veins, straight to her heart. He was intoxicating. A girl could get quite drunk on him.

'I'm no prince. In fact, you'll come to learn I'm more toad than frog so, luckily for you, none of this is real. However, I'll do my level best to duel any dragons that come to your door in our brief time together...' He smiled down at her and everything ignited. 'If you think that'll do. That it's good enough for a woman who was once destined to be a queen. Will you do me the immeasurable honour of becoming my fake fiancée?'

She swallowed the lump forming in her throat and looked down at the ancient cobblestones in this dim back lane, somehow separate from the bustle of London, in a world of their own, and blinked away burgeoning tears. His proposal, for this crazy arrangement, was more romantic than her own real one had been. When she'd become engaged to Ferdinand, he'd simply pronounced, *'It's time we made this official.'*

'Of course,' she said to the stones underfoot.

'I didn't hear you. Don't tell me you're having second thoughts about the sincerity of my false declaration. A man's ego might not stand it.'

She bit her lip to stifle a giggle. Trust Lance to make her laugh. Sara chanced a look at him and he smiled, wide and bright. It was enough to warm her on this chilly day.

He raised an eyebrow, tapping his foot in mock impatience. 'I'm waiting.'

'Yes. I'd love to be your temporary fiancée.'

'Excellent.' He took her hand and slid the ring onto her finger. It was warm from his touch and fitted perfectly. Sara didn't believe in signs, so why did this feel like a portent of...something? She placed her hand to his chest, the strong muscle firm and hot underneath her palm.

'Thank you. For saving me.'

A look passed across his face. Not a shadow, exactly, but something dark and thrilling nonetheless. Then it was replaced by a flash of heat and, even though she wasn't experienced in many things, she recognised that look. The flare of his nostrils as he cupped his hands either side of her jaw. All of this made it impossible to think, witnessing the…intent written over his face. Her lips parted to sip at the air because a tight band had wrapped round her chest and squeezed. His eyes flicked to her mouth, caught there.

'Lance?' Her voice was husky and low, sounding nothing like her at all.

'Let's take a moment to savour this unique event.' His thumbs brushed her cheeks and a tremor ran through her which had nothing to do with the cold breeze blowing down the lane. Then he dropped his head. She knew what was coming and, even though this was fake, she felt a heady rush of anticipation. Sara closed her eyes as his warm breath brushed across her skin, leaving tingles in its wake. Lance was so close the heat emanated from him as he held himself a sliver away. He was waiting for her, she knew, to say no if this wasn't what she wanted. But oh, how she *craved* him.

'*Sara.*'

The whisper of her name brushed her skin and she was lost to him, closing the minute distance between them to press her lips to his, her kindling to his spark, and she ignited. His mouth moved over hers, gentle and coaxing. She sighed into him as his arms slid round her and drew her close, melting as his tongue dipped, touching hers. A question which she answered by opening for him, slipping her arms round his neck and drawing him down. He plundered then, invaded her, and she gasped at the slick seduction of it all, tasting and teasing each other in a lonely lane in the middle of London, where the world rushed round them and could end for all she cared. This glorious moment witnessed only by the old stones.

Sara was lost in it but Lance slowed, his mouth luxuri-
ating over hers before easing to a stop as he drew away. He
glanced up the lane briefly, eyes narrowing, then turned
back to her, removing his hands from her cheeks. She felt the
loss of him to her very core. Her heart pounded against her
ribs and everything tilted on its axis. Did it tilt for him too?
She couldn't really tell, though a slight crease had formed
between his brows. Maybe she'd done it all wrong? She was
scared she had and didn't know why it mattered.

Then he tucked a loose curl behind her ear. Traced the
shell of it with his finger and his touch sparked across her.
His lips tilted into something enigmatic.

'I hope that was better than *moist*.'

She rocked back on her heels. It was about that? A strange
sense of ego? Because her past had no part in what was
going on here. Ferdinand was a mere shadow against this
vibrant, elemental man. She began shivering and it had nothing to do with the chill breeze that swirled around them.

'Come on, you're cold. If we're done ring shopping—'

'Don't you have to pay?'

'John and I have an understanding. Let's say farewell
and take you home.'

They walked back into the shop, hand in hand.

'Congratulations.' John rounded the counter with his arm
outstretched, vigorously shaking Lance's hand. Then he
leaned over and kissed Sara on the cheek. 'I never thought
I'd see the day.'

'Me neither,' Lance said. 'But all it took was a special
woman.'

He looked at her and smiled, and she wanted to believe
in that. She really wanted to believe.

# CHAPTER FIVE

SARA STRETCHED, basking in the cool early morning sunshine that flooded the glorious bedroom of the Duchess suite. It had been a whirlwind since arriving at Lance's magnificent home by helicopter the previous afternoon. She'd been introduced to the small yet enthusiastic staff. George, the butler, seemed especially determined to find out everything about the workings of Morenburg Palace and her own family's manor, her likes and dislikes, so she could feel at home here.

Then there had been a brief tour of the public areas of the house, before a personal shopper had arrived with an array of clothes that fitted the description of what she wanted *perfectly*. It boggled Sara's mind, given the limited time the woman had to pull it all together. It also told her a great deal about Lance's power and influence.

He'd arranged a quiet dinner for her in her room when she'd begun to fade from the stress of the past two days. He was more attentive as a fake fiancé than her real one had ever been. She'd never really felt like royalty, even when she had the chance of being royal. But the way she'd been treated in this house made her feel like a princess...

*Dangerous, Sara.*

She had to keep reminding herself. She knew where romantic delusions had led her once before and couldn't do that again. Believe in love. Be cast aside. She shrugged off those thoughts and peered at the doorway which led to a shared en suite bathroom and walk-in wardrobe separating the Duke and Duchess's suites. Lance had said it was a recent addition to the house, designed by his sister, who'd helped redecorate. But it wasn't the elegant interior design she was interested in. It was the fact that mere metres away Lance had slept...

She held up her left hand in a shaft of sunlight, watching the myriad colours glitter in her engagement ring, which she'd slipped on the moment she'd woken. She hadn't heard him overnight, collapsing into her lavish canopied bed and falling asleep the moment she'd hit the pillow. Her lips tingled and she brushed her fingers across them. Closed her eyes, imagining his coaxing mouth on hers once more. The way his arms slipped round her, holding her tight. It was okay. Her imagination couldn't hurt her, not here. But her body didn't seem to get the message, flushing hot, her heartbeat kicking up at the perfect memory...

Except.

She dropped her hand to her lap. Stood from the too comfortable couch in this beautiful room. She'd been beguiled by dreams before. Powerful, handsome men made false promises. Lance at least seemed a little more honest than most, but she didn't want a permanent protector. Sara wanted to find herself, find her own way. It started today. She and Lance were going to a house an hour or so away. He'd been tasked with assessing the estate. Maybe she'd find something valuable and begin her quest for independence. That was the only thing that should excite her today.

Sara padded across the plush Axminster carpet to the walk-in wardrobe, not sure what to wear for today's expedition. She had mostly practical items, but there were a few lovely dresses she couldn't resist. Her clothes barely took up the allotted space, despite Lance's best efforts. She looked over at his side of the wardrobe. Rows of suits, shirts, ties and shoes, all perfectly curated. She shouldn't…but his domain tempted, through the doorway on the other side. She couldn't help herself…explore a little. What harm could it do? She still had plenty of time.

She brushed her fingers along the rack of exquisite suits hung in perfect order, the fabric soft and perfect. As she moved further into his space, she shut her eyes and breathed in deeply—something spicy and masculine, like cloves, but with a hint of sweetness. She snorted. As if anything about him was sweet. She effortlessly recalled the evil gleam in his eye and the wicked curl of his lip, sending delicious shivers right through her. She explored further, unable to help herself. In many ways he was a closed book, and this might give her an insight. The bespoke fine cotton shirts, hanging perfectly ironed with sharp creases. Silk ties in jewelled colours. She briefly wondered whether he ever wore causal clothes, until she found the worn jeans and soft T-shirts. She traced her hands over the fabric that had touched his skin, unable to help herself.

The door to his room lay *just there*. She peeked through but it was quiet. This was about the only regularly used room of the house she hadn't yet been shown. Her heart skipped at the illicit thrill of it all. But, for the sake of authenticity, shouldn't she, as his fiancée, have free access to his personal space? It made perfect sense, so she boldly walked on through.

If the Duchess suite was feminine, Lance's was undeniably masculine. There was a canopied antique cedar bed, with hangings that made it look as if a king slept there, still unmade. And she couldn't get out of her head that *he'd* slept here. The indentation on his pillow where his head had lain. The sheets, crumpled in disarray.

Had he dreamed about anything last night? Their kiss, perhaps? The warmth of that thought coursed through her. Did he sleep clothed? Naked? That vision embedded in her brain like a splinter, because she'd seen enough of his body in the press photographs to know he'd be magnificent with nothing on at all. And that thought froze her to the spot. She should leave, but she couldn't make her feet move out of the room that embodied him so completely. All saturated, bold shades of greens and blues. Solid yet elegant furniture. Rich, soft fabrics. Decadent and sinful—a perfect reflection of the man himself.

As she stood, staring at the unmade bed where his body had lain, a voice called out from her room, coming closer.

'Sara?'

He walked through the doorway from the walk-in wardrobe on this side. She froze, not knowing what to do, because she was in his space but wore only what she'd slept in—a cute tank and sleep shorts in a silky soft fabric. Great for comfort, but not designed to hide much. His eyes widened as they met hers, then did a slow survey of her body. A lazy smile slid across his face. Her nipples tightened traitorously.

He'd be able to see everything. All she could do was brazen it out...

'I... I was just...'

'Exploring?' Lance leaned against the door jamb, preventing any kind of escape. His gaze flicked to the bed and back to her as the heat rushed to her cheeks. 'Do you like what you see so far?'

Sure, he was talking about the house, but all she could see was him. He wore dark, perfectly tailored suit trousers and one of those bespoke shirts, in a blue and white stripe.

A gleam in his eye and a sensual curl of his lip spoke of all kinds of trouble. He was perfect. She couldn't take her eyes from him.

'It's a beautiful house.' She cleared her throat, and he raised an eyebrow. She tried to get the conversation on track. 'You must be very happy here.'

'We barely spent any time here as children, with my father's ambassadorial work. Sometimes it's nice to be back, but I spend most of my life in London. Is there anything more you'd like me to show you?'

'You must be wondering what I'm doing in here,' she said, sure she was the colour of the prize-winning beetroot the cook had talked of growing in the kitchen garden.

'You're the lady of the house now. For a little while at least. You're welcome to unfettered access.'

The thought of him, naked in bed, granting her unfettered access to his body, flashed through her consciousness. She heaved in a quick breath, heat blistering across her cheeks.

He pushed off the door jamb and came into the room with her, then went to a velvet-covered armchair and picked up the navy-blue bathrobe draped across it. He held it out to her.

'This might make you feel less...exposed.'

She took the plush dark fabric and slipped the robe on. It was warm, soft, and smelled as delectable as him. He walked up to her and took the belt, tying it tightly round the waist, as if she were some child. The garment swamped her. How mortifying. Here she'd been fantasising about him naked in bed and he'd thought she was flaunting herself. She shuffled her feet, looking at the floor.

'Why don't we go into your room now? I have something to show you.' His voice was gentle. When he turned and walked back into the Duchess suite, she followed. She found him sitting on the floral chintz couch, overlooking a view of the rambling rose garden. Sara sat at the other end, but even that was too close.

He pulled his phone from his pocket, flicked to something on the screen and handed it to her.

'What's this?'

'An article in one of the tabloids.'

On the screen was a series of photographs of them in the lane yesterday. His hand to her cheek, looking into her eyes. Then the kiss. The way they looked at each other, simmering, intent. Lance slipping the ring onto her finger. That private moment, invaded. The headline shouted *'Debauched Duke Domesticated!'*

'How?'

He leaned back on the couch, hands behind his head, looking smug.

'There's usually significant interest in me but, on this occasion, I gave them a hot tip.'

She had a nasty feeling in the pit of her stomach, as if something had congealed. Silly. It was an excellent reminder that everything about this was fake. She'd thought maybe he'd been lost in the moment too. But no, it had only been her. Anyhow, what did it matter? Dashing dukes and handsome, aristocratic men weren't on her agenda. She straightened her shoulders and handed the phone back to him.

'So I'm guessing everyone knows now.' Why did her voice sound so quiet and hurt? She cleared her throat. 'Excellent.'

He frowned, then leaned towards her. 'You wanted a scandal, and you certainly have one now. Since it's public information, your parents will no doubt be aware. As will Annalise.'

She hadn't thought of that. When she'd checked her phone she'd ignored all the messages. She couldn't discuss this with Lise, not yet. And perhaps she didn't know yet, being on her honeymoon, hopefully immersed in wedded bliss...

'Thank you. Good job.' She smiled then, but it felt fake to the core. That smile reserved for her parents, Ferdinand. The type of smile she'd promised herself she'd never give again...

'I'm pleased you're happy. Now, back to work.' He didn't look pleased, though. His frown remained. 'We'll be leaving in half an hour. You won't earn a commission if you don't find something worth selling.'

That was fine, excellent even. It was clear he wanted her out of his life. She wouldn't stay anywhere she wasn't wanted longer than absolutely necessary.

'I need to—'

'Put on some clothes... Of course. Take your time, and when you're done—' he stood and moved to the doorway, gave her a wink '—let's go and find some treasure.'

Lance held the steering wheel in a death grip. George had *not* been happy about him driving, had insisted that *Lady Sara* would expect a chauffeur. Good grief. His normally composed butler had finally cracked. Next the man would be breaking out the family Limoges dinner service and demanding they dine in the grand ballroom. It seemed to be all he could do not to wrestle the keys out of Lance's hand and drive them both to the next town for their fossicking expedition.

Lance hadn't really considered what it would be like, bringing a supposed fiancée into the house. Especially not one so...qualified as Sara for the role of Duchess of Bedmore. She was perfect in every way. Lance took his eyes from the narrow country road and glanced at her, staring out of the window, captivated by the vibrant countryside around them. She was wearing some exquisite pale yellow floral perfection of a dress. She looked like sunshine, with what appeared to be a thousand tiny, distracting buttons up the front. He had an irrational desire to undo each one slowly...

No. As much as he tried to project an image of wickedness, he was *better* than this. It was seeing her this morning, that was all. In the past twenty-four hours he'd broken a few of his carefully crafted rules. There were many things he shouldn't have done. Acquiring an engagement ring which slipped onto Sara's finger so perfectly it was as if it was meant to be. Proposing with words that left her eyes gleaming with tears and tugged at his unfeeling heart, seeming all too real for his cynical soul. Kissing her soft lips, which had the hit of a drug and left him addicted and craving.

But the most stupid thing he'd done in this litany of foolishness was freezing like a dumbstruck teenager as she'd stood next to his bed, rather than turning and walking straight out of the room, leaving her be.

He hadn't wanted her to find those articles in the tabloids herself, or that was the excuse he'd told himself. That was why he'd gone to her room early. Then he'd found her and his downfall was complete. She was all glorious blushes and stuttering apologies when he'd been *thrilled* to find her in his space in sleepwear that clung to her beautiful body, looking at his unmade bed with a distant kind of longing that filled him with a surge of heat.

He hadn't been able to help himself. His gaze devouring her long, pale limbs...the golden curls tumbling round her shoulders...the tight nipples pressing against the fabric of her top. He shifted in his seat, the car becoming uncomfortably warm. What he wouldn't have given to sink into the covers, mussed from a sleepless night, and bury himself in her until they both forgot their names...

Which was generally the expectation when a woman was in his room, under ordinary circumstances. But not Sara. He might have spent most of his adult life cultivating a certain reputation but there was no requirement to uphold it, not with her. His job was to protect the woman, not debauch her. As much as he'd failed in the past, he'd make sure he didn't here.

Because as soon as that news story had hit, he'd received a stream of furious messages on his phone. Sara's family, making all kinds of accusations, demands and threats. The accusations he relished, especially from her brother, with whom he had a close to hostile history from school. He took a hand from the steering wheel and rubbed the side of his neck where his scar prickled as a reminder. As for the demands, he ignored—

'Are you all right?' Sara asked, taking her eyes from the road.

'Of course,' he said. Yet a flicker like a pilot light lit inside his chest. That she should care about him, when she was the one in need of protection. Her family's threats… He'd be damned if she was going back to that cold little alpine country where she'd be married off to some dolt who wouldn't care for her. *He'd* care for her, make sure no harm befell her. Protecting her was a chance to begin atoning for his multitude of sins.

They arrived at the stately, if somewhat worn-looking, house. Weeds invaded the gravel drive where they pulled up outside. He did the polite thing and opened the door for her, and then they were let into a dim front entrance by a member of staff. Lance's professional eye immediately began assessing the property. Thinning rugs on the floor. Dust motes glittering in a single beam of sunshine. The place was cold because the heating hadn't been turned on. The house spoke of gradual disrepair.

He'd seen it many times before. Families prioritising keeping up with their peers, forgetting the upkeep required for a property such as this. Then death arrived, with poorly planned inheritance and taxes, which was where he came in. His heartbeat picked up and he flexed his fingers. It always hit him the same way the minute he walked into one of these places. The excitement of the unknown, the quest to find incredible treasures hidden away for centuries.

He hoped it would excite Sara too, bring her out of the inertia that seemed to cloak her in this moment. Her smile was tight, the joy in it somehow subdued. She was probably bothered by the way he'd stared at her earlier like a leering teenager. In truth, he still couldn't keep his eyes from her. The gentle sway as she walked allowed the beautiful dress to twirl about her legs. A bright cardigan was wrapped around her shoulders, embroidered with flowers, her legs encased in boots. She was every country fantasy brought to life. And right now she stood in this drab entrance hall, in the only shaft of sunlight filtering through the smudged windows, brightening up the space with yellow and flowers and her indisputable *glow*. Looking like some glorious spring garden, with her blonde hair a wild and wonderful tangle down her back.

'We'll start in the attic. I'll send my people to assess the rest of the items later.'

The open, lived-in spaces where the obvious treasures would be displayed. His staff could value those, see if there was anything that might be interesting for sale. His speciality had always been the hidden areas—cupboards, cellars, attics—where people hid their treasures as well as their secrets.

'Why here first?' It was the first thing Sara had said in a while, her voice soft and musical, stroking over his skin like a feather.

They were led up a set of stairs that creaked underfoot, and then through several doors that did much the same, as if they hadn't been opened for years. Then they were alone with a large key in a dim, confined space under the roof. There was a dry, aged smell of dust, but it wasn't in as parlous a state as many attics he'd come across. Disappointing—the more dust the better. This looked a little too tidy. He flicked on the light to enhance the natural sun coming through the skylight.

'This is where secrets are kept.'

Sara lifted a dust cover from some bulky piece of furniture and peered underneath. 'You like that, don't you? Finding things out about people.'

'There are too many secrets kept in this world. People who pretend to be paragons of virtue. I like uncovering them, even if it's only to satisfy my own curiosity.'

If he'd done any kind of job uncovering the sins of Vic's husband, she might never have married. She'd have been safe.

'Treasure…secrets… You found a Caravaggio, but what secrets have you uncovered?'

He shrugged. 'Lost loves, grand affairs, erotic collections. You name it, I uncover it.'

'That's almost…voyeuristic.'

'There can be something quite salacious about it that piques my interest.'

He winked and she began to giggle. It was such a bright and beautiful sound. She'd had enough misery. This woman should be smiling for ever.

'You're incorrigible.'

Lance bowed. 'Yes. I'm irredeemable. No matter what will be said about your capacity to reform me.'

'I don't want to reform you, whatever that means. A scoundrel is what I asked for, after all.'

'You might amend your view if you saw the worst of me.'

She leaned up against a mahogany sideboard, cocked her head to the side. 'I'm not really sure I would.'

The moment lingered. It was as if she were trying to reach inside him and weigh his soul. Part of him wondered what she found. Another part dreaded her conclusion. Yet whilst she stood as if trying to judge his worth, all he could see was her next to his bed, looking at the space he'd slept in as if she were imagining him still there.

He broke the silence first, looking around the space. 'Sadly, this attic is too clean to find much. Give me something dirtier. That's where the greatest treasure is found.'

She let out a sigh, hands on her hips as she looked around. The moment passed, and he regretted ending it rather than seeing where it led. 'Where to start?'

'I'll take this end.' He pointed to one side of the room. 'You take the other and we'll meet in the middle. Take notes and photographs, then we'll swap sides and see if we've missed anything.'

They worked in silence. The dust covers hid ordinary things. Broken objects. Nothing of real interest. He glanced over at her. She was clicking a photograph of a painting propped against the wall, arching her back like a glorious cat, blowing an errant curl from her face and tucking it behind her ear. He grinned as she looked over at him, her blue eyes cool and calm.

'You said your father hated you doing this. What about your mother?'

'My mother? The dowager?' He laughed. 'She doesn't much care what I do.'

She had her schemes, of course. Like marrying him off

to continue the inglorious Astill name, to do his duty like some stud bull. That would never happen.

'Will I meet her?'

'No. Come autumn she takes to the villa in Spain and winters there with some of her friends. By the time she comes back, no doubt you'll be settled elsewhere and sick of me. I'll be a distant memory.'

A pretty pink colour flushed across her skin. Maybe not so distant a memory, then. He liked that. He liked it too much.

'And what about your sister?'

'Perhaps at the upcoming charity polo match. She occasionally attends.' Except of late she'd missed so much. He suspected her husband refused to allow her to be seen in public unless she was accompanying him. Sometimes she called, made excuses, her voice tired, distant. A little slurred...

'She has such a talent for design and decorating. Astill Hall's interior is beautiful.'

It was one of the few things Vic's husband had allowed her to do. A job where he thought she wouldn't embarrass herself, something to occupy her so he could pursue his career and other...interests. But Lance hadn't cared, so long as it kept the man away from his sister.

'Victoria has a flair for two things. Interior design and saving abandoned creatures.'

Her husband didn't admire either talent.

'Your sister sounds interesting. I think I'd like her.'

Once, perhaps. Now... Vic's hidden talent was hurting herself, and those who tried to love her. He didn't understand how Sara could remain so seemingly untainted by all the ugly behaviour she'd been subjected to. How could someone still contain all the wonder and hope she appeared to have? Her fiancé, a philanderer and then dead before the wedding. Her parents, still trying to sell her off to the highest bidder to maintain the power and position they felt slipping through their bony fingers.

'Well, I'm done on my side.' She huffed out a breath, blowing a stray curl from her face. 'There wasn't much here. Except...'

The way those words drifted off, making him wait. Making him ask. He smiled. She was playing him at his own game. 'What have you found?'

'All I have is this.' She wandered over to a chest of drawers and rubbed her nose, pulling up an old shoe box. Inside was the flotsam and jetsam of a child's collection—old doll's house furniture, smooth river pebbles and figurines which Sara picked through.

'These—a collection of farm animals.' She lined them up on the top of a chest. They were hardstone, with glittering gem-like eyes. Then she looked up at him again with all that hope. His heart stuttered with excitement because she knew what she'd found and so did he, as much as he could tell from the cursory glance.

'What do you think they are?' she asked.

He smiled. 'You *know* what they are.'

'Fabergé?'

He lifted one; it was cool in his hand. Still in good condition, considering children had played with them. Beautiful. Collectible. Valuable. 'I think you might be right. Congratulations, Lady Sara. If the family's keen to sell, these will be your first commission.'

She stood in front of him, her lips parted, glorious curls framing her face. Looking at him as if he held the answer to every question she'd ever care to ask. She made him feel like King of the world with that expression. Right then, he craved to be the answer to all things for her. In an alternative universe where whatever she wanted and needed he alone would provide.

When had he ever felt this way? Perhaps never. He cherished every moment of the gift she gave him—the belief he could offer something of value. She reached up and pushed some strands of hair from her cheek. A smear of dust was left behind by her fingers.

'You have a mark.' He pointed. Sara rubbed in the general area but missed the smudge marring her face.

'Let me,' he murmured. Lance smoothed his thumb over the spot. Her skin was silky and warm under his fingers.

'All gone now,' he said, about to remove his hand, which had lingered too long. Except she leaned into his touch, her eyes drifting shut in a long, slow blink. He froze, cupping her cheek. They were close, the warmth of their bodies mingling, curling through him. He dropped his head as she seemed to move up onto her toes. It would be one kiss. Celebrating her find. Surely that wasn't too much?

He leaned down and held himself a breath away from her, his whole body tight. The smell of her was like spring in the dusty attic.

'Congratulations, Sara,' he whispered against her lips as she reached for him and their mouths collided, hers soft against his own, opening for him. He slid his arms round her back and drew her hard against his body, her tongue hot and slick against his own.

He groaned as she thrust her hands into his hair, raking her fingers through. The scrape of nails against his scalp. Their mouths and teeth clashing as everything spun out of control. She ground herself against him, no air separating their bodies. He was so damned hard he could barely think, the moment all gasps and questing fingers. There were buttons on her dress, but he fumbled them. Instead, he grazed his palms against her nipples, which were tight and peaked under the fine fabric. His mouth captured her throaty moan, pure bliss to his ears.

They were caught in some kind of madness and the end of the world wouldn't stop him, the desperate noises she made urging him on.

He lifted her, planted her on a covered sideboard which, thank the Lord, was the perfect height. She hooked her booted legs round his thighs and dragged him closer, the heat of her against the hardness of him as she panted his name. She dropped her head back and he kissed the column of her throat.

'You *love* this.'

His lips traced from her pulse point to behind her ear, and she shivered when he kissed her there.

'*Yesss...*' Her elongated hiss drove him on. He slid his free hand up her skirt, teasing at the silken skin of her thighs, slipping his fingers between them till he found her, slick and wet through her underwear. He began to rub her through the damp fabric, stoking all her banked heat. Nothing was more important in this moment than her pleasure.

'There are people downstairs who could hear, but you don't care, do you? I *knew* you'd be like this. So responsive.'

He kept the steady, swirling motion of his fingers against the centre of her, winding her higher and higher. Caught in the maelstrom of Sara's quest for pleasure, her hips moving in time to his fingers.

'How desperate can I make you? What will you do for me?'

He surged against her and she whimpered, her eyes glassy and unfocused. Her cheeks were a delicate shade of pink, the same colour flushing her chest and climbing the column of her throat.

'I need. I need...' It was like a chant.

'I know what you need.'

He didn't give a damn if all of the staff in this house stood at the attic door and watched them. He'd stop for *nothing*. He pressed a little harder, teased her soaked core.

'I have you,' he growled in her ear. 'Come for me like the good girl you want to be.'

She stiffened. Stopped breathing. Arched her spine as he crashed his mouth against hers, capturing her gasping sobs. He kept stroking in a steady rhythm, through wave after wave that had her convulsing in his arms, until she shuddered a final time and fell against him, soft and limp, resting against his aching body. His panting breaths lifted threads of golden curls on her head.

What he wouldn't give to push her underwear aside, slide into her and take her, now.

But sanity inched back. He wasn't a teenager. He didn't have protection. Then a creeping disgust prickled through his veins because he would *not* take advantage of her.

As much as he knew he should move away, as much as he ached for her, he merely held her against him. He felt her relax, stroking her back. Resting his chin on her head and breathing her in. Relishing her long, deep sigh of satisfaction, a bright kernel of glowing warmth illuminating his irredeemable soul.

Sara nestled into Lance's hard chest as her panting breaths eased. One part of her brain screamed *What have you done?* But those thoughts were smothered by the warmth of a man's strong arms round her, of her blood, sweet and thick like treacle, sliding through her veins. Sated. Protected.

She'd never felt like this before. Certainly not with the man she'd been supposed to marry. She knew pleasure on her own, of course, but this had consumed her, burned her, and now she felt new and tender. Easy to bruise.

Lance didn't shift, he didn't move. He just held her, and in his arms she felt like something precious and beautiful. Like the Fabergé animals he'd carefully held and caressed with his fingers. Something of true personal value. Whilst Lance still hadn't let go, she loosened her legs a little. The centre of her was pressed against him and he was still hard. She wondered why he wasn't doing anything. He had an obvious need, the mere thought of which started a tempting pulse low and deep inside her again. As if what had happened had broken something in her and all she could do was want and want and want.

'Are you okay?' His voice was rough, so he cleared his throat.

Okay? Merely okay? The whole of her still soared somewhere in the clouds. And the prickle of uncertainty needled at her as she crashed back to earth.

*You'll never have his heart.*

Those words taunted her, encapsulating the certainty that she was not loved, was valueless other than for what she could provide as a wife. She didn't want any man's heart, not after the painful lessons of her past. But what if she'd misunderstood Lance's desire? No. She couldn't second-guess. He'd looked at her and touched and, whilst she'd been the one to initiate the kiss, he'd been close, waiting for it. And there was no doubt that his body wanted her…

But now all the syrupy lassitude had dissipated with this fear that somehow she'd done something wrong. She pulled back, not quite able to look him in the eye.

'I'm fine.' How gauche she sounded, when what he'd done had ripped her apart. She blinked back the fierce tears burning her eyes, her nose. He'd made her feel…perfect and wanted. Why couldn't she hold her head high and accept it? Because she was worth *something* as a person, no matter what Ferdinand and her family might have thought.

Lance tipped his finger under her chin and she was forced to look into the cool green of his eyes as they tracked over her face, his brow furrowed in concern. If he saw the gleam of tears he wouldn't just think she was a *good girl*, but a silly little girl. Men didn't like those, as her mother had always told her. What they wanted were serene, self-contained women. Well, she could be just that.

'We should get moving. There's a whole house to explore.' She wriggled herself loose of him but, strangely, he didn't appear to want to let her go, slow to remove his arm, his hand. She slid from the sideboard, trying to put herself back together. Straightening her clothes. Reflexively running her hand over her hair.

'We should perhaps wait a few moments. Till I'm more… respectable.'

She looked at him, trousers pulled far too tight across his groin, his arousal impressive—and impossible to miss. She winced.

'Oh, do you need a…a hand or anything?'

He snorted. 'Whilst I haven't had to deal with an inconvenient erection since my teenage years, I think I'll survive.' The blood rushed to her cheeks. She turned and attempted to take a few pictures of the figurines she'd lined up earlier, but her hand wouldn't stop shaking.

'Sara.' He gently placed his hand over hers, steadying it. 'I'm sorry if you're uncomfortable. It won't happen again. We got carried away.'

She took a deep breath. Great, good. Except someone needed to tell her body, which was still tingling all over at his nearness. The whole of her still soft, ready and far too willing to leap at him and demand a repeat performance.

A man like Lance wouldn't want her—if he'd wanted her, he would have done more. And there she'd been rubbing against him as if she were some feline overcome by catnip. Like Ferdinand when they'd spent their disastrous night together, Lance's physical reaction hadn't been to her as such. Any man would react that way to a woman wrapping herself around him and clinging like some rampant creeper. Anyhow, she needed to stand on her own two feet, not fall for her beautiful rescuer. Doing that would be a one-way journey to more heartbreak.

'There's nothing to apologise for, and nothing more to discuss,' she said. She turned to face him because she was going to be an adult about this. Sophisticated. She forced herself to look up at him. His hair was dishevelled, mouth redder than usual from their kisses. He looked down at her with a world of concern shining in his eyes. 'I had a nice time.'

He grimaced. Then nodded. Her hand was steady now, so she turned her back on him and began taking random photographs to give herself some space.

Lance was right. It was simply the intoxicating mix of the excitement of the moment and unrestrained hormones that had led them here. The adrenaline of finding her first valuable antique couldn't be avoided. But her hormones? From now on they were being kept well and truly under lock and key.

They had to be.

# CHAPTER SIX

ON THE DRIVE back to Astill Hall Lance kept up a steady narrative on what they'd found and how much the figurines she'd discovered might fetch at auction. Sara was caught between wanting to scream at him to stop because he seemed so unaffected by what had happened and weeping in thanks that they could pretend nothing had happened at all.

Her body didn't lie, though. No matter how mortified she still felt, it wanted him with a ferocity of desire she'd never experienced before. The ache inside, the heat between her thighs. The prickle of her nipples, now uncomfortable in her bra. As if she was ripe, ready to be picked. If he pulled the car over, dragged out a picnic blanket and wanted to have his way with her under a tree at the side of the road she feared she would agree with indecent enthusiasm.

Proving she wasn't a good girl at all, but *bad*, as he'd first pointed out at the funeral months ago. Even more horrifying, she kind of liked it.

As they turned into the stately driveway of Astill Hall she was relieved she'd at least survived without begging him for a repeat performance or, worse, for forgiveness. The problem was, she wasn't sure how she *should* behave, so she was trying steadfastly to just ignore the fact that she'd orgasmed with Lance's hand stroking between her legs, murmuring those wicked words, making the fire inside her burn hotter…

As Lance parked the car in the expansive garage, George arrived to meet them. He looked from Lance to Sara and back again. Was it obvious something had happened? Surely not, and yet she couldn't help feeling that guilt was written all over her face. The air between them became stiff and uncomfortable as the silence stretched.

'Your Grace.' He nodded to her. 'Lady Sara.'

Lance raised an eyebrow. 'Is this the way things are going to be?'

She wasn't sure what any of this meant. As far as she was concerned, Lance's butler seemed to be behaving entirely appropriately. He would have fitted in with any of the staff at the Morenburg Palace.

'It's only proper.'

'When has anything in Astill Hall been proper?'

George stood a little taller. Glared at Lance. 'You have a fiancée. There are standards to be upheld.'

'You well know I've never been one for *standards* of any kind.'

'Perhaps you can maintain them for a little longer since you have a deputation. From the village.'

Lance snorted. 'Really? I've never had a deputation before.' He looked over to her, a grin on his face. 'I suspect I'm not the person they want to see. They're interested in someone else entirely.'

'Which is why I'm letting you know, in case Lady Sara wishes to…have some time before joining you.'

'Excellent idea. We're both in need of a moment.'

'I'll let them know you'll be with them presently.'

George left and Lance turned to her, his expression serious. 'Do you need anything—bathroom, cold water, a stiff drink? An excuse to avoid the next half hour or so?'

It was time to show him how unaffected she could be. 'No, I'm happy to meet your deputation now. So long as I look presentable.'

They'd cleaned up in a guest bathroom at the manor house before leaving, but she wanted to make a good impression, although she wasn't entirely sure why.

'You could never look anything other than beautiful.'

All her good intentions dissolved with his words, like a flame to candle wax. She wanted to melt to the floor. He held out his hand to her. She dropped hers into it without thinking and the warmth of his palm engulfed her. There was something about him that felt so safe, even though in reality he was her greatest risk.

They walked through the house, hand in hand. It didn't feel cloying, but as natural as breathing. She enjoyed the way he gripped her as if he was intent on holding her, as if she was more than an afterthought and this wasn't just something he was doing for the sake of appearances.

*Dangerous, Sara. Dangerous.*

George was waiting for them inside. He opened the door to a parlour where a small group of people sat. The minute they entered the room, the deputation stood and moved forwards. When Lance smiled it didn't look false and cold, like all the times she'd seen Ferdinand smile at his subjects. Lance's smile warmed the whole room.

'Good morning, Mrs Snow. I hope your husband is improving?'

The woman nodded. 'He is, sir. Our profound thanks for your consideration.'

'Whatever I can do.' Lance's gaze was full of sympathy. 'The village wouldn't be the same without your family.'

The woman's cheeks flushed as Lance turned to the others. 'Mr Bramwell, I hope your daughter's still enjoying university...' He went through the names of the six or so people there, making comments about their lives as they beamed at him as if he were the saviour of all things. 'What brings me this honour?'

Another woman in the group stepped forwards, gaze darting towards Sara. She was older than the rest, with a kind face. *Mrs Hutchins.* 'The honour's ours. We've seen the papers. We never believe what they say about you, but... is it true?'

'Ah, perhaps you should believe some things,' Lance said with a devilish grin. Everyone turned to her, eyes wide. 'I'd like to introduce you to my fiancée, Lady Sara Conrad.'

There was a collective inhale from the little group. Exclamations. Smiles. Everyone crowding her with genuine happiness. It was so infectious she couldn't help but be carried along with it.

'Our heartiest congratulations,' another man said, coming to shake Lance's hand as everyone clamoured around them. It seemed so surreal. She wasn't sure she'd received as much attention and affection in Lauritania when she was destined to be *Queen*.

One of the women passed a basket to Lance. 'It's not much. A few of us put some things together. Small tokens of our congratulations for you and Lady Sara.'

Lance lifted the cover laid over the basket and pulled out a jar topped with checked fabric and tied with a red ribbon. 'Mrs Perkins, is this some of your prize-winning gooseberry jam? You know it's my favourite.'

'It has been since you were a wee boy.' The woman beamed at him. 'But I still won't tell your cook the secret ingredient.'

Lance laughed. 'And I'll continue to ask.'

Mrs Perkins chuckled in response as the chatter carried on around them. Lance seemed to know who had made or grown everything in the basket, from the large brown eggs to the cakes.

Mrs Hutchins came up to her. 'Welcome to our blessed little part of the world. We hope you'll be happy here.'

'Thank you. I've yet to see the village.' What more could she say? She felt like a fraud, lying as she was. How would these kind people react when things inevitably ended? Would they blame Lance, given his reputation? Seeing them with him now, the thought that they might seemed so…unfair.

'You will. Whilst he spends much of his time in London, His Grace still takes a keen interest. I assume you'll be at the charity polo match? He always puts on food and drink for the locals. It's a grand show. He's quite the thing on horseback,' the woman said, lowering her voice in a conspiratorial way.

Sara hadn't thought much about it till now, but she'd seen enough photos when doing her research on him to know that Mrs Hutchins was right. Lance looked fine on horseback. He was, in fact, *fine* in all respects. She lifted her hand to brush back a strand of unruly hair, trying to ignore the blush creeping up her throat.

'What a beautiful ring. You're not wearing the Astill Amethyst?'

Lance joined them, the warmth of his body both a temptation and a strange comfort as he stood close. The pleasure of that heat slid through her as she leaned into him.

'Sara doesn't like purple, so I'd never inflict the amethyst upon her. That would make me a bad fiancé.' A few of the women seemed to blush as Lance's eyes took on a devilish gleam. 'But she looks beautiful in opals. I'll have to drape her in them. She should wear nothing else.'

He winked, and the little group of villagers laughed.

'He was always such a cheeky boy,' Mrs Hutchins whispered with an indulgent smile. 'Could get away with anything, and often did. But always quick to seek forgiveness. Raided my vegetable patch one day as a lad. Found him sitting in the dirt eating tomatoes like they were peaches. There went my attempt at making chutney. But then that afternoon there was a beautiful bunch of roses on my back step. Plucked straight from the bush. Astill Hall had a magnificent rose garden in those days. It's a bit wild now.'

'I love roses,' Sara said.

'That garden should be resurrected. Maybe now you're here…' The woman looked at her hopefully. 'I hope I'm not speaking out of turn. But some of us never thought we'd see the day a woman would grace Astill Hall again. This place hasn't had a family for as many years as I can remember, and it needs one. *He* needs one.'

Sara swallowed, not enjoying the lie she was required to perpetuate. She hadn't really thought through the consequences of accepting his offer, and she suspected he hadn't either. 'Lance is…independent.'

'He's a good man. And we weren't sure. We don't believe much of what the papers write about him, but this…it was too much to hope for, and yet here you are.'

Sara thought she saw brightness like tears in the woman's eyes. Happy tears for sure. It was all such a surprise. He had disdained the role of Duke of Bedmore, yet here, amongst the people from the village, he was warm and kind and…loved.

'Would you all like tea?' he offered behind her.

Mrs Hutchins turned. 'No, we'll be getting along. You'll no doubt have things to do. A wedding to plan.'

The group nodded enthusiastically.

'I'm leaving all of the arrangements in the hands of my capable fiancée, and she tells me there's no rush to the altar.'

The group seemed disappointed. They shuffled and moved out into the hall, leaving the house.

'They adore you,' she said as he closed the door behind them.

Lance turned, his look sharp. 'No. They don't.'

She waved her hand to the door. 'Then why that? There was no need to come here and bring handmade gifts. It took effort.'

He shrugged and said nothing, his jaw hard as if he were grinding his teeth. 'This has been my family's seat for centuries. It's misplaced loyalty, that's all. Don't have any delusions about me, Sara. I'm not a good man.'

'But—'

'They've reminded me there are a few last-minute arrangements which need to be made for the match, and I need to see to the horses. Can I leave you for the afternoon?'

He'd shut the conversation down, his whole demeanour a warning to tread no further. Anyhow, an afternoon away from each other would be beneficial, allow her to regain her equilibrium, because right now she felt like someone on a boat who hadn't yet found their sea legs.

'Of course,' she said. If he wanted to maintain the façade that he didn't care, when it was clear to her that he did, then that was up to him. She wasn't going to be around for long enough to have to worry about it anyhow. But she couldn't help wondering…

Why did he believe he was so difficult to love?

Lance lay awake. It was well past midnight and it seemed sleep would be elusive tonight. He should be exhausted.

He'd spent the afternoon in the stables, working hard with the stable hands to muck out the stalls and clean the tack till it gleamed, not as uncommon an occurrence as some might imagine. He'd always found that hard physical work to the point of exhaustion kept the demons at bay, during the night-time at least. Especially when sleeplessness was a common issue for him in this house, with its oppressive reminders of his unwanted obligations and inexpiable failings.

It wasn't exactly his failings keeping him awake tonight, though. Through the dark cavern of the doorway to his walk-in wardrobe flickered a dim blue glow that suggested Sara might be awake and on her phone. So close, yet so far.

It seemed she wasn't sleeping either. He had a few ideas about what could fix that, for them both, and the less circumspect part of him took the thought and grabbed hold with interest. Those glorious breathy moans of hers, the exquisite flush across her cheeks, head thrown back in ecstasy... Lance couldn't stop thinking about how she'd reacted in his arms that morning. The passion, the pleasure. How responsive she was to his touch, his words. It lit something in him like a fever, leaving him tossing and turning, the crisp cotton sheets scratching rather than slipping over his skin.

Hell, maybe it was these damned boxer shorts he'd put on in case he had to rescue Sara in the middle of the night from...he wasn't sure what. It had seemed like the respectable thing to do with a woman in the room next door. What if a rat or mouse ran into her room, and she was afraid? In such a situation, a lack of clothing might mean she couldn't accept his offer of assistance. He almost laughed at how he'd become so decorous. Except the only rat in the house was him.

This was more than mere desire. It was a vicious craving that flayed him alive. Yet here he lay, gripping the sheets of his bed in his fists to stop himself from going to her, when it was clear she didn't even want to talk about what had happened today, much less engage in a repeat performance. He'd almost made her *cry*, despite her attempt to hide it. The gleam of tears in her eyes was not something he could ignore. He'd been trying to protect her, and now he wanted to debauch her. None of the things he'd done in his efforts to ruin his family's reputation had bothered him before. This? She'd come to him for help and he couldn't keep his grubby hands away from her.

As he rolled over he noticed movement at the door connecting the wardrobe to his room. It was hardly noticeable, the hint of a shadow.

'Sara?' he whispered. 'Is that you?'

'I... Yes. I wondered if you were awake.'

His heart pounded at the soft lilt of her voice. And the memory of her throaty moans left him hard and wanting. But he was stronger than this. He leaned over and clicked on his bedside lamp, wincing at the suddenness of the light.

She stood barely inside his room, swamped in a huge, furry pink robe that looked as if a horde of soft toys had been sacrificed for its creation. He should sack the stylist for bringing such a thing into his house. Usually, the clothes she provided were sheer and tantalising silk, but Sara wasn't a lover who would enjoy the fruits of a fleeting liaison. She was supposed to be his fiancée, and perhaps that was the difference. Now, she looked soft and small like a kitten. Vulnerable and precious. In need of protection.

'Can't sleep?'

She shook her head, looking first at her toes and then at him. Her eyes widened slightly as she took in his naked chest. He grabbed the sheets and quilt and pulled them up slightly higher, as they'd slipped low. She watched every move, her pale blue eyes tracking over him intently. Heat burst across his skin.

'What's wrong?'

'My family's been in touch with you?'

'Yes, they're not happy with me.'

'They're not happy with me either.'

The difference was, he didn't care, whereas Sara appeared to. She moved a little closer to the bed and all his attention homed in on her. Her smooth, curved calves and slender ankles. He wondered then what she was wearing under the robe. That cute little ensemble from this morning, or maybe nothing at all…?

Of *course* she wore something. She wanted solace, not ravishing. He wrestled his imagination under control. He had a duty here. Stray erotic thoughts were not to be involved.

'I expect they won't be, but they seem to think it's all my fault for leading you astray, so you're in the clear.'

She came to the side of the bed slowly. The mattress dipped as she perched on the edge, as if she wasn't sure she should be there. He was sure she shouldn't. Lance gripped the sheets, lest he reach out and touch her. Sara looked down at her fingers.

'I was about to be married, to be Queen, and they're treating me like I'm some runaway child. I could understand why they might want me home if they were really worried, but it's not about me. They don't care about my choices. I've told them…' she plucked at the quilt, looking anywhere bar at him '…but it doesn't matter. I'm not important to them. I wasn't important to Ferdinand either.'

Sara's eyes were wide and sad, gleaming in the lamplight with more unshed tears. 'I liked to dream. Aspired to be the best queen I possibly could be. To serve my country. I hoped I'd finally come to mean something to…' Her voice choked and cracked. 'It all seemed so worthy, but I really didn't matter. I could have been any young, marginally presentable, virginal aristocrat. I'm interchangeable. I was to him, to my family. Perhaps even to my country.'

'No.' He wouldn't take this; she was worth so much more. Another precious woman in her prime, being manipulated for the purposes of others. He knew that script, the ending so painfully familiar. That would not be the ending for her. He sat up, leaned forwards and took her hand, clasping it in his. It was so cool and small. Fragile, trembling like her voice.

'They're the fools, Sara. Ferdinand didn't deserve you. He sought to carry on like his parents, whose marriage was propped up by nothing other than the weight of the crown. You think the King didn't have mistresses? I can give you some of their names. And the Queen. She didn't sit in her chambers knitting whilst her husband was entertaining. Be assured of that.'

Sara's eyes widened and her mouth dropped open, shock evident on her face. Perhaps he shouldn't have shattered her illusions about the now deceased royal family, but he could not sit here and watch her blame herself.

'I might not have lived in Lauritania for years,' he said, 'but my father was one of the King's friends, and Rafe is my friend. Nothing much is secret from me where that family is concerned.'

'So it wasn't his fault; it was how he was raised?'

'Never. It was all his fault. He could have tried to get to know you. Anyone who did that would see what I see. You're a beautiful, passionate woman who hoped for romance, yet understood her duty to her country. What was not to love, or at the very least admire? You deserved that.'

She deserved it all.

She turned away, but not before a tear dripped onto her cheek. 'And what of Annalise? She's married to your best friend.'

He blew out a long breath and thought carefully about his answer, because the truth was important to him, painful as it might be. Kind lies might assuage, but they were lies nonetheless. 'Your Queen was required to marry because of the constitution. Rafe is an ambitious man, a good man, an even better friend, but ambitious and cynical nonetheless. He won't cheat, but I'm not sure the marriage was a love match.'

'So the King doesn't believe in love, but he'll be faithful to their misery. Sounds wonderful.' She huffed and her lips compressed into a thin line. 'Do you believe in love?'

His heart thumped some anxious beats. In his experience, love was nothing more than a negotiation of interests, and never for him. He couldn't be trusted to protect anyone, and when you loved someone it was your duty to protect them for ever. Lance couldn't bear that responsibility, or the pain when he inevitably failed. Victoria's marriage had seen an end to that. But Sara looked hopeful. Did she ask that question because she was looking for love here? His palm began to sweat. He let go of her hand.

'I'm more cynical than he is. But don't ever lose the belief in something more. It's out there, waiting for you.'

'Ferdinand didn't love me. I'm not sure even my family do.'

What could he say? It was probably the truth. She hunched over, looking as if she were shrinking into herself more each moment.

'If that's the case, then they're fools.'

'You're being kind.' Tears glittered in her eyes. He hated them. She deserved so much more. He wanted to lay her down on the bed and kiss them away, turn the sadness into cries of pleasure. Replace that permanent look of disappointment. Make her smile, because her smile lit up the dark.

'Kindness isn't something I've ever been accused of. Do you think it becomes me?'

She huffed, but there it was, the merest raise of the corner of her mouth. For one moment that almost-smile made him feel capable of being whoever she needed him to be. She lifted her eyes to his, the hint of a flush across her face. 'It does.'

A pulse beat deep inside him, a sultry sensation that thickened his blood and made him want in a way that shocked him. He flexed his hands on the covers of the bed. Then her smile faded; it guttered and died like a candle snuffed out in the breeze. As if any happiness was as ephemeral as morning mist.

'My brother was…*is* the favourite. My parents coveted the fact that I'd be Queen, but Heinrich…' She looked at him, her eyes red-rimmed. 'Did your parents have a favourite?'

Her brother was spoiled, entitled and unworthy. As for him? The past, that old wound, ached once more. More bruised than sharp now, it had been with him so many years. Victoria had suffered because of that favouritism.

He shrugged. 'Aristocracy. The male inherits the title, the females are married off. That's the way it is.'

'It's unfair. Would it be too much to ask to be wanted, not for what I can do but simply because I'm me?'

Her voice cracked and against all better judgement he leaned over and hauled her into his arms, wrapping them tight round her. She melted in his embrace, snuggling into him. He felt the warm drip of tears on his shoulder as her face nestled into his neck.

It felt right, *perfect*, but impossible all the same. This was a test, his penance. The price he had to pay for his past failures. Having her in his arms, but not being able to *have* her in the way he desired. Keeping her safe until she found her way, found her feet and left him.

Why did the thought cause something feral to howl inside him?

'Let me torment your family for you.'

'Can you do that?' Her voice was clogged and thick with tears.

'I'm an expert.' He'd made his parents pay for their failings. It was the least he could do for her.

'If you're asking my permission, I'm giving it to you.' She laughed then, a real sound of pleasure, her breath tickling against his neck. He shut his eyes, relishing the sensation of holding her close, the warmth of her against his bare skin. Her left hand was splayed on his shoulder, the scent of her surrounding him, light, bright and floral. His body began hardening, a pulse of desire beating hard, memories of her lips and tongue and panting breaths as she came apart in his hands flooding his mind.

She'd sense his arousal and he didn't want her to feel he couldn't control himself. Lance angled his body and placed her gently down on the bed next to him. Laid out on the covers, her golden hair spilled across the dark sheets, glowing pale and ethereal under the low lights.

'You should go to bed. Dream about your family suffering for their sins.'

He had a choice. To do what was right or what he *craved*. The problem was, in his life he mixed with those who were like himself—hedonists who knew what they wanted and took it without thinking because everyone around them wanted the same thing. Yet he had a greater responsibility.

No matter how much he might want and want and want, his job here wasn't to take from this woman. She stared at him, eyes tracing his face. Lying there, bundled in her soft and fluffy robe, she looked all too innocent.

How he wished he could be innocent again, like her, with the belief that he was in some way a good man. But he was who he was.

Then she licked her lips and the movement punched at the heart of him. A blistering heat flooded his veins, encouraging the pleasure-seeking side of him to take Sara, make her moan. She raised her arms above her head and arched like a cat basking in the sunshine of his worshipful gaze. Almost an invitation to touch. What he wouldn't give to stroke her, make her purr again. Then her lips parted, her voice a breathy whisper.

'What if I want to stay?'

# CHAPTER SEVEN

LANCE WAS TRANSFORMED when she said those words. He froze, not moving at all, as if he were made from ice. When he'd laid her on the bed next to him she'd hoped for something—another searing kiss perhaps? At least something to make her forget. Her family's censure hurt, cutting to the deepest bone and sinew of her. It seemed that so long as she sat down, shut up and did what she was told, they might deign to love her. Heaven help her, wanting something for herself.

But ending up in Lance's arms again? The heat of his touch, his strength…it had coursed through her like molten gold, blistering and precious. And after denying herself time and time again throughout her life, a voice in her head had whispered, *Why not?*

Today what she'd experienced had made her forget *everything*. There had been no pain, no expectation, and she wanted to experience those magical moments of being with him again and again. They were both adults, why couldn't they do this? Yet he made no move to touch her again.

The sheet had slipped to hug his narrow hips, the soft light of the bedside lamp highlighting the shadow-play on his sculpted torso. A body she wanted to trace with her fingertips until they both lost themselves in the glory of the sensation. Still, Lance only stared down at her as if she were an aberration in his bed, not a regular kind of occurrence, as the tabloids would have her believe. His pupils were dark, expressionless. He could have been carved from marble the way he lay on his side, propped on one arm. And realisation dawned. He didn't want her. Not really. Just like Ferdinand. That was why he'd made no move, despite her invitation.

Sara grabbed the front of her robe, clutching the edges together. There was no point making a fool of herself twice in one day. 'Okay. Right. I see.' She'd leave. They'd never speak of this again. She'd go back to her room, curl in her bed and die of embarrassment. She made to sit up.

'Sara.' Lance reached out a hand to cup her cheek, his palm hot against her skin. She stopped, lay back down. A tiny muscle in his jaw pulsed. 'Be sure of what you're asking me.'

She swallowed. A few words and there'd be no turning back. 'I am.'

The corner of his mouth kicked up a fraction. 'I'm not talking about sleeping.'

'Neither am I.'

'Good.' The word was a whisper against her lips as his mouth drifted across hers in an impossibly gentle kiss. When he pulled away, she rose to meet him.

'Patience. We have all night, and I intend to make use of every second of it to make you scream my name. Loudly, and repeatedly.'

She trembled at the thought of a whole night in his bed, in his arms. Lance undid the tie on her robe, opened the soft fabric that had become too hot. What she wore underneath wasn't seductive, practical sleep shorts and a top, because all the sheer nightwear she'd been presented with didn't seem like something you'd actually sleep in, more like something to model and then discard. She hadn't seen the point to it then, but she did now.

Except he looked at her with unalloyed hunger, reaching out a fingertip to circle a nipple pressing hard and aching against the soft fabric of her top. She closed her eyes and arched back into the bright burn of his hand, her breath coming in short, sharp pants.

'So responsive,' he murmured. 'A gift for me to unwrap.'

He slipped his hand under the shoulder of her robe and peeled it from her body, stroking down her back, easing into her shorts and cupping her backside, pulling her flush against him. Her hands roamed against the hardness of his chest, the dusting of hair prickling against her fingertips. He pinched her nipple with his free hand and rolled it between his fingers. She gasped, arching into him.

'You like that. What else might you enjoy for me?'

He did it again and she moaned, heat flooding between her thighs. His lips descended, teasing hers. She parted for him, and their tongues touched as she melted into the rhythm of the kiss. Not hard and taking, but something far hotter, gentle and coaxing, as if he was leading her slowly to anticipate the pleasure he'd promised. The care he showed cracked something inside her, emotion welling through her like lava from a volcanic fissure. He began to pull away and she chased the kiss, not wanting him to see how he was shattering her.

He didn't let her win that little battle between them. Lance rolled on top of her, the sheet and coverlet caught between them. The hardness of him pressed at the centre of her.

'You said you weren't exactly a virgin. What does that mean? It tends to be a state of being you either are or you aren't.'

His voice was kind but the words… They brought that

horrible, humiliating memory rushing back. The searing pain. The disappointment. She shut her eyes, but it didn't stop her recollecting that awful night.

'Sara, we need to communicate. Whatever happened to you, it wasn't good, and I need to know because tonight's *all* about you.'

His thumbs brushed her temples, back and forth, soothing her. She had to get past this, the feeling that she somehow *lacked*, because of the way Ferdinand had made her feel that night. She took a deep breath and simply started.

'He said if we tried it might make our wedding night less fraught.' She wouldn't look Lance in the eye but stared at the ceiling over his shoulder, the ornate cornices embossed with gold leaf. His hands eased into her hair, stroking her scalp in a soothing rhythm. 'It sounded like a sensible idea. So we did. It…hurt a lot.'

The fingers in her hair clenched, and her scalp stung for a fleeting moment before Lance relaxed them.

'Tell me he stopped.'

His words were a hiss through clenched teeth. It had been her former fiancé's one act of kindness that evening. He'd stopped immediately. No attempt to comfort her, just a suggestion that things might be better if she had a few drinks beforehand, maybe at the wedding, then left her. Probably to go to his lover. How she'd tormented herself with that thought over the subsequent days, that her failure in bed had chased him away.

'Yes. He didn't…finish. He went away.'

Lance dropped his forehead to hers. 'Thank you for telling me. I know it was difficult.' His voice was soft, soothing. 'But in this bed I want you only to have pleasure, and to do that I need you to feel able to tell me what you don't want, as much as what you do.'

'What if I'm not really sure what I want?'

The corners of Lance's lips curled in a smile of unadulterated wickedness. His hips flexed into her and the feel of him, hard between her legs, almost made her eyes roll back into her head. As she moved to meet his rhythm, a tantalising pressure began to build deep inside.

'Trust me when I say I have plenty of ideas of what it will take to have you an unintelligible mess of sensation in under ten minutes.'

Her breath caught. There wasn't enough air in the room. Her head spun because the *intent* in his words...

'You sound very certain of yourself.'

He grazed his teeth over the shell of her ear, his breath teasing her throat.

'I am,' he growled. She slid her hands beneath the waistband of his boxer shorts, grabbing the taut muscles of his backside, her nails digging hard into his flesh and trying to pull him closer as he continued to rock against her body.

'Too many clothes,' she panted into his mouth and felt his smile against her lips.

'Greedy. We're doing slow.'

The explosion of that promise roared through her as she shivered with need. He pulled away, and she might have whimpered as he closed his mouth over the fabric of her top and sucked at her nipple, raking his teeth over the tight bud then sucking some more, the sensation arrowing like an electric shock between the juncture of her thighs. He turned his attention to her other nipple, which wasn't quite as sensitive.

'You prefer the left to the right. I'll remember that.' He lifted her top high, settled on the left nipple once more, sucking, teasing with his teeth. Slipping his hand down below the waistband of her sleep shorts, but not to where she wanted him most, teasing but never going far enough. Driving her wild until she twisted and squirmed underneath him, trying to get close, to rub her aching core against him. Then he stopped. She let out a moan of frustration and he chuckled.

'I reward good girls who do what I ask.' Heat flashed over her. If self-combustion was possible, this bed would be her funeral pyre. 'Lie still.'

She obeyed immediately. His smile was pure wickedness as he leaned over her, kissing down her chest, her belly, settling himself between her thighs. He grabbed the waistband of her shorts and she felt his breath at the centre of her as he slid them from her body.

'Open your legs wider,' he murmured, his lips teasing as he skimmed his tongue over her inner thighs. Her legs relaxed as she panted his name over and over. 'That's it. So perfect for me.' He settled between them, easing them wider till she was splayed out like an offering on the altar of his bed.

'I can't wait to taste you. It's all I've dreamed of.'

He'd dreamed of this?

'Please...' she moaned, not caring how wanton it sounded, the burning ache raging between her thighs making her lose her mind, all of her one bright, burning nerve-ending. He didn't move, just looked at her, thumbs circling close, but never close enough, his breath between her legs, warm on her oversensitive flesh. Her thighs trembled in anticipation.

'So sweet and wet for me.' His tongue licked the centre of her and she arched her back, bright lights bursting behind her eyes. There was no time for her to think about what he was doing, or that she should perhaps be embarrassed, with his tongue at the heart of her, his mouth working a slow rhythm. Licking, swirling, sucking. She closed her eyes because she couldn't stand it any more.

He stopped. 'For now, lie back and enjoy. Soon enough I'll have you watching me pleasure you.'

Lance centred on her clitoris. Nothing carried any meaning bar the burst of delicious agony between her thighs, his tongue concentrating on one tiny spot where her world entirely focused. Circling and driving her mad. She thrust her hand into his hair, gripping tight and holding him in place, as if it would end her if he moved away. The harder she held, the slower he went until all she felt was the impossible light flicking of him, and she writhed against his mouth, trying to get closer, saying unintelligible things, begging for release from the agony of it all. He didn't relent, the sensual torture seemingly endless. As if she were the most delicious dish imaginable and he was savouring her. Each time she came close he eased off, and she hated and adored him in equal measure as she trembled in ecstasy.

Then she felt it, at the entrance of her. A finger, pressing and easing inside. Sliding out and moving in again in a relentless rhythm, until it was joined by another. She moved her hips in time with his ministrations, the circling of his tongue, the thrust of his fingers. Then he curled them, touching a place deep inside. Her hips lifted from the bed and his mouth sucked hard at the heart of her. She wailed as the white-hot scorch of an orgasm tore through her body, wave after wave of agonising spasms wrecking her completely.

He brought her down gently, kissing her inner thighs, stroking her as she sobbed, tears streaming down her cheeks and she didn't care.

Losing her mind had never felt so good.

Lance took a glorious moment to absorb the beauty of Sara Conrad, gasping and unintelligible, sobbing with pleasure. Sleep shirt rucked up. Legs splayed wide. He gloried in the sensation, his name on her lips a benediction. Spread out on the sheets of his bed like a wicked offering. Utterly wrecked. He moved up her body, stroking, soothing, as he anticipated the next moments, of *finally* being inside her, hot and perfect.

She moaned at his touch and he allowed her to catch her breath, to glory in the sensation of her first orgasm at the hands of another. Then he kissed her luscious cherry lips and she almost devoured him, arching her body into his palms. He needed fewer clothes, nothing between them, close to being swept away by the wave of passion between them. He wrestled off his boxer shorts, the last vestige of his attempt at respectability stripped away, and carefully slipped Sara's top from her limp, replete body so she lay, flushed and glorious, on the bed before him.

He craved to rush, pound into that glorious soft body of hers till she screamed his name again. But she deserved his time, his selflessness. His hands trembled as he sought out protection and sheathed himself. How long had it been since he'd been like this, almost out of his mind with desire? Like a teenager all over again, when life still seemed full of possibility and promise. All he wanted was to be inside the warm dark heart of her and lose himself, carry them away from the reality of how temporary this was.

He crawled over her. Dropped his mouth to her favoured left nipple and used his teeth and tongue until she was writhing and begging once more, pleading to be sated. He was so damned hard he was terrified he wouldn't last, wanting her mindless again before he entered her, so he could keep his promise that this bed was about pleasure. He slid his hand between her legs, delving inside as she rocked into his palm, so wet and swollen with arousal it almost undid him. Then he positioned himself over her, notched at the centre of her body, and began sliding home, easing inside her until she was praying and moaning his name over and over. He stilled as she gasped. Held, seated deep inside her until she became used to him, kissing her slow, lush and deep.

'Let me show you how I *own* you.'

He moved. Slowly at first, gently rocking, till her legs wrapped round his waist and her heels jammed into his back, driving him hard. He took her with firm thrusts, buried his head in her neck and breathed in the heady scent of flowers and hot, aroused woman. Harder and harder, glorying in the digging of her nails in his back, the slick slide of bodies coming together.

Starbursts behind his eyes told him he was close. The way she clenched round him warned him she was too. He gritted his teeth against the prickle at the base of his spine, wanting her to come first, panting through the impending ecstasy as she ground against him, moaning, *'Please... please...please...'*

He lifted on his arms, looking down on her, head thrown back, eyes heavy-lidded and vacant with ecstasy, taken to some other place he'd soon follow as he thrust, keeping up a relentless rhythm. He dropped his gaze to where they were joined, the eroticism of that sight almost undoing him.

But her first. Always her.

*'Angel.* Look at *us*…look at what I'm doing to you.'

The words were a command and he loved how she obeyed, coming out of her reverie, lifting her head from the pillows to watch between them, her eyes glassy, almost unfocused.

He changed his angle. A tilt and twist and it ended her. She arched, falling back, screaming to the room and convulsing around him. The sensation ripped up his spine, rending him in two. His mind blanked with white-hot ecstasy, her name on his lips like a prayer of thanks.

Lance dropped to her, their bodies slick, pressing feather-light kisses over her neck as she came back to herself moment by moment. Her warm, gentle hands slid over his back as they remained joined. He'd move in a moment, but this... In his long and privileged experience, he'd never enjoyed anything like it. It rocked him, and in a recess of his barely functional brain he knew it was...*more*. This woman in his arms, in his bed, was *everything*. He could barely catch his breath. He wanted her again and again. He was still hard inside her. He could take her now, wanted to. He felt insatiable. It should have terrified him, but all that settled over him was a gloating kind of contentment.

Sara untangled her legs from around his back with a sigh as he slid out of her. Coherence was still piecing itself together, sensible thought blown apart. Somewhere in the fog of lingering pleasure he knew this should be worrying him, but as his body hummed, replete, he really couldn't care.

'Is it always like this?' she whispered, her voice hoarse. A pulse of ego thumped through him, that he'd done this to her.

*Never...*

But he couldn't admit that, or the truth of what they'd both experienced.

'Yes...if you know what you're doing.'

The lie wrapped its sharp tendrils round him, digging in hard, because he was not doing justice to what they'd shared. But there was no point romanticising this for her, or waxing poetic about what had happened in this bed. This was short-term, not for ever. Even though every nerve in his body screamed in violent disagreement that short-term wouldn't be long enough to sate him. Medium-term, he bargained. He'd tire of this before then.

He had to. He couldn't keep her.

A smile curled on Sara's pink, well kissed lips, and an egotistical pleasure curled through him. 'Then you must *really* know.'

'I like to think so.'

He rolled away from her and his confusing thoughts, leaving the bed to deal with the condom. Splashed cold water on his face to bring him back to his senses. Recently, even though he was only thirty-two, he'd felt old. Knew without a doubt he was jaded. But when Rafe had married…somehow imagining his best friend and partner in crime being… *domesticated* made settling down seem almost tempting.

He shook his head. It was a marriage of necessity for the Lauritanian Queen, and one of ambition for Rafe. Still, Lance had assumed that he and his friend would be the last bastions of bachelorhood. But tonight, with Sara in his arms, something else roared through him. As if he were eighteen again, with his whole life ahead of him. It was intoxicating, that sense of possibility, the same as when he walked into an old house full of hidden treasures. He didn't know what to do with that. And it didn't bear thinking about, so he returned to the bed where Sara lay.

She looked at him and stretched, but in her eyes he could see a small shadow of uncertainty. There was no way that could remain. In this bed, Sara shouldn't feel uncertain about anything. He stalked towards her, beautiful and wrecked, her skin flushed pink with grazes here and there from his growing stubble. Marks he'd made. A rush of blood coursed through him. Her eyes dropped to his groin and it was his turn to smile. There were advantages to everything feeling so new and fresh. He was hard for her again and from the way her eyes fixed on him with hunger it was clear she wanted him too.

'I hope you're ready to get no sleep tonight.'

Her eyes widened, and then her lips curled into a seductive smile. He hadn't wanted to touch her, but it was done now. He'd have time for regrets later, when this was over. By then, he hoped to have obliterated all unpleasant memories from her head for ever.

'Weren't we supposed to be doing something tomorrow?'

'Yes.' He'd planned a stroll through the village, but that could wait. He wanted as many of these glorious moments, losing himself in her, as he could get. 'We're spending the day in bed.'

# CHAPTER EIGHT

POLO PONIES THUNDERED ACROSS the field. Bodies clashed. Sara flinched. Lance was in the thick it all, chasing a white ball on the ground somewhere. Her heart thrashed in her chest, part thrill, part terror. He had given her a quick lesson on the rules before they'd left for the charity polo match, organised to raise money for women escaping domestic violence. He said she needed to know when to cheer for him. But she didn't want to cheer. It looked dangerous, with large and seemingly uncontrollable horses racing around, jostling each other. Riders with mallets held high.

A pony broke free of the rough and tumble. *Lance.* Whilst she didn't know much about riding, she knew instinctively the man was an expert. He looked as if he were part of the horse, strong thighs gripping the saddle. She might have had heated fantasises about him, seeing the pictures of him on horseback when she'd searched him online, but looking at the man for real, face intent, directing some huge animal seemingly with the power of thought alone...

The heat of it speared through her and her breathing quickened. He was a magnificent animal himself, all taut, controlled muscle. She ached to have him alone somewhere, anywhere. Who knew she could have become so...wanton? No pretence any more. Working side by side during the day, with the excitement of finding treasure, and their nights entwined with each other. Heat pooled, deep and low, in her abdomen, all of her soft and willing and ready. Those memories. Making love till exhaustion claimed them, snatching sleep, making love again.

No. Not making love. There was no love here, was there. This, them, was only temporary. She'd never really been loved, she recognised. Not by her parents, or Ferdinand. She wondered what it was about her that was so…undeserving. The cut of that thought sliced deep. A sharp pain that could almost cleave her in two. This sensation with Lance *wasn't* love. It was something else. Dark, sultry. Moments of headiness that made her giddy. Though why did the merest thought of it being over make her want to curl in bed for days and weep?

The crowd cheered; they were quite uproarious given the supposed refinement of its members. Though champagne was flowing freely, which probably added to the rowdiness of the group. She took a sip of said champagne, then cheered along with them. Men. Women who stared out at the field. Stared at her, some with curiosity, some with daggers unsheathed. Though most interest was reserved for Lance. He was like the centre of the solar system for everyone there.

The match ended, and it seemed Lance's team had won. He leapt from his current mount, a magnificent chestnut now gleaming with sweat, pulled his shirt out from his polo whites and wiped his face, showing a slice of toned, muscled abdomen she knew came from hard exercise, but also hard work, particularly in the stables.

She shivered, the anticipation of a celebration tonight coursing through her. She wondered whether, in the rough and tumble of it all, he'd have any injuries. She'd kiss them better. She'd kiss him all over. Lance had been a passionate, attentive lover who was not shy about telling her explicitly what he enjoyed. An announcer droned in the background as the crowd returned to other things, drinking, eating. She couldn't wait for the afternoon to end. Because tonight...

'You're a surprise.'

The clipped haughty tone of a woman's voice pulled Sara from her heated fantasies. She turned. A woman with a champagne glass held casually like an afterthought in long, manicured fingers. Everything about her was tailored and perfect. The gleaming golden hair casually curled at the ends, no unruly tangles there. Blue eyes, darker than her own, leaning to grey, were cutting and cold. The smile on her face was sharp like a blade, make-up expertly applied to look barely-there, in a way Sara hadn't mastered without professional help. She was tall, elegant. Everything Sara was not. This woman's looks were a weapon she wielded.

She resembled the women she'd seen on Lance's arm in those tabloid photographs, and the ones that still showed up when she looked online, torturing herself with the untruths about their fake relationship. Initially she'd done it for amusement. To laugh at the fiction they wrote, because it was all a morass of lies. Which led her to contemplate the truth of what they wrote about Lance... But then there were the nastier comments. The talk of inevitable infidelity on his part, comparing her to his bevy of past lovers and finding her wanting in every way.

*You'll never have his heart.*

No, she wouldn't let the cruel memory taunt her. That didn't matter. He might not want her heart, but she didn't want Lance's either. All she wanted was his body. Didn't she? But that didn't deal with the woman in front of her, one brow raised in a supercilious way, almost tapping her foot, waiting for some response.

'Excuse me?' Sara asked.

The woman elegantly waved one hand in the direction of the field. 'Everyone wonders how you caught him. One moment he's the world's most wanted bachelor and the next, well, here we are.'

'Love's like that.'

'Love. *Of course.*' Said with disdain, as if Sara were some kind of fool. The woman took a healthy swig of her champagne and grabbed Sara's left hand. In the shock of the moment, Sara didn't have the wherewithal to pull away.

The woman glared at Sara's engagement ring, her lip curled in what appeared to be a triumphant smile. 'Pretty. But it's not the Astill Amethyst.'

As if that jewel had some kind of mythic status. How did this woman know about it? When had she been close enough to see it? A tightness clenched in her gut, hard and sickening, as if she'd drunk sour milk. Sara wanted to see it now too. Even though, had they been engaged for real, she still wouldn't have wanted it to grace her finger.

The woman looked impassive, cool and poised, like every woman she imagined Lance would spend time with. But it didn't matter. Lance had chosen this ring for her.

*'Beautiful and complex, like you.'*

That was *all* that mattered.

Sara plucked her hand from the woman's grasp. 'I don't have the amethyst because I loathe the colour purple.'

The woman's eyes barely widened a fraction. 'Really?'

The word was loaded with so much that was unsaid. That Sara was too unpolished. Too gauche for a man like the Duke of Bedmore.

'With the greatest of respect...' Sara knew the woman meant none '...we hadn't heard anything about you, and then here you are. From Lauritania as well. Everyone knows Lance despises the place.'

*Enough.* Sara straightened her spine, standing as tall as she could. Whilst her country had a multitude of failings, she still loved it. She'd been trained to be its *Queen.*

'Yes. Here I am. *Engaged.* With a sparkly ring and all.' She wiggled the fingers of her left hand in the woman's direction, feeling more petty than queenly.

The woman said nothing, merely turning back to the field, took another sip of champagne. Sara watched her gaze as it travelled over the players. Lance had removed his shirt. Sara was sure that was a scandalous thing to do, but the sight of his muscular back and the vee of his torso dried her mouth.

'He's a fine horseman. Do you ride?'

The wicked memory of her astride Lance, his head thrown back as she took him deep inside her flickered through her head.

'Horses?' Sara asked with feigned innocence. That was greeted with a supercilious raised eyebrow. 'No. Do you?'

'Of course.' Sara had no doubt this woman would be perfect at everything she did. Unlike her. She was too unruly, too forthright. Too much of everything. 'I'm sure Lance will teach you. He's kind like that. But you do know what they say about him?'

'I'm sure if I don't you'll enlighten me.' A prickle of something cold ran down her spine.

'The Duke of Bedmore. Beds 'em, not weds 'em. Chucks 'em after he—'

'Play nicely, Vic.' That deep, soothing male voice. Lance. Relief coursed through her. She wheeled around and placed her hand on his chest, as much for the ice-cold beauty behind her as for anyone else in the crowd.

'Darling—' she said in a way that might have sounded a little too breathless and a lot too fake, but she didn't care '—

you were outstanding. But I haven't been introduced to...'
She waved her hand in the direction of the other woman in
a dismissive manner, the perfect balance of queenly *and*
petty this time.

The woman smirked, then downed the last of her champagne in one gulp. Lance frowned, but the look in his eyes
was hard to fathom. Distant, sad. Lost.

'Sara, this is Lady Victoria Carlisle. My sister.'

'Your...sister?'

Of all the things she'd expected, that was not it. Victoria
dumped her empty glass on a server's tray. Grabbed another.
Took another healthy sip and raised her glass.

'Pleased to meet you. Welcome to the family. I look forward to the blessed union and so forth.' She turned to Lance
with a brittle smile. 'See? I know how to play nicely.'

Lance took the glass of champagne from Victoria's hand
and gently set it down on a side table before grabbing some
water to hand to her instead. She pouted but accepted the
glass and took a sip. That sadness was in her eyes too.

'Enough.' His voice was soft and low. He turned to Sara,
cupped her face. Dropped his mouth to hers in a gentle kiss.
'I need to have a chat with my sister. Are you safe to enter-
tain yourself for a few moments?'

Sara touched his hand. 'Of course.'

He turned and led his sister away. Something was going
on, something painful to both of them.

Something terribly broken, in need of repair.


Lance took Victoria to a quiet corner, or as quiet as he could
find in the marquee, where champagne flowed and people
were a little the worse for wear. He checked her over as
subtly as he could, because being late to the event usually
meant she'd had an argument with her husband. He was

relieved to see no bruises Vic would try to explain away. However, Lance knew bruises didn't have to be physical. The tongue could lash as mightily as a fist. Because she wasn't wearing sunglasses, he was able to check her eyes. Her pupils were a normal size today, not pinprick. Her voice was clear and cutting, not slurred. To his mild relief, Vic presented nothing other than a cool and brittle aristocratic demeanour.

'She's a pretty little thing.'

Lance hoped she hadn't been too cruel. His sister had a fine capacity to wound, honed to rapier-like precision. He missed the sweet, soft teenager she'd once been, until their parents had destroyed her life.

'Sara's *beautiful*.' And she was. In a dress the same pale blue as her eyes, she glowed. The way she'd looked at him as he'd dressed to ride had almost made him disgrace himself.

'Must be love.' Vic gave an unladylike snort. 'I didn't think our family believed in it. Girl has a spine too. She'll need that in—'

'Leave him.'

Vic's gaze shot to his, a little wide. She was an expert at hiding her emotions, but Lance could sense the fear none-theless. The way she flinched as if under attack.

'Astills don't divorce.' The tone of her voice, those words, were a perfect imitation of their mother.

'You're not an Astill any more, so feel free. *Please*.'

Vic shook her head. 'I've got nothing. You don't under-stand.'

He hadn't protected her back then, but he could protect her now.

'I told you—'

'I'm not taking any of Father's money!'

Vic had always seen the inheritance as tainted. A poi-

soned chalice she would not touch. He had trouble understanding why, when what he had could help her.

'I'm not asking you to. I have my own. I can help.'

'And now I have to rely on the charity of my own brother?
What would everyone say? Look at poor Victoria Carlisle.
Barren... Divorced...'

'Vic, what hold does he have over you?'

She shook her head, her glass of water quivering in her
fingers. 'Nothing you could ever understand.'

'I could try if you expl—'

'No. Leave this be. It's not your concern.'

Yet again, she wouldn't accept his help. Another failure
to add to the litany of shortcomings in his past. Not only his
sister, but Sara too. He'd meant to protect her, look after her,
and what had he done? Taken her to bed. Touched her with
fingers soiled by his genes, by generations of reprobates.
Sara might look at him as if he were all things perfect, as
if he were a god, but he couldn't shake the feeling that she
would be tainted for ever by their association.


'I hope Victoria wasn't...difficult.' The car was warm in
the autumn sunshine. They hadn't spent much longer at the
post match celebrations. Seeing Vic had coloured the rest of
the afternoon, relief and concern all tangled into one congealed mess of emotions.

'Is she often?' No denial then. Sara stared out of the window at the passing countryside.

'She's changed since she was a child.' It was as if he had
to defend her against the cruelties the world had meted out.
Ones he hadn't prevented. 'She was happy once.'

'And then she grew up.' The distant wistful sound of her
voice said a great deal about Sara's current thinking. There

was more in the loaded tone than a mere comment about his sister. 'What happened?'

'Her marriage isn't a good one.' That wasn't breaching any real confidence, but it so far underplayed what was going on there, he couldn't help the stab of guilt.

'Lots of people have unhappy marriages.'

'It was arranged, by my parents. To further my father's career. Mine too, if I'd wanted.'

His parents certainly had. His father had grand plans for Lance. The House of Lords, politics, Prime Minister. Victoria had been the sacrificial lamb. He gripped the steering wheel even tighter.

Sara whipped round then, eyes slightly wide. *'Oh.'*

The way she stared at him said too much. As if she'd peered deep inside him and in some way found him wanting. She reached out her hand and placed it on his thigh, the touch warm and comforting. He wanted to shrug it off. He didn't deserve any respite. His sister had none.

'You can't save someone until they want to be saved.'

'I don't know what she wants,' he said. The pain of that recognition was unrelenting. At five years younger than him, Vic was too young for this life where she seemed to numb her sorrows in a bottle of painkillers. He knew she wanted children desperately. For whatever reason, no pregnancy had come, and each year he watched her fold into herself as if trying to disappear. With a cruel husband blaming her, rather than accepting some things might never be.

'She seems to care about you a great deal. She was only being protective.'

'That's no excuse.'

Another gentle touch of her hand. 'You don't need to apologise for something that's not within your ability to control.'

She was so wise, each word assuaging some of the pain

that plagued him. It wouldn't last, it never did. The taint
of guilt always crept over him. Like a slick of oil he could
never wash free.

'The charity you were playing for...'

'Helping domestic violence victims.'

'Does Victoria have a particular interest?'

What could he say that wouldn't alert Sara to how much
more to this story there might be? The terrible things he
suspected.

'She seems to.'

Sara nodded. 'Then I shall make a donation. For her. To
help.'

'Perhaps you might become friends.'

Or perhaps not. Victoria and Sara might be close to the
same age, but Victoria had few friends now, seemingly
trapped in a world of her own misery. Her only joy appeared to come from her horses, and the other wounded
creatures she tried to rescue along the way.

'I don't believe I'm supposed to be around long enough.'
Her voice was barely a whisper. What was he thinking? The
truth was, he hadn't been. She flummoxed him, unsettled
him, tangled his thoughts when he needed to keep them
straight. Sara was short-term. His duty was to save her, set
her on her feet and then set her free. Nothing more.

They drove the rest of the way in relative silence, even
though he knew Sara had things to say. The way her gaze
kept flicking to him. How she nibbled her bottom lip in
contemplation.

They arrived at Astill Hall and he parked the car. He
couldn't be around her. Those knowing looks, as if she
wanted to *talk* about things. He couldn't deal with that.
How would she feel if she discovered he hadn't protected
his own sister?

So, telling Sara he had to go and tend to the horses, he went to the stables. He helped the groom rub them down, made sure they had no injuries. Once he'd satisfied himself, he went to his room, desire for Sara and disgust in himself congealing in a potent morass of emotion he needed to wash away.

He walked into the en suite bathroom and undressed, tossing his clothes on the floor. Turned on the shower, planted his hands on the wall and stood as the hot water rushed down his back. At least they'd raised over ten thousand pounds today. That would help alleviate some suffering. Assuage some guilt.

'May I join you?'

Her soft voice jolted him from his introspection. He straightened to say something, to say no, even as every part of him became hard and ready for her. Yet his words died in his throat when he turned.

Sara stood in the bathroom, glorious and naked, unruly hair round her shoulders, spilling to the tops of her breasts, her tan nipples beaded and tight, almost begging for his mouth to be on them. She didn't wait for an answer, stepping under the hot spray, her skin pinking as it splashed her. He should turn the temperature down, but she didn't complain, and he was too lost in her blue eyes to do anything but stare.

She reached out and ran her hands over his chest. Despite the heat of the water raining down on them, his skin shivered in goosebumps at her gentle touch. He should tell her to go, that he was dirty and he'd make her unclean too. Any moment now he'd say something...

'It looked rough today.'

'No more than normal,' he managed to grind out, though he wasn't sure she was speaking about his riding.

'I liked it...watching you. All that control. You were...

impressive.' She looked down at him, erect and aching, the drops of water sparkling like raindrops on her eyelashes. 'No one could take their eyes from you.' She licked her lips.

He didn't give a damn if the whole world had been watching. All he cared about was the female perfection studying him now, as if he were her last meal.

'Wondering if I would elicit some scandal from the back of one of my ponies is all.' His voice sounded tight and strained, even to his own ears. She ran her hands over his pectoral muscles and his breathing hitched.

'Did you hurt yourself?'

He couldn't say anything as her hand trailed down his abdomen, lower and lower, till he dropped his head back against the tiles. Then she stopped. He wanted to shout out, but all he did was shake his head.

'I want to check and make sure,' she said, and right now he'd agree to sign his soul over to the devil so long as she continued to caress every part of him. If he hadn't done so already, many years before.

She continued the soft touches on his arm, tracing it. Looking for what, he wasn't sure. A careful inspection of his skin. She placed her hand on his hip and applied enough pressure to tell him she wanted him to turn around. So he did, and she kissed him between his shoulder blades, her tongue licking at the water there before continuing her exploration, running her gentle, questing hands over his back. Down lower. Down each leg, and he knew—he *knew* she was on her knees.

He groaned. 'Sara.'

She stroked over a graze on his hip. Kissed it gently. Kissing him better.

'Turn round,' she murmured against his wet skin.

He hesitated for just a heartbeat before he complied. She

was on the floor before him, looking up. Hair in wavy ribbons plastered to her body. Skin flushed pink all over. Mascara blurred and smudged. Little rivulets of water running down her face. She licked at one running over her lips and he almost lost himself then and there. Then her eyes left his face, looked at him, aroused in front of her. Took him in hand, and he bucked in her warm, steady fingers. She smiled then, like a siren.

'I think you like this.' All he could do was hiss as she tightened her grip and moved her hand like he'd shown her one night, when she'd asked how he enjoyed being touched.

He couldn't take his eyes from her. Her gaze was intent, her mouth so damned close he wanted to beg, to weep, and then the corners of her lips tilted. She moved closer still. Her mouth opened and her tongue licked the head of him. Then slowly, so slowly, she wrapped her lips round him and took him into her mouth.

She had him completely in her thrall. He would give her all the riches he owned, his heart, his soul, everything to ensure she'd never stop what she was doing now. He couldn't stop his hips from leaning into her and she moaned as if she was enjoying it, her eyes closed, wrapping her hand round him, gripping tight and working him till he didn't know who he was or what he wanted any more. Except her. Always craving her.

The base of his spine prickled. Any moment now he'd lose himself completely. He pulled out and she made a small whimper of protest.

'Up here,' he growled. Lance bent down, hands under her arms as she surged to his mouth, teeth clashing as she kissed him, wrapping her arms round his neck as he slammed her against the cool tiles. She lifted her leg and he gripped it, hauling her up his body with both hands under her backside, opening her to him. The panting of their breaths filled the room.

He angled himself, and the heat of her centre began to envelop him as he gave one hard thrust and entered her. She moaned long and low. Her nails scraped against his scalp, fingers gripping his hair. It stung as she tugged, but he relished the pain. Thrusting hard and deep, their bodies slapping and sliding against each other, grappling for purchase. That prickle in his spine started again, something heavy and unstoppable. Sara's legs tightened around his waist as her whole body clenched and spasmed round him. She tore her mouth from his and cried out, tumbling over the precipice. He followed with a roar echoing through the room.

He was spent, legs weak. The only thing keeping him upright was that he held Sara, and he didn't want her to fall, wouldn't let her go. He eased out of her, and she slid down his body, the water still streaming over him. Her lips were red as summer cherries, her body marred by finger marks and evidence of how rough he'd been. She'd wanted to check for his injuries, but he'd hurt her. He stroked his hand over the marks he'd left.

'You'll bruise.'

She smiled, a glorious sight with her bee-stung lips. 'I don't mind. I love your marks on me.'

Marks, they had consequences. A chill ran through him. Consequences. He hadn't worn a condom. He dropped his head to hers. 'No protection.'

She smoothed the hair from his face. Ran her hands over his chest. Was he ready for her again? His heart pounded. She made him insatiable. And, strangely, the fact that he hadn't worn a condom didn't trouble him as much as it should have.

'I'm on the pill and I assume…you've been checked?'

'I have.'

He took his health seriously, the reassurance of his partners even more so. And the secret truth was that, despite the tabloid chatter, he hadn't been with anyone for some time. And he'd *never* been with anyone unprotected.

She brought her lips to his. 'Then let's spend the rest of the afternoon in bed.'

His mouth descended on hers once more. Against his better judgement, he couldn't say no.

# CHAPTER NINE

SARA CURLED UP in a chair in the bright parlour sipping coffee, shoes off, the sunshine warming the room. This was her favourite place in the house, with its yellow-papered walls adorned with little roses, overlooking the rose garden itself, which she'd been talking to the gardener about renovating to its former glory. And if this was her favourite room, then sitting with Lance after breakfast, as he attended to business whilst she looked on, was becoming one of her favourite pastimes. Small domestic moments that made her feel as if she belonged somewhere.

As he did every morning, Lance read the death notices. It seemed like a morbid enterprise, but he'd told her he was always looking to see who'd died and needed their estate *'picked over like a carcass'*. It was an odd thing to say when she found their hunting trips, as she now called them, exciting. She hadn't found anything like a Caravaggio, but she had identified some beautiful, valuable pieces which would hopefully do well at auction. Her parure had been sold. Soon she'd be completely independent of him, as she'd wanted.

She didn't know why that thought sat so heavily on her chest.

Sara took another sip of the rich, strong brew that the kitchen had perfected. She was sure her presence in Astill Hall was keeping Lance away from what he should be doing. His business was in London after all, but he didn't seem to mind being in the country. A complicated man in many ways, he kept so much hidden from her. Only in bed did he lay himself bare, and for those passionate hours she felt blessed. They'd settled into a kind of routine here, working together. Making love. Then when Lance was away, attending to duties around the estate, she'd explore the place herself.

'You'll get in trouble, looking at me like that.'

Lance's gaze hadn't lifted from his phone at all.

'How do you know I'm looking at you?'

He lifted his eyes, and something about them had changed, their appearance liquid and heated. 'I can always feel you looking at me.'

Lance dropped his mobile to the couch, stood and sauntered over to her with a lazy roll of his hips that made her think of a stalking predator.

'You're too far away.'

She put down her coffee and he swooped on her, swinging her into his arms. She laughed. 'Your tea will get cold. I know how you like it hot.'

'The only temperature I care about is yours.' He turned and walked back to his spot on the couch and sat with her nestled in his lap, nuzzling her neck with his lips, the warmth of his breath sending shivers through her.

'See?' he murmured against her overheating skin, as he trailed gentle fingers along her arm. 'Goosebumps. You need warming.'

He liked to play, she realised, take things slow, wind her higher and more frantic until she splintered, screaming his name loud. Right now, she didn't want slow. She wanted fast. As she straddled him, he slid his palms to her backside, dragging her forwards and flush against him.

His hardness nestled between her thighs.

*'Yes.'*

He raised an eyebrow, the corner of his lips quirked in a wicked smirk. Then she gave in to the impossible urge to rock against him. His eyes darkened to the colour of storm clouds before hail.

'You getting any warmer?' The words ground out of him as if he were battling for control. She was about to boil, as he cupped the back of her head and drew her to him, capturing her mouth, his free hand sliding up her thigh under the skirt of her dress. He brushed his thumb back and forth over her panties and she moaned.

'Much better than tea,' he murmured against her lips as she gave in to the burn of her body, chasing the sensation bearing down on her. 'That's it. I love you like this. Hot. Wet. Mine.'

*His.*

It should bother her. It really should. But if it troubled her enough she'd have to stop, and she couldn't. The feeling that she was melting like candle wax all over him was too delicious. Especially because she was there, almost there.

A bell softly chimed in the distance, or maybe it was in her head. She wouldn't be surprised if a chorus of angels started singing, this man brought her so close to heaven. She didn't care as their kisses deepened and he began unbuttoning the top of her dress with fervent fingers.

'Sir!'

She paused. Was that George's voice? She'd never heard him raise it.

'I won't be denied!'

Sara scrambled away from Lance as the protestations came closer. She knew that second voice, although she could hardly believe he was here.

'What the hell?' Lance muttered, adjusting himself and drawing the bodice of her dress together.

The door to the parlour smacked open as her brother stormed in, followed by Lance's butler, looking ready for a fight.

Lance straightened, all the heat bleeding out of him, replaced by something lazy and dangerous. The predator was back, and right now his gaze was fixed on someone Sara had never expected to see here.

'Really, George, why do people insist on disturbing us? Can't a man be the king in his own castle?'

'Your Grace, this man barged in. Would you like me to call the police?'

Her brother Heinrich stood stiff and to attention just inside the doorway.

Lance shook his head and waved in Heinrich's direction as if he were merely an annoying fly.

'Come back in five minutes. We could all probably do with more tea.' Then he glanced at her. 'Or, dare I say, a stiff brandy.'

George raised his eyebrows but backed out of the room and closed the door behind him. Sara clutched at the front of her dress, realising that in her haste she'd fastened the buttons in the wrong buttonholes. Her brother noticed. His scowl deepened.

He poked his finger towards Lance as if trying to punch a hole in the air. 'You!'

'Lance...' She tried to take a breath to calm herself, because the tremble of desire had been replaced by one of fear. 'This is my brother—'

'I know who it is.' Lance turned to her, his voice low, his eyes narrow and cold. Then he whipped back round to her brother, striding forwards with his hand out as if it was

perfectly normal for Heinrich to be barging into their home.
It was a complete change of demeanour.

'Hans! What a pleasure to greet you today as my brother-
in-law-to-be.'

*'Heinrich!'* her brother hissed, looking at Lance's hand
as if it were a snake and not a peace offering. He didn't
reach out his own.

Lance ignored the slight, the disdain flicked off him as
if it were water brushed away by wipers on a windscreen.
Although, by the look of him, it wasn't peace he sought,
standing tall and stiff with his jaw clenched.

'Henry, of course.' Lance turned to her and winked, his
grin cocky and devilish. Heinrich's colour deepened to a
shade of angry purple. Sara couldn't see what on earth was
funny about this. Her brother had been trained in the mil-
itary, an officer in Lauritania's small but efficient army.
There was always a sense of suppressed violence about him,
not so suppressed today.

*'You're coming home, Sara.'* Heinrich spoke in Lauritanian. It was an insult when Lance stood in the room. She
refused to have a conversation with her brother that Lance
couldn't understand.

'I don't think so. Since she's engaged to me,' Lance replied before she could say anything. He spoke Lauritanian?
Her eyes widened and so did her brother's. 'Sara, I know
I've never whispered sweet nothings to you in your native
tongue. I was leaving that surprise to our wedding night.'

'Never.' Heinrich strode forwards, slashing his hand
through the air like a knife. She flinched. The way he
looked at her, as if she were dust on his shoe and he was
disappointed the polished leather was soiled. 'He will never
marry you. It's all false.'

At least Heinrich had something right, though she'd never

admit it. She couldn't say anything because she was a terrible liar. Sara wanted her brother gone, out of this house. The longer he stayed, the more he would taint the memories here.

'It's not false. I've put a ring on it, so to speak,' Lance said, standing straighter and taller, taking faux offence. 'One that's as precious and sparkling as Sara. The light of my life.'

He looked down at her, warm and kind, his eyes dancing with entertainment, and she smiled in return. She couldn't help herself. The man was simply too much.

Lance cupped her cheek. 'Ah. There it is. What I've been waiting for.' He smiled back, and the moment became something precious between them.

'Stop this fakery!' Heinrich shook his finger at Lance as if he were scolding. 'Sara, men like this only want one thing. He's using you and when he's done he'll cast you aside.'

Lance turned, mouth a thin line. 'Like your family used her?'

That stopped Heinrich in his tracks. His eyes widened. 'I have no idea what you're speaking of.'

'I'm talking about another convenient arrangement to shore up your family's power. This time to a man almost twenty years her senior, whilst she was still wearing mourning clothes. Since Sara's first fiancé inconveniently *died*.'

'You're besmirching my esteemed family when your own is such a disgrace, an utter blight on the aristocracy?' Heinrich fixed his cold, cruel gaze on her. 'Sara, you were destined to be Queen, and *this* is who you choose?'

Lance moved in front of her, shielding her from Heinrich's censure.

'I'm from one of the oldest families in the UK. Distantly in line for the throne, as Sara kindly reminded me before we announced our engagement. So you see, Harold, she's not really trading down.'

Sara hadn't spoken up enough in her life, and she didn't intend to be a coward now. She stepped to the side to see Heinrich and Lance glare at each other, like circling bulls pawing at the ground.

'I'm *not* going home,' she said, crossing her arms and trying to look resolute when her stomach churned in a sickening sensation. Her hands trembled. 'I've done my duty. I did it for years. Now is time for *me*. Go. I'm happy here.'

Heinrich sneered at her. 'You turn your back on the family and there will be *nothing* for you. When this man casts you aside and you come fleeing home you'll be no more than the dirt on our soles.'

Even though she tried not to feel the pain of those words, they sliced sharp and true. She'd long suspected her only value to the family was in being sold off to the highest bidder. Today proved it.

Before she could say anything in response, the door opened and George walked into the room with a tray containing a teapot, a trio of cups and a bottle of brandy.

'Tea, Your Grace.' He placed it on a small side table. 'And brandy if so required. Do you need anything else?'

'Thank you. Please wait, I require a moment.' Lance's focus turned to Heinrich once more, his eyes the cold colour of a glacial moraine, hard and green. 'Say what you like about me, but you will *never* speak that way about Sara. George, where are the duelling pistols?'

Sara froze, as if the ice on the surface of Lake Morenburg had cracked and she'd plunged into the frigid waters beneath.

George remained ever the professional, completely impassive in the face of the drama surrounding him. Although his mouth might have twitched at the corners.

'Sadly, we have no ammunition. They haven't been used in two hundred years.'

Lance cocked an eyebrow. 'Hmm. That long?'

'With the greatest of respect, sir, you're not the finest shot.'

'But I am handy with a rapier.' Lance homed in on her brother once more, eyes full of deadly intent. 'Swords, then.'

Heinrich blanched. 'There will be no duelling.'

'You always were a coward. Unlike last time, there's no one to take your place today, so of course there will be duelling. Where are the rapiers, George?'

'Behind you, Your Grace. Would you like me to retrieve them from the cu—'

'No.' Lance stormed to a cupboard and thrust open the doors, frowning. Sara rushed to him, heart pounding. She had to stop this. Heinrich merely paced, clenching and unclenching his hands, muttering expletives all directed at her fake fiancé.

'Lance?' She placed her hand on his arm. His muscles tensed under her fingers. She didn't know what she wanted to say, other than to protect this man who was becoming precious to her in ways she couldn't even begin to contemplate right now. 'He was in the army. He fenced at school.'

'I know.' Lance's voice was hard as he withdrew two terrifying swords from the cupboard. Thin, gleaming blades of steel. 'Your brother and I have a history with weapons like these. It'll be all right. I did fencing too. Don't let your brother dim your happiness. I might become truly angry if he causes that to happen.'

He wheeled round and thrust a hilt towards her brother. 'Take this, Henry.'

*'Heinrich!'*

'I know your name. I simply refuse to dignify you with it.'

'I will not fight.' Her brother clasped his hands behind his back. 'You are being ridiculous.'

Lance dropped the sword in his left hand, which fell to the floor with an ominous clatter. He lifted the other and pointed it, leaving the barest distance from Heinrich's chest. Her brother stiffened.

'Perhaps. Better a fool than a boor and a bully like you.' Lance's stance was lazy yet assured. He brought the blade forwards with a twist and flick. A button flew from her brother's shirt. 'Like the Crown Prince.' Flick. Another button. 'May he rot in hell.' Flick. And another. 'You knew he wasn't faithful to Sara, that he'd never protect her, or love her. Yet you criticise me for *imagined* failings, when yours are very *real* and caused her harm?'

Heinrich stood, marble-white, the same colour as his ruined shirt. Lance stalked forwards, rapier at his side, bringing his own face mere inches from her brother's.

'Before I give you a scar to match my own, run along home like the coward you are.' Lance's hand gripped the sword tight, his knuckles pale.

'You're afraid for your own reputation, not for your sister. But remember, your King is my best friend. Whilst Sara is with me she'll have the full force of his protection, not to mention your Queen's. So take that back to your family, and choke on your aristocratic pride along with it.'

Lance turned his back on her brother, eyes blazing and fierce, like a golden warrior as he focused only on her.

'George, before I do something ill-advised,' he hissed through gritted teeth, 'please throw him out.'

Somewhere, far away in the house, the front door slammed. Heinrich hadn't waited to be escorted from the house, storming out on his own. Sara's whole body slumped in relief. She walked to Lance, his jaw still clenched, all hard and ferocious. She wanted to throw herself into his arms, be held, but by the look of him he wouldn't welcome it.

'What did Heinrich do to you?' she asked, her voice trembling as she tried to control the leftover ripple of fear still coursing through her.

Lance handed his sword to George, who collected the other from the floor and left the room with them.

'We both fenced at school. Heinrich was good, but I was better and he *hated* it. Hated Rafe and I, as all the boys at the Kings' Academy did. One day he challenged me to a fight with rapiers he'd smuggled from home.' Lance clenched his hands then flexed his fingers. 'I don't believe he thought I'd go through with it, but I wouldn't back down. When the time came he claimed to have injured his wrist. Said *I* was the coward if I refused to fight the person who'd offered to take his place. The school champion.'

Sara lifted her hand, then hesitated. The tightness around Lance's eyes softened as she stroked her fingers over the fine scar on the side of his jaw.

'You received this.'

'They wanted to draw blood. Teach me a lesson. It was never a fair fight. Fortunately, a teacher caught us. The school sought to hush up the whole mess. I suspect your family did too, given my father's carefully cultivated friendship with the King. Luckily for me, the blade was sharp and Lauritania had some fine plastic surgeons.'

Sara shook her head. She'd suspected her brother could be devious and cruel, but she'd had no idea what had happened all those years ago at school. There'd not been a hint of it at home.

'Thank you. For seeing him off.'

'I'll do *anything* to keep you smiling.' His voice was a tortured rasp. 'But be warned. I'm no one's hero.'

'You may not think so, but you're a hero to me.'

His nostrils flared, his lips a tight line. It was as if he was still looking for a fight, after her brother's inaction.

'Come with me,' he said. 'There's somewhere I haven't shown you.'

Lance stalked to the door and thrust it open. She hurried to catch up as he made his way through long halls, past room after grand room she'd not yet explored.

'Where are we going?' Her breaths huffed as she attempted to match his long stride. Still he didn't slow down, as if driven by some imperative to keep moving.

'You'll see.'

Lance kept up his relentless pace until they reached the southern side of the house, entering a long room with a rich red carpet. A bank of windows to the right overlooked a stretch of emerald grass that collided with a planted woodland. Scattered through the space were a few plush chaises facing a vast wall of portraits. Lance stopped, turned to the pictures and swept his arm wide.

'I'd like to introduce you to my illustrious family,' he said, his lip curled almost in a sneer.

She stared at the array of pictures. They seemed the same as the Morenburg Palace portraits, and those of her own family home. The aristocracy cataloguing their imagined magnificence for all to see.

'Why bring me here?'

'You should meet some of my ancestors.' Lance paced restlessly before stopping at an impressive gilt-framed portrait of a man dressed in scarlet trimmed with ermine, his robes bejewelled with pearls and rubies, elegant hand at his waist, one finger touching a golden key hanging from his belt.

'The Fourth Duke of Bedmore, an incurable hedonist. There's nothing he wanted that he didn't acquire. Married the beautiful young Mary to get himself an heir, then made it his mission to strip her considerable fortune.'

Sara studied the portrait. Its subject was handsome, even to the modern eye, standing with a familiar, almost amused look on his face.

'That's how things were then. I don't think many in the aristocracy married for love.'

Lance didn't acknowledge her, entirely focused on the painting. 'Mary was said to be desperately unhappy. She'd been meant for another man, but the Duke made certain promises to her and she fell for them. As did her family. Sound familiar?'

Sara shrugged. 'It's nice to think in some ways things have changed.'

'Have they?' Lance wheeled round, raising a sardonic brow. 'When he tired of Mary he locked her in her apartments. Demanded servants pass food through a barred door he refused to open. Would release her on rare occasions, only if she "behaved", and who the hell knows what that meant? He's smiling. This portrait shows his hand on the only key to her chambers. For years the portrait was kept in her sitting room, above the fireplace. A *reminder* to her of what he could do if he wanted to. That there was *no one* to stop him.'

Sara's breath caught, a sickening sensation twisting inside her as recognition flowed through her. Had her own life been much different? Engaged to a man who'd only wanted her pedigree, her ability to bear his heirs. Parents who hadn't cared that Ferdinand was unfaithful, their only response the cold reminder that she'd marry, become Queen and do her duty. Whilst she hadn't been locked in a tower, she'd been trapped nonetheless...

'That's horrible.' She was unsure whether the words were for Mary or herself.

Lance jabbed his finger at the wall, continued describing a litany of his family's sins, not sparing the past Dukes in any way. He was right. They had all been drinkers, gamblers, adulterers and fornicators, as he'd warned months ago. Some of them had been even worse. When he came to the last portrait, his own, he stopped.

'That's my *history*, Sara. There was not a shred of good in any of my ancestors.' He shook his head. 'Don't ever call me a hero when there's ample evidence that I'm as bad as the rest.'

She must realise now. There was no way she couldn't when faced with the evidence of his family's infamy. Chasing off Sara's brother had been no heroic act. It was the *least* he could do; any other man would have done the same for her.

Yet rather than look at him with distaste, she cocked her head, placed a hand over her heart. 'Both of our families, even Lauritania's royal family, have profited from the misery of others. Do you think I'm immune? I haven't examined my past in detail, but there's ugliness there too. All we can do is try to be better.'

Lance ran his hand through his hair. 'You don't understand.'

He had to make her, for her own good.

'I do. You say you're a bad man. But you can't control my thoughts.'

She was achingly beautiful, in a blue dress covered with little roses. The portraits of his ancestors were at her back, the ghosts of his past watching them. It was time to show her the truth of being an Astill. The Eighteenth Duke of Bedmore. He'd spent most of his adult years cultivating the role, slipping into it with ease because, no matter what she thought of him, it was who he was born to be.

'What if I wanted us to continue what was interrupted earlier? Here. Now. Told you to strip from your dress with the eyes of my ancestors upon you.'

Her mouth opened. Closed. Pink bloomed on her cheeks. Then she began to stroll towards him with a sultry roll of her hips, her fingers working the buttons on the front of her dress, one after the other. He wanted to shout at her to stop, all the while silently begging her to continue.

Sara shrugged the dress from her shoulders, the fabric sliding over her body to the floor as she stepped out of it and stopped in front of him, wearing nothing but sheer blue lace underwear. Desire mingled with the remnants of his anger, a potent mix that scorched through him with blazing heat.

'I'm not afraid of the dead, Lance. They can't hurt you.'

She glowed in the light pouring through the windows, the angel he'd called her in every way. A sickening burn of disgust rose to his throat. He couldn't do this, not here in the presence of his cursed past. Not to her. He closed the distance between them and wrapped his arms round her, burying his head in the side of her neck, drinking in the intoxicating scent of her like redemption.

Sara sank into him with a sigh and the fury of the morning bled away. Lance swung her into his arms. He was damned if he'd let anyone hurt her. She should be cherished. He could do something right—he would prove it. He'd look after her till the time came for her to leave.

Even though he feared the person he needed to protect her from most was himself.

# CHAPTER TEN

LANCE SAT IN his study, looking over the books. Everything had run seamlessly until now, with this pretence that he was leaving bachelorhood behind him. Who knew being a proper duke took so much work? His workload had seemed to increase exponentially since his pretend fiancée had entered his life. Or perhaps they were simply the demands of his staff trying to make things perfect for Sara, because she'd become beloved by them all.

Now George had given him some sort of report about Astill Hall. He'd never had a report about the particulars of running the house before. He trusted his staff implicitly to do their jobs, and nothing they'd ever done had caused him to question them. But George had insisted, inundating him with information about meals and things which needed to be done on the estate. The place was becoming unrecognisable. His efficient butler had tried to involve Sara in their meeting this morning, but Lance had refused. There was no need to disturb her when she was somewhere else about the house, probably in the kitchen garden with the chef, talking about vegetables.

It was all so domestic. The pleasure of that observation slid through him till he beat it away. What on earth was he thinking? Not much, bar the satisfaction of having her here. The house, which had been a mausoleum, causing him to spend most of his time in the bright lights of London, was beginning to feel like a home again. Every night spent together, limbs entwined. There was no pretence any more, the Duchess suite now unused unless they wanted a change of venue. It was all too satisfying, too comfortable. Yet... Once that might have given him an itch, now he gloated about it all. Life with Sara felt like something gloriously never-ending.

Except it had to end. The mere thought raised a howl deep inside him. But what was he, if not a man of his word? Still, her smile over coffee in the morning, glimpses of her as she explored the house and garden, set his heart alight. Perhaps he was selfish, but right now he didn't care.

Then he felt the glimmer of something. A sensation that spoke of a future which was concrete and permanent. The feeling of solidity he wanted to nurture and keep, not crush and destroy. He let it unfurl inside him, a far more interesting idea than listening to the cost of polishing the bloody chandeliers, which George was now discussing with him. As if he needed to know. But since Sara had entered the house it seemed the staff took their obligations of accountability terribly seriously. And rather than talking about said chandeliers and their repair he wanted to find her. Perhaps take her to their room, peel off whichever pretty dress she wore today. Make her gasp his name. Of course it didn't really need to be in their room.

He stared at the gleaming surface of the desk he was sitting at. Couldn't get out of his head the memory of Sara splayed out for him on the desktop, skin flushed, the glorious taste of her on his lips as she writhed under his tongue. Really, this room was no longer a place of work but a playground for his fantasies. And he had plans for every flat surface of his home. A dinner for two in the grand dining room, where he'd lay her out on the table and—

'You're not listening to a word I say.'

Could George imagine what might have been distracting him? Perhaps. He was canny like that. The man had been with him for years.

'No. You can do what you want with the chandeliers. You always have. Why now?'

'Lady Sara was raised to be a queen.' How much better would the Duchess of Bedmore sound? *Perfect.* And where had that thought come from? He shut it down. George went on. 'She will have high expectations, and all of us at Astill Hall are determined to exceed them.'

'I think she's merely happy to be here. I don't believe she has any expectations.'

Though Lance wasn't sure. Was she happy? He wanted her to be. It seemed imperative to discover whether she was. Immediately.

'Perhaps I should find Lady Sara and ask her?' George asked.

Lance gave a wry smile. 'Not if I find her first.'

His butler gave a knowing smile in return. 'If I may say—'

'Nothing's stopped you before.'

George cleared his throat. 'You've done well. Sara is a delight. We, all of us, are genuinely happy for you. It's a pleasure to have her in the house. And we've been wondering, would you like us to resurrect the nursery?'

'The *what*?'

The words were almost strangled in his throat. Except the thought of the nursery with a cot and mobile and pretty wallpaper didn't fill him with dread as he thought it should. He rubbed at an ache in his chest that felt something like yearning. For little cherubs like her. Hell, he couldn't be going there. But now his mind was filled with a vision of Sara, belly round with his child, sitting in the nursery in a rocking chair, nursing a baby. Of them running through the once silent halls, chasing squealing children. Little angels like herself. Those visions he'd had on the plane, as they were flying over here mere weeks before, coming back with a vengeance.

They made him glow with a satisfying heat, rather than cringe with cold dread. He should put an end to this talk, but somehow he couldn't. The words wouldn't come out to stop what he knew was foolishness and fantasy.

'Perhaps you should ask Sara what she'd like to do.'

There, he'd leave it with her and shut down these unfamiliar feelings. She'd tell George to wait, and that would be the end of that.

Lance stood, and his phone began to ring. He frowned. 'It's Victoria. I have to take it.'

George nodded and left the room as Lance picked up the phone.

'Vic. How are you?'

'Lance…' The sound was hollow with a slight delay, as if she was far away, her voice quiet and uncertain. 'It's only a quick call to let you know. I'm not allowed to talk for long.'

*Allowed.* A prickle of concern marched down his spine.

'Where are you?'

'Switzerland. A…a…clinic. Bruce thought it best.'

Hearing those words was like being thrown from his polo pony. The shock, then landing with a bone-jarring thud. That husband of hers, he'd never thought of what might be best for Vic. Ever. Only himself and his career. Even if it crushed Vic in the process.

'Why? What's happened? Why is it best?'

'I need some time.' Her voice was so tired, as if all the life had leached out of her. She'd been such a vibrant young woman, once a bright and shining light like Sara. Then she'd married and everything had dimmed.

'Mother agrees. Bruce is going through a lot at the moment, what with the campaign and my inability to fall pregnant, and I'm...'

Politics. Parents and a man who didn't cherish his wife.

'It takes two to make a baby, Vic. That's not your fault.'

'It was.' Her voice was knotted and choked. 'The fall. You know it did something.'

She'd been in intensive care with internal injuries after an incident involving one of her rescued horses, and all anyone could worry about was whether she'd be able to get pregnant when she recovered. As if she were some brood mare and not a young woman to be loved and cherished.

He clenched his fists tight and gritted his teeth till he managed to hiss out the words, 'That was an accident. No one's fault. You could have IVF.'

'Nothing's worked and I'm tired. So tired.'

'You're not happy. I'll say it again. Take your chance now. I'll help you. *Leave him.*'

'But the horses. My other animals. They're...' It was what she didn't say. She was more afraid for the pets she loved than she was for herself. 'You know how Bruce feels. If I'm not there...'

Was that what he held over her? No, there had to be something else, something Vic wouldn't tell him. Lance didn't care any more. He would gather every animal she owned, make sure they were safe. Then he would bring her here. Bring her home.

'I'll come and get you. You can stay with me.'

'*No.* You're engaged now.'

'That doesn't matter.' *Nothing* mattered, apart from doing what he should have done in the beginning—protect her.

He heard the murmur of a voice in the background and the muffled sound of Vic's reply, as if her hand was over the phone.

'I've got to go. I won't be able to talk for a while. They say I need no contact with anyone. I'll call you when I can, but—'

'Wait! Vic. What's—'

'It'll be fine, Lance. I promise. I…love you.' Her voice cracked. 'It'll *all* be fine.'

The line went dead. He closed his eyes, taken back to that damn cathedral. She'd looked so beautiful and fragile walking down the aisle in her wedding dress, and he *knew* he should have grabbed her then, stopped the wedding. But he'd been too tied up in his own life to listen to his gut feeling and now here she was—far away from home, in some prison of a clinic where she wasn't even allowed to use a phone. The embarrassing wife being locked away by her husband whilst he campaigned. Who the hell knew what would happen to her there? All because of his failure to act.

The reality lay before him, stark and endless. He knew how to throw legendary parties; he knew countless ways to make a woman scream in pleasure; he knew what the tabloids wanted to hear to keep him on the front page. But he didn't know how to look after a woman, how to protect her. He couldn't protect anything or *anyone*.

His selfishness and thoughtlessness would destroy everything in the end. No one should ever place their care in his hands. Especially not another bright and beautiful young woman, one with her whole life ahead of her.

Again, all he could selfishly think about was Sara, barefoot and pregnant, in his house. But why? She probably didn't even want that. She'd been engaged to that man since birth. She didn't need to be trapped by another. His failures had ruined Vic. He couldn't be trusted. He'd ruin Sara too. And if he did that he'd never forgive himself.

Sara stood in the portrait gallery once more. She adored the whole house, enjoying her daily explorations when they weren't out working, or if Lance wasn't corralling her against the nearest flat surface to undress her and make her scream his name. Frankly, not satisfied till she did.

Egotist.

She loved it. Was addicted to it. Addicted to him.

And yet here was where she came to ponder the man she'd slowly and inexorably fallen in love with, despite her best efforts. The whole of her existence in the house, the clear lines she'd set for herself, were blurred and smudged like a pastel picture.

She stared at the portraits before her. A gallery of his ancestors, stretching the length of the long wall. She'd studied them one by one, trying to figure out the family, endeavouring to understand *him*. This morning George, Lance's highly efficient butler, had come to her, asking about refurbishing the *nursery*. That wasn't the issue so much; the staff all came to her now with questions about Astill Hall, her preferences. As if she, not Lance, ruled the home. Assumptions made by the ring on her finger.

No, it was that *Lance* had directed him to talk to her.

When George had asked the question, she'd blushed. After what they'd done together, Lance completely unabashed and comfortable in himself and, in turn, making the passions of her own body come alive, the talk of a nursery and the prospect of babies made her flush red. Embarrassed like the virgin she well and truly wasn't any longer.

But a *nursery*. What did it mean? Lance could have an-

swered that question with a short, sharp *no*. Yet he'd in-
structed George to seek her out, as if it were her decision.
As if it was a question he wanted her to answer for him.
And that answer whispered in her ear seductively.

*Yes.*

The breath was jagged in her throat. That couldn't be the
answer. It really, truly couldn't. Yet the idea of him, of her,
together in this house, a real marriage and children, spoke
to her louder and louder. She hadn't meant for this to happen. All she'd wanted was freedom, and yet something about
the fake situation she'd walked into felt all too real. It was
a reality she didn't want to walk away from.

Because she felt free with Lance.

So she'd said yes. And George had smiled and practically
skipped on his way. Which had led her here, to the gallery
of Lance's ancestors, trying to figure him out.

She strolled down the line of paintings to his portrait.
Each one sent a message, but his… If she didn't know better,
she'd say it screamed a kind of warning. His picture made
no pretence of dignity. The man in the portrait lounged,
dissolute, almost indecent, as if a lover had just left him.
Shirt half open, a lazy gleam in his eye, a smirk on his lips.
Looking louche and untrustworthy, bent on destroying everything formal, right and proper. It was an exquisite picture
that had her standing in front of it far too long and too often.
Because it was all irony, a joke on everyone who looked at
it and only saw what they wanted to see.

She knew he wasn't the man in the painting, but someone else entirely. A man who cared for those who couldn't
care for themselves. Someone serious, who hid his true self
behind a veneer of humour and carelessness that he wore
like a layer of ice over a lake, leaving everyone unaware of
the depths beneath.

A man she craved to learn with every atom of her being.

'You spend too much time here.'

She whipped round. She hadn't heard him come in behind her because she was too absorbed by the picture. Lance leaned against a wall, arms crossed, jaw hard and somehow disapproving. Seeing him in the flesh eclipsed the picture. He was life, a force of nature that made everything else pale to sepia. But catching her out like this embarrassed her in a way she couldn't explain. How many times had he witnessed her here, staring, trying to figure him out because the real man confused her?

'Why do you say that?'

'My ancestors could corrupt by their pictures alone.'

'You are not the man in that painting.'

'Yes, I am. I'm exactly that man, and you'd be wise to remember it.'

Sara shook her head. She wouldn't be cowed. Never again.

'You like to pretend not to care. The problem is you care *deeply*. About the village, the estate... Your sister.'

*Me.* She hoped he cared about her.

'Angel, I'm good at pretending to have an interest when I don't, in anything much other than myself.' His voice sounded like a sneer, and she hated that he used the word *angel* like a weapon rather than a term of endearment. 'However, I don't wish to pretend any longer.'

'What do you mean?' She didn't understand any of this, but the look on his face terrified her. It was detached, cool. Not the heated way his eyes usually flared when they looked at each other.

'I'll be travelling to look at some horses, then I'm off to Switzerland.'

None of this had been scheduled in the obsessive diary he kept, the one he'd shared with her. This had to be new.

'Does this have anything to do with Victoria?'

His eyes widened almost imperceptibly, then settled back into the lazy, bored charm he always fooled others with. Never her. Until now.

She didn't like it.

'George, I presume?' He raised a supercilious eyebrow.

Yes, George had told her in cautious tones that Victoria had called. As if she'd need to repair the damage after the conversation was done. But nothing appeared irreparably broken. Yet.

'He really oversteps the line,' Lance said. 'This has nothing to do with my sister, and everything to do with the future.'

Her heart rate spiked. 'Did he overstep in asking me about the nursery?'

Lance's brow furrowed to a frown, before smoothing again.

'He did say you suggested he talk to me,' she said.

Lance shrugged, a lazy nonchalance tainting him. 'It doesn't matter now.'

She wouldn't let that stand. She'd spent so much of her life accepting what was handed to her. Now she wasn't afraid to fight for what she wanted. If she didn't, who would?

'What if it matters to me? What if I told him yes, that the nursery should be refurbished?'

She held her breath as Lance's face shuttered, entirely devoid of emotion.

'I'd say it was a mistake. You want love. We know that's something I don't do.'

The words sliced to the heart of her, sharp and true, as she was certain they were meant to.

*'You'll never—'* No. She wouldn't let that voice intrude again. Sara ignored his words and focused on how he'd treated her, his actions. He'd been so kind, protective. Passionate. All he'd done for her over the weeks she'd been here told her that Lance felt something for her. But she suspected he didn't believe he was a good man, that he was capable of softer feelings.

'Are you sure? Some things here felt very much like love to me.'

'That's sex. Which has nothing to do with love.'

'But what we have—'

'Is chemistry. You've confused that with something deeper. So let me be explicit...'

He was disavowing her. Her mouth dried, her heart pounding frantically in her chest.

'Don't. Don't demean this. Us.'

He raised an eyebrow, his expression disdainful. As if she were a silly little girl who needed educating. 'I'd never demean sex. I'm an enthusiastic supporter, as you must have learned. But sex with a person is like your favourite meal. You might love it, but eat too much and you'll get bored eventually, and want to try something different.'

The impact couldn't have been worse if he'd taken a rapier and sliced her off at the knees.

'You're...bored of me?'

'You're an intelligent, charming young woman, but...' He shrugged her off as if she were nothing.

*'You'll never have his heart.'*

Of course. She'd been a fool to think this had meant anything. She took a deep breath, battling the burn in the back of her nose, the prickle in her eyes. She wouldn't cry. Not with all his wicked ancestors witnessing her misery.

'I thought...' She let the words trail off because she was

really talking to herself. Lance didn't care. All along he'd treated this like a huge game, when she'd thought he was trying to make her smile, to chase away her sadness. Instead, he was probably mocking her. And, like with Ferdinand, she'd ignored the truth, hoping and dreaming that this could be something more, when she'd been nothing but a few moments' entertainment for a bored rich man.

He swept his arm wide. 'Yes, all of this gallery is filled with shysters and conmen who encouraged people to think and dream things they shouldn't. But, if you remember correctly, I never encouraged you with any false hopes.'

No, he hadn't. He hadn't encouraged her at all. He'd never whispered quiet words of love as he'd worshipped her body. He'd made no promises for the future. And she'd fooled herself into believing things because she was desperate for love. The trap she'd told herself she wouldn't fall into again.

'And now for my trip,' he said, and all she wanted to do was scream at him to be quiet, put her hands over her ears because she didn't want to hear any more.

'Please feel free to stay here for as long as you choose. I'm unlikely to be returning in the near future. My home is usually in London, after all.' Sara barely heard the words. They'd made love this morning, and now this? 'Astill's Auctions will pay the commission on your finds and will provide you with introductions to some of the finest auction houses in Europe, if you wish to find a job at any of them.'

Her humiliation was complete. He was paying her off like someone cheap and disposable. She wouldn't take it. She couldn't.

'I don't want your money, or your help.'

Lance flinched, before settling back into his cool, businesslike demeanour.

'It's what you deserve.' Money. Not love. *Never* love. 'You're exceptional at what you do.'

Sara couldn't let him see how much this hurt. How it wounded her to her soul. Deeply, irrevocably. She'd known the first moment she'd set eyes on him that he was trouble. Yet she'd sought him out, chased it. Well, she was reaping the tainted rewards of their liaison now. She looked down at her finger, to the opal there. *Beautiful and complex.* It burned, as if taunting her with what might have been. She wanted to tear it off. Instead, she carefully slipped it from her finger.

'You should have your ring back.' She held it out. He merely clasped his hands behind his back, staring at the exquisite piece as if it meant nothing at all.

'Keep it. If I were truly getting engaged I would have given my fiancée the Astill Amethyst.'

She felt like a fool now, standing there with the ring in her fingers, as if begging him to take it. She'd beg for nothing from a man ever again. She clenched the jewel in the palm of her hand when all she wanted to do was hurl it at him. But it represented something precious, a fleeting moment when she'd *believed* she was worthy. She wouldn't treat it with the disdain he'd shown her...

'I don't *need* it. I want nothing of yours. I can make my own way.'

'That, I don't doubt.'

She closed her eyes for a moment, holding back the tears she refused to allow to fall. He might claim not to doubt her, but in this moment she doubted everything. No. Not any more. No relying on others when she should find her own way, no relying on men to steer her course, letting her life be run by them.

It was time to be on her own, because she realised now

she would have given Lance everything and left nothing of herself.

'I'll leave this afternoon.' She'd been raised to be a queen, to control her emotions. She would not let this overcome her. 'I've clearly outstayed my welcome and I shall leave you to your life.'

'There's no—'

Sara held up her hand. She mustered all the cold disdain he'd shown to her. 'Let's not be any more of a disappointment, shall we? How's this as a new moniker, Lance—the Disappointing Duke? I think it has quite the appeal.'

She turned, straightened her spine as her royal training had taught her and walked away from the man she'd thought she loved, the old diamonds of her engagement ring cutting into her palm as she did so.

# CHAPTER ELEVEN

SARA WANDERED THE damp cobbled streets of Morenburg old town after the end of an early shift at the palace. She drifted through the antique markets on the way to her apartment. Sadly, on this dreary late-autumn day, they held no interest. A shard of pain sliced through her, a reminder of the things she tried to forget. On most days it was more like a bruise, dull and deep. But here, amongst all the sellers and the antiques and people looking for treasure, the universe liked to remind her of what she'd lost.

The breeze picked up, cutting into her. A distracting kind of sensation prickled the back of her neck. She wrapped her coat more tightly round her to ward off the chill. It seemed colder than normal. The rest of the crowd bustled round her, people laughing, going about their lives. Her life seemed permanently on hold now, when in truth she was *trying* to move forwards, after moving back home with a healthy bank balance and little more, to a country which didn't feel like hers any longer.

She'd left home behind in a person, not a place.

Now, everything reminded her of a man she couldn't have. A man who, she'd come to realise, after days of sobbing and self-recrimination, didn't love himself enough to love her the way she deserved. Sara had taken a while to accept that certainty. After his cruelty to her, pushing her away only hours after it seemed as if he wanted her closer. None of it had made sense, except that vicious voice in her head that told her she'd never have his heart. But after time away other memories apart from those of that awful last day invaded her consciousness.

How he'd protected her. How he worried for his sister. His staff, who loved him even if it didn't seem he could reciprocate. The villagers who spoke of his enduring care and kindness. How he'd always tried to keep her smiling, even when she'd wanted to curl into a ball and weep. If she could ignore his cruel words, that she was now sure had been designed to force her away, his had been the *actions* of a good man. The truths others believed were self-evident, Lance couldn't see for himself. That he simply wasn't the Dastardly Duke he pretended to be.

And in the end her heartbreak became more about his loss than hers. If Lance couldn't accept that he was a good man with the capacity to love, he'd never accept it from someone else. Having experienced being in love, Sara couldn't imagine now living without it in her life. But sadly, two months after she'd walked away from Astill Hall, she still had trouble contemplating her world without Lance in it. Still, some things you couldn't have, no matter how much you wanted them...

She sighed. There was no point to these ruminations. Not any more. Sara made her way through the milling crowds, past a kitschy tourist shop selling royal memorabilia. She hesitated. Little Lauritanian flags adorned the window, pictures of the still new yet quickly beloved King and Queen adorned random items on display—mugs, eggcups, tins of sweets. Then there were items commemorating the deceased King, Queen and Crown Prince, the past and the present colliding. One of those portraits could have been her, and she didn't even have a twinge of loss at the thought of what might have been. That sense of lost opportunity was for another person entirely.

A shadow passed her shoulder. Another prickle of awareness, this time hinting someone was close. Even though she'd tried to melt into obscurity, people still saw her as a minor celebrity here. The death of her fiancé and failed fake engagement meant she was a kind of tragic heroine. The woman who would have been Queen, still looking for love.

Sara took a deep breath, pasted a smile on her face. Prepared herself for the questions from a public that was mostly caring, if not sometimes intrusive. She looked up and glimpsed a tall, broad reflection in the glass of the shop window that choked the breath from her lungs.

'Ferdinand really was a fool, and not the only one.'

That voice. Her knees buckled, before she firmed them, her heart tripping then pounding. She took a long, steadying breath. It should probably have been no surprise that he was here. She'd heard the rumour that he was back in the country, had known he was working with the royal family, auctioning unwanted items from the palace, since the country's finances had been in a shockingly bad state and Lise and Rafe had been fighting to restore the economy.

'It's wrong to speak ill of the dead,' she said. Part of her craved a glimpse of him in the flesh, and another part knew she should leave well enough alone. But it was as if everything around her had stopped. The cold breeze, the sounds of people going about their lives. In this moment there was only her and him, as if the universe was waiting. And she couldn't ignore Lance any longer.

She turned, forgetting the full force of him.

He looked as heart-stopping as she remembered. More so. The curve of his bottom lip that had obsessed her for so long, had haunted her dreams. The green eyes that seemed to peer into the very soul of her. His jaw, now shaded with fashionable stubble. A man who knew more of her secrets, her desires, than any person alive.

But it didn't matter. He'd been clear that they had no future together, and she deserved more from life, someone who could love her with his whole heart, even if right now she couldn't contemplate loving anyone at all. Other than Lance, of course. But part of her hated him too, for playing on her fears. For having made her believe, once again, that she was something *less*. Before she'd realised that she had a future and a value.

That she was enough.

'I'm only speaking the truth. You know I can be cruel. Whereas you're too kind.'

Today he was dressed as if for business, standing there in a dark coat over a suit. No tie, the neck of his perfect bespoke shirt open, showing a tantalising hint of his chest, a sprinkling of hair. She was taken back to the times when she'd rested her head there, listening to the thump of his comforting heartbeat as it lulled her to sleep.

'It's not a bad thing to be kind, but it can be misplaced.' She shrugged. 'I think you believed the greatest act of kindness was your cruelty.'

'The Despicable Duke.' His eyes tightened, but otherwise his face remained blank. 'I told you they were right.'

He still underestimated himself, perhaps always would. And no matter how much she'd wanted a future with him, there would be none so long as he pitched himself as a bad man. Because in his mind he'd never truly deserved her love.

She shook her head.

'Still trying to find the good in me?' he asked.

'That's not my question to answer.'

It was whether he could find some good in himself that was important.

'Some would call me irredeemable, for things I've said.'

The breeze in the little lane picked up, a few late autumn leaves skittering about their feet. His words to her in their final conversation still pricked at her consciousness. He'd wanted her to walk away without a thought of turning back. He'd ensured it. So why did she crave to run to him and hope he caught her now?

She wrapped her arms round her waist, needing to leave but fixed to the spot. She looked towards the exit of the lane, anywhere except Lance. In the distance a small group began drifting down towards the tourist store.

'I should have thought you'd be happy with that. Your reputation soiled even more than before. Isn't that what you were trying to achieve?'

'Once, perhaps...'

A couple of people looked from her to him, as though in recognition. She didn't want this to become some spectacle, but didn't want to walk away either. She'd dreamed about seeing him, about what she'd say, since shortly after she'd left his house. Strangely, now it was as if her tongue was tied in knots. Then the truth began screaming loudly at her. Even after everything, she still didn't want an end. She wanted a beginning.

Lance frowned as someone in the crowd raised their phone as if to take a photograph. He turned his back on them and manoeuvred himself so any view of her was blocked by his height and breadth.

'Whilst I deserve public humiliation, you don't. Is there somewhere we could talk in private?'

Two equally tempting answers, yes and no, pitched a battle inside her. It was a terrible position to be in, wanting to toy with fire but not wanting to be burned.

'Are you going to be cruel to me again?' She tried to sound firm, but her voice was quiet and cracked.

He shut his eyes for a brief moment and flinched as if in pain. When he opened them again the intensity and heat in his gaze almost incinerated her on the spot.

*'Never.'*

That one simple word ground out of him with vehemence.

She was like Icarus, hurtling directly into the sun. She didn't care about the consequences. In the end, the side of her entirely disinterested in self-preservation won over common sense.

'Then follow me.'

*'Are you going to be cruel to me again?'*

Since his sister's marriage, Lance had spent his life trying to live without any more regret or self-recrimination. Now, Sara's words cut through him, jagged and deep, representing one of his greatest shames. He'd hurt her, calculatedly, deliberately. He'd played on her insecurities and fears in a misplaced desire to protect her from himself. At the time, it had held a twisted kind of logic. Then she'd walked out of his house with her head held high, like the Queen she had once been destined to become, leaving behind her engagement ring, her clothes, and a perfectly pressed handkerchief embroidered with his initials on his bedside table...

It was the handkerchief that had almost undone his resolve in that moment. The realisation that she'd kept it with her since the wake, like something precious. A memory of him. Still, in the days after she'd left, he'd kidded himself into believing that what he'd done had been in her best interests. It was only much later that he'd come to realise he was as bad as her family or Ferdinand, because he'd not given her a choice. He'd taken it from her in a moment of breathtaking arrogance and paternalism, treating her as if she were a child, and not an adult woman who could make decisions for herself about what she wanted in life. Even worse, he'd done it because he was a coward.

The mere fact that she was still willing to speak with him now showed a graciousness he wanted to deserve.

'Was finding me today a chance, or deliberate?' she asked.

He could lie, but truth was all he had left, even though it exposed him. He'd tortured himself over the past months, agonising over Sara's wellbeing. Whether she was safe from the machinations of her family. Whether she was doing well. In the end, appraisal of unwanted items from the Lauritanian royal collection had given him an excuse to be back in the country, and being back in the palace where she worked had made it easy to find out what time her shift finished today...

'Entirely deliberate.'

She sighed. 'Well, that's something, I guess.'

Good or bad, he couldn't be sure, when the full extent of the truth was that he'd been unable to stay away.

Lance followed her like a man being led to his doom, but the barest hope of reprieve kept him putting one foot in front of the other. Even now, she was like a beacon, with her golden hair vibrant in the dim lane ahead of him, wearing a coat the same vivid blue as Lake Morenburg. She had always been the light in his darkest places. Only he hadn't realised it till he'd forced her away and all the light had simply been snuffed out.

He'd learned then how much he loathed the darkness.

They stopped at the door of one of the stone terraces for which the old town was famed. She looked over her shoulder at him, her teeth grazing her lower lip. 'This leads to my apartment. I hope that'll do.'

He'd been desperate to see what she'd made of her life. Rafe and Annalise had been his only means of answering that question, and they'd been naturally protective, telling him little other than confirming that Sara had a job in the palace, curating the art collection, and a place to live.

'I'm humbled you'd have me in your home.'

She hesitated as they reached the top of a narrow flight of stairs, as if about to say something before thinking better of it. Then she unlocked another door to a beautiful airy loft. She walked through the door, inviting him in. The whole space was light and bright, with mismatched rugs on the floor and decorated with well-worn antiques she'd clearly found in the markets below.

'It's not like you're some villain in a dark fairy tale,' she said.

'There I might beg to differ.'

'And that sums up the entire problem.'

She stood in front of windows overlooking the town and the soaring Alps in the distance, every move stiff and weary. He'd done that to her, taken this beautiful, open woman, whose life should be one filled with joy, and somehow left her closed-off and shattered. Of all the things he needed to atone for, this sin was one of his greatest. It started now with his deepest truth. He loved her, to the nucleus of every cell in his body. A sensation so marrow-deep it radiated within him and there was no turning back from it. The heart he'd thought withered, cold and dead could beat again, because she'd shocked it to life.

'You redeemed me, Sara. That was a sin I found hard to forgive when I'd spent so much of my adult life fighting against any kind of salvation. Especially after Victoria.'

The heating in the loft was warm. Sara slipped off her

coat and moved to an armchair, draping her coat over it. She gripped the back, fingers digging into the fabric.

'How…is she?'

'She seems to be doing better.'

It had taken six weeks of fighting to be allowed to see Vic in the clinic. He'd gone there to tell her two things. News that he'd ensured the safety of her animals, and news of his broken engagement to Sara. For the first, she'd closed herself in the bedroom of her small suite and came out again ten minutes later seemingly composed, yet with her eyes red-rimmed. As for the second…

*'I'm sick of people martyring themselves over me. I refuse to allow you to be another.'*

She'd said plenty of other things too, like how he was a fool to pass up a chance of love, and she wouldn't be responsible for his future unhappiness. All whilst hugging him like the warm, adoring young woman she'd once been.

He'd recognised then that he'd given Victoria no agency to help herself, trying to fix things rather than supporting her decisions—good or bad. Perhaps one day she'd tell him what her husband held over her. Perhaps not. For now, he'd done what he could to ensure she was safe, that she had options. She didn't need his guilt. What Vic needed was his love and unquestioning support because his guilt made her trauma about *him*.

Just as with Sara. It had never been about her in the end. He hoped to change that today. If not, he'd walk away only half a person and try once again to live with the sins of his past.

'I'm happy for you and for her.'

He shook his head. 'All this time I'd convinced myself I hadn't saved her. It directed my actions every day. Then you walked into my life, and I knew I had to save *you* or

I'd never forgive myself. Yet I was terrified I'd fail and let down yet another person who'd become vital to me.'

Sara's eyes widened a fraction. 'I don't think I was the one who needed saving.'

She was right in every way.

'You and my sister are some of the wisest women I know. And I'm a fool.'

She released the back of the chair she'd been crushing in her hands and turned to look at the view, framed by the soaring mountains in the distance. Her shoulders lifted and fell.

'What do you want, Lance?'

He'd tried living life as the worst version of himself and, in doing so, the cursed memory of his father always won. No more. He raked his hands through his hair.

'I'm trying to make amends. Another fool made you doubt your ability to be Queen here, and yet you *are* a queen because you rule my whole heart. You always will.'

She couldn't look at him, *wouldn't*. If she did, she'd likely run into his arms and never want to leave them, when there was more to be said.

Time and tears had taught Sara many things. Her own value, her own strength, and that she was deserving of love. She'd promised herself when she'd left Astill Hall that she'd only look ahead, and now she needed to clear away that past to make sure she could build the future she craved.

'It was only sex, you said.'

A long exhale hissed in the burgeoning silence between them.

'For a man who prided himself in dealing brutal truths, I told the most terrible lies. When we were together, you reached in and grabbed my soul. I had *never* experienced anything similar. It wasn't sex, it was a connection so intense it consumed me. I was terrified I couldn't protect you. That I'd end up hurting you, yet that's what I did anyway. For that, I can't forgive myself.'

'Of all the things you said, that's what cut the deepest.'

Sara bit into her lower lip. Outside, the sun broke over the mountains and their snow caps gleamed a fierce, blinding white. A tingle at the back of her neck, that sixth sense always attuned to him, told her Lance was closer than before.

'What I should have said is that I love you, Sara. I don't want to slay dragons for you, I'll trap them and train them and have them lie at your feet. The food on my plate, the air that I breathe, it's all ash. I forced you away, and the colour in my life leached to grey.'

A slide of warmth drifted down her spine. The heat of another body standing close behind her. She shut her eyes, absorbing the pleasure of it, swaying back till she bumped against a hard chest. She couldn't move away, not now. She leaned into him and Lance wrapped his arms round her, holding her tight. Right back where she belonged.

'Say something, *please*.' Lance's voice was low and gentle.

'I think…that I'm not the only one who needs their dragons tamed.'

'I hate to admit it, but you're right. Are you offering to carry out that task? If so, I think you'd look rather fetching in armour, wielding a sword. Both of which I could supply from Astill Hall's armoury if you were so inclined…'

She couldn't help the laugh which broke free. Lance had the uncanny ability to fill her life with joy and fun. His arms round her waist squeezed tighter for a second. The weight of his chin rested on her head.

'You have no idea how I've longed to hear that sound again.'

'There hasn't been much laughter for me recently.'

'Let's change that, shall we?'

He loosened his grip on her, gently turned her round and cupped her jaw in his hands. Only now she noticed the bruised quality under his eyes. How the lines of his face had etched deeper. She guessed there hadn't been much laughter for him either.

'Sara, I asked once to be your fake fiancé, but what I want is real and true and permanent.'

Her heart fluttered like a butterfly caught behind her ribs.

'What are you saying?'

'I'm offering you my heart and my soul, if you'll have them. My love and adoration, from today and for as long as I have breath in my body. A ring on your finger and a big wedding if you wish, and if not I don't care. I want you to be mine and me, yours. And some time in the future I hope for little cherubs with blue eyes and golden curls like their magnificent mother.'

The nursery. She knew it. He *had* wanted her to decide. Wanted it as much as she had on that day.

'What if those cherubs take after you?' she asked.

Lance dropped his hands from her cheeks and rubbed one over his face, chuckling. 'Then they'll be little devils and I'll love them all the same. But if you don't love me now, then feel free to reject me as cruelly as I did you. It really is nothing less than I deserve, being the Disappointing Duke, as you so aptly named me.'

Somehow, that title didn't fit any more. It probably never had. She could think of so many more adjectives to describe him, if only he'd believe them himself.

'Do you think you deserve my love in return for yours?'

He hesitated, blew out a slow breath.

'With you, I can achieve anything. It's time to let go of

a past that's bound me for too long, and to forge our lives together. Being the best man I can be.'

The last flurry of reserve melted away like the snow in spring. All that bloomed inside her was love and certainty of a future that lay bright and beautiful before her.

'Then you *are* a fool.'

He cocked an eyebrow, the corner of his mouth curving in a wry grin. 'If playing the jester will make you smile, then I'm a fool every day for you. Never doubt it.'

'You're a fool because you've always been the best man for me. My whole problem was that I never *stopped* loving you. Wanting you.'

'I see no problem at all. And you'll have me. Always.'

She put her hand to his chest, the warmth of him pulsing through her. 'My Dashing Duke.'

'Devoted is a better description.' Lance smiled as he bent down and brushed his lips over hers. She sighed when he pulled away too soon, craving more. Craving *everything*.

'If you're going to be the most Delectable Duchess of Bedmore you should probably have the Astill Amethyst.'

'I'm thinking "Disobedient" sounds better. I don't much like the idea of doing what I should. And I hate purple. But I do *love* opals.'

'Whatever you want to be, you're perfect.' Lance reached into his pocket, brought out a small velvet box and opened it. 'Luckily I have this.'

In the afternoon light the old diamonds sparkled. The opal itself, full of fire. He took her left hand in his own and slid the ring onto her finger.

'There, back in its rightful place.'

'My rightful place is with you.'

He sank to his knees. The look on his face was so full of

adoration she almost dropped to the floor with him as her legs could barely hold her upright.

'Let's see what we can do about that then. Angel, will you give me the immeasurable honour of becoming my real fiancée, and wife as soon as we can humanly arrange it?'

'Yes, now and for ever.' She smiled, her heart so full of joy and love she thought she might never see a sad day again. 'There's no one else I'd rather be.'

\* \* \* \* \*

# COMING SOON!

We really hope you enjoyed reading this book. If you're looking for more romance be sure to head to the shops when new books are available on

## Thursday 13th April

To see which titles are coming soon, please visit

**millsandboon.co.uk/nextmonth**

MILLS & BOON

# MILLS & BOON®

## Coming next month

### THE ITALIAN'S INNOCENT CINDERELLA
### Cathy Williams

"Explain," Maude whispered, already predicting what he was about to say and dreading confirmation of her suspicions. "What...what was in the paper, Mateo?"

"I debated bringing it, but in the end, I thought better of it."

"Why?"

"Because we're engaged."

Maude's mouth fell open and she stared at him in utter shock.

"Sorry?"

"It would seem that I found the love of my life with you and we're engaged."

"No. No, no, no, no...no..."

*Continue reading*
THE ITALIAN'S INNOCENT CINDERELLA
Cathy Williams

*Available next month*
www.millsandboon.co.uk

# LET'S TALK

*Romance*

For exclusive extracts, competitions and special offers, find us online:

- **f** facebook.com/millsandboon
- **𝕏** @MillsandBoon
- **⬛** @MillsandBoonUK
- **♪** @MillsandBoonUK

Get in touch on 01413 063 232

For all the latest titles coming soon, visit
**millsandboon.co.uk/nextmonth**

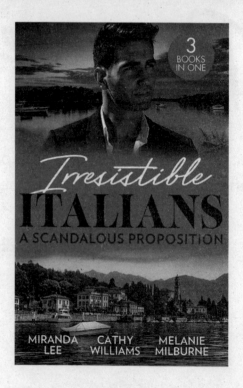

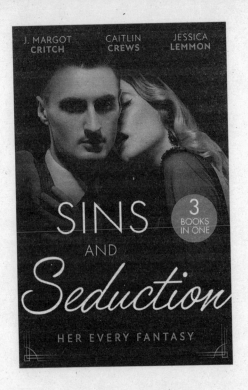

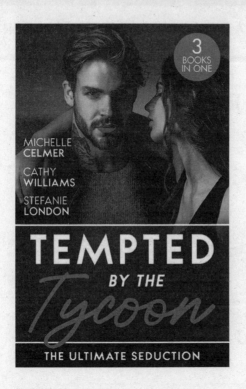

# MILLS & BOON

## THE HEART OF ROMANCE

---

## A ROMANCE FOR EVERY READER

---

**MODERN**
Prepare to be swept off your feet by sophisticated, sexy and seductive heroes, in some of the world's most glamourous and romantic locations, where power and passion collide.

**HISTORICAL**
Escape with historical heroes from time gone by. Whether your passion is for wicked Regency Rakes, muscled Vikings or rugged Highlanders, awaken the romance of the past.

**MEDICAL**
Set your pulse racing with dedicated, delectable doctors in the high-pressure world of medicine, where emotions run high and passion, comfort and love are the best medicine.

*True Love*
Celebrate true love with tender stories of heartfelt romance, from the rush of falling in love to the joy a new baby can bring, and a focus on emotional heart of a relationship.

*Desire*
Indulge in secrets and scandal, intense drama and plenty of sizzling action with powerful and passionate heroes who have it all: wealth, status good looks...everything but the right woman.

**HEROES**
Experience all the excitement of a gripping thriller, with an intense romance at its heart. Resourceful, true-to-life women and strong, fearless men face danger and desire - a killer combination!

To see which titles are coming soon, please visit
**millsandboon.co.uk/nextmonth**